# AMERICA'S BRAVEST

# KATHRYN SHAY

Copyright © 2013 Kathryn Shay

All rights reserved.

ISBN: 1939501105
ISBN 13: 9781939501103

Kathryn Shay spent five years riding fire trucks with a large city fire department, eating in their firehouses and interviewing hundreds of America's Bravest. Read the books that resulted from her intense relationship with firefighters!

# Praise for America's Bravest from readers and firefighters

*"I would recommend these books to anyone who loves romances."*

*"This series is really good. I could not put my kindle down. I can't wait to read the rest of the books written by Kathryn Shay."*

*"I couldn't put these books down. I'm a firefighter in Tennessee some of this hit home to me. Thank you for a great series."*

*"I'm a firefighter at heart so I loved the fact that the story outside of the romance was so researched and the author was very knowledgeable. The stories make the romance even better!!! I couldn't wait to read the next one I could find from Ms. Shay!"*

*"Thoroughly enjoyed these books. Would highly recommend this series. I'm in the EMS world so I found these to be pretty accurate."*

# AMERICA'S BRAVEST

### By KATHRYN SHAY

Copyright 2011, Kathryn Shay
Cover art by Patricia Ryan

This ebook is licensed for your personal enjoyment only. This ebook may not be re-sold or given away to other people. If you would like to share this book with another person, please purchase an additional copy for each person. If you're reading this book and did not purchase it, or it was not purchased for your use only, then please return to smashwords.com and purchase your own copy. Thank you for respecting the hard work of this author.

# In Too Deep

Novella number one in the
AMERICA'S BRAVEST SERIES

**KATHRYN SHAY**

# CHAPTER 1

DREADING THE NEWS he was about to give, Captain Gabe Malvaso stared out at his group of firefighters, who sat in the big couches and stuffed recliners of the common room of Firehouse 7. In the back by the door to the kitchen stood the Hidden Cove Fire Department brass. A warm July breeze drifted in through the many open windows, but the soothing morning wasn't going to help Gabe's cause. His men and women trusted him, and so far in his eight years as their officer, he hadn't had to deliver any bombs about cutbacks. From the rear, his cousin Mitch, now a battalion chief, nodded his encouragement.

Gabe cleared his throat. "Let's get started. There's been a lot of rumors going around and you can probably tell from Chiefs Malvaso and Erikson being at this little gathering that something's coming down. And yeah, it's what you expect."

Murmurs rumbled through his group: Felicia White, his serious, aloof lieutenant who he already talked to about this; his paramedic, Brody O'Malley, a lively ladies' man that everybody liked; firefighters Tony Ramirez, quiet and excellent at his job, Sydney Sands, their feisty rookie and, finally, Rachel Wellington—sometimes called *Princess* because of her classy background. She was a good firefighter and sensible at work.

And with her steel-blond hair and wide eyes, she was about the sexiest thing he'd ever seen. *That* had been causing Gabe problems for a while now.

O'Malley spoke up first. "So, somebody's going to get the ax on Rescue 7, right Cap?"

"Yep. And on Quint and Midi 7, too." Those were the other two rigs in the firehouse, the first performing fire rescue operations, the latter a medical truck. The groups who rode them also had separate officers. "They're having their own meeting. But we're all cutting back on each shift."

Sydney, the group member with the least experience at the on the squad, shook her head. "Oh, hell!"

"Syd, you'll still have a job, though it'll be another station house. You have some seniority in the department as a whole; plus we're expecting retirements soon."

She lifted her chin to keep up a good front, but her young face tensed, telling Gabe she was upset. The twenty-three-year-old already had had a lot of tough stuff to deal with in life. "I'll have to break in a new bunch of clowns."

The others didn't joke. Losing a brother—or sister—that you fought fires side by side with was serious business in any fire department. And theirs was a special group, an experiment of sorts in affirmative action. Their rescue squad, which went to every fire in their area, was comprised of three men and three women to demonstrate how liberated the department was and to promote the recruitment of women. So far, after eighteen months, the experiment had worked well.

From behind Sands, Tony Ramirez put his hand on her shoulder and squeezed it. She covered his briefly with hers. The two often paired up inside a building and they'd become fast friends.

"I know this is hard for all of us," Gabe added. "But we got no choice, guys."

"Yeah, we don't have to like it, though." O'Malley's tone was angry. Brody was a good guy but he couldn't censor his words, and he caused Gabe grief from time to time.

"Chief Erikson is here today to give you some more information on what's gone down and to answer any questions you have." He nodded to the back of the room where Cal stood with Mitch. "Ready, Chief?"

Erikson pushed off the wall. "As I'll ever be." The tall, powerfully built man strode to the front with a commanding presence. Though Gabe wanted to climb the HCFD ladder as quickly as possible, he didn't envy the chief today. Designated by the top fire guy, Noah Callahan, all the battalion chiefs would be answering tough questions this week.

"Hi, all. I'm not going to mince words. You've heard the rumors. For budget reasons, the mayor's cutting ten percent of the fire department. But it gets worse. The town newspaper, the *Hidden Cove Herald,* which recently went to online publication, has been running a daily blog by a reporter, Parker Allen. She named the thing *Make It Right,* which galls me. Of course, she's in full agreement with the cutbacks but wants more of our hide."

O'Malley raised his hand.

"Yeah, Brody, what?"

"Do the powers-that-be know without a sixth firefighter, we're all in more danger than usual?"

"I think they do."

"Hell, Cal, firefighters were everybody's heroes when our guys ran into the towers on 9/11. Now we're just another organization to be cut."

At the mention of 9/11, everybody went silent. The events of that day had changed Americans, none more than firefighters. Gabe and several members of the HCFD had gone down ten years ago to work at the pile, and some of the people sitting before him had lost relatives or close friends. O'Malley seemed to take it the hardest every year.

Cal's expression was grim. "Life isn't fair, I know."

"I don't mean any disrespect, Chief. Honest. But it galls me where the government chooses to cut. My brother Ryan says the same thing is happening in the police department. Ten percent across the board."

"I know about the HCPD and I don't like it any more than you do. And you're not going to like what else Lois Lane is bitching about."

More grumbling. Gabe didn't know what the chief was referring to.

"She's making noise in that blog of hers about our *downtime*. She wonders why people see us in supermarkets shopping together" — because it was the only way to get groceries for the meals they had to eat at the house — "and why we're seen at Subway Station" — to have a freakin' meal out once or twice — "and why we're on Facebook and Twitter and other websites while on duty."

Felicia raised her hand. One thing Gabe liked about his second in command was that she only spoke when she had something to say.

"Yeah, Lieutenant?"

"I'm guessing we can be more circumspect about being seen too much around town for a while, but the Facebook thing is totally bogus. We're always waiting for a call, and it can be tedious. No reason why we shouldn't be online after we do housework and training."

Gabe remembered an adage about the fire department: *A firefighter's job is hours of boredom, seconds of terror.*

Felicia wasn't done. "I'd like to spearhead some kind of publicity campaign to have our routine better understood by the public."

"Good idea, Lieutenant." The chief scanned the others. "Anybody want to work on that with Felicia?"

Sands spoke up. "I will, even if I'm at another firehouse."

Wellington, who rarely said much, also jumped in. "I'd help, but then it'll be the women taking over again. That sucks."

The guys laughed. Brody tossed out, "We volunteer Ramirez. He's as pretty as the rest of you."

More chuckles around. It broke the tension, and Gabe was glad for the levity. The group had dubbed Tony and his spouse Sophia *the beautiful people* because they both were, well, beautiful. He reminded Gabe of a young Jimmy Smits and she resembled Jennifer Lopez.

"All right, go for it," the chief finished. "And I appreciate you not getting on me too badly. Believe me, the HCFD administrators are furious about the cuts and Allen's crusade. That's all I have to say."

Gabe went back to the front. "Why don't you take an hour to decompress, shoot the shit about the news and then we'll start housework."

"Oh, that cheers me up," Sydney groused.

"Come on, girl." Ramirez tugged on her arm. "You can have the first piece of the coffee cake Sophia sent in."

They dispersed, except for Wellington. She stayed seated and looked over at him. Jesus, those eyes of hers about killed him sometimes. Though he couldn't see their color from here, he knew they were hazel with specks of gold in them. He braced himself for the full onslaught of her presence—especially if she had on that bath lotion she wore after a shower—when she stood and took a step toward him.

• • •

RACHEL WAS TRYING to stay away from the captain of her group, really she was, but she had to talk to him now. She only hesitated because he was visibly upset. He'd lost kids in fires—a firefighter's worst nightmare—and once when a tanker crashed, spilling gasoline all over a highway, he'd laid foam on the flames with a steady hand. Even when the red devil reignited, it hadn't fazed him. Now, he was concerned for his group, and he wasn't afraid to let it show. Which was one more thing that she found unbelievably attractive about him. Before she could reach him, though, his cousin came up to him from the other side. "Hey, buddy."

Rachel backed off and sat down when they hugged.

Gabe smiled broadly. "It was great seeing Megan at the camp."

The Hidden Cove firefighters and police officers had begun a summer camp, Hale's Haven, for the children of slain department members three years ago, and the organization grew bigger every year. Rachel had volunteered for a week this year but not the one Gabe had worked at. Intentionally.

"Yeah, she's busy with our toddler, her job and my teenagers," Mitch told him. "I'm glad she could get away to work at the camp."

"I hear Sabina's been a great help."

Mitch had bought his mother's house when he and his cop wife married, and now grandma took care of her namesake, their three-year-old, Sabby.

"She has." He patted Gabe on the shoulder. "Gotta run. I just wanted to touch base. You did as good as you could today."

"Thanks, cuz."

When Chief Malvaso left, Rachel stood again and crossed the short distance to Gabe. "Hey, Cap."

Up close, those dark chocolate eyes focused on her intently, sparking with remnants of anger in them. His brown hair was a little longer than he usually wore it. And damn it, his woodsy aftershave filled her head.

"Hey, Wellington."

She noticed he never used the *princess* nickname and always called her Wellington. That was common among firefighters, especially when they were in a burning building with another group who might have a Rachel or Tony inside the structure. But Gabe *never* used her given name.

"I, um, wanted to ask what housework I'm assigned today, because I'm taking two extra days of furlough besides our four days off. I'm leaving at noon. Not a good time, I guess, to do that."

"It's fine. This shit with the reporter is making me crazy, but I refuse to deny my squad the time they need off for doctor's appointments or the like."

It wasn't a doctor's appointment, but she'd be damned if she let her group know where she was going. "Thanks. I'll do my chores now if you tell me what they are."

"Felicia made up the list today. It's already posted."

"Oh, okay." She hesitated, not wanting to leave him yet. That had happened a lot lately. "I'm sorry you had to be the bearer of bad news."

Sighing, he shook his head. "I can't believe society is so down on us after all those accolades in 2001. Hell, some states are even trying to take away our collective bargaining rights."

"People always go back to their old ways when a crisis is over."

He gave her a little smile that jump-started her heart. "You're pretty young to be that cynical, Wellington."

"I'm older than my years. In any case, you did a good job, like your cousin said."

"Thanks." She was shocked when he reached out and touched her arm. Oh, he showed affection to other group members, but rarely to her. "Is everything okay? With the time off you need? You're not sick, are you?"

"Nope, it's a family thing."

Cocking his head, he studied her, his intense gaze making her nerves jitter. She tried not to fidget. "You've been working here eighteen months and we still don't know much about your family."

"That's okay. You don't want to. You're lucky to be part of the Malvaso clan." She gave him a weak smile. "I'll head out."

He nodded. "Take care, then."

Rachel left, thinking about the Malvaso family gatherings and the fun escapades they had together, which were legend in the department. But comparing her family to them wasn't the worst part of being around Gabe Malvaso.

Her main concern was that she had the hots for her captain. Her feelings were totally unprofessional, not to mention more than stupid for a woman in today's fire department.

• • •

THE ABANDONED BUILDING on Jay Street was already filled with smoke when Rescue 7 pulled up to the site. As soon as the truck stopped, Gabe hopped off and headed to Incident Command. Cal Erikson was already directing the action from a computer on the hood of his Jeep. The machine contained the blueprints of the building filed with the city.

"What's the status?" Gabe asked the chief.

"The structure's abandoned. But you know what that means."

"Homeless people inside."

"Engines 17 and 23 are laying hose. Truck 5 is getting ladders up and broaching the front access. As soon as they're in place, take your group around back." When Gabe started to walk away, Cal stopped him. "Be careful. These old buildings—"

"Hello, Chief."

Glancing to the other side of Cal, Gabe saw a tall brunette, her cheeks flushed with excitement, had come up to them.

Cal stiffened. "Ms. Allen. Chasing fires now?" His voice was cold and sarcastic.

"I am." Her violet eyes flashed at the battalion chief. "Since you keep emailing me about how brave and worthy your guys are, I thought I'd come to a few calls and see for myself."

"Emails and calls you never answer."

Gabe said, "Chief, my guys need to talk about back entry."

Subtly, Erikson gave Allen his back, effectively closing her out. Gabe's group needed no such thing, but Cal would be glad to be rid of Lois Lane.

In five minutes, Gabe's group was inside the building. The interior of the former department store consisted of large open spaces, which might make finding trapped victims easier. The fire was rolling, but the smoke wasn't yet thick enough to blind them, as often happened. "Keep your gear tight and SCBA secure," Gabe said through the radio attached to his face mask. "It'll be bitchin' hot in here, but don't loosen up."

Though their turnout gear was heavy, they needed the fireproof protection of helmet, bulky coats, pants and bunker boots. Air tanks, of course, were vital.

They went slowly, all six of them. When they'd gone about twenty yards into the room, Gabe spotted a stairway leading to the second floor. "White, take Sands up with you. See if Truck 5 needs some help on search and rescue. O'Malley and Ramirez go left on this floor. Wellington, you're with me."

They separated and Gabe said a brief prayer that his group would be safe. He led the way through another corridor and reached an open doorway. The basement. "Stay here, Wellington, while I test the steps."

As soon as Gabe went down a step, he realized it was spongy. But when he took a few more, he realized the staircase was too unsteady to hold up. They'd need ropes and backup to check the basement.

A loud boom rocked the building, then a second one. The entire structure shook, and the steps shifted beneath him. Gabe realized they were going to cave before he could get back up. When he turned to signal Wellington, he bumped right into her.

In seconds, the staircase collapsed and they fell with it.

# CHAPTER 2

RACHEL AWOKE COUGHING. Total darkness surrounded her. For a minute, she didn't know where she was. Then she remembered. Oh, shit. The staircase had collapsed. Gabe had told her not to follow him, but she had anyway, and now they were both trapped.

Gabe! Where was he? Since she could see absolutely nothing, she felt around her immediate area. Her gloved hand came upon something clunky. Rounded, with a hose. Her air tank. It must have come off with her helmet and SCBA. Before she could search farther for Gabe, she heard movement, a groan of pain. On her knees now, she followed the sound. About five feet away, she touched an arm. "Gabe, are you all right?"

"Don't know." His words were grunted out. "Wellington?"

"Yeah. I, um, followed you down the steps." She wished she could see him, but she couldn't. She held on to his arm because the contact made her feel better.

"You disobeyed a direct order, Firefighter!"

"I know." She unsnapped her turnout coat and shrugged out of it, and her gloves, because the air was stiflingly hot down here. "You can put a letter in my file." If they ever got out. Which at this point was not a given. "Tell me what hurts."

"My back. My mask and helmet are gone but the tank's digging into me. Help me get it off." More groans as she turned him to his side and blindly wrestled with the gear. "That's better," he mumbled, and she could sense him lie back down.

"Let me check out the rest of you." Gently, she prodded his left arm and shoulder. Then his right side.

"I'm just sore," he said.

Opening his turnout coat, she felt his chest. Crazily, given their situation she thought about how she'd dreamed of touching him like this, only in different circumstances and without clothes on. Still, she patted down one leg, then up the other. When she got to his abdomen, he barked, "Enough."

"Your stomach hurt when I touched it?"

"No. I'm good." His reply was curt, as if she was doing something wrong.

Sitting back on her haunches, she took in a deep breath. More aware now, she noted a stale musty odor. "Nothing's broken that I can tell. I can't see you though. You have any cuts or bruises?"

"My left temple."

"Maybe you should lie there a while."

"I said I'm good. I need help sitting up, though. I'm dizzy and my back hurts."

"Okay." Inching over in the direction of his voice, she scooted to his shoulder and slid an arm under him from the right side. With the action, his face turned into her breasts. She stilled, and he said, "Jesus Christ."

"Why do you keep yelling at me?"

"Just help me up, Firefighter."

Shrugging, she got him to a seated position, then slid her hand over the wall behind him. "There's a wall about a foot from you. Can you ease back?"

"Yeah. Is it dry?"

She put her hand on the wall again. It was crumbly and pieces of cement came off in her fingers. "Uh-huh."

"At least we're not in a wet basement."

Since they couldn't see each other, she could only hear him shuffle to a different position. "I'm against the wall now." His voice was less harsh, if still raspy.

Rachel settled next to him, could feel the slight brush of his shoulder against hers. She heard him slap his leg. "The lights on our helmets would help!"

"They must have gone out in the fall. I'll find them." Again, she got to her knees and crawled forward, sweeping her hand around in front of her for the helmet. Gloves gone, the debris on the floor scraped her palms and fingers. "I got one." She tried to switch it on. "No luck."

"Search for the other."

Still kneeling, she rummaged around. Dirt and dust that had settled from the cave-in flew up, making her eyes water. She proceeded until she found the second helmet. "I got it." She switched on the lever.

"Great!" he said.

Eerie, that's what the single beacon of light was, shining into such complete darkness. She caught a glimpse of Gabe's big form slumped against the wall. Cautiously, she crawled back to him. Careful not to shine the light in his eyes, she set down the helmet. "You've got a cut on your forehead. Scratches on your neck. The arm of your coat's ripped. That's it." She chuckled. "Your face is filthy, Captain."

"Hand the helmet to me." He scanned her with the light. "Your hair's a mess. You have a bruise on your cheek." He checked her hands. "Scratches, is all."

"It's a freakin' miracle we're not injured other than your back." Though her shoulder ached some.

He coughed from the dust, which still clung to the air in little particles that they could now see floating before them in the light. "Let's hope our luck holds out with the radio." Into his lapel mic, he said, "Rescue 7. Malvaso and Wellington reporting."

Nothing. He tried again. Still nothing. "I'm not surprised. We're boxed in pretty good to get any reception. Or it broke in the fall. Try yours."

She did, with the same negative result.

He swept the area with the light. "Walls are ten courses. Area's about eight by five. Chunks of concrete and timber sealed us off."

Sealed off. Which meant they had limited air. And she bet the makeshift walls were thicker than iron. Her heart rate sped up.

In the dim light, they met each other's gaze. "This isn't good," she whispered.

"Nope," he answered. "It isn't."

• • •

HIS BACK HURT like hell as he maneuvered his coat off, then went for his turnout pants. After he refused her offer of help, Rachel shed her pants and boots, too, as the temperature in the closed-off space had spiked. He thought about how she'd touched him through the heavy material. Even in dire circumstances, having her hands press his cock, and his face buried in her breasts, affected him. How could that be when they were in so much trouble?

When he was down to his white shirt and navy pants, he managed to lean back against the wall again.

Wearing just her uniform, too, she began to unbutton her light blue shirt. Hell. "W-what are you doing?"

Without looking up, she said, "I got a clean white T-shirt under my uniform. I'm going to tend to that cut with it."

"Want me to close my eyes?"

"No need, unless you feel like it. You can't see much anyway, but I've got on a sports bra, and it covers as much as what I exercise in at the house. But go ahead, Galahad, if you want."

"That's Sir Galahad to you."

Chuckling, she removed the outer shirt, reached to her waist and yanked up the tee. He didn't avert his gaze and was treated to a hazy view of her toned skin and even more toned breasts. After she re-dressed, she sidled in close and knelt up. "I wish I had water." Gently, she touched the wound on his head. It stung. "I'll get the worst of the grime off, though."

"You know that no water down here means more than not being able to clean my cut."

She sat back and looked him in the eye. "I know. We can't hydrate and we could run out of air before they rescue us."

"If they rescue us." He reached for her hand. Squeezed her fingers. "We entered the building at ten a.m." He checked his watch, which miraculously hadn't broken. "Eleven. They won't know where we are. I didn't relay our whereabouts when we headed down here." He shook his head. "The fire was really rolling. They probably had to evacuate and might not even have a head count yet."

"They'll put it out, Gabe." Her voice was full of bravado. "And find us."

"I hope so. But we need to be realistic. We're in pretty deep."

"Should we, I don't know, try to dig ourselves out?"

He scanned the area with the light again. "Too much debris to make a dent." Silence. "We should conserve the light."

"Well, we might as well get comfortable before we go dark." She stood, grabbed their turnout gear and formed their coats into two piles, their pants like a pillow of sorts.

"Good idea." If they were going to die, at least they'd be resting easily. Besides, they could conserve air by lying still.

They both slid onto the makeshift beds, and Gabe switched the light off. The area around them turned pitch black. "Holy hell."

"It's scary," Rachel commented. "I wonder why. We work in total darkness a lot of times in a fire."

"Yeah, but we know we're in open air most of the time, we have on our breathing masks and psychologically we understand we're not buried in some cave."

He felt her shiver, despite the heat. Reaching beside him, he found her hand and placed his over it. "That better?"

"Uh-huh."

"So, what do you want to talk about while we wait?"

"I don't care."

"If they don't find us soon, you'll miss your furlough."

"No big loss." She didn't sound sad about that.

"What were you going to do?"

She shifted. He could feel the weight of her body move. "Promise you won't laugh."

"Scout's honor."

"My parents are...were...taking my sister and me to Positano for four days."

"Positano, like in Italy?"

"They call me *Princess*, remember?" Her tone was disgusted.

He chuckled, the sound magnified in the small room and in the darkness. "Does it bother you, the teasing?"

"Nah. I understand where it's coming from."

"How rich are you?"

"Rich enough to fly to Italy for a few days. Old money. On both sides, so there's a lot."

"Lucky woman."

She waited a beat. "Not as lucky as you."

"What do you mean?"

He heard a heavy sigh. "I envy the Malvasos, Cap. You're so loving toward each other."

"Yeah, you wouldn't say that if you knew about our knockdown drag outs. A few years ago, before my cousin Jenn married her hubby, her brother Zach physically attacked Grady on Thanksgiving Day because Jenn was pregnant."

"Tell me more stories about them. It'll pass the time. And make me feel good."

He began talking, filling her in on his extended family. When she asked about his immediate one, he recounted how his two brothers lived out of town, how he supported his mother; and when she asked for information about his ex-wife and kids, he told her only some of it. Man, he hated his discussing his failure as a husband, the hurt he'd caused his kids. Especially now, when those might be some of his last memories.

• • •

LATER, THEY WERE still resting on the piles of clothes, and Gabe had gotten Rachel to tell him about growing up in the sterile environment of the Wellington household. They'd turned to face each other and she could feel the fan of his breath on her when he spoke.

"You're right," he said after she finished. "I'd envy the Malvasos, too." He sighed. "I'm glad you have your sister to commiserate with." Her only respite in the Wellington World was her beautiful, doctor sibling, Alexis, who felt exactly as she did about their overbearing parents.

Conversation lulled, neither wanting to voice the topic they were avoiding. Finally, she said, "It's been a while. Check and see how long."

His watch told him three hours.

"They had to have gotten the fire out," he told her. "They're probably bringing in drilling equipment as we speak."

"If they know where we are."

Her despairing tone of voice killed him. He grabbed her hands this time and held them tight. "We're gonna get out, Rachel, and when we do, I'll take you to our next Malvaso gathering. You can get some good home cooking, and a lot of hugs."

She whispered, "I could use a hug now."

A long pause. "Inch over then."

Without thinking about the breach of protocol in the request, she slid closer to him. His chest was as solid and muscular as she thought it would be, the crook of his arm and shoulder as comfortable as she imagined. She cuddled in. "Don't tell anybody about this when we get out, Captain."

"I think we should be on a first-name basis, down here, don't you?"

"Oh, okay." A pause. "You always call me Wellington. Why?"

"Hush and close your eyes. I'm exhausted and you must be, too. If we're not rescued in an hour, I'll explain it all."

"It's a deal."

She heard him inhale. "Your hair smells like lemon, even now, down here and amidst the dust."

"I'm getting whiffs of the aftershave you put on this morning."

Those were the last words they spoke before Rachel drifted off.

While she slept, he figured out that in a five-by-ten-by-ten room, they'd have about 18 hours of air. Divide by two, nine each. Carbon dioxide would be slowly replacing the oxygen. He wondered if their drowsiness was caused by that. Holding Rachel near, he closed his own eyes.

• • •

GABE AWOKE WITH a start. He was dreaming Rachel had cuddled up to him. He'd felt her nestled against his chest. No, wait, she *was* nestled against his chest.

But she roused, too. "What—where are…? Oh."

"We're in the basement of the abandoned building." He said the words soothingly as he rubbed her arm up and down.

"I remember. What time is it?"

"Move over and I'll check." He picked up his helmet and shone the light on his watch. "It's three o'clock. We've been down here four hours."

"That's not good, is it? That they haven't found us yet?"

"No, Rach, it isn't. And I hate to be indelicate, but I have to pee."

"Me, too."

With as much discretion as could be managed in a small space, they both took care of business on the farthest side of the room and covered it with debris.

When they settled back on the clothes, she said, "I figured in my head how much time we have left."

"I did, too, earlier." He tugged her close again. "Don't think about that."

"Tell me why you always call me by my last name, Gabe." Her voice was thick with emotion. "Tell me why you never touch me on the back or shoulder like you do everybody in the house. And you rarely hug me when we have a save."

"I'm your captain. I'm very careful with women."

"I've seen you hug Licia and Sydney." She waited. "You said you'd tell me if we weren't rescued." She tugged on his shirt. "'Fess up."

No response. Every instinct he had told him they shouldn't be doing this. He shouldn't tell her about the feelings that he'd developed for her over the eighteen months she'd been at House 7. But they could have only a few hours to live, and nausea, disorientation and drowsiness could claim them anytime.

"If you're shy, I'll start. Remember when we pulled that baby out of the burning house six months ago? You forgot about your distance and hugged me then. Didn't let go for a while. I liked it."

"So did I. A little too much."

Now she went silent.

*All right,* he thought. *Who knows what's going to happen?* "Remember when you first got here? The guys took your clothes when you were showering because they wanted to haze you like they would any male firefighter. You came out of the locker room wrapped in a towel, your hair wet? I practically swallowed my tongue."

"The other guys laughed at me."

"What can I say? Maybe they don't see you as I do."

Rachel started talking again. "One time we were working out in the weight room, you took off your damn shirt. I couldn't keep my eyes off your arms and chest."

He chuckled, then sobered. "Last year, you got hurt when that girder fell. We couldn't get you out right away and ended up using the Hurst tools. I about lost my mind. O'Malley asked me why later."

"What did you say?"

"That you were one of mine. That I'd react the same way to any of my crew being pinned."

"Oh."

"I lied."

"Oh!" Silence. "Your ex-wife is beautiful."

Now he stroked her hair. He couldn't see it, but knew the strands were steel-blond, not dyed, and thick and silky. "Not as pretty as you. And certainly not as feisty, independent and strong as you."

"Thank you, Gabe."

"That guy who picked you up for a date last week? We called him pretty boy. He's more handsome than Ramirez."

"He's an underwear model."

"Shit."

More silence. She was probably deciding whether or not to go further, as he'd been. "I changed the week I was going to volunteer at the camp because you signed up for the same one."

"Ah. I wondered what happened to you. I was looking forward to seeing you in shorts and a bathing suit."

They passed time in the same vein, only the confessions got more intimate, more personal. Finally, he checked his watch again. "Time's running out."

She buried her head in his chest and he cupped her neck, drew her closer, tighter.

"I'm not sure we're gonna make it out of here, Rachel."

"We should probably lie still, then. Not talk, even, to conserve air."

He was silent for a few seconds, then said, "Me? I think we should use what's left of our time wisely."

A girlish giggle bubbled out of her chest. "I agree. So, Captain, do you like doing it in the dark or with a light on?"

• • •

*SHE WAS A beauty*, Gabe thought as he stared at her naked form in the dim light from the helmet. He ran his hand down her arm, over her torso and her flank. Her skin was like watery silk; leaning over, he caught the scent of the lotion she used. Gooseflesh formed as soon as he touched her. If this was the last time he got to have sex, he was going to savor it.

"I never expected this to happen," she whispered as he continued his exploration. Her voice was hoarse with arousal, which only increased his. As did the way she glided her hands along his naked back and butt!

"It wouldn't have. We're breaking every rule in the book."

"As if it matters now." He caught the sheen of tears in her eyes.

Not once in the months he'd known her had he seen her cry, not even when she was pinned under that girder.

"Shh. Don't think about that. Think about me. Us together, this unexpected gift."

To distract her and, hell, to please himself, he cupped her incredibly toned breasts, kneaded them. They filled his hands nicely. He massaged them with increasing pressure. She sighed and he knew she was there, with him, not worrying about what was going to happen. Finally, he replaced his hands with his mouth and suckled a hard nipple. Closing his eyes, he enjoyed the feast.

She arched forward. "Ahhh…"

Against her skin, he whispered, "You like?"

"Oh, I like."

He moved lower, tongued her navel, kissed her firm belly and lay his cheek there, savoring the taste and feel of her. Then he slid his hand between her legs and ground his palm against her. This time she bucked. Moving back, he closed his mouth over her. She squirmed on the makeshift bed. "Gabe. Jesus. Oh, God!"

Rachel was so close, so close…but she wanted more. More of him. More time. No, no, don't think about that. He increased the pressure of his mouth and she let herself go. In seconds, she exploded into acute pleasure that went on and on, converging into one long stream of sensation.

After she came back to consciousness, she smiled up at him. He was braced over her and grinning. His eyes were dark liquid, and sweat dampened his hair, which was a mess from her hands. "I'm so glad I got to see that."

She ran her fingers over his jaw. It was scratchy by now. "I want to watch you, too."

Sliding her hand between them, she grasped on to his hard length. He was hot and full, heavy and ready. She rubbed up and down, up and down. His eyes closed, and his jaw slackened. "Oh. Jesus. Hell." Pushing her hand away, he opened her thighs and thrust inside her. "Ah, Rachel, baby."

He filled her completely. To increase the sensation, she pressed on his butt and urged him deeper, made him push harder. He groaned, grunted, then lost control and pounded into her. Rachel felt taken, consumed, possessed. His face was taut, his body unbelievably rigid. Suddenly, she tensed again. And sparks ignited inside her. She went with it, murmuring his name, encouraging him, and they crashed over the top together.

A while later, slick with sweat, he rolled to the side, taking her with him. Still connected, they held each other tightly. "That was one of the most wonderful things I've ever experienced, Gabe," she said softly.

"Me, too, sweetheart." His hand brushed down her now-damp hair. "Worth the oxygen we used."

Then the light went out. She startled and he drew her closer, their bare chests melding together, their legs entangled. "It's all right. I'm here. Close your eyes."

"Will we just drift off, Gabe?"

"Let's hope so. The symptoms at the end are…not pleasant." Already he felt sleepy. And now that he was conscious of his condition, his stomach felt queasy. "Close your eyes and try to relax."

When she did, he said, "Thank you so much for giving this to me."

"I feel the same."

Then they slept.

• • •

CRASHING SOUNDS. LOUD, louder, very loud…

Gabe thought he was dreaming about the cave-in until he startled awake. Rachel awoke, too, and grabbed hold of him. Pitch blackness surrounded them and they could see nothing. But the noise was loud. And they both coughed at what was in the air. Dust.

"What...Gabe what...is the building falling in on us?"

He got his bearings and assessed the situation. Nausea roiled inside him, and his head felt light. His throat was clogged. "No, that's excavation equipment."

"Excavation...you mean..."

He grasped her by the arms. "We're being rescued."

"Oh, thank you so much, God. I thought we were going to die."

"Hallelujah!" he shouted enthusiastically, hugging her to him.

Then they both drew back.

Reality dawned.

She said, "Uh-oh."

A pause. Then, "Yeah, uh-the-fucking-oh!"

# CHAPTER 3

"I STILL THINK you two should go to the hospital. You might need a hyperbaric chamber to restore oxygen in your system." Zach Malvaso, Gabe's cousin, was working the night shift and took Gabe's pulse for the third time. He and Rachel had been given oxygen from a portable tank. His nausea and light-headedness receded quickly. The consensus when they were pulled out was that some air had to be seeping into their cocoon. Thank God, or they'd be dead.

"I don't need to rest," he said shortly. "And I don't need an oxygen chamber. I feel good." He nodded to the other cot. "How about her?"

Casey, Zach's dark-haired wife, took Rachel's pulse again. "I think she's fine. More than fine. I'm shocked you two could be in such carbon-filled air for so long and still be in good condition." She smiled at Rachel. "What'd you down there? Sleep to ignore the stress of almost buying it?"

Damn. Rachel felt herself blush. And Gabe's guilty glance didn't help. "No, we're seasoned firefighters accustomed to crisis situations."

The other four members of Rescue 7, Group 3, hovered outside the truck, pacing, looking inside, scowling. They'd been at the fire ground all day, even after their shift ended, waiting to see if their captain and colleague survived. It was nine p.m. and night had fallen.

Ramirez shook his head, his eyes bleak. *"Querido Dios, usted dos podrían han muerto."*

Leaning against the rig next to him, Sydney touched his arm. "But they didn't die. Be happy about that." She shrugged and called into the truck, "Though if you hadn't gotten out, Princess, I might not have had to transfer."

"Sorry to disappoint you."

"Kid-ding." Sydney had bounced back first from the day-long worry and was the most upbeat among the other four members of their crew.

Rachel breathed in the warm air sneaking into the Midi. "That feels so good."

*That feels so good, Gabe. So, so good. I can't believe you're touching me like this.*

If Gabe remembered her words, and similar ones of his own, he wasn't showing it. Instead, he was ornery and bossy—unlike the fireman's firefighter he was. Normally, he was so even-keeled, everybody loved him.

Zach hopped out of the Midi. "Okay, if you're not going to get checked out, at least go home. Your shift ended hours ago. I'll drive you, cuz."

"No." He climbed out of the truck right behind Zach. "I'm going back to the fire station with the group."

Thankfully, it had taken the specialty crew a half hour to break through the last layers of rock and sludge to open up the basement. Once Gabe and Rachel had realized what was happening, they'd had time to dress. Now, back in the real world of their jobs, she couldn't believe the impulse they'd acted on.

Tony helped Rachel down from the truck and she leaned into his hug. Then she saw a black Mercedes pull into the parking lot. *This* was all she needed. Slamming the door, her father exited the car, and even though their daughter could have died a few hours ago, her mother waited for him to open the passenger side. Both tall and slim, they were dressed in country club casual. Their strides were purposeful as they approached her.

The equipment was loaded onto the rigs, and other crews were beginning salvage and overhaul to clean up the building, but Henry Wellington was oblivious to the commotion. "I cannot *believe* this! Are you satisfied now, Rachel Anne? You've ruined our vacation and almost got yourself killed."

Rachel was stupefied by his outburst. The adrenaline rush of being saved was wearing off, and her knees went weak. "Please, Father, not now." And not in front of her squad.

Catherine moved in close and put her hand on Rachel's arm. "Are you really all right, dear? You gave me quite a fright."

"I'm fine, Mother. I'm going back to the firehouse to get my car and go home."

"Nonsense." Her father again. "We called Madison. He's meeting us at our house to check you out." Madison King was a doctor friend they socialized with. Her parents knew not only medical personnel, but lawyers, judges, TV personalities, who were at their beck and call.

"No, thanks. I want to go home."

"I won't have this!" her father stated. Some of the huge lights set up suddenly went out, casting him into partial darkness.

Gabe stepped up to her side. "Mr. & Mrs. Wellington. I'm Captain Malvaso, Rachel's supervising officer. I assure you our paramedics have checked us both out, and we're fine.

All Firefighter Wellington needs is some rest. Now, if you'll excuse us, she's required to come back on the truck to debrief." Turning, he took Rachel by the elbow and led her to the rescue rig, leaving Henry Wellington sputtering behind them.

Bending his head, he spoke into her ear. "Don't look back; they'll go away."

"Th-thanks, Gabe. I don't stand up to them well."

"So I saw."

Before they reached the rig, she stopped and touched his shoulder. "We have to talk, Gabe."

He stepped away immediately, so different from the man who'd touched her, sank his body into hers and relished her response to him. His face was set in hard planes and angles. Gone was the tenderness and care with which he'd made love to her. "Oh, God, no. Let's forget what happened."

Though his curt comment cut her to the quick, she'd be damned if she let it show. Firefighters were good at blocking. They had to be. "I see. Like, what happened in the basement stays in the basement?"

"Um, yeah, I guess."

Unaware of what she was interrupting, Felicia approached them and slipped her arm through Rachel's. "Come on girlfriend, let's go home."

Brody looped his arm around Gabe's neck. "We're gonna take you out to celebrate."

They all piled into the rig and took up their assigned positions—Gabe in front with Sydney, who was driving, Rachel in the middle seat between Tony and Brody, Felicia in the back with Syd. After a minute, Tony put his hand over hers, where it rested on the seat. Brody did the same on the other side.

"Jesus, we were afraid…" Brody began.

"I know, buddy. So were we."

Which was why she'd acted so inappropriately, she thought. Now that she'd calmed down, she realized the last thing females in the department needed was to confirm the false reputation that they slept around.

Who knew, though, how she and Gabe were going to deal with what they'd done.

• • •

OUTSIDE OF BADGES, the firefighter and police bar of choice, hence the name, the night was warm, and Gabe was glad to be alive. He'd taken a long shower, dressed in jeans and a red shirt rolled up at the sleeves, and had O'Malley doctor him up again. All told, he came out of the incident with a cut on his forehead, which needed only a bandage, and a few scrapes on his cheek and neck. But he knew in his heart he wasn't the same man who had rushed headlong into that burning building. In one short afternoon, he'd compromised his principals and slept with a firefighter under his command. Not only that, all those months of keeping himself in check around Rachel Wellington were lost in a dark room that he'd thought they'd never get out of. Which explained why he'd bought a pack of cigarettes and wandered out here with a beer.

"Jesus, give yourself a break, asshole," he muttered, disgusted with his self-recriminations. "You thought you were gonna die."

"Talkin' to yourself?" His cousin Mitch had joined him on the patio. "Did you get hit on the head harder than we thought?"

"Yeah, maybe."

Mitch dropped down across from him in a chair at the wrought iron table, then nodded to his hand. "Thought you gave that up years ago."

"I did." Gabe smiled at the guy who'd been not only a relative but a close friend all his life. He took a drag then held up the butt. "For the life of me, I can't figure out why so many firefighters smoke. We breathe in enough shit as it is every day."

"There's a psychology behind it, I'm sure." Nonchalantly, Mitch leaned back, crossed his ankle over his knee and linked his hands behind his head. "So, are you really okay?"

"Yeah, I am. Shaken some. That's natural."

"How's Wellington doing?"

"As good as me, I'd guess." He didn't want to look at his cousin, so he rubbed his hand on the steel of the curlicues in the tabletop. "Why do you ask?"

"She lit out of the house in a flash." Mitch shrugged. "Maybe she had a date."

Shit. Gabe took another drag.

Staring over his shoulder, Mitch got a faraway look in his eyes. "I remember when me, Zach and Jenn got trapped in that warehouse three years ago. It put everything in perspective for us. I ended up with Meg, Jenn and Grady got together and Zach found Casey."

Hell, could his cousin read his mind? "Lucky you."

"So, Gabriel, what are you gonna change about your life?"

"Not much. I'm happy as I am, Mitello." Their mothers had given them their Italian names then shortened them.

"Your divorce was five years ago. You need a woman."

*I just had one. And it was some of the best damn sex of my life.*

"Yeah, I guess I do."

Mitch watched him for a minute, then checked out their surroundings. Some bluesy jazz drifted out of the bar, but no one else was on the patio. "I can tell you're holding back. I always knew when you were keeping something from me. And I'm a pretty good sounding board."

"It's bad, Mitch. Professionally. And you're a BC in the department."

"Fuck it. I'm your friend and cousin first. I won't tell anybody. Whatever you say stays here."

*What happened in the basement stays in the basement.*

"I didn't think I was gonna get out." His voice sounded heavy, somber.

Mitch waited.

"Something else is goin' on with me." A pause. "I've had…feelings. Hell. No, I don't know, maybe…"

"Spit it out. Gabe."

"I've been attracted to Wellington for months. Kept a lid on it good enough so nothing happened, nothing even showed. Apparently, she'd been doin' the same thing." He took another drag then butted out the cigarette. "The lid blew today. For both of us."

Mitch's brows hiked up and he sat forward. "Holy shit, I didn't expect that."

"Neither did we. I can't believe I breached professional ethics like that."

Mitch's eyes narrowed. "You can look at it that way. Or you can see it as two desperate people finding solace with each other when they thought they were gonna buy it. My guess is anybody would pick the latter."

"Maybe. But I went against my values, my beliefs."

"You're only human, Gabe. Like you said, give yourself a break."

He nodded.

Bracing his arms on the table, Mitch leaned forward. "The question is what are you gonna do now?"

"Forget about it. I told her as much when we got a minute alone after we were rescued."

"How'd she take it?"

The image of Rachel's distraught expression and the trembling of her lips when he reacted badly assaulted him. He might as well admit everything. "I think she was hurt. Probably more with my delivery than the actual meaning. Hell, Mitch, she's one of the top female firefighters in our department. Other women like Sands look up to her. She can't be glad we were so…indiscreet."

"Again, circumstances. Are you gonna be able to go back to what it was before between you?"

"I hope to God we can. I don't know what I'll do otherwise."

• • •

RACHEL LET HERSELF into her condo on Hidden Lake, a twenty-minute drive from the firehouse. The first time she'd invited the guys out here, Gabe included, they'd teased her mercilessly about her trust fund digs on the water. Her place was expensive because she had part of the beach, too. The interior was huge, and the back of the house sported a screened-in porch with furniture groupings and a wall of windows opening to a patio and deck.

From back there, a light shone, and her sister called out, "I'm here. Don't get scared."

Sighing, Rachel trudged to the rear of the house; she found Alexis on one of the couches. Her eyes welled at seeing the person she loved more than anyone in the world. "Thanks for letting me know. I'd say I've been scared enough today."

A pediatric surgeon, Alexis still wore her hospital-blue scrubs. She rose from the sofa, set down her BlackBerry and crossed to Rachel. Her hug was strong and safe, and for a moment, Rachel clung to her. "Thank God you're all right. I don't know..." Strong and competent Dr. Wellington had a soft spot for her younger sister, too. All their lives, they'd only had each other to deal with their self-centered parents.

"Sit. I'll make you tea."

"I'd rather have whiskey."

"I can do that."

After Alexis fetched both of them drinks, they sat on the wide-cushioned couch, face-to-face, mirroring each other's cross-legged position. "Was it awful?" her sister asked.

"Some of it. Did you know what was going on while you were at the hospital?"

"Yeah, they brought in hurt firefighters all day from the explosion. There were six vagrants in the building, but only a few needed treatment. The rescue personnel got whacked."

"Oh, Lexie, I'm so sorry. That must have been terrible for you."

"Bad enough. Plus our parents called a million times to tell me I had to talk some sense into you when you were rescued." Alexis had the same hazel eyes and steel-blond hair as Rachel, only her sister was more feminine, with a slighter build. "Tell me all of it, sis."

Tears welled in Rachel's eyes again, but this time they spilled over. She swiped at them impatiently. The adrenaline rush had subsided, and she was shaky, uncertain, even cold, making her shiver despite the warm air that filtered in through the open screens.

Grabbing a throw, Alexis put it around Rachel's shoulders. It was as soft as a kitten's fur. "Jesus, I don't think I've seen you cry in years. I'm sorry, honey."

"We're trained in confined-space maneuvers, and besides the space wasn't that small. Still, being trapped was awful."

"How big was the area?"

Rachel looked directly at her sister. "Big enough to have sex in."

Alexis's eyes widened. *"What?"*

"I was with the hot captain I told you about." There were few secrets between the sisters. "He confessed he felt the same about me as I did about him. I told you before I thought that might be true. We, um, thought we weren't going to get out."

"So you gave in to your feelings?"

"Uh-huh." She sipped the drink that had gone untouched on the table. The tart liquid gave her the punch she needed. "What a mess."

"First, tell me how good it was."

Rachel smiled at Alexis's mischievous expression. "He's got great hands. He was so tender, then at the end, so... forceful. Hell, I sound like the heroine of the romance novels you're always reading."

"Romance novels got me through med school, girl."

"Anyway, he was wonderful, and I haven't felt that close to a guy...in I don't know when."

"It certainly wasn't with Awful Edward."

The man Rachel had been engaged to. The man who'd dumped her when she wanted to join the fire department.

Couldn't have a CEO of a major corporation with a woman who smelled like smoke half the time. Rachel had given up a lot to be a firefighter, and now she'd jeopardized all she'd fought Edward and her parents to achieve.

"So what are you going to do now?" Alexis asked.

"Forget about what happened between me and Gabe." She held up her hand, palm forward. "Before you give me the 'firefighting isn't everything' talk, know that as soon as we were rescued, Gabe turned cold and abrupt. When I said we needed to talk, he gave me the complete brush-off." She took another sip of the whiskey. "Shit, I would have suggested we forget what happened if I'd had a chance, but he turned into a typical boy bastard."

"I'm sorry, Rach. Really. You could look at it this way—you had some hot sex with a hot guy."

"For which I'll pay dearly. How can I face him every day?"

"You have time to mull that over. Remember, we have four days off, both of us."

"Yeah, I forgot. Think we can stay below the parents' radar?"

"Yep. We've always been good at that. I say we hole up here with our phones off, sit out in the sun, swim and drink wine."

Rachel heartily agreed to the time she'd have alone with her sister, an unexpected treat. Deciding to throw herself into that, she ordered herself not to think about her ordeal in the basement with Gabe Malvaso.

# CHAPTER 4

ON THEIR NEXT shift, a night rotation, Firefighter Wellington breezed into the station house so bright and bushy tailed that Gabe wanted to snarl at her. He'd had a hell of a time during their four-day furlough and she looked rested and tanned. Even her hair sported pretty blond highlights. Had she gone to fucking Italy after what they'd been through? He, on the other hand, had walked around his house simultaneously kicking himself in the butt for his unethical actions and remembering what she felt like under him. With little sleep behind him, Gabe was ready for a fight.

"'Afternoon, everyone." She set two big, pink boxes on the table. "Got us a treat from La Belle Gourmand."

"Hey great," Ramirez told her. "Sophia loves the pastry from that place."

"Take her home a few," Rachel said, smiling.

O'Malley looked up from a magazine he was reading. "What's the occasion?"

"Dummy." This from Ramirez, who'd gotten up to hug Rachel. "She cheated the dark force. She's still celebrating."

Across the room at the big urn, Gabe turned his back, poured coffee and tried not to listen. It was useless, of course.

"Yeah, Wellington, tell us how you spent those extra days." Sands again, in that teenage wheedling voice that belied a very good firefighter. "Did you get away for a few days with your main man?"

Coffee sloshed over Gabe's hand and he swore.

"You okay, Cap?" Ramirez called over.

"Just peachy." He turned, but they weren't watching him. They all exchanged looks. Rachel mouthed, "What?"

"Cranky." Brody whispered the word. "Big time."

"I heard that," Gabe said, joining them at the table. "'Morning, Wellington. Nice treats." He faced O'Malley. "You'd be out of sorts if you'd almost died, too, Firefighter."

Rachel gave him a wide smile. "But we're alive, Captain. Something I intend to remember. My new mantra is *No Bad Days*."

"Good luck with that." He pointed to the open box. The scent of pastry filled the air. "I'll have a half-moon cookie."

Sands passed him one as Felicia entered the kitchen. "Hey, don't eat those. I got dinner all planned."

The guys rolled their eyes. Firefighters were robust eaters no matter what snacks they consumed.

After she greeted Licia, Rachel grabbed the newspaper and buried her nose in it.

Later, she got up to help Felicia.

During dinner, she was all sweetness and light to everybody but Gabe, acting as if he wasn't even there. As if he hadn't touched her everywhere. Been inside her. She even approached their training—a review of the newest machine to test for anthrax—in a good mood, chatting happily all through the drill. Her Pollyanna act wore thin—and so did being near her, smelling her scent, seeing her eyes crinkle with humor—so as soon as the training was over, Gabe changed in the locker room and made a beeline for their workout area upstairs. He'd get on his boxing gloves and knock the shit out of a punching bag.

When he went inside the well-equipped room, he found Rachel had beat him to the punch, so to speak. Dressed in a pair of clingy white shorts and a dark navy muscle shirt, she danced around the bag hanging in the corner, making it sway with her attacks. Gabe raised his eyes to the heavens and said silently, *Gimme a freaking break!*

But as he watched her, he realized they couldn't ignore the strain between them. So he locked the door and crossed to her. When she acted as if she didn't see him, he grabbed the bag.

"Hey!" Finally she looked at him. Her eyes were fiery and her face moist with perspiration. "What are you doing?"

"I wanna talk to you."

Cocking her head, she asked, "As my captain or as a man?"

"A man."

"No thanks." She gave him her back and started in on the bag again.

Jesus. At a loss for what to do, he caught sight of the rack beside him. Hell, why not? Maybe it would help release some of the tension smoldering between them. Quickly, he suited up, then butted her arm with a helmet like the one he'd donned. "Here, put this on."

"I don't want to."

"Don't be childish. You might as well take shots at your real target."

She arched a delicate brow. "That has appeal."

When she was ready, she faced him. "Give it to me hard, Malvaso," she said swinging first and landing the punch on his shoulder.

He was so surprised by her suggestive remark and her quick offensive, he didn't even raise his hands to block the attack.

Next time, he was ready and feinted left when she swung, then he did a counterpunch to the side of her helmet. "That what you want, Princess?"

She punched back, pulling it low to get him on the chest. He stumbled. "Yeah, now shut up and do your best."

"I always do my best, but then you know that firsthand, so to speak."

Her blow hit square on his jaw.

After fifteen minutes, they were both covered in sweat, and Gabe was sore as hell, so she had to be, too. Neither had taken it easy with the other. He stepped back first.

"Done?" she asked, challenge in her voice.

"Yeah, and so are you."

"No, I'm not. I'm going to do some weights."

He wrested his gloves off, removed his helmet, then grabbed her wrist. "Now I'm your captain. You're done exercising, because you won't be able to lift your air tank if you work out any more."

"Fine." She whipped off her helmet and threw it on the rack. Her gloves were next and hit the floor. Her antagonism didn't surprise him, after how he'd acted in the aftermath of being stuck in the basement with her. In fact, it told him plenty. As she took a step toward the door, he pulled her back by the shoulder. "We're gonna have this out."

She whirled on him. He wished her cheeks weren't so flushed, her hair not damp like it got after sex. "What?"

"You know damn well what. You wanted to talk after we were rescued and I wasn't ready. I am now."

"Tough shit. I don't wanna talk anymore."

"I'm sorry if I was abrupt and unkind in what I said." He tried to soften his tone, but she was being a real brat, and it made him mad. "I don't want to hurt you, Rachel." He couldn't help himself. He ran his knuckles down her cheek.

She ratcheted back. "Don't you *dare* touch me in this house! And don't try to charm me out of being furious with you. We weren't even on solid ground yet when you regretted what we'd done. What was it you said? *Uh-fucking-oh.* You never use that word around us. Then after we were rescued, you said we should forget all about having sex in that cellar. You treated me like yesterday's trash."

"I—"

"Well, you got your wish, Captain. I've forgotten all about our little tryst."

Her words sparked his own anger. "Yeah, with who? The guy you spent the last four days with, getting that tan?"

"I don't believe you. Talk about dog in the manger."

Gabe couldn't believe his behavior, either, what she brought out of him. He had to get control of the situation. "I admit I was a jerk."

"An asshole is more like it."

"Okay! I got it!" He ran a hand through his hair. Who knew she had such a temper? She'd never once shown it around the house. "Look, I apologize. I want to talk about where to go from here."

"We go absolutely nowhere, Gabe. Nowhere. If you'd been halfway decent to me, I would have said then what I'm saying now. We *do* have to forget what happened. I can't possibly be involved with my officer. My reputation in the department would be ruined if we hooked up. It was over between us, really, before it got started."

He never expected that. "Then why are you so mad?"

"Because you were *offended* by what we did as two consenting adults." She shook her head. "And here I thought you'd be decent to women. I envied the dates you brought to department events, was jealous of your wife. They're welcome to you."

Turning, she stormed to the door. Yanked on it. It wouldn't open. Over her shoulder, she spat out, "Don't ever do something like this again. Being behind locked doors with you will cause untold speculation about us."

"The group's outside playing basketball."

"Don't do it again." She undid the lock, then faced him. "As soon as I step out of this room, I'm going back to being respectful and cooperative with you. But don't mistake that for anything more than what it is. Duty and responsibility."

As she left, he muttered, "Fat chance of forgetting that."

• • •

FELICIA WHITE WAS a force to be reckoned with. Cool, calm and determined, she was the best person to present what she, Sydney and Rachel had come up with. They sat around a conference table in the battalion chief's office down the hall from the firehouse proper, to discuss their publicity idea. Noah Callahan had assigned the problem of Parker Allen to Erikson.

Rachel was satisfied with their proposal and refused to be distracted by Gabe's presence. He'd asked to be at the meeting, probably because he felt responsible for everything. Now he sat across from her, and instead of watching him, she examined the Manwaring print on the chief's wall. Rumor had it the framed photo from the popular firefighter artist was real, which would be costly.

All week, she'd tried hard not to think about the regrets she had for behaving badly with Gabe when they'd boxed, but today they'd come back full force. She and Gabe exchanged no more unprofessional talk, and it was good to stay distanced, really it was, even if he looked big and masculine in his crisp white shirt, had gotten a haircut and a bit of sun.

Licia spoke up. "We want to start a blog of our own to retaliate against Parker Allen. We'll make it clear that's the purpose by titling the first blog entry *Make It Right or Got It Wrong?* All the women in the department have agreed to take a day to write an entry—on their own time—and discuss their lives as firefighters. Readers will be invited to respond. If we get good feedback, it'll be ammunition for fighting against the shrew."

"Why single out women?" Gabe asked. When forced to look at him more closely, she noticed a nick from his razor on his chin. "The whole point of our experiment at House 7 was to integrate a gender-equal team to prove that we can work together as well as all guys."

"And we'll discuss that, Gabe. But fire women have a unique story to tell that'll appeal to the public. We'll advertise on all the fire sites as well as some global sites that the general population goes to. Word will spread. We can start with the history of women integrating the fire department, then narrow down to the HCFD and our experiment at Rescue 7. We'll also talk about our daily lives as firefighters in and out of the station houses." She gave what passed for a smile from Licia. "Besides, can you see Ed Snyder and his cronies over at Engine 4 writing about their feelings?"

The question needed no answer verbalized. That group would shun the blog, maybe even work against it.

"And this way," Rachel put in, rubbing her hand over the padded armchair made of nubby fabric, "It's more controllable."

"I guess that makes sense. None of this will be done on work time, right?" Gabe clarified.

"That's what we said, Captain," Rachel said coolly. You'd never know how pissed they'd been at each other.

"What do you think, Cal?" Felicia asked Chief Erikson.

"I think it's worth a shot. God knows we're not getting good coverage in the *Herald's* news section or from Allen's blog." He nodded to Gabe. "They barely interviewed you and Wellington about what it was like being trapped in the basement of a burning building, thinking you'd die."

"Not much to tell, really." Rachel jumped in to answer. "It was dark and scary. Your officer was brave and stalwart."

Gabe gave a half smile. For some reason, it made her sad.

"All right. Go for it. I need to see that first post, though." Erikson's brow furrowed when Felicia frowned. "Is that all right?"

"Well, if you don't trust me to oversee this." Felicia's tone was glacial. Rachel was glad it wasn't directed at her.

"You know I do. Okay, you're on your own. It is okay if I check the blog when it's posted?" His tone was teasing.

"Of course, Chief."

"Do you have a name for the website?"

Felicia tossed a sideways glance at Rachel and Sydney. "Girls Gone Wild?"

"What the hell?" The question came out of Gabe's mouth before he realized the women were playing *gotcha*. They shared a laugh at his expense, which felt good, then told him they'd chosen to label it Fire Belles.

"I objected to the frilly sound of the term but got out voted."

"It's cool," Sydney said, "and a great play on words."

The meeting wound down and the three women left together.

"A word, Wellington?" Gabe called out as he left the office, and Rachel walked a few feet ahead of him.

She sighed. Just being close to him bothered her big-time. Sometimes, he'd sidle past her in the kitchen and she'd catch his scent. And she'd remember smelling it on all of him. Watching him after he'd showered, she wanted to tousle his damp hair. And she had to resist the urge to run her fingers over his pecs, even his bare arms, when he was within touching distance.

"Yes, sir?" she said when they were alone, a few paces down from Erikson's office.

His dark gaze was intense, and the expression in them made her recall another kind of heat she'd seen there that afternoon in the cellar. "Does your compliment in there mean you're not still mad at me?"

She glanced over his shoulder and watched the trees through the open side door. "Yeah. I lost my temper that day in the workout room. I'm sorry. I plan to be better."

"Good." Relief shone on his rugged features. "Then it'll make working together easier. And for the record, you were pretty brave down there, too."

At least they'd formed a truce of sorts. It should make life easier all around. She just wished she didn't feel so bad about their decision to do the right thing.

# CHAPTER 5

IN THE YARD outside her condo, Rachel sipped from a cup of beer and watched several little kids gather around the two picnic tables she'd set up for them. The lake shimmered in the background on this late July afternoon, and the warm air soothed her frayed nerves.

Tony joined her, looping an arm around her neck. His cheek was scratchy, but she liked his openness. He was easy at affection and had great relationships with everybody. His wife was one lucky woman. "Hey, lady. Thanks so much for letting us have Miguel's party out here. The kids love the lake."

"I know. They had fun last summer when our group came out for a picnic."

He scanned the crowd, his dark eyes full of joy. "I'm glad you invited the squad and their families."

"We always seem to flock together, don't we?"

The joy in Tony's eyes dimmed. "Sophia says, too much."

She drew him around. "Really? I had no idea she objected to socializing with us."

"*De nada*. She loves you guys. I think all firefighter spouses feel left out where their group is concerned. It shows more when the crew is together."

"Well, I wouldn't know much about married life."

Laughing, he poked her in the ribs. "You gotta get yourself a man, Wellington. How old are you anyway?"

"Twenty-eight. So I got plenty of time for babies if I want them."

"Um, excuse me."

She didn't even have to look at the owner of that deep, male baritone. Their captain had arrived. When she turned, the expression on his face was intense, and his stare wended its way inside her. Today he wore khaki shorts and a red-striped golf shirt. The color highlighted his dark hair and made his eyes look liquid.

"*Buenos Días*, Capitano."

"Hey, *bombero*." He gave Rachel a nervous smile. "Hi, Wellington."

"Captain." Rachel peeked around Gabe. "Hello, Lily, Joey."

Gabe's kids were adorable. At eight and nine, they were dark haired and dark eyed, like their dad. She saw them every so often when he had them after work or at a party like this. They'd become good friends with Tony's son and daughter.

"Thank you for letting us come here again," Lily said shyly.

"Me, too." Joey asked his father, "Can I go see Miguel, Dad?"

"Sure."

Lily grabbed on to Gabe's legs. He hunkered down to meet her at eye level. His gentle way with his daughter made Rachel's throat clog. "Don't you want to go with Joey, sweetheart?"

The little girl shook her head.

Standing, Gabe gave his daughter's shoulder a gentle squeeze. "She's shy."

Tony held out his hand. "Hey, baby girl. Mari's been waiting for you to get here. The other kids are mostly Miguel's friends, but she invited you especially. Want to go see her?"

"'kay."

Tony looked to Gabe. "I'll take her over."

Gabe handed Tony the two presents he'd set on a picnic table off to the right. "Take these to the birthday boy."

Rachel shifted uncomfortably when they were alone. Not only was the nearness of his body discomfiting, but his scent—something dark and sexy—caught in the breeze and teased her senses.

"Thanks for doing this for Tony. He and Sophia need it right now."

She cocked her head. "Something wrong?"

"Um, no, I don't know why I said that."

"If it's private, Captain, say so."

"Yeah, it's private. And I only have a few suspicions." He nodded to the keg off to the right. "Need any money for that?" For anything?"

"The O'Malley boys brought the beer." She nodded to the sandy beach behind her house. "They're like kids themselves." Right now, the brothers were punching a volleyball to each other over a net they'd also brought and set up. Both were dressed in dark bathing trunks and no shirts and looked young, healthy and happy.

"Don't stare too long at them," Gabe said with an edge in his voice. "You work with them."

"Not with Ryan." She glanced at Gabe. His brows furrowed. "Besides, I can judge for myself what to do and not do."

"You couldn't three weeks ago."

"Touché." She sighed. "Let's not fight. Or talk about that."

"In a minute." His gaze darkened and he drew her farther away from the crowd, pitched his tone purposely low. "I heard you talking about babies."

"Yeah, to Tony."

"Hypothetically?"

"What do you…?" She could feel her face flush. "Oh, yeah. I see. No, Gabe, don't worry. I got my period last week. No unwanted results of our basement thing." She smiled, but it was perfunctory. "I have to go check on the kids' drinks. Have fun today."

"You, too."

*Son of a fucking bitch*, Rachel thought as she left Gabe. It was a good thing that they didn't talk much. Every time she saw him at the firehouse, she wanted to jump his bones. She expected her reaction to weaken by now, but it hadn't. What on earth would she do if she couldn't get over the feelings she had for him?

• • •

GABE WALKED INTO Rachel's house to change into his swimming trunks. His mind was imprinted with how she looked in her bathing suit, a sleek, black one she wore with a pink-flowered skirt that tied around her waist and hit her knees. The top showed off her beautiful breasts. Her skin had been kissed by the sun, and a few freckles peeked out on her shoulders and chest. His hands itched to touch her, and it about killed him not to.

He made his way through the porch and sliding doors to a state-of-the-art kitchen with gleaming appliances and a parquet floor. He'd been to her home before, so he made his way down a hall to the bathroom. He tried the knob.

"It's me, Sophia, in here. Rachel said we could use the bath off her bedroom, too."

Oh, swell. Seeing her private space was just what he needed. Still, curiosity got the best of him and he went farther down the hall, where he found the door open. He stepped inside, and immediately, her scent assaulted him. Along with it, came the memories....

His face was buried in her breasts. *Mmm, you smell so good.*

*Bath gel my sister sent me from Paris.*

*It makes me hard just smelling it.*

She'd cupped his neck in a gesture so tender it caused his heart to beat faster and not because he was turned on....

Shaking himself free from the images, he scanned the room. It was *her:* well-appointed but no frills, no nonsense. A huge bed took center stage, covered with a deep-rose-and-green—what was it called?—a duvet. He walked over to it and ran his hand across the soft down. More gorgeous wood on the floor and ceiling. A ribbon of windows faced the lake with a pretty view. Walls were painted a deep green with white trim.

Disgusted with himself for devouring her surroundings, he found the bathroom, a huge thing, with—oh, great—a Jacuzzi tub. He swallowed hard at the vision of her and him in deep sudsy water. On the heels of that came an unwanted thought. What man—or men for God's sake—had she bathed with? Worse, *would* she bathe with?

He focused on what he was doing as he slipped into a black-and-white swimsuit and black T-shirt. He left the room hurriedly, but the scents of Rachel followed him.

For a long time, he played with his kids in the sand, squishing it between his toes with Lilliana and Mari, then he took them into the shallow water while he kept a weather eye on Joey, who swam out further with Tony and Sophia.

"You're different with your kids," he heard from behind him.

Turning around, he found Sydney dipping her feet in the lake. He glanced down. Syd had her two-year-old girl by the hand. "Hey, Syd."

"Captain."

"Lily, look here's Daisy."

Lily and Mari both rushed to the baby. "Hi, Daisy." They nudged Syd back, and each took one of Daisy's hands. "Can we play with her in the sand, Daddy?" Mari asked.

Checking Syd's reaction, he said, "Sure."

"I'll watch them, Gabe. I've been playing volleyball while Rachel took care of my little one. Why don't you go join the team and have a little fun?"

He glanced out at the lake. "Joey's still in."

"Tony's out there with them. Go ahead, let down some."

That sounded good to Gabe right now, and so did exercise, until he walked to the makeshift court. Ryan O'Malley, along with a friend of his from high school and Rachel played on one team. The other consisted of Felicia, a woman and man he didn't know and Brody.

"Hey, Cap," Ryan yelled out, using the familiar term because he was at the firehouse so much. "Come on, we need a fourth."

Wondering who was sending him this punishment, Gabe ended up next to Rachel again. He didn't know how much he could take of being near her in a social setting and keep his emotional distance. It had been a mistake to come to the party.

• • •

THE SUN BEAT down on them as Rachel stood in the server's box, tossed up the ball and punched it over the net. Felicia managed to slide in the sand and a pop it back. Brody sent the thing hurtling over the net.

Not to be outdone, his brother dived for the ball and lobbed it up; Gabe spiked it over so nobody had a chance for a save. Damn, he was good at everything.

*This feels wonderful, Gabe.* She'd smiled. *You're so good at this.*

Even though she was trying hard, she couldn't stop the memories that came out of the blue, sensual ambushes, which struck without warning.

"Hey, Rachel baby, where are you?" Ryan asked. "You missed an easy shot."

"Oh, sorry. It won't happen again."

Like her and Gabe. *It won't happen again.*

Forcing herself to concentrate, she made two saves and a spike on the next plays. After the latter, Ryan raced over, picked her up and twirled her around. "Hey, there, girl, you're hot today."

She hugged back. Over Ryan's shoulder, she caught Gabe's stare. Intense and...jealous.

This wasn't what she wanted at all.

• • •

GABE SAW HER go into the house from where he sat at a picnic table eating a hot dog with Cal, who showed up late.

"The blog's going pretty well, don't you think?" the chief asked.

"Like gangbusters." Gabe's smile was genuine. "Do you know they got a million hits last week? I have to admit, some of their stories are funny."

"And moving." Brody was nearby. "Licia's account of the women involved in the 9/11 search-and-rescue operation made me bawl."

"I read Wellington's post about being trapped in the basement," Cal put in. "Pretty scary."

"We got through it all right." He glanced to the kitchen again and could see her in the window. Rising, he said, "I'm gonna go get another hot dog. Want something?"

No one did.

Instead of heading to the grill, he detoured into the house and found her washing pans at the sink. Her back was to him and he admired the feminine curve of her spine, the toned muscles of her calves. He remembered how soft and smooth all that skin was. "Need some help?"

She glanced over her shoulder and swallowed hard. "No. Go back outside."

Instead, he leaned against the counter and folded his arms across his chest. "Why?"

"You know why. It's hard to be around you."

"Is it?"

She turned and seeing no one was nearby, she faced him fully. "What do you want me to say, Captain? That it kills me to witness how tender you are with your kids. How terrific you look in that T-shirt. How I—" She stopped short. "Jesus. I'm sorry."

Acting on need and not thought, he moved in closer but didn't touch her. For a minute, he stared at the soap dribbling from her hands to the floor. "At least you didn't have to watch while another woman put her hands all over me." At Rachel's questioning look, he added, "God's gift to women, Ryan O'Malley. Hell, he couldn't stop touching you."

"Really? I didn't notice."

Gabe wasn't going to back down. "This isn't working. The last three weeks, today, have been hell."

"I know. What are we going to do?"

"Maybe one of us has to transfer."

Her eyes turned hot. "That would be me. I only moved to our house eighteen months ago. I'd be off the affirmative action test case. I'd have to break in a whole new crew."

"I can't leave." He stepped closer still and whispered, "If you did, maybe we could—"

She recoiled back. "Don't even say it. If I moved and we got together, everyone would know I transferred because of you, that something happened between us. That would confirm all the nasty things people say about having women in the department. My public shame would make it hard for the rest of our females to convince others that they're serious firefighters, not in the job to sleep around."

He inched back. "Okay, I get it." At her still-fuming expression, he added, "Pardon me for trying to find a way for us to be together."

She shook her head. "I'm not going to transfer, Gabe. We'll have to work this out. We'll be stronger."

"Yeah, well, good luck with that." Giving her his back, he walked toward the door.

# CHAPTER 6

THE O'MALLEY TWINS sat across from Rachel and her sister Alexis. The two guys looked like a million bucks. Well, two million. They wore blazers, one gray, one taupe, that matched silk T-shirts, and knife-pressed trousers. Were it another time in Rachel's life, she'd be drooling like most of the other women in the Lakeside Restaurant who got a glimpse of them. She was glad to see Alexis enjoying herself as Brody's date.

"So, you think this is working, sweetheart?" Ryan's light blue eyes twinkled when he spoke. He'd asked Rachel out last night after the picnic at her house, and given her state of mind, she'd said yes. When he'd wondered if she had a girlfriend for Brody, they'd decided an all-sibling evening would be fun. So far, it was.

"Yep, Sergeant, I do." She nodded to the remains of Beef Wellington the four of them had shared along with scalloped potatoes and a Caesar salad. "Super food."

As they drank another glass of good merlot, they told stories about growing up, though the O'Malley escapades were a lot more interesting than the Wellington adventures. At one point, Alexis laughed so hard, she attracted the attention of other patrons. "You were fifteen and caught naked in the boathouse of your parents' cottage? What did your dad do?"

Ryan chuckled. "First he got rid of the older women we were with."

"Older women?"

"Yeah, two college freshmen who took a shine to us when we crashed a frat party." He grinned at his twin, as if remembering. "They, um, didn't know how old we were. After they left, Dad gave us the *responsibility* talk."

"And told us to respect women." Brody's eyes narrowed. "Rach, don't tell anybody about this at work. I'm already considered a womanizer."

Rachel sipped her wine. "Work's off-limits tonight. So vice versa. What happens here, stays here."

*What happened in the basement...*

No, she wouldn't think about that. Rachel *had* to forget about work and a certain captain; thoughts of him were driving her crazy. Which was why she'd accepted Ryan's offer of a date tonight.

The O'Malleys told the rest of the story, and Rachel was duly entertained. Later, after dessert of terrific Baked Alaska that melted on your tongue, the guys suggested dancing at a club over in Camden Cove, where Brody and Ryan had grown up. She and her sister readily agreed. They stopped at the ladies' room on the way in and the brothers went ahead to get a table.

As soon as they finished their business, Alexis pulled Rachel to a settee. "I wish you were having a better time."

"I'm having—" At Alexis's knowing stare, Rachel stopped the lie before it left her mouth. "Okay, I'm *trying* to have a good time. You don't think Ryan noticed, do you? He's a nice guy."

Alexis snorted. "He's a player. Watch out for him. He'll try to get you into bed as soon as you're back at your house, no matter how preoccupied you are."

"Oh, God." The thought of another man's hands on her made her ill.

"Things no better at work?" Translated — with Gabe.

Shaking her head, Rachel scanned the pretty peach lounge. "Worse. We had a fight last night at a birthday party at my house."

"What about?"

She gave her sister the details.

"Hmm."

"Hmm, what?"

"He offered you a way out of this, then."

"Not one that I'd accept. I can't risk what an affair with a firefighter — my boss — would do to my reputation. To the reputation of all the women in the department."

Alexis got that *doctor look* on her face. "I know firefighting's important to you, sweetie. But there are other things in life."

"Lexie please, I don't want to get into this." She stood. "Let's go dance and have fun."

Out on the floor, the O'Malley twins were terrific dancers — of course. Ryan swept Rachel up into a swing, which she knew how to do thanks to her mother's insistence on dancing lessons. Her short, royal blue halter dress swirled around her knees, and she giggled at the dips and turns and antics of her partner. When a slow song started, Ryan pulled her into his arms. "So, who's the guy?"

"Excuse me?"

"Who've you been thinking about while I'm trying to work my magic on you?"

"Nobody."

"I been in the game too long a time, sweetheart, not to recognize moping. Who's the lucky guy?"

"Not somebody I can have."

"You sure? 'Cause if I can't distract you, something really serious is going on inside your head."

She chuckled. "Can we drop it? I am having fun."

"Okay, I'm not one to talk anyway."

"Never found anybody you liked enough to settle down?" She knew he and Brody were six years older than she.

"Haven't tried. Besides, if you have to look, you aren't ready. It should just happen."

A few minutes later, as the band played loudly and the lights captured dancers in movement, two women walked by. Ryan's eyes gleamed, and when Rachel tracked his gaze, she said, "See something you like?"

"They're both gorgeous."

"Don't you know who they are?"

"Should I?"

"They work at our firehouse. Sands and White. Sydney and Felicia."

"Wow, they clean up good."

"Wanna go talk to them?"

"Sure. Though White doesn't seem to like me, which I totally don't understand." He said the words so deadpan Rachel smiled.

Her colleagues had stopped at the edge of the dance floor. Felicia did look great in a one-piece, black clingy thing, and Sydney had outdone herself in a short, ruffled, gray dress that hit way above the knees. She wore it with stacked heels so the dress seemed even shorter.

"Hey," Rachel said, coming up to them, holding Ryan by the hand. His palm was big and warm, but not...Gabe's.

Felicia rolled her eyes. "Oh, shit, we're all here and look girly."

"Nothing wrong with that, darlin'," Ryan said as he touched the lieutenant's arm.

Felicia gave him a scathing look until he moved his hand. "Save it, O'Malley. I'm immune to your charms, thank God. I'm only here because it's Syd's birthday and she wanted to go clubbing."

"Why didn't we know about this at the firehouse?" Rachel asked. "We always celebrate birthdays."

Sydney shook her head, her dark hair shining under the lights. "I didn't want razzing about being only twenty-three. I deal with enough rookie barbs."

"How about if we all dance?" Ryan suggested.

"Oh, Lord." Felicia's protest went unnoticed as they dragged her to the floor.

They formed a circle, Brody and Alexis joined them and the boys took turns twirling each of the women. Even sour Felicia was laughing, though Ryan was right: it was well-known in the department she didn't care for him. She was close to Brody, though.

Rachel was glad, at least, to have this respite. Now if she could keep it up—for the rest of her life—she'd be fine.

• • •

GABE STOOD OUT on the deck he'd built for his mother, staring at the backyard full of summer flowers, listening to the nightly chorus of crickets, when he heard the sliding doors whisper open. Angelica Martino joined him at the railing. She carried a filled wine glass in her hand. "So," she said in their first minute alone tonight, "are you as embarrassed by all this as I am?"

Despite the circumstances, he liked the pretty, sophisticated woman. Angling his head toward the house, he gave her a small smile. "You mean the fact that your mother and my mother had to set us up at this stage in our lives?" Angelica was nearing forty, about his age.

"Yep." She rolled her pretty dark eyes, compliments to her raven hair. Too bad Gabe kept thinking about steel blondes. "Nothing against you, Gabe, but she wore me down."

"Back at ya." He perused her pretty silver dress and high heels, suddenly wondering what Rachel looked like all gussied up. He'd never seen her dressed for a night out. "What I don't understand is why nobody's scooped you up yet."

She sighed. "Still carrying a torch for somebody who didn't want me."

His jaw dropped. "That's hard to believe."

"Cheating spouse. Dirt bag." She shrugged delicate shoulders. "But thanks for the compliment. My battered ego needs them."

Lifting his beer, he clinked their glasses. "Let's drink to something really rotten happening to the guy."

"How about you? Why are you being set up?"

"Divorced. It was rough. But a long time ago."

"So what's your excuse for the long face tonight?"

*A beautiful woman I can't have.* "I can't seem to meet anybody I like enough and is free."

"Free of what?"

"Responsibility."

"How enigmatic. Want to talk about her?"

"God, no." He scowled. "I'm not good company, Angie. I'm sorry."

"We're in the same boat. Don't worry about it."

Turning, he leaned against the railing and saw his mother at the sink, pretending to do dishes but checking them out. "What do you think our mothers would say if they knew what we're talking about?"

"We're wasting our youth. To get on with our lives. I wonder if things were easier in the romance department in their day."

"They were certainly simpler."

Her eyes sparkled. "What do you say we leave? We can pretend we're going out together and split up when we're away from here."

"Well, dinner *is* over."

"Deal?" She extended her hand.

He took it and held on. "Yes. And Angelica?"

"Hmm?"

"I hope you find someone else who treats you well."

"Same here. For you."

Gabe didn't hold out much hope for that, though. Since he couldn't get his mind off a cute little firefighter, there wasn't a chance he was going to find someone else he wanted to be with.

• • •

"FUCK THIS!" BRODY O'Malley tossed out the epithet from where he sat at one of the computers in the common room at the beginning of their next tour on Monday.

From the couch where she sat watching *Jeopardy!* Felicia asked, "What's wrong?"

"It's Allen's blog. *Make it Right,* my ass. Come look."

Rachel frowned from the other end of the room where she was reading a new edition of *The Heart of Hidden Cove,* a magazine that came out quarterly and focused on the positive aspects of the city. Their battalion chief's best friend, Max Delinsky, was its publisher and the rag had become wildly popular. "We aren't supposed to be using the Internet on company time."

"I don't care. Come over here, too, Rach."

Ramirez and Syd sauntered in, so the five of them huddled over the computer. The blog topic read: *Working Hard? Cops and Firefighters Frolic on the Weekend!*

Beneath the heading, several pictures had been downloaded. Brody, shirtless and shoeless, hugging Sophia. Felicia spiking a ball at Ryan. Gabe, bending down to talk to his daughter. Hell, Sydney holding a beer and carrying a baby on her hip.

"How the hell did Parker Allen get these pictures?" Felicia asked. Her voice shook with barely controlled rage.

"I have no idea." Rachel looked to the rest of them. "Nobody posted anything about the party on Facebook, did they?"

They hadn't. They knew better.

"She musta been spying on us." Tony ran his hand through his hair. "Sorry about this guys. It was my shindig and we shouldn't have been in a public place."

Rachel straightened. "We weren't. The party was at my *home*, Tony." Her blood pressure spiked at the thought. "That woman had no right to invade our privacy. She must have taken pictures from the lake."

Pacing now, Felicia finally said, "Well, we can't let this go unanswered."

"Yes, we can." Gabe stood in the doorway, his face like thunderclouds.

"What do you mean, Cap?" Syd asked.

"If we fight back, it will only give her more ammunition." He crossed to them. "Listen to me, all of you. We did nothing wrong by having a good time on our day off. My guess is Allen's pissed about the women's new blog. It hit her pretty hard." His features were set in stern, hard lines. "We use that to fight her. I got an idea. I want some time on the new site. I'll post about our schedule, our days off, even our downtime and how we're entitled to *that*." He pointed to the computer.

"Hey, maybe we can have a 'Captain's Corner' once in a while." This from Felicia. "You can give the boring details of our existence."

"I think that's a great idea," Rachel put in.

"Holy hell." This from Brody again who was scrolling down Allen's site.

"What now?" Gabe asked.

"There's more pictures."

Gabe peered over Brody's shoulder. "Those weren't taken at the picnic."

"Um, no. They're from Saturday night."

"Hell," Felicia said. "I knew I shouldn't have gone to that damn club."

"Jesus." Gabe's voice raised a notch. "It's the four of you, Ryan and another woman dancing."

Brody flushed. "We, um, went out to dinner then to a local hot spot in Camden Cove."

"You and Wellington?"

Brody's face reddened. "No, I'd never date a group member! Nothing but trouble in that. Me and Wellington's sister. Ryan took Rachel."

Tension was back in Gabe's shoulders and his hands fisted. "Oh, great. Just great."

Syd put in, "Hey, at least we look good."

Gabe stared at the screen, then his gaze flew to Rachel's. She froze at the fire in it. After a moment, he turned and stalked out.

"What was that all about?" Sydney asked, offended.

"Guess the blog's getting to him, too."

It was more than the blog. Rachel knew what she saw in his eyes, and she wasn't happy about it. Man, wasn't this going to get any easier?

# CHAPTER 7

ONE OF THE reasons Gabe was a good officer was because he had a sixth sense about the people who worked for him. And after yesterday, Rachel admitted tension was building among the group and not just between her and Gabe. So, she wasn't surprised when the crew arrived the next day that Gabe greeted them warmly but directly. The Quint and Midi were out so they were alone.

"Good morning, everybody. Get coffee. Sit. Help yourself to the donuts I brought in." The scent of the strong morning brew and the pastries made Rachel's stomach growl. "Then we need to talk."

Rachel wondered what their captain was up to. But she avoided his gaze and he ignored her. Sitting next to Felicia, she took the gooiest, custard-filled pastry in the box and bit into it. The others followed suit, then they all looked to Gabe.

"I was in a foul mood yesterday for a shitload of reasons." He scanned the five of them, focusing for an extra minute on Rachel. "So were some of you. We all bring personal conflicts to work, and all of us, me included, need to remind ourselves to leave them at the door. I think problems get heightened when there are other kinds of tension around us. The danger we face. Victims we don't save. Those things we can't do anything about. But we can address our own stresses and those from Parker Allen." He tossed Rachel a warm smile. "I think you said it first, Wellington. No bad days."

Rumbles of agreement.

"I want to reiterate what I said about Allen yesterday. We keep at our goal of counteracting her through the blog." He smiled at Felicia and Rachel's heart did a flip-flop. "Thanks, Licia for giving us a mechanism to fight back with. I wrote a great blog about us last night."

"You're right," Ramirez agreed. "We gotta stick together."

Others nodded.

"I'm glad you all agree. So, today, to put us all in a good mood right off, we're starting with the Joke Jar."

Groans from the women. Each group in the station house had their own traditions, like Mitch Malvaso's crew, who, when things got tough, told old firefighter stories of past saves, or ones that had been floating around the department for a long time. Mitch had started the ritual with his kids, and it had spilled over into the firehouse. Rachel had heard the story of the origin of Gabe's Joke Jar.

Years ago, when Gabe became captain, he decided the firehouse needed lightening up. They had a series of injuries and more losses that year than any other. Gabe instituted the jar for everybody to bring in firefighter jokes, and when the group was particularly down or when they plain wanted to have fun, they'd read some aloud. Over the years, the game transformed into putting in a dollar with each joke entered, and every time jokes were read, they'd all vote on the best one. Whoever put in the one chosen got the cash. Some of the guys brought in sexist jokes, which the women pretended to be outraged about.

"It's a little early for juvenile male humor, isn't it?" Felicia asked, donning a fake grumpy facade.

"We have to live in the present, appreciate things more, Licia. That's what we're gonna do today. We'll start off this way, then I got a surprise for you for lunch. Maybe we can leave here in a good mood for a change."

Gabe passed around the big jar Sydney had decorated with flowers and rainbows. Each person took a slip of paper.

"I'll start." Gabe quietly read his joke. "The captain said to the rookie, 'How can one person make so many mistakes, probie?' The firefighter gave him a big grin. 'I get up early!'"

Tony poked Sydney in the ribs. "One on you, *bonita*.

Her eyes narrowed. "Fine. 'Cause I got a male one. An older firefighter was schmoozing a new woman in the department at the Fireman's Ball. He said, 'Where have you been all my life, darling?' The pretty young firefighter drawled, 'I wasn't born for half of it.'" Sydney was grinning when she finished.

"She gotcha, guys." Tony perused his paper silently "Aw, crap…"

"Read it, *bombero*."

"Okay, but I don't agree with it." He continued, "A firefighter approached the eighteenth tee. 'I'm really eager to hit this shot. That's my mother-in-law in the clubhouse porch watching.'

"'Hell,' the captain playing with him said. 'You can't hit her from here. It's over two hundred yards away.'"

Brody guffawed. "Ryan would love that one."

Felicia rolled her eyes. "Spoken by one of the twin Peter Pans who'll never grow up."

"Here's one for you, Licia," Brody retorted. "Did you hear about the female EMT who is so conceited she takes a victim's pulse then subtracts ten beats for her effect on them?"

Gabe jumped in again. "I'm gonna read one for Cal, since he's busy this morning."

"No fair," Rachel whined, teasing.

"Hush, Wellington," Gabe said. "A blond, female firefighter visited the doctor and said 'Every time I have a cup of coffee, I get a stabbing pain in my eye.' The doctor fixed her a cup. 'Here, show me.' After the demonstration, he said, 'Take the spoon out of the cup first.'"

"That's stupid." This from steel-blond Rachel. "And insulting."

Brody shrugged. "If the shoe fits, Wellington."

Felicia grinned evilly after she scanned hers. "A sign on the wall of the shower room in a firehouse reads, 'A firefighter's wife's definition of retirement: Twice as much husband, half as much money.' Not a good deal, I'd say."

Rachel could see that the jokes, stupid though they were, had indeed put them all in a good mood. The joke about the blonde won, of course, four to two, with Gabe voting for Cal. It had been turned in by Brody, so he got the money. But the exercise worked its charm.

When the call came for a flooded basement, a really crappy job, they approached it in a good mood. Even Rachel, who'd reveled in the laughter and smiles on Gabe's face. He'd been right, they needed this lightheartedness.

• • •

ALL THE WHILE he fixed lunch, Gabe kept picturing Rachel's face this morning. She had a beautiful smile, one he hadn't seen much of lately. And she'd teased him, warmth emanating from her dark eyes. "Argh...."

Brody entered the kitchen, disrupting his thoughts. "Hey, no bad days, Cap."

"I know. It snuck up on me." Like she always did.

"Gabe, is it okay if I invite Ryan over for lunch? He loves turkey."

"Sure. I invited Mitch, and Tony asked Sophia, but she has surgery." Tony's wife was a surgical pediatric nurse.

Mention of Ryan made Gabe picture Rachel in the short dress she'd had on in the photos, being dipped by the guy on the dance floor last week. Gabe had gone online to look at the pictures again after work that night. He'd stared at them until he'd gotten aroused by the sight of those slim legs and toned body. At least he hadn't printed out the photos.

"Brody, can I ask you something serious?"

"Sure."

"No harm intended, but is Ryan interested in Wellington? I'd hate to see her get hurt."

Brody plucked a piece of celery from the mound Gabe had cut for stuffing. "Nah. He's not ready to settle down, and he won't, what's the word, *trifle* with a firefighter in the group. We were all bored, so we made plans to get together." He chewed on the stalk. "Besides, he said she was preoccupied with some other guy and even he couldn't charm her out of her mood."

"Is that so?" *Hoo-rah!* "Um, set the table will you?"

Brody asked as he got out plates, "Are you worried about Wellington?"

"Not her specifically." *Liar.* "Unrequited love wreaks havoc on station house life." He should know, only his feelings weren't exactly spurned. He could still remember how she responded to his touch.

By one o'clock, after another short call while the bird cooked, Gabe's group as well as the members of the Quint and Midi sat at the table with succulent turkey, spicy stuffing and tart cranberry sauce in front of them. Cal came in and Gabe waited for him to get his plate.

"Geez," Sydney said, staring at the feast, "I hope we don't get a call. I've been smelling this all morning and I'm famished."

Cal shot Mitch a glance. Gabe didn't get why. "We won't," Mitch said, forking some turkey onto his plate. "Cal got the chief to take you out of service for an hour."

"Super. What's the occasion?" Felicia asked.

Cal lifted his ice tea. "To a job well-done in all our calls." Then he murmured. "And for handling the piranha out to get us."

Sydney smiled. "Parker the Piranha. It has a nice ring to it."

They ate, and when Mitch finished, he lazed back in his chair. "Hey, cuz, you ever tell them about the pop-up turkey pin thing that happened to us in our rookie year?"

Both Gabe and Mitch had served a few years in the FDNY together. When 9/11 happened, they'd moved out here but stayed friends with the city guys.

"No, you tell them."

Mitch stood, crossed to the stove and got the little button thing off the turkey, then sat back down. "When we were green and on the line in New York, one of the battalion chiefs came in to talk to the rookies. I don't know where he got these, but he gave each of us an un-popped turkey button. He described how the things popped in turkeys when the internal temperature hit three hundred and fifty degrees. He told us to put them all in the bands on the inside of our helmets and after the next fire we went into, to check them."

Gabe grinned. "Anybody got a guess to what happened?"

"The fuckers popped, right?" Ryan shook his head and threw his twin a look. "Hell, bro, you work in three hundred and fifty degree heat? Unbelievable."

Mitch said, "Anytime people like Allen start to give you shit, remember what we really do."

"Want to write a blog on that story, Chief Malvaso?" Felicia asked.

Mitch's smile was broad. "Yeah, I can do that. I'll get points with my wife for it."

Gabe glanced around the table. His crew was all relaxed. Then his gaze snagged on Rachel. She was talking quietly with Sydney. Her features had softened. She caught him looking at her and gave him a private smile. "Thanks," she mouthed.

"You're welcome."

Damn it to hell, he longed to put that smile on her face again but for very different reasons.

• • •

RACHEL DIDN'T KNOW what was worse, fighting with Gabe or having fun with him. The jokes and the turkey yesterday had soothed tempers and put everybody in a good mood. The mellow mood only made her want him more.

The next morning, a call came in at seven o'clock. "Rescue 7, an incident on Granger Drive. Male, fifty-five, needs medical attention. Extrication equipment needed. Specific details are unavailable."

The team hurried out, got on the truck and sped to the scene. When they arrived at a two-storey home on the outskirts of the city, they entered the back bedroom as a group. Gabe went in first, with Brody at his side. They stopped short, so Felicia, Tony, Sydney and Rachel bumped into their backs.

Because on the bed was a sight to behold.

The bedroom looked like any normal one in a modest home, except that a gray-haired man was handcuffed to the four poster. Both his legs and arms were bound. He was totally naked. Rachel bit her lip at the sight of his floppy penis. An assortment of sex toys graced the nightstand. Two women were off to the side, dressed in robes, their makeup smeared, their hair a mess. She guessed them to be in their fifties, too. This was a Sex Call. All fire departments got them once in awhile, and details of the events were passed around year after year.

"What's going on here?" Gabe asked gruffly, stifling his mirth.

"We, um, were having some Morning Delight, I think you called it, didn't you, Henry?"

"Yeah. Hey, my chest hurts."

"Probably a heart attack from too much excitement," Felicia muttered under her breath.

Already at his bedside, Brody took out a stethoscope.

Gabe asked, "Why didn't you unlock him?"

"The key dropped into the register behind the bed," one of the women told him, her face flushing.

Gabe ordered saws brought in.

"And call 911," Brody ordered. "I think this is serious."

Rachel and Tony brought back a power and handsaw. Sydney was with Brody at this point, giving mouth-to-mouth on the guy.

"Heart stopped," Gabe said. "Hurry."

Power saw sounds rent the air, making Rachel's teeth hurt. But her blade cut through the metal like butter. Then they worked on his feet bindings. By the time the ambulance came, Brody and Syd had him breathing again, he was free of his restraints and the women were cooing over him.

"All right, we're done here." This from Gabe. "I'll meet you all at the truck." Rachel let the others go but stayed back while Gabe approached the women. "Ma'ams. Next time you do this, have a spare set of keys."

"Oh, we will, won't we, Mona? Can't have anything happening to our dear Henry."

Gabe turned and Rachel saw his cheek was puckered. He was biting the inside of his jaw. "Come on Wellington," he said and took her elbow to hurry her out. They reached the back of the truck before the laughter bubbled out. The others were already hysterical. "Holy hell," Gabe got out. "They sound like they're at a garden party."

"And they're no spring chickens." Felicia said.

"Yeah, Cap, they gotta be your age. Didn't know the elder set went in for kink."

"I already forgot more than you'll ever know, O'Malley."

Swells of laughter. When it subsided, he said, "Okay, back on the truck."

When he turned to the rig, Gabe's eyes rested on Rachel. They twinkled. Then, without his conscious consent, she guessed, they dropped to her breasts.

And she remembered how true his response to Brody was. He knew a lot about how to please a woman.

• • •

## GABE'S BLOG

*Hours of Boredom and Seconds of Terror.*

*You've probably heard the saying before, maybe applied to soldiers in war, but it's true about the daily life of a firefighter, too. Every time we come to work, we wait around for a fire call (sometimes an hour, sometimes five minutes) only to be faced with flames that can burn at 451 degrees Fahrenheit, walls collapsing, searching for victims in smoke so thick and black it blinds you. We suffer all kinds of maladies from headaches to cancer from inhaling noxious chemicals that we're exposed to every day. We come back to the firehouse, ill and exhausted. At that point, we need to crash.*

*Recently, on a blog which shall not be named, we were criticized for attending a birthday party for one of our sons on our day off. Not unlike teachers, whom I have the utmost respect for, people don't understand the necessity of downtime, and the reasons for it. Every day the fire department is asked to take on more responsibility. Recently, it's been as first responders to terrorist attacks. (Do I need to go into details about what America's Bravest did on 9/11?) Every local fire department has learned more about dirty bombs, anthrax, skyscraper rescue than we thought we'd ever need to know. EMS used to be part of the ambulance crew's responsibility, but now all firefighters are trained EMTs and paramedics. We conduct classes in school on fire safety, interface with the community and participate in parades and benefits for the city. The list goes on. We also have to eat together in case we get a call, which happens during a meal frequently. Hence you see us shopping for food to cook at the firehouse, or occasionally we take a lunch at a restaurant. We've been known to pay our bill, only to have to leave our meal in the middle for a call. I will NOT apologize when you see us out in the community breaking bread together.*

*Finally, I'd like to say a word about our Fire Belles. In my opinion, they are the bravest, strongest and most accomplished women in the city. They do what was always known as a man's job, and they do it well. The fact that you see them out dancing in pretty dresses speaks even more highly of the ability of women to be feminine and do a dirty job like ours. You've seen them profiled on this site, heard their stories. Listen carefully to what they say. They are our beloved sisters and we treat them as such. You should, too.*

*Sincerely,*

*Captain Gabe Malvaso, Rescue 7.*

After reading the blog Gabe handed out later that day, Rachel took the paper, went into the bathroom and cried.

# CHAPTER 8

ON THE LAST day of their tour, a voice came over the PA system. "Rescue 7, Quint and Midi 9 go into service. Backup needed at the scene of an accident on 490. Multiple vehicles involved. Three alarm." Which meant three fire houses were ordered in. The call was a big deal.

The six firefighters of Rescue 7 rushed to the bay, empty of all but their truck. Jumping into turnout pants and boots that were set up and waiting, they climbed into the rig and were out of the station house in three minutes. Ramirez drove with the siren blaring, while Gabe read the printout he'd ripped from the computer on his way from the station house. Rachel nervously ran her fingers over the soft material of her Nomex hood, and she noted how most of her group were fidgeting.

"Tanker overturned, so there's a gas spill," he told them. "Engine 4's on site with foam. Three cars skidded off and hit guardrails. Multiple passengers."

They made it to the site in under five minutes. Thankfully, cops had arrived and shut down the highway to prevent harm to rescue personnel. Ryan O'Malley was in charge. Rachel was glad because despite his playboy image, he was good at his job and they needed people to respect the rescue ground.

"Get out the tools while I head to Incident Command," Gabe said. "Looks like Chief Callahan is in charge."

Sure enough, the top firefighter was directing the action. Tall and robust in the morning sunlight, he was commanding action to the assembled rescue personnel.

"Must be bad," Brody commented.

In minutes, Gabe returned. "We got the white SUV. Let's go."

Brody grabbed his Advanced Life Support medical bag and the others took a variety of tools to the vehicle. A firefighter from Quint 5 brought over a stepladder as they reached the Cherokee, which was tipped on its side.

Loud crying shrilled from the interior. Shit! Kids were trapped. Rachel couldn't see into the backseat because of the car's angle; it was taller than all of them.

"Kids are screaming, so they're alive," Gabe called out.

Felicia circled to the front of the vehicle. "Female driver's slumped over the wheel."

"Do nothing until we stabilize the SUV." Gabe's voice was strong and sure. Like always, his calm tone made everybody feel confident while the others waited. Holding off was excruciating in situations where work had to be done before they could pull out victims and most firefighters had difficulty staying back.

While the captain and Lieutenant assessed the situation, the rest of them ran back to the rig and yanked off big blocks of wood, called chocking. When they returned, they had the car secure in seconds.

"White and Sands, cut out the front window," Gabe ordered. He glanced at the others. "We need somebody light on top. Wellington, climb up and tape the glass. Ramirez and O'Malley, stand by for victims."

With the sound of screams in her head, Rachel removed her turnout coat and hurried up the ladder that Gabe heeled;

out of the corner of her eye, she saw Ryan O'Malley bringing over a backboard. Brody handed her up tape so she could stripe the window, which would keep the glass from shattering on the kids. With a razor-sharp knife they also provided, she cut the pane around its edges then moved aside as it fell backward. She went feet first through the opening and found two kids strapped in car seats. She maneuvered in front of the closest. The boy was about three and wailed into her ears while she un-clicked the seat belt. Brody was on the car now and handed her a neck brace. The child fought it, but Rachel won. As carefully as she could, she drew him out of the seat and he got a stranglehold on her neck. "Easy, buddy," she said kissing his head. "I'm here. You're going to be all right." She managed to hoist him up to O'Malley, who lifted the kid to safety.

Then she froze. The other child had stopped crying.

Vaguely aware of Felicia and Syd removing the woman from the front, Rachel slid over to the second car seat. The child of only a few months lay with his head lolling to the side. She took his pulse. He wasn't breathing. Tilting his chin back, she executed a jaw thrust maneuver she'd done before but not on anyone this small. From above, she heard Gabe call out, "What's going on Wellington?"

Glancing up, she saw him through the window, on top of the car. "Kid's not breathing," she said, massaging his tiny chest, then began giving him mouth-to-mouth. Once, twice, three times.

"That's right, Rachel," Gabe said calmly. "Give him air to revive him before you try to get him out."

Suddenly, what sounded like firecrackers came from the front of the truck, and Gabe slipped and fell to his knees. The car rocked. She heard shouts from people outside.

"Get away."

"Abandon the vehicle."

"It's going to blow."

Gabe yelled, "There's fire near the engine. Out now, Wellington."

"I can't." She gave the kid more air. These seconds were crucial for the boy to survive.

"Now!" the cap said.

"Please, Gabe."

"Three more seconds."

"One..."

"Two..."

"Thr..."

The baby started coughing. Rachel yanked him from the seat—thank God he wasn't stuck—and handed him to Gabe. There was no time for a collar or backboard.

Gabe gave the baby to somebody, told whoever to run and grabbed Rachel under the arms. He got her up and out enough so she could scramble down on her own. Everybody else was a safe distance away.

Grabbing Rachel by the hand, saying, "Run!" he kept hold of her as they dashed away. They were clear when the car burst into flames.

All six of them froze, Gabe and Rachel on their knees now.

"Jesus!" Felicia said, "That was close."

*"Dios Mio."*

"The woman?" Gabe asked.

O'Malley answered. "Broken collarbone but she and the other kid have no life-threatening injuries."

"The baby?" Rachel's voice was squeaky.

"In the ambulance, but he was breathing," Sands said. "Woo-hoo, Wellington, you got a save."

"We all got a save."

They let the emotion bubble out. Adrenaline ran high. Hugs all around. More firefighters and some cops surrounded them, slapping them on the backs, offering genuine praise for their actions.

When he got free, Gabe picked Rachel up in a big bear hug. "Way to go, Princess."

She held on tight. Breathed in the firm, solid, and once again, *alive* feeling of him. "Thanks, Gabe."

His arms stayed round her. "I thought I was gonna lose you."

Before she could answer, the group crowded them again. But she knew what her answer would be. She thought he'd die, too. And that was something neither could ignore.

• • •

THEY MET UP at Badges after their shift ended. The roomy bar was crowded and the rumble of conversation, some of it loud, filled the air. People were generous tonight with high fives and toasts as several firefighters gathered at tables analyzing what had happened at the accident scene. The tanker driver made it and the victims survived.

Opinion bubbled out of the rescuers who included the cops.

"Man, I knew that tank was gonna blow...."

"The foam around the tanker needed two coats to smother the flame...."

"The SUV was toast. I was sure some of us were gonna buy it...."

Miraculously, no firefighters had been hurt. Everything was good. Grateful, Rachel only half listened to the cheerful comments. Instead she watched Gabe in the corner of the room, talking on the phone. He'd showered off the grime and, like all of them, was dressed in civilian clothes—soft denim jeans, like her, and a tight, black, long-sleeved shirt.

He'd taken a flurry of calls during the hour or so they'd been at the bar and reported how psyched the brass was, how a local news station had been on scene and pictures of the rescue had gone viral on the 'net, which should shut up Parker Allen for a while. As she remembered how Gabe had trusted her judgment, how he'd held her close after they were safe, she was stunned by a sharp pang of the hopelessness over their situation. So she snuck away to the Ladies' Room.

*It's only hopeless if you let it be,* an inner voice commented.

*There's nothing I can do.*

*You almost died tonight. Is this how you want to live your life? Running away from situations because they're hard?*

*This is more than hard. It'd ruin my career.*

*Not if you don't let it. You might take a hit or two. You'd have to change groups, but wouldn't that be worth having Gabe in your life, maybe even a baby or two?*

Thinking of the woman with the babies they'd rushed to the hospital—there was still no word on the infant—Rachel didn't know where her head was at anymore.

When she returned to the table, she saw Gabe click off his phone yet again. "Drinks on me for all of you. I got great news."

She stopped several feet away from him.

"Rachel, come here while I tell this."

Walking over, she took her place next to him. He put his arm around her, right in front of everybody. "The baby that was in the van is gonna be fine."

Cheers went up.

"There's more. Guess who the mom is?" He waited. "The deputy mayor's daughter-in-law." He peered down at Rachel, whom he kept at his side, and, God, if she didn't like it. "She's so grateful to you, Wellington, to all of us, she's gonna write on our blog about what we did tonight. She mentioned our girl here by name."

Good-natured boos and a chorus of "Teachers pet!" all around.

"Hey, Rachel saved that baby." He grinned boyishly. "After I told her to get out, mind you." He smiled broadly. "Go ahead and celebrate, guys, and if you drink too much, I'll hang around to drive you home."

"I can do it," Ramirez said. "I'm designated driver."

"Then have a good time."

Finally he let Rachel go. She looked up at him, overcome with emotion from the night. With the good news for the department. With being hugged by Gabe again. Tears sprang to her eyes.

His dark brows furrowed. "What's wrong?"

"Nothing. Just feeling emotional. I'm gonna go get some air."

She hurried outside and headed to her Mitsubishi. She'd reached it when from behind, Gabe called out, "Wait up."

*Oh, no.*

Facing him, she swallowed hard. "Go back inside, please, Gabe."

"I got a better idea." He grabbed her arm and dragged her to the far side of the parking lot where his truck sat under trees. Clicking the locks, he opened the passenger door. "Get in."

She shook her head. He gave her a nudge. Too tired and overwrought to argue, she hiked up and slid onto the buttery soft leather.

Slamming the door, Gabe circled around back. He didn't let himself think about what he was doing as he got into the driver's side. He was acting on gut, on instinct. And a high so incredible he thought maybe he could leap tall buildings.

Instead of starting the engine, he faced his woman. "Look at me, Rachel."

Again, she shook her head. Gently, he tugged her around and tilted her chin. Her eyes were wide and wet.

"We almost bought it again tonight. That gas tank could have blown and we'd be dead."

Tears coursed down her cheeks. "I can't bear the thought of you dying."

He swiped at the droplets with his fingertips, then ran them over her sculpted brow, her cute nose, and brushed his knuckles down her cheeks. "I feel the same about you. Not about other things, though."

"What do you mean?"

"I can't forget about us, Princess. I don't want to anymore, and I'm willing to compromise. I'll ask for transfer from House 7."

"What? You've been at that fire station for fifteen years, even before you got on the Rescue Squad."

"I don't care. If I have to give that up to have you, I will." He frowned. "But a transfer doesn't address your problem of having slept with your captain. About the female firefighters' reputation in the department."

"Suddenly, that seems so small in comparison to how sad I am missing you. And the scare I got tonight."

"I know what you mean." He couldn't help it. He drew her close and kissed her hard.

She returned the kiss and more. When he let her draw back, her face was animated. "Maybe we could stack the deck."

"How?"

"Get Syd and some of the other women on our side. Felicia will have a fit and is well respected among the female HCFD. I'll take some shit. But you can persuade the Malvaso clan, especially your cousin Jenn, to back me."

He grinned.

She stared hard at him but didn't smile.

"What?"

"It seems stupid for you to leave the group. Sydney will still have to go, too, because you'll need to be replaced with an officer. Maybe it would be better all around if I transfer somewhere else."

"You might not get on another Rescue Squad."

"There'll be another opening sometime."

He shook his head.

"What's wrong?"

Emotion clogged his throat. "I can't believe you'd do this for me."

"You were willing to do it for me. Besides," she said climbing over the gear shift and straddling his lap. "You can spend a lot of time making my sacrifice up to me." She kissed him this time, long and sweet.

Afterward, he was overcome with tenderness and gratitude. It wasn't going to be easy, telling the higher ups, having her switch houses and be the target of slurs. He could even be demoted. But he didn't mention any bad things right now. Instead he held her close to his heart like he had in that basement a month ago and basked in the promises they'd made to each other.

• • •

# Hot Shot

Novella number two in the
AMERICA'S BRAVEST SERIES

KATHRYN SHAY

# CHAPTER 1

"YOU SURE YOU want to do this? We weren't always nice guys in high school."

Brody O'Malley toed the gravel in the parking lot with his hand-tooled boots and glanced over at his twin brother, who'd spoken the concern. They didn't look exactly alike, but both were over six feet, muscular, with sandy blond hair and blue eyes, though Brody's were darker than Ryan's. "It's only a reunion. What can they do to us?"

Angling his head to the front door, Ryan shrugged. "Some of the girls we scorned are probably lined up inside picketing our arrival."

"They don't know we're coming. The invite said anybody could drop in Friday night."

"There is that."

Shaking off thoughts of their wild days, Brody straightened his shoulders. "Anyway, we weren't complete jerks. We liked to play the field is all. I'm going in. Don't let me show you up."

The latter comment was one of the reasons the two of them had been such bad boys in their teen and young adult years. They were always trying to outdo each other.

"That'll be the day."

Both men headed into Camden Cove Country Club, which was hosting this Labor Day weekend shindig.

They'd grown up in town, though neither lived or worked here now.

"You ever been to this place?" Ryan asked at the door. Their family was nowhere near country club rich.

Brody scanned the area, which sported a big entryway with dining rooms in front and to the left of them, with a bar to the right. Fancy chandeliers hung in strategic spots, and the moldings were beautiful hand-carved wood. "Yeah. We had our Senior Prom here, remember?"

A hostess approached them, and they got The Onceover, a look often directed the twins' way when they were out together. Twice the sex appeal. Twice the fun. "You gentlemen here for the reunion?"

Ryan winked at her. "Yes we are, darlin'."

"Your classmates are on the patio."

Teetering on heels that made her legs look great, she led them through the bar to the back of the club. A cocktail party was in full swing on the outdoor patio overlooking an expansive golf course. September had stayed warm. Balmy night air surrounded them as stars twinkled down from the sky.

"Here we go," Ryan said, and they headed outside.

After he took a few steps, Brody stopped short. He knew he was in for a razzing tonight. It was one of the reasons neither of the brothers had been back to a reunion. What he *hadn't* expected was he'd come face-to-face, as soon as they arrived, with a woman who didn't seem to have changed at all in a decade and a half. On closer inspection, though, her reddish hair had turned more auburn but was still cut short. Makeup-less blue eyes looked up, and the smile on her face died as soon as her gaze landed on them. Pure shock suffused her delicate features, making Brody feel like a first class shit.

"Oh, I didn't know...didn't see...um, hi, guys." Emma Walsh recovered quickly. She was—had been—too nice to do otherwise.

"Hi, Emmy," Ryan said first.

She blinked at the nickname.

But Brody couldn't find his voice. He was completely caught off guard by the only girl he'd ever loved—and ditched—because he didn't want to be tied down.

• • •

DESPITE THE SURPRISE of seeing Brody O'Malley again, Emma brought herself in check. "Let's start again. Hi, to both of you. Nice to see you again." She studied them quickly. Damn it, they both still looked good. Better, even, than in their high school days. Then, they'd been cute, hot teenagers; they'd grown up to be sexy, virile men. For a few years, she'd seen them from a distance around town now and again. But not in a while. Their parents had moved out of Camden to the renovated cottage—now a nice house—on Hidden Cove and the boys had settled there, too.

Ryan nodded and Brody stepped forward and took her hand. "Hi, Emma."

His touch was unfamiliar, bringing forth a spurt of nostalgia over what they'd lost. "Come on over to the reception desk. Get name tags."

She didn't precede them but finagled her way next to Ryan and as far away from Brody as she could get. Just his presence disturbed her.

"So, how you been?" Ryan asked.

"Great."

"Are you still in the area?"

"Yes, I'm a teacher at Camden Elementary. I, um, heard you majored in criminal justice and are a cop."

"A sergeant. I'm on the streets, still in uniform and train rookies. I've also done some special projects like being the liaison in arson investigation."

"How cool."

"Brody's a firefighter."

"I heard that, too." She shot Brody a glance and smiled weakly. "Both noble professions."

He rolled his eyes. Nobility was not a word that would have applied to the O'Malley brothers fifteen years ago.

"We're bringing our fourth grade classes to a fire station here in Camden Cove at the end of September."

"Yeah, we have kids come visit ours all the time." Brody smiled. "The guys bitch about it, but I kinda like being looked up to."

"Since I haven't talked to you two, let me say I'm sorry about the colleagues you lost in 9/11."

"Yeah, thanks." Ryan touched Brody's shoulder. "This guy took it pretty hard."

Soon, they reached the registration desk at the end of the stone patio, thank God. Emma smiled graciously "Hey, ladies, look who's here."

The two women who'd organized the event glanced up. Karen's eyebrows rose. Amy's face got red. They'd been two of the O'Malley brothers' casualties. Before Emma, but casualties nonetheless. She wondered if Ryan and Brody realized the damage they'd left in their wakes.

"Hey, is that you, Rye? Brody?"

Turning, Emma smiled at the guy who wouldn't break her heart if his life depended on it.

Brody frowned and glanced at his name tag. "Mark Adams? Wow, you look different."

"Yep, I grew into my looks, my mother says."

He had. Gone was the nerd with glasses. He'd filled out, gotten contacts and a great haircut. His features had matured him into a handsome guy.

Sliding his hand around Emma's waist, Mark smiled broadly. "Surprised to see you here, though. You haven't come to a reunion before."

Brody's gaze dropped to Mark's hand and where it rested intimately on Emma. "Um, yeah. But this was our fifteenth and all."

"Then, welcome." He moved in even closer to Emma. "Right, Em?"

"Sure, of course." To them she said, "You'll want to mingle."

"Have fun." Mark tugged on Emma's hand. "Come and see Joey Calder. He's a coach at Hidden Cove High School. A teacher, just like us."

Emma left the O'Malleys, thankful to be distanced from Brody's still-overwhelming presence. At least she'd be able to collect herself. God, she hated her reaction to him after all these years. Holding on to Mark's hand, she let this very dear man lead her through the crowd and away from the guy who'd hurt her like no other ever had.

But as they stopped to talk to Joey, amidst the murmur of voices and a piano playing some cool jazz, Emma couldn't forestall the memory of her last contact with Brody all those years ago. Maybe seeing him with their old classmates caused images to come unfiltered....

On graduation night, in the boathouse of the cottage his family owned on Hidden Lake, Emma and Brody had gotten dressed after a bout of lovemaking. He took her hand and shrugged his shoulder, a telltale sign she wasn't going to like what he was about to say. Still, she hadn't suspected the news.

"I'm, um, not gonna be around soon," he said casually.

She brushed a hand down his caramel-colored hair. "I know, silly. We're both heading off to college." She'd been so innocent then.

"I mean this summer. Rye and I are going to backpack through Europe. A graduation present from Mom's rich brother."

A scowl breached her mouth. "You have a job as a lifeguard lined up."

"I know. This was a last-minute gift. And, um, look, Emmy. You know I care about you. A lot. But, I think we should be, you know, nonexclusive. Now and when we go to school."

For a moment, she hadn't understood. "Nonexclusive?"

At least he'd reddened with embarrassment.

"As in dating others?" Her tone was incredulous. "*Sleeping* with others?"

"Um, yeah." At the tears that immediately formed in her eyes, he added, "Look, honey, you knew the score. I told you when we started dating I wasn't a tie-me-down kind of guy."

"Eight months ago. You told me that eight months ago and proceeded to be exclusive the whole time. Or I never would have slept with you."

He fidgeted. "I don't feel like settling down. I love you but—"

She hadn't even railed at him. Hadn't even said what a schmuck he was to have had sex with her before dropping his little bomb. Instead, she'd walked out of the boathouse, gotten in her car and left him behind....

It had taken her a long time to get over him, to trust men again. Damn it, she hoped this didn't cause her a setback. After a period of depression, she'd vowed not to waste another minute crying over Brody O'Malley. And that was a promise to herself that she intended to keep.

• • •

BRODY WASN'T HIS usual upbeat self as they raced toward the Rescue 7 rig. A compressor had blown in a factory that made light fixtures, a fire had broken out, and there was a whole night shift inside. The Quint and Midi from Firehouse 7 were called, too, as well as two other trucks from different locations. The incident was serious.

"You okay?" Felicia White asked on the way out. "You're quiet. You've been quiet for days. Is it because 9/11 was last week?"

Firefighters all over the country had a hell of a time on the anniversary of the terrorist attacks that changed their lives. Brody included.

"Partly, I guess. But I got a lot on my mind."

"At least you're a thinker." She snorted. "That brother of yours is all reaction and no thought."

Needling their lieutenant was a favorite past time of Brody's. So after they jumped into their turnout gear and climbed on the truck, he continued their conversation. "For the life of me I can't understand why you don't like Ryan. Most people do. Hey, maybe you have the hots for him and you're pretending to hate him like a first grade girl."

"Bite me! Besides, it's his type I don't like."

"Rye and I couldn't be more similar and you like me."

"Nah, you're a better man."

He gave that some consideration as they sped through streets slickened by rain. It was true in some ways, especially concerning women. Ryan could be a dog. He had a rule of six with them: never spend more than six hours with a woman you didn't like, never let a relationship go on for six days if you hadn't slept with her, and break off all but the best matches after six weeks. Once or twice, he'd dated someone for six months, but they didn't go any further.

Then there was the fact that Ryan had been one of the reasons Brody had broken up with Emma Walsh, whom he couldn't stop thinking about after seeing her at the reunion. His brother had razzed him during his and Emma's entire relationship and nagged him to ditch her before the two of them went to Europe. Brody hadn't fought too hard. At eighteen, he wasn't ready to settle down. Still, he'd missed her like crazy on the whole trip and through the first semester of his freshman year.

Now, he missed her again, which was ludicrous. But Felicia was right. He'd been quiet all week. Introspective. Nostalgic. The unexpected meeting with Emma had affected him — a lot. And he hadn't even gotten to talk to her again that night. She was either in deep discussion with her beau of two years, or she was working on details of the event. But he had a feeling she was also avoiding any contact with him. Meanwhile, he couldn't keep his eyes off her.

Their captain's grave voice from the front seat brought him back from the memories. "This is gonna be a long night, guys. Lots of injured people, the update from the chief says." They reached the site and the cap hopped off the truck, barking orders. "O'Malley, go right to Incident Command. The chief wants you working with the other medics."

All of the HCFD were now trained EMTs, but there were more than a few with advanced certification like his as a paramedic. Jumping off the truck into the cool mid-September night, he strode to IC and found Battalion Chief Erikson directing the scene. "Hey, O'Malley, glad to see you. You're going inside."

"How bad is it?"

"The medics in the building report people pinned under machines and some buried in debris. Enter through the front door and go left. Factory work stations are at the far end."

"I'm on my way." Donning his mask and air tank and buttoning up his turnout coat, Brody raced inside. The thick, black smoke meant the chemical elements in the building were noxious. Breathing in that shit was dangerous. Dropping to his knees because of the heat and the fact that he couldn't see anything, he crawled his way down the corridor, running his hand along the wall to find his way. He bumped into some chairs but finally reached the factory.

He called out, "Yo, O'Malley here."

"Straight, O'Malley." His friend, Zach Malvaso, another paramedic, yelled the directions.

Brody inched over. Malvaso's voice was tinny through the mask. "Male, looks to be around forty. He just stopped breathing. Take over CPR." Zach eased back and stood. "I got more where this came from."

Staying on his knees, Brody began his chest compression. Meanwhile, the water slapping on the fire, shouts, and falling debris created a cacophony around him.

"One-two-three-four-five.   One-two-three-four-five." His hands pressed on the guy's chest in time with his counting. After some mouth-to-mouth resuscitation, he got the man breathing. He whipped off his mask and gave the guy air. Over the next half hour, Brody alternated sharing his own oxygen and taking some for himself. When he didn't have his mask on, he coughed violently. So did the victim.

Finally, a crew came in with the Hurst equipment. A generator rent the air, and soon, rabbit tools were prying the weight off the man's legs. "Come on, buddy," Brody whispered as the man was freed. "Stay with me."

Behind him now, White and Sands handed him a collar; after he secured the guy's neck, they lifted him to a backboard. "You two take him out," White told them. "I'm heading to the next one."

Brody eased off his air tank and set it on the stretcher so the man could have air. Carefully, they hefted him, crept around debris and skirted smoldering timbers. He coughed and choked.

Sands stopped. "Take some of my air," she shouted and started to remove her mask.

"No. Keep going. We're close to the door."

At least they could see better, which meant the fire was must be nearly doused. Sands caught her foot on something and stumbled, causing the air tank to fall from the backboard. Brody reached for it but missed, and several pounds of metal hit his foot instead. "Jesus." Though it was almost empty, the contact hurt like a bitch.

When everything was right again, he hobbled with them to the front exit.

Once outside, another team of medics relieved them of the patient, and Brody fell to his knees, choked and coughed again. Sands came over and forced some oxygen on him. His lungs felt better, but his eyes stung and watered. He held on to the fact that he was feeling shitty, but at least they'd had a save. After a few minutes, he put the mask down and breathed clean air, hoping the symptoms would abate. Now that the emergency had abated, his foot hurt like hell.

About fifteen minutes later, Gabe approached him. Bending down, he looked Brody in the eye. "You okay?"

"Yeah. Haven't had a mouthful like that in a while."

"You should have shared air with Sands. It's going to cost you in recovery."

"How's the guy?"

Even though his vision was blurry, Brody could see the grim expression on Gabe's face. "Sorry, Brody. He crashed in the ambulance. They couldn't revive him."

# CHAPTER 2

AFTER SEEING THE O'Malley brothers at the reunion, Emma had experienced a disconcerting three weeks. She'd been preoccupied at school, short with her mother and distanced from Mark. So she was glad for the distraction of herding forty-five fourth grade students off the bus and into Camden Cove's Fire Station 1, despite the inevitable excited screeches they emitted. Thankfully, this was not Brody O'Malley's house—or even his department—because he was the source of her irritability.

"Ms. Walsh, come on," little Terry Miller said. Rambunctious and hard to handle, he seemed to listen more to her than his parents or even the school administrators.

She reached out to him for safekeeping. "Hold my hand, Terry."

Together, they entered the bay area. In preparation for the trip, Emma had researched firefighting equipment and terminology and taught some of it to her kids—so she knew what to expect. Three garage-type doors opened up to an engine that carried water and a truck that handled ladders and tools. One big space to the left was empty. Folding chairs had been set up facing a row of firefighters, two men and a woman. They hailed the kids, and as she and her colleague Sara Carson got the little ones seated, Emma faced forward again and saw Brody O'Malley had joined the group. On crutches. Damn it all, why was this happening to her? There was no way he should be here.

"Good morning, people," the short wiry officer—she knew because he wore a white shirt—said. "I'm Captain Falcone. Welcome to House 1." He pointed to his left. "This is Firefighter Ames, next is Firefighter Wellington and finally, Paramedic and Firefighter O'Malley." Who looked ridiculously handsome in navy pants, light blue shirt with a navy T-shirt peeking out. She'd never seen him in his uniform, and it did something to her insides.

Terry bounded up. Without waiting to be called on, he stood. "How'd you get hurt, Mister Firefighter?"

Brody dropped down on a chair, folded his arms across his chest and stretched out his feet—one encased in a soft shoe. "I was carrying an injured man out of a fire, and my air tank fell on my foot."

"Isn't it supposed to be on your back? Ms. Walsh showed us pictures."

Brody gave the boy a half smile and Emma's response to it was visceral. She remembered vividly how everything she did in high school brought on a smile of approval from him. She'd thought he was genuinely interested in her. Really cared about her. "I put my air mask on the wounded guy. My tank went along with him on the stretcher."

"Aw…" Terry, of course, was hoping for a more exciting scenario.

Hell. Emma tried not to think about Brody running into burning buildings. He'd joined the fire department right after college, and though she'd gotten over him by then, she'd worried for a while about his safety. Finally she'd stopped thinking of him altogether except when someone mentioned him. Now the danger he was in every day doused her like cold water in the face.

"If we can get back to the lesson," Falcone said somewhat impatiently. "You're gonna split into groups and visit three different areas that will demonstrate what we do. Firefighter Wellington will show you the machines that we use to pry open cars."

"The Jaws of Life?" someone besides Terry called out.

"Yes. You've been taught well," Brody put in.

"Next is the equipment we use to fight fires, including the trucks, which you can sit in after we finish. Finally, our paramedic—he's like a doctor—is going to demonstrate some of his duties and what's in his ALS bag. That means Advanced Life Support."

Since Emma and Sara had been informed about how the day would go, they'd already spilt the students into three groups. Fifteen kids headed to each area while she, Sara and an aide accompanied one. Thankfully, she didn't get the medical station first. And she made a quick decision to ask the others to let her stay with the woman and her gear.

Firefighter Wellington was pretty, with steel-blond hair a shade or two lighter than Brody's and kind hazel eyes. Had she ever hooked up with Brody?

"This is the breathing mask," Wellington started with.

"It's a SCBA," Terry called out. "Like diving equipment without the U."

"Yes. Those letters mean self-contained breathing apparatus. Would someone like to volunteer to try it on?" Each kid's hand shot up and Firefighter Wellington picked a shy little girl in the back.

Later, she hefted up a tank. "This is filled with air. Let's see who can lift it."

Several volunteered again.

When it was time to switch areas, Emma waited for Sara to come to her group so she could ask about exchanging places, but instead her friend stayed behind, talking to Brody. Sara was young and pretty and single. And Brody still looked like dynamite. She tried not to watch the two of them together, the flirting that came to Brody as natural as breathing.

"Come on, Ms. Walsh. Let's go." Terry again.

Emma resigned herself to her fate.

Brody's gaze locked on her when she reached his space. "Good morning, Ms. Walsh. That pink sweater looks beautiful on you."

Damn her light complexion. She blushed. "Thanks, Firefighter O'Malley." She cocked her head. "How did you happen to be here today? You don't even work in Camden Cove."

"But I'm in your county, and the Fire Academy services three fire districts. I've been at the Academy on desk duty and when I heard your group needed a medic today, I volunteered."

On purpose? To see her? She'd told him she was visiting a station house in Camden.

He smiled at the students, and Emma's heart did another little flip-flop. "Now, who would like to see Ms. Walsh be my patient?"

He had to be kidding.

But every hand shot up.

"Want to come over here, pretty lady?"

"Oooo…"

"Miz Walsh. The fireman likes you."

Even the kids caught the sexy tone of his voice.

When she went up front, she whispered, "Please, don't undermine my authority, Brody."

His beautiful eyes rounded. "Oh, sorry. I was joking."

"Teaching is serious business. So is firefighting."

"Well, you know me. It always was hard for me to take things seriously."

She arched a brow. "And I've got the scars to prove it, in case you've forgotten."

His face turned dull, like the light went out of it. "Would you lie down on the mat, Ms. Walsh?"

Thankfully, Emma had worn khaki slacks, so she dropped to the floor. Before she stretched out, he added, "I think you're going to have to remove that sweater. I need to use the blood pressure cuffs."

It was a demonstration, so he could indeed check her blood pressure through the light sweater. Still she removed it, and having a short-sleeved blouse on, most of her arm was bared.

Taking his time, he hunkered down beside her. And sniffed. "Sweet," he said to her quietly, and to the students, "We call this examination the ABCs: Check the person's Airways." He opened her mouth and shined a light in it. "Her Breathing." He touched her throat and laid an ear near her chest. His thick hair tickled her jaw, and it smelled lemony. He had on an aftershave that was…wonderful. Then took held up the blood pressure cuff. "I'm showing you how to use this little thing to see how her blood's pumping, so gather close."

He taught the kids. He didn't just demonstrate. And he really took her blood pressure. "Hmm, BP is one-forty over eighty. A little high." He gave her a knowing look which she ignored.

He grinned up at the kids. "I think she's alive."

They laughed.

She didn't have much choice in the other things he forced her to participate in: for a suspicious situation or when there was blood, he dressed her in the universal precautions of a face mask, gloves and goggles.

When he put her eye gear on, his breath fanned her ear, causing her to shiver.

But by the time he was done with her, she needed to fan herself.

The morning ended with a boxed lunch for the kids. When they were all seated at long tables set up for them, she pulled Brody aside. "What was that all about?"

Dimples claimed his cheeks. "Illustrating my moves, babe."

"Yeah, they were moves, all right. It was embarrassing."

"The kids loved it." He gazed down at her eyes. "Didn't you?"

"No. I got over loving anything about you when you broke my heart." She started away. But he drew her back.

"I'm sorry, I didn't mean any harm."

"It doesn't matter. You cause harm even if you don't want to. You always did."

"Look, I tried to talk to you at the reunion, but you didn't stand still long enough."

"I had responsibilities."

"You avoided me."

"I did not."

"Then prove it to me. I'm off and tomorrow's Saturday. Have lunch with me."

"No! I'm not interested in renewing old acquaintances."

He asked seriously, "What if I am, Emmy? I've been thinking a lot about my life after I lost a victim. I—"

"Well, this was fascinating."

Brody looked up and Emma turned around. A beautiful woman with skeins of dark hair and shrewd violet eyes had approached them. She was dressed in a designer business suit. "Parker?"

"Emma? What are you doing here?"

"I'm one of the teachers for the kids. You?"

"I came to get some shots of this community service activity, I think the chief called it."

Brody's eyebrows skyrocketed. "Parker? As in Allen?"

"Yes. You know who I am?"

"We got pictures up of you in the firehouses with targets on them."

She blinked.

"How do you know Lois Lane, here?" he asked Emma, his voice deadly cold.

"We were sorority sisters," Parker said, and hugged Emma. "So nice to see you again."

• • •

OKAY, SO HE hadn't planned to come on so strong. He'd volunteered to help out today—requested the duty, really—because he wanted to see Emma again. He'd thought about her *a ton* over the last couple of weeks so he'd acted on impulse. Now, as she sat with her students for lunch, he remembered the sweet scent of her when he'd bent over to do his patient assessment. Her pupils had dilated, telling him his nearness affected her. And that she was embarrassed.

"What was all that about?" Rachel Wellington asked from his side. She bit off a section of a peanut butter and jelly sandwich, like those they were feeding to the kids.

He dragged his gaze from Emma and focused on his friend. "What do you mean?"

"Spare me. You were all over that pretty little teacher. And in front of her students."

He winced. "Was I inappropriate?"

"No, I'm busting your balls. But what's going on? I miss hearing about your love life."

"Now that you have one of your own, you don't need to poke into mine."

"Touché."

Last summer, Rachel Wellington had unexpectedly transferred from their tight-knit group on Rescue 7. Rumor had abounded that something was going on between her and the captain, and he'd also heard Malvaso was taking grief for it. Finally, she and Gabe had talked to the four remaining members and confessed they'd become involved after they'd been trapped together and thought they might die. Because they'd decided to go public rather than sneak around with their unexpected romance, the department had reacted, some positive, some negative. Brody was happy for them both.

"Sorry to tease you. For what it's worth, I don't think you should be taking shit for falling in love."

"It's better now." She shook her head, sending her hair swirling around her shoulders. "I'm worried about Gabe, though. Did you know they put a letter in his file? No disciplinary action yet."

"I don't think anybody really cares about what happened. Gabe's well loved." He grasped her neck. "You too, Rach."

She smiled. "Now, back to Ms. Walsh."

Brody sighed as he looked at Emma. She was talking softly to a boy who he'd noticed was energetic. Her head bent, he could see the bare skin on her neck. She'd been sensitive there, long ago, when he kissed her. "My first love."

"Yeah? What happened?"

"I wasn't ready to settle down. Christ, we were eighteen."

Rachel tracked his gaze. "Huh! She looked at you like a woman looks at a man she cares about."

"No shit?"

"No shit. Life's short Brody. We both know that." Her gaze was intense. "I heard about the guy you lost. It must have been hell, after having kept him alive so long."

"It was a tough one." That had affected him greatly.

She gestured toward the group—and Emma. "So, if you have something with her, I say go for it."

Rachel's words stayed with him as the school kids finished lunch, took their turns with the engine and noisily headed to the bus while someone honked the horn. Walking out behind them on his crutches, he managed to catch Emma by the arm as she helped the kids board. She hadn't put her sweater back on; her skin felt like silk. "Can I talk to you a minute?"

She swallowed hard, and the pretty light complexion of hers blushed again. Her eyes were wary and he hated putting that look there, but he needed to say some things out loud. "Please."

Nodding, she stepped away from the bus.

He thought of Rachel's comment. "I lost a victim in a fire. I'd been giving him my air for a while. He died after he got out."

That warm sympathy in her eyes made him remember how he'd depended on her to make tough situations better, like the time in high school his dad had had a heart attack and she hadn't left his side for three days. And he'd had a strong urge to talk to her after 9/11. "I'm sorry, Brody."

"It made me think long and hard about my life. About my future."

"That's good, isn't it?"

"Yeah. Would you *please* have lunch with me?"

She shook her head. "No. I don't want to restart anything with you. And besides, I'm involved with Mark."

He watched her. What could he say? Abandon your boyfriend so we can see if we're still good together?

"We had our chance Brody, and it didn't work out. Good luck with your life, but I don't want to be part of it."

An incredible feeling of sadness came over him. Stunned by his extreme reaction, Brody swallowed hard. "Oh, okay. You have a nice life, too."

Standing on the blacktop, he watched her board the bus. She was slender, yet nicely built. Suddenly he could remember what she felt like all those years ago in his arms. Then he remembered how he'd hurt her. The *noble* thing to do would be to let her go without protest. That would show he'd truly changed after the fire last month.

Shit. He turned away from the sight and hobbled back into the bay, shaken to the core by Emma Walsh.

# CHAPTER 3

"ARE YOU EMMA Walsh?"

A delivery man had come around the back of her house. She'd just started the lawnmower, and the ear-splitting roar had covered up his arrival. He wore a uniform and carried a floral arrangement wrapped in green paper.

She smiled. Flowers from Mark. "Yes. Are those for me?"

The guy nodded and set them on a teak umbrella table. "Enjoy."

"Wait a second. Let me get you a tip."

"Already paid for with the bouquet." He made his way out.

That was so like Mark. He was considerate and thoughtful and never failed to take an opportunity to spoil her. In the mild September afternoon, Emma tore off the paper—but frowned. Carnations. Pink ones. Lots of them.

Inhaling the scent that was like no other flowers, her heart started to beat at a clip, with a visceral response. She'd never told Mark those were her favorite flowers, or used to be, until she and Brody broke up. Even as a teenager, he'd showered her with them.

She opened the card. "I'm sorry I imposed on you. I won't do it again. Good-bye, Emma."

For some godforsaken reason, her eyes welled. Damn Brody O'Malley. He didn't play fair.

• • •

"WHAT BUG'S UP your ass?" Ryan spoke from the other side of their parents' twenty-five-foot boat.

He and Brody had gone out early this morning to do some end-of-the-season fishing. The lake was choppy but well suited to catch the little buggers. Brody loved the scent of seaweed and the sound of the waves lapping over each other. Though they wore light jackets, the sun was beating down on them.

"Nothing." Brody rarely lied to Ryan, but now seemed a good time to do it. He didn't need a lecture.

"Like hell. You haven't been on a date since the reunion. Even after…oh, damn. Oh, shit. It's Emma Walsh, isn't it?"

So much for lying. He should have known better, given their twin intuition. "I guess."

"Jesus, Brody, you need to get a grip. I don't want to go through *that* again."

Frowning, Brody looked up from his pole. "What are you talking about?"

"When we went to Europe after you broke up with her, you were a lost puppy."

He didn't like the image. "I was not."

Ryan's gaze zeroed in on him. "You were in a rotten mood the whole time we were in Paris. You wouldn't sleep with those two Norwegian models. And I caught you staring at Emma's picture all through Italy."

Ah, now he remembered. "I punched you in the face because you stole it and threw it in the Trevi Fountain."

"Uh-huh. But no, you weren't a lost puppy." Sometimes he hated Ryan's sarcasm.

"I got better when we went to college."

He and Ryan attended John Jay College of Criminal Justice in New York City, both planning to be cops. Then when they graduated and returned to Camden Cove, Brody gravitated toward the fire department, passed the entrance test with flying colors—of course—and got his paramedic certification.

"You were okay until we got home for break. You acted like a baby every time you saw her around town."

A pain pierced his heart. He recalled the feeling of loss in the pit of his stomach when he caught a glimpse of Emma across the street or at a movie.

"Okay, it's Emma. I couldn't get her out of my mind after the reunion, then I lost that guy in the fire and started thinking more and more about her. I, um, volunteered at the firehouse last week after she told us that night her class was visiting one in Camden Cove."

"Shit, bro, why'd you do that?"

"I don't know. I'm acting so out of character, I don't even recognize myself."

Ryan stared hard at him. "Are you ready to settle down?"

"I hadn't thought about it."

"Then get your act together. The worst thing you could do is lure Emma back and then find that out you didn't want a June wedding and babies."

Well, that was true. Rye understood him like no other, and Brody always listened to him. "Yeah, it is. Thanks for talking this out." A tug on his pole. "About time," Brody said, starting to reel the fish in.

"See, things are lookin' up already."

• • •

"THIS IS FUN." Emma meant the words as she stared over at Mark. "Ready?"

"Yeah. I'm so glad you came with me tonight."

"You help me chaperone elementary school events all the time. It's the least I can do." Mark's high school was sponsoring a Fun Night at a place called Play Station in Hidden Cove. A huge warehouse, it was filled with games, this rock wall and a variety of video and carnival-type attractions, providing a wonderland of play for teens and adults alike.

"Let's go," Mark said.

She put her foot in the first steel rung, which jutted out from the wall for the climb up. Then, she grabbed onto the handhold. Carefully, but steadily, she ascended the steep incline. Mark lagged behind, probably letting her get ahead of him. He always did nice things like that.

The memory came out of nowhere.

*You should let me win!* she'd told Brody jokingly when they were getting in shape for his baseball and her softball season by racing around the high school track.

*Oh, yeah, like you let me win at Scrabble. Get moving, beautiful.*

Her hand slipped. *No*, she told herself. Not here. Not now. No more. One of the reasons she'd hesitated to come tonight was because Brody lived and worked in Hidden Cove—and he'd frequent this kind of place, probably with his brother and two cool blondes. And she'd made a decision, hadn't she, when she threw out the flowers in the garbage before she even brought them into the house?

Fiercely concentrating on her climb, she beat Mark to the top. Sweaty and out of breath, she made her way back to the ground. The exercise felt good.

"Hey, Emma," her colleague Sara said. She dated a high school teacher, too. "Want to go play the skee ball machines?"

"Go ahead," Mark told her when he hit the ground. "I've been challenged to a pinball game with a kid who really needs my attention."

So she and Sara headed to the skee ball area. "It's fun to see you having a good time," Sara commented.

Emma scowled. "I always have a good time."

"Nah, you've been down lately, though you think you hide it. But I've known you too long. Is everything okay with Mark?"

"Why wouldn't it be? He's perfect."

Sara scowled. "You say that as if it were a crime."

Emma stopped short. "Oh, no, of course not. He's wonderful. I'm a lucky woman."

They reached the crowded skee ball room. People were rolling the balls up a miniature lane with an incline, trying to get them into one of the concentric circles, each having a different point value. Sounds of wood hitting wood and shouts of joy came from some lanes, groans from others. Rock music was piped in the background. They found free alleys next to each other, and as Emma picked up a ball, she glanced to the side.

About five rows down, dressed in jeans and a Yankees T-shirt revealing sculpted muscles, Brody O'Malley pitched a ball down the lane, and a perky blonde stood next to him, cheering him on.

• • •

CARRIE WAS ALL over him when he caught sight of Emma on the bowling machines. Wearing simple jeans, sneakers and a T-shirt that read *Camden Cove High School*—he'd seen several at Play Station tonight—she looked like a teenager herself. Which, of course, catapulted him back to their time together. She'd noticed him and gave a brief smile, and he limply waved back. Hell. This was all he needed. Her, too. She didn't want to see him again.

Extricating himself from his date, Brody turned back to the lane and spent five minutes racking up points. When he finally looked again, Emma was gone. Well, good. Fine. They both needed the distance.

Which didn't explain why he said, "You play for a while, Carrie. Some people I know are here and I want to talk to one of them."

"Don't be gone long." She smiled and gave him a kiss on the lips.

He found Emma in the batting cage. He'd headed there because in high school she played softball and he played baseball and they used to frequent batting cages. It was one of her favorite activities, other than sex with him. Well, once he learned how to make it good for her. He grinned, remembering their bumbling attempts all those years ago. He knew a lot more now and could… Damn it!!!

For a while, he stood out of view and watched her beat the hell out of balls, which came at her fast from the automatic pitching machine. When the thing stopped, she was red-faced and sweating. He opened the door to the cage, stepped inside and leaned against the chain link. "You still got it, Emmy."

She looked back. "I do," she told him, and reset the machine. Another ball flew at her; she focused and slammed that one into never-never land. He waited while she tore the covers off several more balls, until the machine shut down again.

"Want to go another round?" he asked her.

"No, I'm tired. I've got to find Mark."

Brody couldn't let her go. He just couldn't. So when she started toward the door, he blocked her way. "I wanted to say hi."

He liked that she didn't avert her gaze, but stared right into his eyes.

"Did you get the flowers?"

"Yes, and the message that you were going to leave me alone."

"I know." He gestured around the place. "It's kismet that we met here."

"Dismal luck, you mean."

"Why?"

She threw down the bat and it clattered to the cement floor. "You know damn well why. Since the reunion and seeing you at the firehouse, I can't stop thinking about you, dreaming about you. The last thing I need to see is you here, on my turf, with your pretty babe."

For some reason, her tirade pissed him off. "It's my turf, Emma."

"Which is why I almost didn't come." When he saw tears in her eyes, he grasped her arm. "Hey, I didn't mean to upset you."

"You always upset me. You always did."

Against his better judgment, he moved in closer. Something drove him that he couldn't control. "I did more than that with you. I want to again."

A tear escaped. "Please, Brody, don't do this to me. I have a good life and I can't let you into it. Go away."

She said *can't*, not *won't*. Hmm.

"Look, could we meet and—"

"Em? Are you okay?"

Brody pivoted. Mark Adams stood behind the chain-link fence.

Emma immediately stepped back from Brody. "Yeah, Mark, I'm great. But I'm finished."

The guy bristled, probably at the sight of her tear-stained face, and came inside the cage. "Brody, what are you doing here?" His tone of voice was definitely colder than at the reunion.

"Came for a night of games, like you all did."

Mark glanced at Emma. "Why are you upset?"

"She missed a lot of pitches is all. She's still competitive."

"Not so much anymore." He gave Brody a once-over and took Emma by the hand. "But I am. Come on, honey. The bus is leaving soon. Brody, I don't much like you upsetting my girl."

Brody didn't respond. The *honey* and *my girl* said enough.

• • •

"CAN I COME in?" In the dim light from the outdoor lamp she'd left on, Mark stood with Emma on her front porch. He expected to stay over, like he often did.

Emma felt as if weights were crushing her shoulders. "Would you mind if you didn't? I have a headache."

Reaching out, he rubbed his hand along her temple. "Isn't that the oldest line in the book? If you don't feel like making love, you can tell me."

"What did I do to deserve you?" Her lips trembled. "You're so sweet, so kind. I care so much about you, Mark."

"But something's happening. You haven't been the same since seeing O'Malley at the reunion. It's been over a decade, and I never thought…"

She leaned into him. He ran his hand down her hair. "All right, he's...bothering me, I guess."

"What does he want from you?"

The crickets sounded loudly in the lawn around her. Finally she said, "He wants to see me alone. He's been flirting...."

"You've had contact with him other than tonight?"

She explained about the visit to the firehouse.

"Damn him." His gaze zeroed in on her. "Why didn't you tell me about all this?"

She shrugged. "I don't know."

"I think you do. It's all right if he upsets you, but don't even consider seeing him alone." He moved in close and kissed her soundly. "I'm not letting him take you away from me, Emma."

For some reason, that made her feel better. "Okay."

Cupping her jaw, he kissed her nose. "This is a little bump in the road, honey, from seeing him for the first time in years. We'll get through it. Now, go in and get some sleep." He smiled. "And dream of me."

Emma watched Mark go, her heart breaking. If only she *would* dream about him and not the man who'd broken her heart and wanted a chance to do it again.

# CHAPTER 4

USUALLY, BRODY LOVED Halloween. He dressed up and went to parties or threw one at his place; often, he decorated the outside of his house and met kids at the door in an uber-scary costume. But this year, he was in a vile mood and instead of celebrating the day, he offered to work for Zach Malvaso as a medic on Midi 7 so Zach could go trick-or-treating with his kids.

Brody's friend Grady O'Connor walked into the common room after answering yet another kiddy visit and found Brody sitting at a table-and-chair grouping, putting together a puzzle. "You look like you lost your best friend," Grady said, not to needle him, but with concern. Grady was a hell of a good guy. "Women problems?"

"What would you know about those? You've been married three years and are still on your honeymoon."

The man's grin was infectious. He'd fallen in love with his best friend, Jenn, sister in the Malvaso clan. "We are. And, damn, it's great."

"How come you're here tonight?"

"Only one of us could get a sub. I let her off the hook. She and Angel are trick-or-treating with Mitch's family." Brody studied him. "How old are you, Brody?"

"Thirty-four. Though I'm feeling seventy tonight."

"Time to settle down then."

"Maybe."

"Never met a girl you cared enough about?"

He pictured laughing blue eyes, messy auburn hair and a toned body in jeans and a school shirt. "Yeah, once. I blew it." He rolled his eyes. He found it easier to talk to Grady than to Ryan, who never thought Emma was a good idea. "I met up with her a couple of times in the last two months. She makes me grumpy."

"No chance of rekindling old flames?"

"Not on her part. And I know I'm being a jerk, that I should leave her alone. She had a tough time when I dumped her after high school graduation. Now she has a boyfriend who's a great guy."

"Ah, then it was puppy love."

"You know, it wasn't. She understood me, accepted me. If I recall, we never had one fight the whole time we were together."

"That's a real loss."

"Not gonna tell me I should go after her?"

Grady shook his head. "Nope. Sounds like she made a good life after you ditched her. I'd say find somebody else."

"There aren't a lot of Jenn Malvaso's out there."

"Jenn O'Connor now." Another shit-eating grin. "And you're right, she's one of a kind."

The buzzer sounded in the kitchen. "More Halloweeners." Grady stood. "I'll go."

Disgusted with himself, Brody picked up a copy of *The Heart of Hidden Cove* laying off to the side, but its message was too upbeat, so he went back to his puzzle. After a minute, Grady came back...with Mark Adams in tow. Holy hell!

"You have a guest." Discreetly, Grady left them alone.

Leaning back from the table, Brody tried for nonchalance. "Hi, Mark. Do I even have to ask why you're here?"

Mark shook his head. "At least you're honest." He took a seat, a gesture of civility instead of looming over Brody. "You're upsetting Emma. I want it to stop."

"I'm sorry. That isn't my intention."

Easing back in the chair, the guy looked more confident than Brody would have liked. "You always were the nicer one."

"What do you mean?"

"Of you and Ryan. There was a real carelessness about your twin, an attitude that he didn't have to be nice because he was handsome, athletic, sought after. You were a cocky son-of-a-bitch but I always thought you were considerate of people." His eyes narrowed. "And as far as women were concerned, Ryan treated them like disposable plastic bags — use them and throw them away."

Though he didn't like the guy dissing Ryan, Brody didn't want to start a fight. "I don't know what to say."

"Do you remember facing down the soccer team when they went after our chess club? I think you singlehandedly stopped their bullying."

What Brody remembered was how proud Emma had been of him. How they'd made love that night, and it had been the most satisfying experience they'd ever had to that point. For him, it had felt good not to be the bad boy.

"I'm asking you to find that guy now, Brody. Somewhere inside you, he's still there."

"And leave her alone."

"Yep. She was happy before you came along again."

"Was she?"

Reaching inside his pocket, Mark withdrew a box. A ring box. Fuck! When he opened it, Brody saw a sparkling diamond, set on a band encrusted with smaller ones. He had the ludicrous thought that he wouldn't have chosen something so traditional for Emma. "I bought this last summer. I was waiting for her birthday."

"Tomorrow. All Saints' Day. I used to tease her she was one, too."

"She is, in so many ways." Mark stood. "I wish you luck, Brody, and I hope you find someone as good as Emma in the future. But you can't have her. She's mine. So back off. Really, this time." Mark didn't wait for an answer and walked out of the common room.

Suddenly, there was a movement on the couch, the back of which faced him. Felicia White sat up. She was subbing tonight, too, in the officer position. "I'm sorry, truly. I fell asleep and woke up in the middle of the boyfriend's visit."

"That's okay. My humbling is complete now."

"I won't spread it around." She rose and came to the table. "For what it's worth, I agree with him about you and Ryan."

"You alluded to that before."

"I also agree with him about Emma. You lost your chance with the girl. Let her be happy. Find somebody else."

"I know that's the right thing to do."

"Then do it." She socked his arm. "Come over to the couch. I want to show you my next blog. One woman asked in a comment if it was hard working with such cute guys." She shook her head; her expression turned disgusted. "I hope she didn't find out about Wellington and Gabe. Now *that* has set us back light-years."

"Give them a break, Licia. They're happy. And you can't control who you love."

"Sure you can."

He grinned. "So what did you say to the woman?"

"That we managed to behave ourselves. I thought maybe you might want to write something about working with such hot chicks."

He laughed. "Sounds like fun. Let me see the blog."

• • •

FINALLY, EMMA TURNED the lights off on the front porch. She was exhausted from doling out candy apples and pumpkin cookies she'd made for the neighborhood children.

And from not sleeping. She'd moped around most of the day, cleaning the house, making her treats. Mark hadn't come over last night, or today. She knew he was giving her space and she appreciated his thoughtfulness. She'd been trying to deal with the fact that she'd sent Brody packing and that he was out of her life. She chose Mark over him and knew it was the right decision, but that didn't make her sense of loss any less.

As she was heading upstairs to crash, the doorbell rang again. She sighed. Maybe she wouldn't answer it. She went up two steps and the sound continued. Then pounding on the heavy wood. What the hell? She retraced her steps, looked out the side window and saw the caller was Mark, so she swung open the door.

He stood before her in a tux, bow tie, top hat and cane. His brown eyes were smiling. "Trick or treat."

She burst out laughing. "What are you doing?"

"Don't worry, I borrowed the outfit from the drama club costumes."

Coming inside, closing the door, he took her in his arms and kissed her. It felt good. Right. "Hi."

She nestled into his chest. "Hi."

When he pulled back, he set her away and withdrew something from his pocket.

Oh, my God, it was a ring box. Slowly he dropped to one knee and opened the lid to reveal a gorgeous diamond ring. "Emma Walsh," he asked, his throat thick with emotion. "Will you marry me?"

• • •

THE CALL CAME in at three o'clock in the morning. "Quint and Midi 7, Rescue 7 and Truck 8. Fire at 33 Jay Street. Multiple injuries. Gunshots fired. Police on the scene."

"Fuck," Felicia mumbled as they bounded out of bed.

Quickly the group donned uniform pants over the boxers and T-shirts both sexes slept in and hurried downstairs. Being awakened out of a sound sleep meant grogginess; there was no discussion and they stepped carefully. But by the time they met in the bay and geared up, they were wide awake. Felicia ducked into the office and came out with the computer report; they climbed into the rigs and sped off.

Rain slicked the streets and beat a steady pattern on the windshield of the Midi. Over the radio, he and Grady heard, "Fire started in the cellar. Gang was freebasing."

Gangs were rare in Hidden Cove but had started to come up from New York City.

"Police on the scene. Shots fired. GSWs." Gunshot wounds.

Brody's heart picked up speed. Then he remembered Ryan wasn't on duty tonight. His brother had a date with a model in the Big Apple and had made a crack before Brody left for work about getting adult treats tonight. Brody's worst worry, more than for his own safety, was his twin getting hurt.

When they reached the site, it was orderly and well directed, but there was a buzz in the air. Not a good one. And the rain seemed to increase the tension. Brody felt a shiver creep up his spine. The battalion chief in charge, also a sub tonight, was stiff and appeared anxious. Brody didn't know him. The guy barked orders and sent Brody to the rear of the building where other medics were working on the injured. Grabbing his own ALS bag, Brody put on his helmet and jogged to the side of house. As he rounded the corner, a shocking pain seized his back. Just for a second, then it was gone. Oh, my God!

He raced to the men and saw three firefighters hunched over two bodies. The downed men were uniformed cops. Closer still, and his heart beat ratcheted up.

Because he saw his own new boots, which his brother had borrowed a week ago and never returned, on the feet of one of the victims.

Ryan had been shot.

# CHAPTER 5

ON SUNDAY MORNING, Emma could barely drag herself out of bed. Her eyes were puffy and she was achy from the tension her body had held for the last twelve hours. She'd cried herself to sleep, woke up and cried some more. When she did doze off, it was only to dream about Mark's wonderful face when she told him she couldn't marry him. His proposal had been a turning point for her—seeing the ring, seeing the hope and trust in his face. She couldn't dissemble any longer. She wasn't in love with him. And she knew, if she accepted the proposal, it would only hurt him more than telling him the truth. He'd been kind, warned her about Brody and left with the graciousness that was as natural to him as breathing.

Slipping into a fleece bathrobe and slipper socks, she trudged downstairs, made coffee and stood staring out at the autumn morning. The end of October leaves on the trees were beautiful hues of gold and red. Whoops, no. It was November first. Oh! Her birthday, which she'd forgotten in all the emotional drama of last evening. Dear Lord, how was she ever going to deal with her parents' call from Florida and her sister's Skype from Paris? Well, at least she didn't have to face them in person, when they'd know right away how devastated she was. At least through machines, she'd have a chance of keeping the worst of it from them.

Sick of her thoughts and recriminations, she considered a shower, even went upstairs to have one, but instead, she got back in bed again and turned on the TV with the remote.

"Breaking news from downtown Hidden Cove. At approximately three a.m., police and firefighters were called to the scene of an explosion in a house on Ambrose Street. Allegedly, a group of men were in the home cooking drugs—it's called free-basing—and tried to escape the structure when the fire began. By the time they found their way out of the burning building, police and firefighters were on the scene. A shoot-out ensued and the two perpetrators fled. Two firefighters were injured, along with two of Hidden Cove's Finest."

Emma closed her eyes. *Please, please, don't let Brody have gotten hurt.*

"Firefighters injured were Jim McNally from Engine 4 and Juan Gomez from Truck 2."

*Thank you, God.*

Injured police are Officers Carla Lopez, Rick Shank, Denzel Johnson, who were released after treatment. One cop is in critical condition. Sergeant Ryan O'Malley was shot twice, and we're awaiting news of his recovery."

Emma froze. Brody's brother had been hurt? She thought about the robust guy who loved women—lots of them—and didn't apologize for it. He'd always been there for Brody, even when they disagreed. She remembered the stories of how the two of them physically suffered when the other was hurt. Once, Ryan had known Brody had fallen skiing because his own leg had begun to ache.

What must Brody be going through now?

• • •

HE COULDN'T EVEN think about Ryan dying. And he certainly couldn't talk about it, so he stood off to the other side of the private waiting room of Hidden Cove Hospital and stared out the window seeing only mages of him and his brother—sharing a womb, a crib, a bunk bed, a college dorm room and now a duplex, learning about girls together, playing ball on the same teams, breaking rules their parents had set down. Though they had differing views on a lot things, they were rarely distanced. Could he survive if he lost the other half of him?

"Hey, buddy, how you doin'?" A hand on his shoulder.

Turning, he saw his tall, gray-haired father, Jimmy O'Malley, behind him. His dad's eyes were bleak and his usually animated face taut.

"I'm hanging in there, Pa."

"Don't kid a kidder. I can see how you're hurting."

Brody's throat clogged and he couldn't answer. Jimmy knew his sons well and drew Brody into a bear hug. Over the man's shoulder, he saw his brothers, Sean, Timmy, Danny and Joe spread out in the waiting room. Right now Timmy was holding his mother's hand and showing her pictures of her grandchildren. Timmy's wife had brought albums to the hospital this morning to distract his mom.

Brody drew back and caught sight of his lieutenant, Felicia White, sitting on a couch using her netbook. She'd come to the hospital at the end of her shift. "I think I'll go talk to Licia, Dad."

Crossing to the room, he dropped down next to her.

She squeezed his arm. "How you holding up, buddy?"

He shrugged. "You don't have to wait, Licia. It's gonna be a while."

"We're not leaving you at a time like this."

"We? Oh, I get it. The group's gonna take shifts and sit with me."

"Uh-huh. Whether you like it or not. So don't even bother protesting."

He nodded to the computer. "What are you doing?"

"What else? Want to hear something that takes nerve? Parker Allen commented on our blog."

Anger was easier than gut-sick pain. "What the fuck is wrong with that woman?"

"I don't know. I think we should—"

Before she could finish, Brody bolted up. The surgeon who'd spoken to them four hours ago had walked into the room. A big sturdy woman with a no-nonsense attitude, she strode toward his parents. The O'Malley clan gathered around her. Without preamble, she said, "Ryan made it through surgery. It was touch and go for a while because one bullet lodged near his spine. We managed to get it out and we don't think we did any more damage. The other bullet went right through his shoulder, so that didn't give us much trouble."

"How's he doing?" Brody asked.

"He's going to live. I don't know about everything else. He hasn't awakened. We have to wait until he does to determine the extent of his injuries."

His mom gripped his father's arm. Fatigue etched itself on every one of her features, making her look older than usual. "What does all that mean, Brody?"

"It means she doesn't know if Ryan will be able to walk again."

Everyone gasped.

"I'm not gonna sugarcoat this," the doctor put in. "But we shouldn't be pessimistic, either. It's great news that the surgery went well and we got the bullet out."

Brody was trying to be strong for his family, but he knew the implications of what the doctor had and hadn't said.

His mother turned her face into her father's chest, and his dad looked at him bleakly. "How soon will we know?"

"Can't tell, Dad." At his father's bereft expression, Brody felt his own throat clog. "We have to do what we've been doing. Wait and pray."

After the doctor left, Brody stayed tough, answering his brothers' questions, comforting his parents. But when they dispersed, he felt like he was going to combust, and he couldn't let them see him fall apart. He had to get out of the room. "Going to the john," he said to his brother and strode out hurriedly.

Down the corridor a ways, he leaned against the wall, closed his eyes and tried to breathe easier. But, dear God, what would he do if Ryan couldn't walk?

"Brody?"

Opening his eyes, he saw a vision and was sure it wasn't real. Then she came closer and touched his arm. "I just heard. I'm so sorry."

"Emma, w-what are you doing here?"

"I came to be with you."

"Why?"

"Because I could always make the bad times easier for you, and I want to do that now."

Emotion gushed out of him. Her words, her being here, released feelings he'd kept dammed up since he saw Ryan lying on the ground. As they flooded him, he threw himself into Emma's arms.

• • •

"OH, MY. WELL, look, here's Emma." Brody's mother came up to Emma and encompassed her in a bear hug. *The daughter I didn't have*, Mary O'Malley always called her. Emma let herself inhale the familiar powder Mary always wore and basked in the woman's affection.

"So nice to see you again, Mary. I'm sorry it's under these circumstances."

When they parted, Brody's mother clasped more tightly the rosary beads she held in one hand. "My Ryan will be fine. We trust God."

"That's good." Though Emma believed God worked through man and didn't perform any miracles, she knew another kind of faith brought comfort to this family.

She was equally welcomed by Brody's dad with another big hug. His brothers and their wives were particularly effusive. At one time, all of them expected her to be part of this large, boisterous and loving family with little kids of hers and Brody's running around with theirs. A pang of disappointment and grief for what had never been made her tense.

"You've changed some since we last saw you," Jimmy told her, his hand still on her shoulder. "When was that?"

Brody spoke up. He hadn't let go of her hand since he'd taken it in the hall after she'd found him there. He'd cried like a baby and she'd held him for a long time. "High school."

"Um, no. Since you all moved from Camden to Hidden Cove, Jimmy."

Cocking his head, Brody frowned. It hurt to look at his slumped posture and the desperate expression on his face. "You saw my family after we broke up?"

"Of course." His dad again. "She came over on college vacations, and then when she moved back to town, we saw her until we left Camden Cove."

"I didn't know any of that."

Timmy pointed to his watch. "Brody, it's yours and Danny's turn to go inside."

"Do you want to come, Emma?" Brody asked.

"No, you go ahead."

"Okay, but don't leave."

"I won't. I promise."

The rest of them sat as someone else walked into the waiting area and up to them. Timmy stood and shook his hand. "Hey, Tony, thanks for coming."

"No problem. How's Ryan?"

His dad gave the man the somber news. "Seems to be resting easily, though."

"It's nice of Brody's group to take turns coming here on a day off," Mary told him.

Emma asked, "You're from the firehouse?"

"Yeah." He held out his hand. "Tony Ramirez."

His dad grinned. "This is Brody's old girlfriend."

"Emma?"

Startled, she stared at the handsome man. "How would you know that? We were sweethearts fifteen years ago."

"Sometimes on late shifts, me and Brody stay up and talk about stuff. I met my wife in high school, too, only we got married."

"Lucky you." The words were out of Emma's mouth before she could censor herself.

A knowing glint came to Mary's eyes. And the brothers' who heard the comment. She had to try harder to keep her emotions hidden. Hell, she didn't even know what they were.

When Brody returned, he looked even worse. Emma kept vigil by his side. She talked him into eating—he was the only one who hadn't—and they watched some TV. As the night wore on, Mary stretched out on a double couch and the brothers busied themselves on their iPhones. Tony talked to Brody alone, sat awhile, then left. At a table, she and Brody set out a puzzle of an Irish Wolf Hound someone had brought in.

"Remember Wolfy?" he asked as he scattered the contents of the box.

"How could I not? You loved that dog."

"My parents have Wolfy the Third, now."

She chuckled and picked up a piece of what could be a nose. "They were on Wolfy the Second when they moved."

"It was nice of you to keep in touch with them."

"I loved them, Brody."

"I know. They thought I was crazy when we broke up."

"Let's not talk about anything bad tonight. Let's catch up while we work the puzzle. These things always calmed you down. Tell me about college. Why you went into the fire department, became a paramedic, that kind of thing."

They traded stories till four in the morning, getting coffee, assembling half the dog. Finally, at five, when Emma knew she had to leave to go to school, the doctor came out again. The news was evident on her face. "He can move his legs," she said with a big grin. "He'll be walking in no time."

His father jumped up. "Hot damn! Holy hell!"

His mother had come awake minutes before and held the rosary to her chest. "Thank the dear Lord."

Blesses and curses abounded.

A couple of his brothers cried, and his dad's eyes got moist. Brody let a few tears fall.

When his parents went in to see their son, Emma took Brody aside. "Listen, I have to leave."

"Leave?"

"Yes, the worst is over. I have to go to work."

"Work? Oh. I didn't think... You haven't had any sleep. And you never did finish telling me about your sorority."

She smiled. "Some other time."

"Can you take the day off?"

"I'd rather not on such short notice."

Brody didn't really need her now that they'd gotten the news they'd been praying for. But more so, Emma wanted to get away from this group who were treating her like family again. And this man who was acting as if nothing had changed in fifteen years.

Holding her hand, he walked her out of the waiting area and down the hall, where he pulled her into a little alcove. The hospital was waking up; nurses buzzed around, and pages sounded over the PA.

Brody's navy blue uniform was wrinkled and his eyes bloodshot; a night's growth of beard stubbled his jaw. "Emma, I need to know something. Mark came to see me last night."

Her throat got tight at the memory of the man she hurt. "Why did he do that?"

"To warn me off pursuing you."

Her eyes teared. "He came to see me, too."

Brody picked up her hand. "No ring?"

She shook her head, sending auburn locks into her eyes. He brushed them back. "How come?"

"Because I'm not in love with Mark. I thought I was, but when he asked me to marry him, I knew I wasn't."

She wouldn't tell Brody how he'd figured into the decision.

She didn't have to. He gave her the same knowing look of his mother's. "When this all settles down, can I call you?"

Unable to ignore the feel of his arms around her, Emma felt herself slipping under his spell again. She hadn't thought much about where to go after last night. She'd blindly rushed to the hospital because she knew she'd be a comfort to Brody and damn the consequences. But now she needed to be careful. Very careful.

"Give me some time, Brody. I have to think things through."

His face tensed and she could tell it was hard for him not to bulldoze her like he used to. Though she wasn't so easily bulldozed anymore, she was glad he held back. "All right. But think about this while you take your time."

Grasping her arms gently, he drew her to him. He lowered his head and brushed his lips over hers with intention. He increased the pressure by increments, then drew her even closer and nipped and bit and brushed some more. By the time he let her go, she was breathless.

"Good-bye, pretty lady." With that, he turned and walked down the hall.

His fingers on her lips, Emma watched him go. She'd think about him, all right, probably more than she wanted to, but the notion didn't make her sad anymore.

# CHAPTER 6

"YOU'RE BEING A baby. Buck up, Rye." Brody spoke the words from the foot of a bed in the spare room of his parents' home on Hidden Lake. They'd brought Ryan here to recover and he'd been a terrible patient.

Ryan's face flushed. His brother's feelings had always been easy to pinpoint. "You're right. But I can, you know, let go with you."

Already regretting his words, Brody sat on the bed opposite Rye's, where he'd been sleeping, or trying to, for four days. "I know. I shouldn't have snapped. I'd be doing the same thing."

Leaning back, Ryan stared at his brother. "I think I know why I'm so grumpy."

"Tell me. It might help to get it out."

"I almost died, Brody. Or I could have been in a wheelchair for the rest of my life." He looked away, but not before Brody saw his eyes glistening with moisture. "I've been thinking about my attitude toward life, what I've done with mine."

The two of them had shown emotion in front of the other before. But Ryan's reaction rocked Brody this time. Probably because he was tired and cranky, too. Still, he answered candidly, "Nothing wrong with that, Rye. We all need to reassess once in a while."

Ryan shook his head. His hair was limp and his skin was pale, indicating he was still early in his recovery. "I haven't lived as good of a life as you."

"What do you mean?"

"I'm not...I don't know, as nice as you are. I always admired how you treated women better than me."

Felicia White and Mark Adams had both said the same thing. And he knew secrets about Ryan and a couple of girls that really painted his brother in a bad light.

"How come we never talked about this?"

"Maybe I didn't want to believe you were a better person."

He never lied to Ryan even when the truth hurt. "Then start being nicer."

"I'm not sure I know how."

"Of course you do." He got up and socked Ryan on the arm. "If you need any pointers, I'll help."

Ryan laughed, which was Brody's intention. "I'll start by telling you to go home."

"You want me to stay. It's okay."

"I do. But you've been here your whole time off. Go sleep in your own bed. I'll be fine now." He arched a brow. "I heard Emma Walsh came to the hospital."

"I didn't want to tell you. You never liked her."

Glancing out at the lake, which shone in the rare November sun, Ryan shook his head. "I was jealous that she took you away from me so much."

"I didn't know that!"

"Listen, go home. Or go see her."

Brody nodded. When he finally did leave his parents' house, he thought about Emma all the way back to his place. He hadn't heard anything from her and he'd been run so ragged by Ryan's demands, he didn't have much time to worry about where they stood. Besides, he said he'd give her more time. Now he wondered where she was, what she was thinking and if she'd decided anything about seeing him. When he got home, he crashed on his bed face first. His last thought was he wanted another chance with her.

• • •

WHEN SCHOOL STARTED in September, Emma had organized a yoga class in the elementary school gym, where she now sat on her tie-dyed mat. The hour and a half began at three-thirty to accommodate all district personnel. The teacher, who demonstrated up front, was a retired yoga instructor, which was why she'd offered classes here at school. Lights down, about twenty people were in attendance.

In a true lotus position—it had taken her years to be able to execute one—she closed her eyes and breathed in deeply. Exhaled out slowly. Told herself not to think about Brody.

*Good luck with that.* Tired blue eyes and disheveled sandy-colored hair intruded on her meditation. On most everything these days.

She stood when instructed to and slipped into a downward dog. As she pushed back on her hands, her arm muscles strained, so she tried to transfer her weight to her legs. More comfortable now, she admitted some things to herself. She wanted Brody back in her life. So what was she waiting for?

Well, for one thing, she vowed to save face for Mark. He'd been gracious about her refusal to marry him, and she wouldn't run into Brody's arms as soon as she was free.

*You could keep it on the QT for a while.*

But she hated the thought of sneaking around.

Pressing into a lunge, she sneaked her leg under for pigeon pose and held it. As others achieved the difficult pose, groans rumbled through the class. And honesty came fast and furious to Emma. Okay, she admitted to herself, her hesitancy wasn't only about Mark. She was afraid to let Brody back into her life. She was terrified that he might leave her as he had the last time she'd fallen in love with him. She didn't really know what kind of man he was, yet somehow she believed he still had that inner core he'd shown her in high school. But as a man, was he ready for a relationship? She didn't want to be a fling for him — again.

By the end of class, one thing was clear — there was no sure way to determine if Brody O'Malley would break her heart again.

• • •

MOST PEOPLE DIDN'T know that seasoned firefighters were required to train in fire situations off the fire ground. Brody stood outside the Academy training tower, a four-storey concrete structure where administrators simulated fires using mist functioning as the smoke. He was glad to be busy today because giving Emma time to decide whether or not to see him again was harder than he guessed it would be. A week had gone by. He was a man not used to waiting for anything, especially a woman. But he forced himself to give her the space.

Fully dressed in turnout gear, and assigned only an ax to carry into the building, Brody was waiting for orders when he heard Gabe's voice over their radios. "Trapped woman on floor five. Firefighters O'Malley and Sands respond. Victim's having breathing problems."

The *trapped victim* was a training dummy named Harriet, who they used for various maneuvers. This would be a simple search and rescue. Pulling on his face mask, he said to Sands, the rookie he'd been paired up with, "Let's go."

"Right behind ya."

The house was full of thick, white mist, but he could see a hazy outline of the stairs. When he reached them, he dropped to his knees to climb up. It was cooler this low to the ground—they'd cranked up the heat—but it was slow going, and he didn't know how much air was in his tank. The trainees had turned their equipment over to the cap who'd drained a few tanks, fiddled with the breathing masks and literally broke equipment—all things that could happen during a real fire. Brody knew from experience none of those situations was fun. The brass had probably gone for Sands, though, because she was still learning.

Despite their snail's pace ascension, they were both breathing hard when they reached the top floor. Up here, it was completely dark. Every window had been covered, and the mist was thicker, making it impossible to see anything.

They heard a loud moan from a room to the right, which would be made by an officer observing them. Once inside, the sound was repeated from over in the corner. Using the wall, Brody felt his way to the "body." Another moan in front of him, so he dropped down and searched for a victim. "Got her," he told Sands. "Pick up an arm on your side, and we'll drag her out." No movement. Huh! Harriet was stuck. He felt her lower body and found it had been covered with heavy timber. A lot of it. They'd have to dig her out. His heartbeat escalated, which was odd because he'd dug out victims before. Being watched, evaluated and tested increased blood pressure and heart rate, he guessed.

And, Jesus, it was hot in here.

He gave Sydney orders.

"Fuck, I can't see anything," she said.

"Calm down. We've been blind before. Feel your way."

"Okay. I guess I'm nervous because this is training."

Brody felt his way into position. He'd learned to picture what he was doing when working blind. He yanked at a timber. Nothing. He tried another.

"I can't get them off her," Sands said.

"Me, either. They're heavy as hell. We'll have to pry them. Let me try first." Taking his ax, he maneuvered it under the top piece of wood. It budged slightly. "Try to loosen the top piece with your tool while I go at it from this side."

In a minute, Sands said, "I can't get the wood to move." There was an edge in her voice.

"Stay calm and keep trying. I felt some give."

Suddenly, the wood loosened but it sprung up, hitting Brody's face mask and knocking him back a bit.

"We got one!" Sands exclaimed.

"Keep going."

He inserted the long ax under another piece, and it took them a while to get the damn thing freed. Experience told him this was taking too long. He was about to remove his face mask to give Harriet his air when his PASS alarm—personal alarm safety system—went off. It blared out a smoke-alarm type noise that killed his ears and grated on his nerves. He turned if off. "Fuck."

Someone appeared out of the midst. He could feel but not see the officer. "Air's down, O'Malley." Gabe's voice.

"Get out of the building. Sands, you're doing good. Keep at it."

Shit. Standing, Brody made his way to the door and into the hall. And started to get pissed. Why the hell was he the target and not the rookie? Adrenaline pumped through his veins and he told himself it was because he was angry. Distracted by his thoughts, he realized he was out the door in the hall. He went left. Felt for the stairs.

And didn't find them. Instead he encountered a wall. Shit, he'd gotten disoriented, which happened to the best of them, but he was embarrassed to have done it in practice. Of course, that was why they *had* practice.

By the time he turned and headed the other way, he was struggling for air. Damn it to hell. If he could only find the steps.

He couldn't, so he must have taken another wrong turn. Was he in another room? He had no idea. Though he'd get grief for this, he knew the drill and spoke into his radio. "Mayday. Mayday. Out of air, and don't know where I am."

Later, at Badges, he did indeed take the razzing. While the jukebox blared some eighties music, his colleagues were making comments while Brody sat at the bar, his back to all of them.

Tony Ramirez slid a full beer in front of him. "Got lost like a cherry."

"Yeah, yeah, yeah."

From Felicia: "Sands found her way out easy. Showed up by a rookie. God, I love our women."

The cool brew went down smooth and helped him hold his tongue. Any response would egg them on.

Sydney clapped him on the back. "I gotta say, buddy, I never expected you to pee your pants."

He'd get back at her for that lie.

"O'Malley peed his pants?" someone yelled. "Who-hoo."

Gabe dropped down on the stool beside him. "Doing okay, buddy? I don't think they're anywhere near done."

"I got thick skin."

Sighing, Gabe sipped a coke. The guy looked younger these days. Happier. A woman could do that for you. "I got disoriented once in real time and had a Mayday incident, too."

"No shit?" Gabe was an icon in the fire department. He never made any mistakes.

"I was in a fun house at that amusement park near the lake. Mirrors, things jumping out at you in the dark. I totally didn't know where I was."

"Yeah, I can see why."

"I got teased mercilessly. Nobody was hurt and my cousin Mitch, who I worked with at the time, came in after me. It's why we do these trainings with seasoned firefighters."

"I know. I can take the heat. Besides, I'd do the same to them if things were reversed."

For a while, Brody enjoyed the camaraderie if not the teasing, but then a thought snuck into his head. He wanted to share this experience with Emma. Her eyes would light up and maybe even twinkle at his expense. This time he didn't need comfort. He needed a companion, a friend, a woman who cared about him, to be part of all aspects of his life.

And that was a lot bigger deal than wanting to get her in the sack again.

• • •

TEN DAYS AFTER Halloween, on a rainy Saturday morning, Emma did something she hadn't done in fifteen years, had never let herself do, in all that time. She walked into one of her spare rooms, opened a closet that she used for storage and pulled down a couple of big boxes marked High School. She stared at them for few seconds, knowing what was inside would sway her one way or the other. The contents would reveal how shallow her relationship with Brody had been or remind her that they'd had something special together. Sitting down on the floor with her back leaning against the bed, she lifted a cardboard lid. Sachet she'd put in ages ago still wafted up a faint sweet scent. On top was a photo album with Flowers scrawled across the front. Now she remembered. She'd pressed a few petals between the plastic pages from every bunch of blossoms Brody brought her. When she opened the book, she found groups of pink carnations labeled with dates. Oh! He'd sent her a bunch on the first of each month, starting with her birthday in November. Cute little cards were attached: November..."For my birthday girl." December..."For my favorite Christmas present." January..."For the newest and best thing in my life." She'd forgotten how romantic he could be, even as a boy. Turning the pages, she came upon some daisies. He'd picked them for her after they'd had sex outside in a field of flowers. She'd been nervous, but he'd coaxed her into it. Under the yellow blossoms was scripted, "I love you." That had been the first time either of them said the words.

Photo albums followed: the dances they'd gone to, senior activities they'd worked on and participated in. One of her favorite pictures was of her in her softball uniform and Brody in his baseball uniform standing back-to-back smiling. The shots had been taken for the yearbook when their respective teams voted them captains. Slowly, she traced the outline of his smile. Hers matched his. God, they'd been happy.

In another book, she found cards for every occasion, all signed, "Love, Brody." And, oh, wow, she'd forgotten about these. Sexy little notes he wrote to her at odd times: "Physics sucks. I'm thinking about getting physic—al with you. Get it?...I'm waiting in the cafeteria for baseball practice. You're out sick today. I miss you, Emmy....I'm in bed writing this. Ryan would freak if he knew I did this at night. I think about you, honey, all the time."

For some reason, Emma counted the notes as she read them. She stopped at thirty. There had to be more than a hundred of them.

Leaning back against the bed, she sighed heavily. If they'd been this much in love—which was what she remembered and the evidence before her supported—why had he left her so callously? Why hadn't he gone to Europe with his brother and come home to her? Their colleges were only a few hours away—they could have dated during the whole four years, then gotten married. Lots of couples made it under those circumstances.

A dark thought invaded her mind: If he'd break up with her back then after so many declarations of love, would he again profess his undying interest in her, then drop her when he was tired of her? Was she willing to risk her heart on him again? Or would she say no, play it safe and walk away?

Emma ran her hand over the cover of the album that held the notes. Suddenly, she knew in her heart she was sick of playing it safe.

• • •

FROM A TABLE by the window in Hidden Cove's Lakeside Restaurant, Emma watched the waves crash and peak on the shoreline. She loved winter, when snow dusted the streets and the lake created a live landscape painting. The Hallmark Card setting didn't calm her though, and the reason walked through the door and looked around. Brody spotted her and a big grin spread across his face. He'd dressed up in a gray silk shirt and black pants. A darker gray sports coat accented his broad shoulders. When he reached her, his scent—something so masculine it made her stomach clench—filled the space around them. "Hi, there, pretty lady."

"Hi, hotshot." She used to call him that because of baseball.

He dropped down into the adjacent seat, held up his fingers and started counting them off. "You look beautiful in that blue dress. I missed you. Ryan's doing well. I'm sorry you've had to deal with this emotional turmoil because of me. There, now that's all out of the way, I can't wait another minute to hear what you've decided. Give it to me quick, even if it's bad."

When she laughed aloud, he closed his eyes and leaned back. "So it's yes?"

"It's yes."

The expression on his face was intense. It took her a second to realize he was too moved to speak.

"With one caveat."

He shook himself. "Anything. Though I hope it isn't no sex."

"We can't broadcast that we're dating. I don't want Mark to be embarrassed publicly. People in Cameron Cove know we broke up, but they think our relationship ran its course."

"So that means I can't take your hand right now, huh?"

"I'd rather you didn't, though we are in Hidden Cove."

He just stared at her, his gaze intense. "It's a small price to pay for what I'm getting in return. What made you decide? This whole thing has happened pretty fast."

"After I saw you at the reunion, I couldn't stop thinking about you. And in my heart, I wanted to be with you." She rolled her eyes. "I realized you're the only man I ever loved. *Boy*, really." She gave him a serious look. "Brody, I'm risking my heart here, and it's scary. Tell me this isn't a passing fancy."

"God, no. Like I said, I haven't been able to stop thinking about you, either."

"I can't figure it out. We've been separated for fifteen years."

"I've been trying to come up with something, too." He bent forward and the old cocky Brody surfaced. "Though I can tell you, Emmy Walsh, you've turned into one gorgeous hunk of woman."

"Lord, I forgot how sexist you could be."

"I'm not, though. There's this blog the women in the department started. They say I'm quite liberated."

"I've been reading the blog. It's really cool. And I read your companion piece to the women's about working with good-looking guys."

"I was honest. And fair, I think."

"Yes, I agree."

Glancing around, he asked, "Are we eating?" He winked at her. "For some reason, my appetite came back."

"Oh, sure." Well, she didn't expect him to sweep her out of here and into bed. Not really.

They ordered a seafood platter for two and a bottle of white wine. Over lettuce wedge salads, he shook his head. "I've got to distract myself from the thought of getting you in bed. Tell me about Parker Allen, your sorority sister. Nobody can figure out why she's on a rampage about us."

"You know, she was always aloof. We were surprised when she wanted to pledge for Delta K. I was glad she got in, hoping maybe she'd open up. She didn't really, only once or twice when we worked ourselves through a keg. Something happened to her family, I know. And she was pretty much alone in the world. Oh, yeah. I think she dated a firefighter after college. Maybe even married him."

"This is all because of *a woman scorned* kind of thing?"

"Imagine what I could have done to you."

His didn't laugh. "I'm so sorry, Emma."

"That was dry humor, Brody. I don't remember any more details about Parker's life."

"At least it's some information. Maybe I'll try to find out what happened to her family. We already googled her, but not much came up. It galls me that she's slanting things against us. And that the blogosphere has taken to her."

"You still have a lot of adoring little fans in my class."

He smiled.

Reaching over, she touched his hand. "And a big one."

A brow arched. "That's good to hear."

When they finished dinner, he stared hard at her. "So, darlin', where do we go from here?"

"How about to your place? It's outside of Camden Cove, and I want to be with you."

"How?"

Geez, he was going to make her spell it out. "I'm ready to make love, Brody."

"Thank the good Lord. I'm dyin' to have you." He glanced around and snagged a waiter. "Check please."

• • •

FIRELIGHT KISSED HER hair, highlighting the deep red strands. Her cheeks were flushed and her skin glowed. Brody sat with his back against a sturdy chair he'd moved closer to the fireplace, and she was straddling him.

"Watch me, love," he whispered hoarsely. "Look at me when I come inside you."

She held his gaze. "Don't take too much time. I'm almost there."

How could she not be? He'd spent an hour relearning her body, exploring every inch of it, talking naughty about what he wanted to do with her. He was granite hard and struggling to control himself.

Lifting her hips, he slowly brought her down on his cock. Her warmth closed around him, and when she clenched her muscles, the impact was almost unbearable. He didn't remember sex ever being so acute it almost hurt.

"Hmmm," she whispered and closed her eyes. "I never forgot how this felt. Maybe because you were my first."

"Stay still for a minute or I'll go off like I did that time."

"You'll make up for it." She met her forehead with his. Her skin was moist. "You did then."

He chuckled, then groaned when her movements pushed him farther into her. They'd fumbled around for a long time before he figured out how to make sex good for her. The memory of the first time she came when he was inside her juxtaposed with the woman who'd now impaled him, and of its own volition, his body jerked. He gripped her hips. "I. Can't. Stop."

They both went at it hard, harder, really hard. He groaned, grunted and swore. She encouraged him with sexy words. Just before Brody's body exploded, he felt her spasms begin.

Their moans joined like their bodies and he surrendered himself to the wonder of being with Emma again.

• • •

"WHAT'S THE MATTER, Brody? You shy?"

"Jesus, where did *this* side of you come from?"

"It's only a little camera."

"On your computer." Which she'd had in her car.

"We can watch what we video together on the screen later."

"Now, *that* is kinky." Emma pictured him smiling.

"Shut up, Brody, and get in position."

The *position* was Emma on her knees, draped over an ottoman in his bedroom; he was also on his knees, behind her. They'd had adventurous foreplay before she suggested this kind of sex around midnight. Emma had decided to throw caution to the wind and have Brody fill her fantasies. "You said to pick one thing I always wanted to do."

"You got me there." He chuckled as he poised himself for entry.

Inch by inch, he slid inside her. He felt bigger, for some reason, maybe because she wasn't opening as much by virtue of her position. When he completely filled her, she gasped.

His chest met her back. It was slick and muscular. "Like that?"

"It's more intense this way."

He began to move.

"Oh, wow. Yes, Brody, right there."

He took advantage of the sweet spot he'd found and stroked it from within. Lots of moans, groans, even shouts when Emma totally surrendered herself.

Suddenly, she felt him tense, and as he plunged harder, she said, "Smile for the camera."

• • •

"HEY, I LOOK pretty good." After getting some wine for both of them, Brody watched the laptop situated on the bed. "And I've never seen a prettier sight than you taking me inside your body."

"God, look at your muscles bulge. And they *glisten*. It makes me hot watching us."

Smiling, they clinked glasses, sipped and then both gasped when the two of them really got going on screen. "Jesus, are you…?" she asked.

"I guess. I don't exactly remember."

"Your hand's… Holy crap, Brody, I never did that before."

Turning to her, he threaded his fingers through her hair, inhaling its flowery scent. "This is one of the sexiest things I've ever seen in my life, sweetheart."

She kissed his chest then licked a nipple. "Want to do it again?"

Emma took care of their glasses, and Brody set the computer on the night table then turned her over on her back. "You don't have to ask me twice, love."

# CHAPTER 7

AS THEY STOOD in the throng of people on Fifth Avenue watching the Macy's Thanksgiving Day Parade, snowflakes kissed Emma's nose and tongue when she stuck it out to capture the light precipitation. Being in New York City for the annual event was only one of the gifts Brody had given her in the two weeks they'd been seeing each other. She'd told him once when they were teens that she'd always wanted to come to the city at this time of year, and he'd bought the plane tickets as a belated birthday gift.

She spoke over the chatter of the crowd and the announcements. "Think your parents are mad at us for not spending the holiday with them?" Hers were in Florida and didn't expect her to join them. She was going south for Christmas, though.

"Nah." He kissed her forehead. "They're so glad we're together again, they would have paid for this trip."

"I wish you'd let me pitch in."

"You can buy me some puzzles at F.A.O. Schwartz tomorrow." He pointed to the stage where Broadway numbers were performed. "There's Spiderman."

She leaned her head against his shoulder as familiar music wafted over to them. "It was so much fun seeing that with you last night." In truth, it was fun doing everything with Brody, and she must have repressed the memory that it had always been this way when they were together. Though they hadn't gone public yet because of Mark—she'd decided they could after Christmas—she and Brody had had a wonderful few weeks.

As kids squealed at the Disney float of Rapunzel, Emma thought back to the dinners in Hidden Cove, the trip they'd taken to a Bed and Breakfast in the Catskills and the nights spent in one of their beds.

When the parade ended, he took her hand. "What would you like to do now?"

Shivering, she said, "Have hot chocolate by a warm fire."

He cocked his head. "Our hotel has a fireplace in the common area."

"Or we could get hot chocolate in the room."

His grin was a killer. "Hmm, I'd forgo the fire."

The walk back to the Marriott was crowded and noisy, so she held on to Brody's hand and enjoyed the sights and sounds of the city. When they reached the big hotel, they took the elevator up to the seventeenth floor. Once inside, he asked, "How about we take a Jacuzzi together?"

"Sound wonderful."

"Call for hot chocolate. I'll do the bath."

When the water was drawn and the hot chocolate had arrived, they climbed in the tub, which he scented with the jasmine oil provided by the hotel. Its sweet scent was enhanced by the hot steam and the pulsing jets. The warmth on their cold muscles was heavenly. "Aren't you afraid you're going to smell like a girl?"

"Nope, not if this makes you happy."

She opened her eyes, from where she was lying opposite him against the foam pillow. "You make me happy, Brody O'Malley."

Brody was glad to hear her say those words aloud. For him, the past few weeks had been a sexual haze interspersed with good, clean fun. Even Ryan admitted he'd never seen Brody so content.

Gently, he lifted her leg and took the hard sponge thing—she'd called it a loofah—and ran it over the soles of her feet. She moaned. He couldn't imagine ever getting tired of the sound. The woman who was Emma fulfilled all the potential she'd shown as the teenager he'd loved. She was an excellent teacher—he knew from her class's visit to the firehouse—a considerate daughter and a loyal sister. With him, she'd shown she had a sense of humor and was sexually curious. All in all, Emma Walsh was one nice female package.

He sighed. "I hate to think about going back to Hidden Cove after spending all this time together."

"We have two more days here." Emma winked at him. "We'll make the best of them."

"Lift up." He retrieved a sponge and began to wash her leg. "I know we have more time. It's not only that. I hate to have to be so careful about where we are, what we're doing."

"I'm sorry. It's only been a few weeks. I don't want to embarrass Mark."

He picked up her other leg. "Do you, um, see him?"

"I'm on a multi-grade-level reading committee that he chairs."

Brody stopped the motion of his hand. "I didn't know that."

"Um, yeah." She held his gaze. "We've had coffee together after a couple of the meetings."

"And you didn't tell me. Why?"

"Because I knew you'd get the pouty look on your face that's there now. I intend to stay his friend, Brody."

"What if I don't like it?"

She stilled. "Then you'll have to find a way to deal with my decision." She splashed water at him. "And I'll be extra attentive in bed."

"You get any more attentive or inventive in bed, I'm going to drop dead of exhaustion." Though he chose to tease her, it burned him how she dismissed his objection to her seeing Adams.

Later that night, when she made good on her attentive comment, it hit him that he was jealous of her old boyfriend. Jesus, when had that happened? He couldn't ever remember feeling the emotion.

• • •

THREE WEEKS AFTER Emma had gone to the city with Brody, she was on a train back to the Big Apple to meet her sister at Penn Station. Lucy was flying in from Paris to spend a week with her before the Christmas holidays. When school got out, they'd both go to Florida and join their parents to celebrate the holiday. She wished she could be with Brody on Christmas, but it wasn't going to happen. He had special plans for New Year's Eve, though, and she looked forward to coming back for them.

As she peered out the window at the snowy scenery, she hoped she didn't have her period when they brought in the new year. She basically had a four-week cycle. Had she gotten her period before or after her birthday? To check, she reached into her black, ruffled leather bag, which sat on an empty seat, and pulled out her calendar.

Okay, she had her period in October, right before her birthday. So it was due at the end of November. Huh. She flipped to December. Today was the tenth. Yikes, she was late!

Shaking her head, Emma blew out a heavy breath. There really wasn't anything to fear. She'd been late before, stress or even joy affecting her hormones. And she and Brody had used condoms every single time they made love, even when she recorded them together. Thinking about that experience, a grin split her face. The only drawback to having Lucy here would be she wouldn't spend any nights with Brody.

*We can have quickies, though,* he'd teased her.

Maybe even tonight. Lucy would probably fall asleep early because of jet lag, and Brody had suggested she sneak over to his place for a tryst. Briefly she thought about a way to make their limited time together exciting. She liked keeping him on his sexual toes. Yes, she knew exactly what she'd do.

• • •

BRODY HAD BUILT a fire when the doorbell to the half of the house he shared with Ryan rang. Hmm, Emma was early. He hoped nothing had gone wrong with Lucy getting into town. Whipping open the door, he found his brother on the porch. Ryan had long since moved back from their parents' house to finish his recuperation at home. His brother was dressed like him, in a heavy sweater and cords. "I can't find my key to your place." He held up a six-pack of Yuengling. "I'm going stir crazy. Wanna share this?"

"Sure, at least until Emma gets here."

"Ah, my competition." Ryan said the words kiddingly, but Brody caught the ring of truth in it. He'd had little time to spend with his twin since Emma had reentered his life.

They settled in the very masculine living room, which Brody had remodeled, putting in a conversation pit, similar to the ones that had been popular in the seventies; he liked the uniqueness of it. Prints of modern art graced the walls. Big, dark leather couches absorbed their large frames as they sat. Over the gas fireplace was a fifty-inch television.

"So, what's the word on returning to work?" Brody asked.

"January one. Maybe desk duty. I'm still sore as hell."

"Sorry."

"Where's the lovely Miss Emma?" Rye asked.

Brody explained about her sister. "I thought we'd have both of them over here, and you could help me entertain them."

"Man, I can't believe the change in you. You're smitten. Now it's dinner parties for her family. Soon, I'll be hearing about June weddings and due dates."

The beer stopped halfway to his mouth. "Due dates?"

"Babies, my friend. I know you use protection, but condoms break."

"Not mine. I get the heavy-duty, extra large ones."

"Yeah, well, that's good. Don't want any unintended consequences." Ryan popped a beer. "Wanna watch the Syracuse basketball game until she gets here?"

"Yeah. Sure."

But something niggled at Brody during the first half of the game. Something to do with what Ryan had said about babies. He couldn't put his finger on exactly what bothered him, so he tried to focus on Syracuse trampling Georgetown.

Emma showed up as the game ended and Ryan left. Her hair was dotted with snow and her cheeks red from the cold. She wore a long dark coat.

"Hi." He kissed her soundly.

"Hi."

"Want a drink or want to go to bed?"

"Bed." Kicking off her boots, she stooped over and slid down her pants then stood and slowly unbuttoned her coat. Under the heavy wool, she wore the sexiest one-piece, black lacy thing, which barely covered all her assets. "Man, you kill me, woman."

Pushing the coat to the floor, he dragged her to his room upstairs.

After some incredibly hot sex, he faced her on the bed, arm crooked, head in his hand. Sheets covered them. "How did I get so lucky?" he asked.

"Me, too. I'm so glad I found you again." Tears welled in her eyes, sparkling in the light at the bedside.

"Hey. What's going on?"

"Nothing. It was emotional seeing Lucy. The holidays are here. I tend to get weepy."

"Maybe you're getting your…" He trailed off, his hand lightly brushing her hip.

"What?"

A zillion things went through his mind. And suddenly he realized what he was trying to capture during the game. They'd been dating about five weeks and she'd not had her period since they'd been together.

• • •

"BRODY, YOUR WHOLE body went tense."

He just watched her, frown lines deepening on his brow.

A frisson of alarm went through Emma. He'd asked how he'd gotten so lucky to have her, and then he seemed to have frozen up. She cupped his cheek. "Brody? What are you thinking?"

"Ryan came over earlier."

"And?" No answer. "You said he was better about us."

"He is. He was busting my balls, though. He said something about weddings and babies."

"That's premature, isn't it?"

"I think so. I hope you do, too."

"I don't understand."

"When you said you're emotional, I wondered about PMS."

Damn it, she blushed. "It's funny you should say that."

His eyes widened and he lay back on his pillow, stared up at the ceiling. "Don't tell me you're pregnant. Please God, don't."

Pain pricked at her heart. She certainly didn't want to have a child before they solidified their relationship, but she also wouldn't pray to God for it not to happen, as if pregnancy was a terminal illness. For self-protection, she brought up the sheet around her breasts. "I'm late is all I know."

"How late?" He still wouldn't look at her.

"Three weeks."

"Jesus Christ."

*Think rationally, Emma. Don't fly off the handle.*

"There's no reason to think I'm pregnant. We used protection each time."

"So did both my brothers and they each had a surprise baby." His tone was so disgusted it shocked her. And so cold. Very cold.

Emma lay back, too. "Well, I'll give it a few more days. If I don't get my period, I'll do a pregnancy test."

Suddenly, he whipped off the covers. "No, you'll do one now. I'm going to get a kit."

She sat up, too. "Do you really think that's necessary?"

He stuffed his legs into his pants and dragged on the sweater. "If I ever want to get any sleep again or have some measure of sanity for the next few days, then, yes, it is."

"I see."

"Stay right where you are. I'll be back soon."

Brody hurried out.

And Emma burst into tears. He was treating her like a…problem. Like a woman who was going to trap him into something he didn't want to do. He'd been abhorred at the thought of her being pregnant with his child. She didn't want that, either, not now, but it wouldn't be the end of the world.

He was gone twenty minutes, during which she dressed in her pants and one of his shirts, stuffed the teddy in her coat pocket and vacillated between anger, fear and understanding. When he burst back into the bedroom, she didn't show any of those emotions. Wordlessly, she took the kit and walked into the bathroom.

Peed on the stick.

Stayed there until the results came in. Then she walked back into the bedroom.

Calmly, she handed him the stick.

And just like that, he turned back into the man he was an hour ago. "Whew! That's good."

"Yes it is." *Her* voice was cold now.

"It's the most accurate one. I knew that from studying for my paramedic recertification."

"Oh, good."

He didn't take her in his arms. He didn't say, "Let's discuss what happened here." Instead, he stood there and shifted from one foot to the other.

Emma lifted her chin. "I have to get home. An early day tomorrow."

"Oh, yeah, sure. Say hi to Lucy."

Head high, Emma walked out of the bedroom.

# CHAPTER 8

"SO, HOW'S EMMA?" Ryan asked the question as he and Brody rode the chair-lift up the slope of Mountain Tree Ski Resort, about an hour from Hidden Cove. "I'm kind of surprised you wanted to come with us."

"I'm surprised you went this year. You can't ski yet."

"Nah, but I enjoy the air. I don't mind taking the ski lift back down. It's fun being on the mountain after I was cooped up for so long. So, why're you here?"

Bracing wind whipped Brody's face as he turned to his brother. "I love to ski. And I haven't seen your cop buddies in a while."

"What's Emma doing today?"

Brody shrugged a shoulder encased in a warm, bright blue ski jacket. "I don't exactly know. We're taking a little break."

"Is that why you've been so available for a week? I thought maybe it was because her sister's here."

Fuck! Brody didn't want to deal with his relationship with Emma today. All week, he'd been blocking what had happened in his bedroom the night Lucy came to visit. The night he and Emma were supposed to have a hot little quickie. Not only had he panicked when she'd told him she'd missed her period, but he'd let her leave without talking about his reaction, admitting he'd acted like a jerk, trying to determine why. She had to be hurt by his abrupt behavior.

Not to mention the fact that he hadn't called her all week.

"Things were going too fast between us," he told Ryan as they moved through the crisp morning air. "I think we need to slow down."

"Does she agree?"

Body couldn't look at his brother, instead stared down at the white snow beneath them. "I um, I didn't talk to her about it."

"Jesus, Brody. You can't just stop calling her after she gave you another chance."

Because he knew he was wrong, he snapped at Ryan. "This from the guy who's left a stream of broken hearts from here to New York?"

"Now that's a low blow. You know I've changed."

"Yeah, well, I thought I had, too. I thought I wanted to settle down." He shook his head. "That pregnancy scare did me in, Rye. I'm not ready for a baby in my life."

"And she is?"

"No, she said the opposite."

The lift reached the peak of the snowcapped mountain. With the sun crystal clear above them, Brody hopped off the lift and took a deep breath. "This is what I need. To make some tracks."

Ryan grabbed his arm. "Brody, think about what you're doing here."

"I am. I'm going to race down the slope." He pulled his goggles over his eyes, set his skies, hunched over his poles and took off. The freezing cold numbed him, which was exactly what he wanted. He wouldn't think about Ryan's words or the shit he was at having left Emma alone all week after a pretty disastrous experience.

One *he* had caused.

• • •

"I HATE HIM!" Lucy sat across from Emma in the whirlpool of the gym Emma belonged to. The steam rising and the hot water bubbling around them was supposed to make them relax, but Lucy's face was taut with anger. "I told you it was a bad idea to start seeing him again, when I called from Paris."

Her sister had had a front row seat to Emma's devastation when Brody had broken up with her in high school.

"Apparently you were right." Emma couldn't believe that Brody hadn't called her or come over or set up a time for dinner with her and Lucy. She never expected the cold shoulder, even after his hurtful behavior that night in his bedroom. And she was mad, too. If anyone had a right to be distanced, it was her.

Leaning back against the ceramic edge of the tub, Lucy sighed. "I wonder what he plans to do, just never see you again?"

Emma's eyes stung. "Could be. In any case, I need to stop thinking about a future with him. Even if came groveling back, how can he explain his overreaction that night and freezing me out this week?"

Lucy suggested, "Maybe he's trying to get his head on straight?" Her sister loved her and was trying to be fair for Emma's sake.

"Well, it looks to me like he did exactly what he said he wouldn't do—have a fling with me." Tears coursed down her cheeks. Emma scooped up some of the water and splashed it on her face.

"The bastard." Lucy reached for her hand. "I'm sorry."

"Yeah, me too—that I ever believed he'd changed."

• • •

"THE HOUSE WAS on fire. There was a kid inside. I went." Brody faced down his battalion chief with a carelessness about his job that he hadn't known he possessed. He'd always approached his work with the utmost professionalism.

Erikson's light complexion reddened in contrast to his stark white shirt. "Against strict orders by me that the house was fully involved and evacuation was in process."

There was that. Brody shifted his stance. "I couldn't leave a kid in there, Chief."

The BC cocked his head. "Brody, this isn't you. You never act so irresponsibly."

"I don't see what I did as irresponsible."

Again, the chief surveyed him. "Well, I do and that's what matters. You're suspended without pay for two days. Starting right now."

"I'm calling my union rep."

"Go ahead. Meanwhile, get out of here and clear your head. It's usually on a lot straighter than it is now."

With the chief's words echoing in his brain, Brody stormed from the office. Grabbing the duffle he'd left on the kitchen table, he stormed outside. He blanked his mind and refused to question his actions; he was right to have saved that kid. Just ask her mother.

*What are you running from?* Ryan asked after word got around Brody was in trouble because of his actions in the fire. Rye got on Brody's ass about it, too.

But he wasn't running. He was doing his job.

His behavior on the line had nothing to do with Emma Walsh.

• • •

EMMA LITERALLY BUMPED into Mark in the teachers' cafeteria of the elementary school. She was staring down at her tray of food and didn't see him. He grasped her arms to steady her. "Hi, there." Though his words were cheerful, his eyes showed the hurt she'd caused. And for what?

"Hi, Mark. What are you doing here?"

"Meeting with your principal about a peer tutoring program between our two schools."

"That's nice." She shifted her tray.

He studied her face. She knew what he'd see there—dark circles under her eyes, taut skin, frown lines. "Are you all right?"

"Yes, of course."

He shook his head. "Em, I know you well enough to see something's wrong." He motioned to an empty round table across the room. "Let's sit. I'll get my meal and be right back."

She wasn't sure why she agreed. Maybe she needed a man to be nice to her again.

After he returned and while he ate, she picked at her meal.

"Tell me what's going on."

"I feel bad seeing you again, Mark. I wasn't very nice to you."

"Honey, you were great, as always." He averted his gaze to the window where snow fell in big fat flakes. "I wish Brody O'Malley hadn't come into our lives when he did, though."

In so many ways, she did, too. But the least she could do was to keep her regrets from Mark. She'd done enough damage to him.

So, she put on a fake smile. "What are your holiday plans?"

"Going back to Nebraska to see my mom and sisters. I, um, don't have New Year's Eve plans now, so I'll stay for the whole vacation."

She sucked in a breath. "I'm so sorry, Mark."

"Hey, I'll get through it." He winked at her. "There's this cute English teacher who's been making excuses to come to my office. People, um, know we broke up. Thanks, by the way, for not broadcasting about you and Brody."

"It was the least I could do."

"How about you? What are your plans for Christmas?"

Emma thought about the upcoming holiday without Brody. It stretched grimly before her. Still, she disguised her sadness. "Lucy's here. We're going to Florida for the break. I'm looking forward to it."

"Tell her I said hi."

They made small talk as they finished their lunches, and Emma remembered how easy it was to be with this man, how there was no drama in their interactions, no subtext lurking beneath the surface.

Which was why, when he walked out of the cafeteria to go to his meeting, her throat felt like a sock was stuffed in it.

What had she done to her future?

• • •

ON HIS FIRST full day of suspension, Brody put in new garbage disposals for him and Ryan, tore up his living room rug in preparation for installing hardwood floors, and at ten, when he still wasn't exhausted enough to sleep, he headed for Badges. He'd have a drink and let the comfort of his favorite place soothe him.

When he walked in, some Doors music blared from the jukebox and there was loud chatter from the dozens of patrons tonight. He was surprised to see Tony Ramirez at the bar. "Hey, Tony, what're you doing here? It's pretty late for an old married man to be out."

"Having a beer. Sit. I'll buy you one." Brody dropped down on a stool next to him. "Hey, sorry about the suspension," Tony said after he ordered a Coors for Brody.

"Yeah, well, I deserved it."

Tony stared into space, not really seeing the mirror behind the bar or the two bartenders. "It's hard, isn't it, putting our own safety ahead of a victim? I'm not sure I wouldn't have done what you did with the kid."

"Thanks for saying that. But the beautiful Sophia would have your ass for it."

"You got that."

Something about his tone alerted Brody. Besides, he and Tony talked sometimes, late at night, when the others were asleep. He spoke of his wife as if she'd hung the moon. "Problems at home?"

"Things have been brewing a while." He looked at Brody, his brown eyes bleak. "I'm not sure any firefighter's wife ever truly accepts the job."

"I thought yours did."

"I thought so, too." He shook his head. "Let's not talk about this. Tell me about Emma."

"Nothing to tell. Our relationship is a mess. I've been blowing it."

"Well, I'm not exactly in the position to give advice, but I—"

"Hello there, gentleman. Can I buy America's Bravest drinks?"

At first Brody didn't recognize the woman who'd slithered up to the bar. The long luscious hair. The sparkling violet eyes. But then Tony said, "No thanks, it would be like consorting with the enemy, Ms. Allen." He stood. "I'm leaving." He socked Brody on the arm. "Come with me."

That's right. Now he recognized Parker Allen, the reporter waging war against the fire and police departments. To Tony, he said, "Ah, no. I think I'll consort a bit."

The woman laughed and took Tony's stool when his friend left. "If it isn't the hero. Hear you got your hands slapped."

"I did. It was worth saving a kid."

"Can I quote you on that?"

"Sure. Go ahead. If I can ask you something."

"I might not answer." She gave him a look Brody recognized as one of pure female interest. "Then again…"

"Why this vendetta against the fire department?"

Her color rose. "It isn't a vendetta. I think public employees have a good gig going, and I'm not sure it's always deserved."

"Tell that to the mother whose kid was in the fire."

"Touché."

She snagged the bartender's attention. "I'll have another shot of bourbon. And get my friend here one."

Five shots later, Brody ended up in a Lexus belonging to the reporter. He'd gotten his shirt off and unbuttoned hers, where he found another layer of clothing, when she stayed his hands. "Brody, stop for a minute. This is fun but I'm not...just stop."

The statement was a bucket of cold water on his head. He was blinded by a flash of Emma insisting they have *fun* with the video camera, Emma asking for different positions when they made love, Emma insisting they order some toys from an online catalogue.

What the hell was he doing making out with another woman?

Shaking his head, he drew back. "You're right. We have to stop."

Her keys were in the ignition, and he was sober enough to remove and pocket them. Taking out his cell phone, he punched in numbers. After several rings, he heard a groggy, "'ello."

"Rye it's me. I had too much to drink and so has my companion. I'm in the parking lot at Badges. Come get us."

• • •

EMMA FACED HER kids on the last day of school before Christmas vacation. Miserable, she was trying to put up a brave front so she'd dressed in a bright red Santa sweatshirt and pasted on a smile. "I thought we'd do our reading lesson with the book *The Polar Express*." She held up a copy of the popular Christmas story. She was comfortable sharing this book for the Christian holiday because she'd read Kwanza books and Hanukah tales, too. "How many of you have read it?"

Almost all hands went up.

"Oh, dear," she said, sounding disappointed. "I guess we should pick something else."

Twenty-five faces scrunched in dismay.

"No, no Ms. Walsh."

"Please, we *love* that story."

More of the same from the rest of them.

She grinned. "Then push the desks out around the perimeter and sit on the floor." Her room sported a nice Berber carpet. "It'll be like when you were little kids." They were all of nine now.

Controlled chaos abounded as chatter filled the room, the excitement of vacation hard to quell. At least their antics took her mind off Brody, his reaction to the pregnancy scare and his disappearance from her life. Damn him. At one time she'd pictured him reading a story like this to their kids. Shopping for toys for their little girl and boy. Spending Christmas morning as a family. Now, none of that would ever happen. She remembered the conversations she'd had with her sister this week.

Lucy thought Brody had been leading her on.

Lucy believed neither O'Malley brother could commit. Emma had forgotten her sister had skid marks from dating Ryan when they were in high school.

And Lucy contended that Brody was still the same self-absorbed teenager who'd broken up with Emma to play the field. As soon as there might be something serious to deal with, something that might require a commitment, he'd freaked.

It all fit, and though Emma felt incredibly sad about the fact, she wasn't going to delude herself about the kind of man Brody O'Malley really was.

When the space was cleared, Emma sat down in a group with the kids and asked for quiet. Then she began to read the story of the boy who takes a midnight train to the North

Pole. Once there, Santa gives him some sleigh bells; he puts them in his pocket, but he loses them on the trip home. They turn up on Christmas morning, but only he and his sister can hear the bells jingle. Their parents can't.

"So, what's the message of this story, guys?" she asked after she closed the book. Twenty-five excited faces greeted her and made her smile genuine.

Two boys raised their hands. "Peter."

"Christmas is great."

The kids and Emma laughed. "What else? Tommy?"

The boy, who was very precocious, said, "Grownups can't hear the bells because they're too busy shopping."

"*Very* good."

After more suggestions, Emma added, "I think the story also shows that you can't forget what's important to you when you get busy for the holidays. What should be more important to you than presents?"

"Nothing!" little Terry, the boy who'd wanted to know about Brody's injury at the fire house that day, answered.

"Mom and Dad." A girl wrinkled her nose. "My brother, too, I guess."

"That's right. This is a book about priorities. Do you know what they are?"

"My mom says my dad's priorities are messed up. It means he works too much."

Story time wound down and Emma put on some Christmas carols as the kids moved the desks back in groups, then went off to music class with an aide who'd come to get them. The fourth-grade and fifth-grade students were presenting a concert to the school this morning. Emma planned to head down to the gym/stage in fifteen minutes.

Sitting back down at her desk, as she listened to the season's tunes, she thought about priorities. Christmas *was* too full of material things. She and Brody had decided not to swap presents but give to an annual firefighters' Toys for Kids in the city. For the hundredth time, she wondered if his priorities had shifted from her to...whatever? Or was she ever really important to him?

"Emma." As if she conjured him from a genie bottle, she looked over and saw him at the doorway. Her heart skipped a beat, reminding her of how he'd broken it.

"Hello, Brody."

"I watched." His voice was a bit hoarse.

"What?"

"I watched you read to the kids. I stood off to the side so they couldn't see me. You're great at vocalizing parts."

"I was a bit distracted today."

Entering the room, he shut the door behind him. "Yeah, I bet I know why."

She glanced at the clock, trying to calm her pulse. "I've got about ten minutes before I have to go to the gym."

Nodding, he came close. He'd showered, dressed in nice jeans, a ski sweater and vest, but his eyes were bloodshot and his face drawn. Even his color wasn't good.

"Rough night?" she asked.

"Rough few days. For you too?"

She nodded, trying to determine his mood.

"I came to apologize for what happened at my house the last time we were together."

"Apology accepted. Sit down."

He took the adult chair she kept against the wall and drew it close to her desk. "I'm sorry I haven't been in touch." He linked his hands between his knees and stared down at the floor. Then back up at her. "I, um, flipped about the pregnancy scare."

"Yes, I got that."

"Actually, I went off the rails. You might as well know everything. I was suspended from work." He told her about the kid he'd saved.

"I can't say I'm sorry you saved a baby, but your chief's right. You told me firefighters know their boundaries and don't cross them in fires."

"This time, I didn't know mine. I've been acting crazy for days." He ducked his head sheepishly. "Last night, I almost did something really stupid."

Her pulse escalated as he told her about Parker Allen. Heartache was replaced by anger. "You almost screwed the woman who's singlehandedly trying to destroy the fire department?"

He shrugged a shoulder, and she could see him turning on the O'Malley charm. "I think *almost* is the operative word."

"Do you know how she could use that against you and all of your friends?"

His face blanked. "I, um, hadn't thought about that."

"And now," she said, gathering steam. "Now, what do you want from me?"

"I'm not really sure. I just know I bungled it between us."

"But you're not sure you know what you want?"

Running his hand through his hair, his expression was annoyed. "Look, all I know is I woke up today and had to see you. Had to make this right between us. I want to start going out again."

Emma watched the man she once loved in high school, the man she maybe loved again. "This is by far the worst apology, the worst attempt at asking for a second chance that I've ever heard." Standing she threw down her pen. "You know what, Brody, go to hell. *I don't want to see you again.*"

With that she stalked out of her classroom.

# CHAPTER 9

TEXT #1, WHILE Emma and Lucy waited for the plane to Florida: *You're right, it was a lame apology. Guess I'm not used to making them :)*

Text #2, when she landed in Sarasota: *Hoping you've been flying. Text me back. Say I have another chance.*

Text #6, while she and her mother sat on the back porch Christmas Eve day. *Look, okay, you have a right to be mad. I blew it on Friday, too. Please, please, text me back and tell me you'll see me again so we can at least talk.*

Text #11, Christmas Day: *Happy Christmas, love. Can't believe I'm not with you this year. Did you know every Christmas we were apart those fifteen years, I thought about you?*

Text #16: *Work today was tough. We lost a victim in a fire. I was good, though, no heroics. I'm learning, babe. And changing.*

Text #20: *Please, I'm dyin' here. I can't eat or sleep. Contact me.*

• • •

"ANOTHER TEXT, DEAR?" Cara Walsh, Emma's mother, lounged next to her in the sand under a rainbow umbrella at Siesta Key Beach where the two of them had gone to relax while Lucy fished with her father. Emma's mom was sixty but looked a decade younger. Though her hair was shot with silver, it went well with her almost unlined face. She wore an orange tankini suit.

"I'm afraid so." Emma closed her phone and flipped down her sunglasses against the glare coming off the Gulf. Its waves whooshed and receded, which usually calmed Emma but didn't today. "Why doesn't he stop trying to contact me?"

"Why don't you delete the texts before you read them?"

Emma smiled over at her mother. All her life, the woman had been able to prod her daughters into admitting what they'd prefer go unspoken.

"I should. I honestly believe he's not committed to this relationship. He never was. But he still wants me in his life. And damn him, his texts make it impossible for me to ignore him."

"Hmm. Then that's a problem. I guess you have to think about why he's able do that to you."

A cool breeze wafted over to them from the water, ruffling Emma's skirted bathing suit. "What do you think?"

"I was very sad that he broke your heart when you were teens. But as I told you then, I thought you were too young to be committed, and that he was right to date others."

That time came back to her in Technicolor. The hurt curling inside her when he first uttered the words. The fear that she'd been just another one of Brody's girls. The incredible ache at missing him. "I remember all that. But I meant what do you think about now?"

"You say he's shown he's not ready to commit, but he seems to want to give the relationship more time. Can you take a chance on that, honey?"

"I don't know. Maybe I want to. But he did exactly what he said he wouldn't do—treat me like a fling—and his contrition sucks."

"I'm guessing that boy doesn't know his way around an apology. Him or his brother, Ryan." Her mother's smile gave the sun competition. "If it were me, I'd make him grovel."

"Then what?"

"You, sweetie, have to decide if you can try again with him. But don't let him go because he made an ass out of himself. He is a man, after all."

At her mother's advice, for the first time since Brody had run out to get the pregnancy test kit, Emma felt a spurt of hope that there was a chance for them.

• • •

It had been six days and thirty-seven texts since Emma left town and still no word from her. Brody clicked off his phone, vowing he wouldn't contact her again unless he heard from her first. Damn it, *this* was not what he wanted. Loneliness so acute it hurt him during the day. And erotic dreams at night that made him wake in a sweat.

"You still moping around here like a kicked puppy?" The question came from Felicia, who, he knew from experience, had little patience for matters of the heart.

"I think it's time to stop."

"Thank God." She sat down at the kitchen table and buried her nose in *Firehouse* magazine. After a moment, big hazel eyes peeked over the top of the pages. "Wanna talk about it?"

"Maybe." She put down the magazine.

"You ever been in love, Licia?"

"Nope."

"That was a pretty quick answer. How come?"

"Too cautious." She shook her head. "I got engaged to this guy early in my career as a firefighter. I thought I loved him, but he said the only thing I was really committed to was the fire department. I broke it off."

"So you *didn't* love him?"

"I wouldn't *let* myself love him." Her expression turned thoughtful. "I'd completed my arson investigator certificate and wanted to climb to the top of Fire Investigation, similar to what Eve Callahan did before she joined the HCFD as our lead arson person."

"Yeah, I knew you did that. What happened to the goal?"

"I missed actual firefighting. A lot. So I went back to the line." She gave him a pointed look. "Be careful if you don't want to grow up and be like me."

"Gimme a break. You're only five years older than I am."

"Really? I think of you as a kid."

"Very funny."

Grinning, she indicated the Joke Jar. "Let me tell you a few to cheer you up."

"Sure, why not? I couldn't feel any worse."

She stood and went to the counter to get the jar and drew out a big sheet of paper. "I wonder who put this in. It's big." She scanned it. "Oh, it's a series of shorts. Here we go." She read them to him.

Q. How can you tell when a firefighter is dead?
A. The remote control slips from his hand.

Q. What does CHAOS stand for?
A. The Chiefs Have Arrived On Scene.

Q. How many firemen does it take to change a light bulb?

A. Four. One to change the bulb and 3 to chop a hole in the roof.

Q. A Mexican fireman had two sons. What did he name them?
A. Hosea and Hoseb.

By the time she was finished, Brody was laughing at the dumb quips, as had been her intent. She turned back to *Firehouse* magazine and Brody wandered into the common room to watch TV. It had been a light day; cleaning and rig care and training were done by noon, and they'd had only one call to a fire in a cemetery. They'd frozen their asses off putting out the burning storage shed. Dropping down onto the big leather couch, he flicked on the set.

But he couldn't concentrate on world news. Since the remote was his favorite toy—hence he thought the joke Licia told was funny—he thumbed through the channels. An ad for a restaurant for New Year's Eve came on. He'd planned to take Emma out to a fancy place, though she wasn't impressed by glitz and glamour. And now he wouldn't even be able to try to spoil her. She was apparently done with him.

Flip, flip. A ski resort in Aspen played some awful jingle while advertising that they still had openings for their New Year's Eve singles bash. Hmm. He wondered if he could get a flight out. Nah! Even if he could, he wasn't interested in free-flowing booze and women out for a good time. Lately, he'd felt past that phase in his life.

Ryan was going to a gala at the Holloway House with a new woman in his life and said Brody could tag along. But that meant putting on a monkey suit, and he didn't want to dress up for anybody but Emma.

Briefly, he considered flying to Florida and confronting her in person. His presence might push her to reconsider their relationship. But he didn't want to bully her into seeing him again. Contrary to what she now thought of him, he had some integrity. Sighing, he picked up the phone to call Rye to tell him he'd go along on the thirty-first, changing the channels as he waited for his brother to answer.

His finger stopped at an ad on QVC. He stilled. Hmm. *Hmm.* An idea hit him. Maybe one more try. Just one more.

• • •

TWO DAYS BEFORE New Year's Eve, Emma was alone in her parents' house because she'd begged off on a bike ride with them and her sister. Instead, out on the lanai, she read one of Lucy's romance novels and enjoyed the squawk of birds and the warm breeze drifting in through the screens. A pelican even came to the door once and seemed to look in at her. Emma almost didn't start the novel because the guy on the cover reminded her of Brody. And once she got into the story, she should have put it down because the book was about finding true love. The content was making her more depressed as she read on. She was glad when the doorbell rang. Rising from the chaise, she padded to the front door and opened it.

A FedEx guy held out a package. "Delivery for Emma Walsh."

"Oh." She accepted the five-inch-by-five inch box and signed the slip. Returning to the lanai, she set the package on the table and looked at the return address. QVC? She hadn't ordered anything from the shopping channel. Maybe Lucy had bought her a late Christmas present.

Ripping open the box, she found another rectangular one fastened with a big white bow. Inside that was tissue paper. It rustled as she drew the thin covering back and found a silver handbell inside. The surface caught a beam of sunlight and sparkled brilliantly. The outside was woven with delicate curlicues around the handle. When she picked it up, it tinkled. On close inspection, she saw the bell had been engraved.

*To Emma. I hear the bells now because of you. Please believe me. Brody.*

She'd never expected something so poignant from him. Touching. Meaningful. How was she supposed to resist the gesture?

• • •

BRODY RAN HIS finger around the inside collar of his dressy shirt, trying to loosen it.

"Stop fidgeting," Ryan grumbled from beside him, where they stood at the bar watching Hidden Cove's elite mingle.

"I'm uncomfortable." For a lot of reasons.

"I wonder who Kathleen *had* to talk to," Rye commented.

Brody checked out the dark-haired beauty a few feet away, chatting with Ryan's date, Kathleen. "Lisel Loring, the Broadway star who moved to Hidden Cove. Remember, a few years ago, there was this big story about her getting stalked by a fan? Hey, look, they're coming over."

The two women approached. "Ryan, I wanted you to meet Lisel Loring. She's a dancer for the New York City Ballet."

Extending her hand to Ryan, she shook his. "It's Lisel Woodward now."

Brody introduced himself. "You're married to the battalion chief in charge of our Fire Academy, aren't you?"

"You bet she is." Ian Woodward rolled up to them in his wheelchair. The BC had been in the FDNY and was sidelined by terrorists in 9/11. Because of that, he was an invaluable resource for teaching probies and seasoned firefighters alike. Smiling, the man slid his arm around his wife's waist, touching her rounded belly.

"Happy New Year, Chief," Brody said affectionately. He liked this guy. A lot. Everybody did. "And congratulations. When's the due date?"

"Two months." Lisel looked like a million bucks to be that far along in her pregnancy.

For a minute, Brody pictured Emma carrying his child. She would have glowed like Lisel, and he'd be as sappy as Ian. Shit, why hadn't he handled the baby scare better?

Ian nodded at someone behind them. "Hey, Derek, come join us."

Brody turned and saw a man and woman had reached them. He did a double take. "Wow!" he said, forgetting his manners.

"Holy shit!" Ryan added.

"Close your mouths, boys." Derek Dennison, another battalion chief from the academy, touched his date's elbow. "Ian, you've met Felicia White, but I don't think your wife has."

Dressed in gold from head to toe, Felicia's close-fitting strapless gown flattered curves. After she greeted everyone, she looked from side to side. "Brody, are you, um, alone?"

"Yeah, a threesome with my twin and his date. Pathetic, huh?"

For some reason, Felicia seemed surprised.

Derek asked, "Where's Eve and Noah? I haven't seen them tonight."

"Eve was called to an arson case before they were about to leave."

Ryan cocked his head. He'd been on some arson cases, too, as police liaison. "I hear she's doing a great job since she took over."

"Of course." Ian beamed with pride at the compliment to his sister.

The two couples drifted away and Ryan and Brody watched them leave. Rye said, "Who would have thought the lieutenant could be such a fox when she dressed up?"

"She cleans up good." Brody frowned. "She never said anything about dating Dennison."

"They aren't dating," Kathleen told them. "They accompany each other to social events like this."

"Friends with benefits?" Ryan wanted to know.

"No, at least I don't think so. Come on, Rye, let's dance."

Ryan looked to Brody.

"Go ahead, I'm gonna get some air."

"It's freezing out there."

"I'll be fine. Go do me proud."

Wending his way through the crowd of dancers, Brody slipped outside onto a stone patio that traveled the length of the ballroom. Shivering with the first flash of cold, he looked out over the snow-covered golf course and thought about the sorry state of his life. Everybody in there was a couple. Why the hell had he let Rye talk him into coming here? He was miserable.

This was stupid. He'd leave. Circling around the outside of the building to go directly to his car, he planned to call Rye on his cell and tell his brother he'd slunk home.

Brody reached a second patio and the door opened from the inside. Out stepped a woman in black. Hair a little spiky. Cute nose. Pretty… Oh, dear Lord in heaven. "Emma?"

"Hi, Brody."

"W-what…?" Jesus, he felt his eyes sting. He swallowed hard, trying to keep the emotion at bay. "I thought you were in Florida."

"I came back today. With the ticket you bought me."

His throat convulsed. "H-how'd you know I'd be here?"

"I called Felicia. She said you were coming with Ryan."

His whole body slumped. "I…I don't deserve this."

Emma sensed an emotion emanating from Brody that she'd never witnessed before. It was powerful, profound and…humbling. His reaction to her presence made it easier to do what she'd come to do. "Maybe not, after how shitty you behaved. But I'm here to say I'll give this relationship another shot. See where it goes."

His mouth dropped. Gone was the charming easygoing Brody O'Malley. He didn't move to touch her; instead he stood there staring at her. Operating on instinct, she stepped into his arms. He encompassed her, totally. Despite the cold, she was warm from the heat of his body. He didn't speak, just buried his face in her neck and held her close. She grasped on to him tightly. Finally, he drew back, his eyes suspiciously moist. "Did you get the bell?" he asked in a gravelly voice.

"I did."

"I meant what I said. My priorities are in order now. Finally." He brushed his knuckles down her cheek. "I'm so sorry I hurt you when you thought you could be pregnant."

"I already forgave you for that, Brody."

"Then why did you tell me to go to hell? And not answer texts?"

"Because I'd decided that I couldn't risk letting you hurt me again. I couldn't trust you not to use me and throw me away."

Stepping in closer, he put his hand on her shoulder. "I won't, baby, I promise."

"You know what? I don't want that promise from you. You really can't be sure you won't. I'm taking the risk with my eyes wide open."

"Why? Because of the bell?"

"No, though that spurred me to act. I've missed you, I've been miserable and I want to see where this goes."

"I missed you. I've been miserable and I want to see where this goes, too."

She smiled.

He smiled. And glanced at his watch. "It's eleven. Where do you want to be when we bring in the New Year?"

She arched a brow.

So did he. "You're on, Emmy." Grabbing her hand, he tugged her toward the parking lot.

An hour later, they snuggled in her bed, watching the stars in the clear, winter sky sparkle down at them through the skylights in her ceiling. Brody eyed the clock. "It's twelve."

She kissed his lips lightly. "Happy New Year, Brody."

"Oh, it will be. Because of you."

"And you. Us together."

Reaching over, he picked up the champagne she had in the fridge and poured for midnight. Emma pushed herself up with the sheet secured around her. He sat so he was facing her, his sheet slipping low on his naked hips. Clinking her glass with his, he whispered, "I love you, Emma. Before, still and in the future."

"Oh!" They were words she never thought she'd hear from him again. And hadn't realized she wanted to. Her voice was husky when she said, "I love you, too, Brody. Very much."

They sipped the champagne from the glasses, then tasted the bubbly on each other's lips. Emma knew loving this man wasn't going to be easy, had never been easy, but it didn't matter anymore. A part of her had always belonged to him. She might as well give him the rest and hope for the best.

"There, now that's over." He set aside their glasses, then yanked down the sheet. "Let's get to the real celebration."

She smiled as he eased her onto the mattress. "Yes, hotshot, let's."

• • •

# WORTH THE RISK

Novella number three in the
AMERICA'S BRAVEST SERIES

## KATHRYN SHAY

# CHAPTER 1

AN EAR SHATTERING blast rent the air and Lieutenant Felicia White, the officer in charge, yelled, "Duck!" into her lapel mic to the other four members of her crew. Simultaneously, she dove forward as far away from the explosion as she could get. The room shook and smoke filled the back area of the Hidden Cove Library where a fire had broken out approximately thirty minutes ago.

She shook her head to clear it and waited for her hearing to come back. When it did, sounds of sirens outside told her help was on the way to assist Quint and Midi 7, the fire trucks that had gone on the call along with her rescue rig. She spoke into her radio again. "Rescue 7, respond and give me your status."

Nothing. Felicia's heart rate escalated as she rolled over and sat up. Jesus, she couldn't lose these guys. She just couldn't. The run had been designated as a small, self-contained blaze of origin unknown. When they'd arrived, the smoke in the building was light and she thought they'd have it under control in no time. Until the explosion. What the hell could have happened?

"Repeat, Rescue 7 firefighters check in with me *now*."

"I'm okay, Lieutenant." Another female voice came over the radio. Rookie Sydney Sands sounded hoarse but alive.

Felicia barked, "Everybody else?"

"Ramirez here. I'm good. What about O'Malley and Hutch?" Jim Hutchinson was the sub in for Gabe Malvaso today.

Coughing over the lines, then Hutch managed to say, "I'm alive. My arm hurts like a bitch, though."

"O'Malley can tend to you. O'Malley, report in."

No response. "Brody, answer me. Are you hurt?"

Nothing. "Anyone who can move, start looking around." Which would be harder for her because the light on her helmet had gone off when she hit the ground, though the smoke was abating. Had the Quint guys ventilated? "Anybody got light?"

"I do," Sands responded.

Blinking, Felicia could see outlines. Rows of shelves had toppled over scattering hundreds of books everywhere. She began to crawl, feeling in front and to the side of her. Thankfully, gloves protected her from the junk, some of which was jagged.

"Can't find anything, Licia." Sands' now anxious voice broke the silence.

"*Nada.*" This from Ramirez.

Felicia dragged herself closer to the pile of debris and managed to stand. She was still light-headed and disoriented. Smoke vanished by the minute, though, and her vision was better. She scanned the rubble before her. A few feet away, her gaze landed on an arm sticking out from under a fallen shelf and a pile of books.

She'd found O'Malley.

• • •

NO USE IN *panicking. Been here, done this.*

Despite what he told himself, Ryan O'Malley's pulse was triple timing and his throat had gone dry. Not even an hour ago, he'd gotten a weird sense of foreboding and then a shooting pain through his back so he knew immediately his twin brother was in trouble. Ten minutes later Mitch Malvaso called saying that Brody had been hurt. A second update reported that his twin was at Hidden Cove Hospital. On his way over, Ryan phoned Emma Walsh, the woman Brody was head over heels for, and told her to meet him here. As he strode through the ER doors, he prayed Brody was okay. Anything else was unthinkable. He found the Rescue 7 crew hovering at the door to the treatment area. Ramirez approached him first and clapped him on the shoulder. "We don't know anything, Rye. He wasn't conscious when the ambulance took him from the site."

Ryan spotted Felicia White heading toward him. Tall and lithe, her long stride was purposeful. Her expression was soft in a way he hadn't seen before, maybe because her brown hair was down around her smudged face. "I'm sorry, Ryan, we're still waiting. We didn't get here much sooner than you." Their clothes and the dirt that clung to them confirmed they'd come right from the scene of the fire. Its stink gave the hospital smell competition.

Swallowing hard, Ryan nodded. Usually he gave the woman a hard time, but he couldn't think about anything but his brother. "What happened?"

Felicia looked over his shoulder. "Here's Emma. I'll tell you together."

Brody's woman walked quickly over to them, her face pale but her chin up. She was tough in ways you'd never guess from her girlish freckles, short hair cut and slim build. "Is he all right?"

"We don't know any more than I told Ryan on the phone, Emma." This from Felicia. "I was about to fill him in on what happened. Let's sit."

Ryan shook his head and slid his arm around Emma. "No, I wanna know how he got hurt right now."

Felicia gave them a brief rundown. "It happens like that a lot. You get hurt when you never expect it." Not too long ago, Ryan had been the victim of a gunshot wound from gang members free basing in the cellar of a building which caught on fire.

Emma leaned on him. "We have to have faith he'll be fine. Maybe we *should* sit."

The two of them broke off from the others, crossed the room and dropped down onto a double seater. Emma said, "We were here for you last fall."

Six months ago. "I know. Bad karma."

"Brody and I talked a lot about safety since then. How firefighters do everything they can to protect themselves. He promised me no more heroics."

"I'm glad. This was probably a freak accident." He took her hand. "It'll be okay, Emmy. I feel it."

An hour later, a doctor came out; Ryan knew Laura Spencer from police work he'd done here. She headed toward him and Emma. "Hi, Ryan. He's okay. Nothing broken. A concussion, bruised back, other lacerations. But he'll be fine."

"Thank God." Emma sagged in to Ryan's arms.

"Two of you can go together," Laura told them.

Ryan looked to the crew, who'd gathered around the doctor. "Emma and me first, okay?"

"Of course." Felicia had stepped back and her face was blank. Must be her reserve returned now that the crisis was over.

Giving them a weak smile, Emma said, "I'll come out soon so one of you can go in."

Ryan scowled. "I'm not leaving his side."

A flicker of irritation crossed the lieutenant's face but she said nothing.

Ramirez clapped him on the back. "We know you gotta stay with him, Rye."

Sands nodded and took a seat. Gabe Malvaso was missing, but Ryan didn't take the time to ask about him. Instead, he grabbed Emma's hand and they hurried back to the treatment area.

They found Brody half-lying, half-sitting on a bed in a curtained-off area. Someone had made a cursory attempt to clean him up and his face was blotched with bruises. A stark white bandage slanted over one temple and another covered his hand. His eyes lit when he saw Emma come into the room. "I'm good, honey," he said even before she reached him.

With a phony smile pasted on her lips, she crossed to one side of the bed, Ryan to the other. Emma grasped Brody's un-bandaged hand. "I know. The doctor told us."

"I didn't do anything wrong, either."

She swiped at his hair, still sprinkled with soot. "I know, love. You got knocked down by Proust and Albee and Shakespeare."

He laughed. Ryan did not. Adrenaline fading, he was still shaky and in no mood for jokes.

Glancing at him, Brody shook his head. "Shit, Emmy's doing better than you."

For once, Ryan didn't have a rejoinder. He took a breath and put his hand on his brother's shoulder.

Immediately Brody covered it, catching on to Ryan's state of mind. "Hey, buddy, I'm all right. Get rid of the grim look."

Emma looked askance. "This from the guy who cried in my arms when Ryan got hurt."

"He was worse off than me." Brody's eyes darkened. "Wasn't he?"

Finally, Ryan found his voice. "Yeah. You know me... with, um, you."

Brody gave him their twin smile, the one of understanding that often passed between them. "Sit, Rye."

Both he and Emma took chairs. Brody continued to hold Emma's hand and Ryan found himself jealous. Not because he was envious of their closeness—he wanted the best for his brother. And he never believed he'd feel this way, but lately, Ryan wished for the same kind of relationship Brody had with a woman of his own woman.

It was a longing he hadn't gotten used to yet.

And, truth be told, didn't like too much.

• • •

COOL AND COLLECTED, Felicia entered Brody's hospital room with a smile on her face. Emma had come out to fetch coffee for her and Ryan and she'd told Felicia to go in for a while. Emma would make a good firefighter's wife, as she seemed to accept Brody's closeness to his brother and sister smoke eaters.

Felicia stopped in the doorway. Brody lay in bed, bruised but not too badly. He and Ryan looked more alike than usual. Heads bent, she could see Ryan's hair was a little darker, his features sharper. Brody had turned toward his twin and they were holding hands and speaking quietly to each other. The scene was touching, and she felt an unwanted spurt of sympathy for Ryan. "Am I interrupting a private moment?" she asked wryly.

Ryan looked up with blue eyes lighter than Brody's. His cop's uniform heightened their color. He was a sergeant on the force, so he could wear a suit to work, but Brody said he preferred department blues. He trained new officers in field work and also took on special projects for the police.

Brody said, "Hey, Licia." Smoke had made him sound like a two-pack-a-dayer.

Smiling, she walked toward him and dropped down in the empty chair. "I imagine you feel like shit."

"Like a ton of *books* fell on me." He frowned. "What happened?"

"I don't know. We'd gotten halfway across the classics' room when an explosion went off somewhere near us. The shelving and books toppled, along with some of the ceiling. It took us a few minutes to find you." Felicia shivered with remembered fear.

"Everybody else okay?"

"All our guys are fine. But Hutch broke his arm."

"Shit, and he was doing Gabe a favor when he agreed to sub at the last minute so Gabe could go with Rachel to her parents' party."

Felicia stiffened. Not everybody accepted the romance between their captain and Rachel Wellington, who was forced to transfer to another group when the two of them fell in love. Most of the women in the department were concerned that the match-up would taint the reputation of females as serious and equal firefighters. Felicia told Rachel she herself agreed that hooking up with her officer was a foolish move. Rachel brusquely commented that Felicia must not ever have been in love if she could be so narrowed minded about what had happened. The encounter had been unpleasant and they'd been only civil to each other when forced to be together.

Ryan's phone rang. He let it go.

"Might as well get it now," Brody teased with a smile. "They'll just keep calling."

The cop rolled his eyes.

"Who?" Felicia asked.

"One of the many women after him. Let's see, I bet Buffy. Or maybe Mitzy."

Felicia snorted. "They sound like teenagers."

Ryan had no comment. Hell, the guy must be really worried. Finally, he answered the nagging tones. "Hi. No, we're not on tonight. My brother got hurt. I'll call you tomorrow." And he clicked off.

"Brody ruin your date?" Felicia always felt the urge to needle this guy and now they knew Brody was okay, she could do it. She didn't like him for a lot of reasons, one being his Rule of Six philosophy, which she thought demeaned women. No date went over six hours, six days was a limit for girls he only wanted to screw, six weeks for somebody he liked and no one after six months. Brody had been joking about it to Tony Ramirez and she overheard the conversation.

"No big." He looked at his brother. "You comfortable? Can I get you another pillow?"

"You can get me out of here."

"No, he can't." The same doctor who'd come out to the foyer was standing in the doorway. "You have to stay overnight, Brody."

Brody began to whine.

"Shut up," Ryan said harshly. Felicia rarely heard cross words between the two of them. "You need observation! You have a concussion!"

Brody and Felicia, who talked a lot, exchanged glances.

"Okay, Rye." Brody squeezed his brother's arm. "Get a grip, though."

The doctor checked Brody's chart. "We're putting you in a room because the ER's unusually busy."

"I'll sleep all night in the chair."

Brody didn't argue with his brother this time. Neither did Dr. Laura. She obviously knew the two of them.

And again, Felicia didn't tease Ryan. The guy was obviously overwrought about his twin's accident. It made her look at him differently.

When she got up to leave a few minutes later so someone else on their squad could come in, she was bemused. She couldn't think of another person in the world she felt as strongly about as these twins did for each other. And she had a brother, Garth, but rarely saw him.

The notion made her oddly sad.

# CHAPTER 2

BRODY WAS PUT in a room around nine, three hours after the fire broke out. His group had gone back to the firehouse to shower, then returned to the hospital and came up together, visited and finally, on Brody's orders, left to go home. Of course Emma stayed behind.

Darkness had fallen and they'd put the lights low but Ryan could see his brother brush his fingers down Emma's cheek. "You should go home, too, sweetheart."

Lines had etched around Emma's mouth. "I took tomorrow off so I'm fine."

"You're exhausted." He cupped her jaw. "Please, get some rest."

Feeling like an interloper, Ryan stood. "I'm going to get something to eat. How much time alone do you two want?"

Brody shrugged. "A half hour would be good."

Giving them a sham frown, he snorted. "No hanky-panky in here."

"He's not up for that," Emma said innocently.

Both men chuckled.

Ryan commented, "I won't even go there."

Once in the hallway, he saw that the hospital corridor had quieted down and only the low murmur of the nurses and some custodians filled the silence. The place still smelled like antiseptic, but the muted atmosphere was soothing. Noting the signs for the cafeteria — he hadn't left Brody's side all day and suddenly was starved — Ryan headed down to get some chow. Adrenaline had long since drained from his body and he knew the effects of the plummet. His shoulders ached and his head started to hurt. He needed food.

After he bought a BLT, French fries and coke from the serving line, Ryan looked for a table. He scanned the eating area, empty except for a few scattered medical personnel. As he headed for a spot, he noticed a woman at a table in the corner, working on her laptop. Huh, Felicia White. Why the hell was she still here? Then he remembered — she'd waited with Brody when Ryan was hurt. He crossed to her.

Since she was focused on the computer, he took note of how her light brown hair had several streaks of blond in it. He'd never noticed before, and wondered if they were natural or done in a salon. Some flowery scent wafted up to him — very feminine and sexy. "Hey."

She glanced up. Her light brown eyes were muddy with fatigue. "Hey, Ryan. Brody okay?"

"Yeah. He wanted time alone with Emma."

"Sit." When he did, she smiled. "You're staying all night, you said."

"Look, I know it's silly. But..." he shrugged "...I just am."

"Doesn't sound silly to me."

That wasn't like her. "Why are you still here?"

"I thought I'd get something to eat and then head out."

He noticed an empty plate on the table as he took a bite of his sandwich. The bacon was juicy and the tomatoes sweet. "What are you doing on the computer?"

"Our blog. It's going great guns."

In reaction to a series of attacks by Parker Allen, an online reporter who had a grudge against the fire department, the HCFD female firefighters had started their own blog about what it was really like to be a firefighter, and had garnered tons of followers. The blog had worked to counteract some of the reporter's headway into making people believe the fire and police departments were overpaid, had too much down time and unwarranted benefit. It galled Ryan that she was spewing that view and people were buying it.

"I know about the blog. It's good." He smiled. "Brody's entries were great."

"Yeah, and very popular."

"What's the flack from Allen today?"

"She's majorly pissed." A smirk flirted with her lips which were full and sensuous. "She's digging in her heels more. Suggesting brown outs."

"Damn." A brown out was the shutdown of one station—either police or fire—for a week. Nearby houses to the one gone dark would take up the slack. "I hate hearing that."

"We're fighting the measure, but a lot of cities are doing them."

"They're a very a bad idea."

"I wonder if–"

"I thought I'd find you here." Ryan looked up at the battalion chief of House 7. "BC Erikson."

"Hello, Chief."

"Felicia. Ryan. How's Brody?"

"Doing good," Felicia answered. "It's a precaution keeping him here overnight."

"Glad he's okay."

Felicia asked, "Did you come to visit him?"

"Yeah, I'm going up soon. But one of the guys told me you were in the cafeteria so I headed here first."

Ryan watched her as light brown, nicely sculpted brows, lifted. "Really, why?"

The chief shifted from one foot to the other. "There's been a development in the case."

Ryan tensed. "What do you mean *case*?"

"Eve Callahan declared the fire at the library incendiary."

"Arson?" Felicia breathed out.

"Son of a bitch!" This from Ryan. "Somebody hurt my brother on *purpose*?"

"Yeah. There's more and Licia, this concerns you. You know Captain Callahan's partner had a heart attack last week."

"I heard in a briefing he's out for a while."

"Eve's on top of this, of course. She's the best arson investigator we've ever had, given her background at the state investigative bureau. She has two assistants working with her but they're handling the leg work."

Felicia frowned. "I hope you're not going where I think you are, Cal."

"I am. She wants you to help out."

Ryan watched as her friendly façade disappeared. "I made it clear that I'm not interested in working in the arson division."

"You're a certified arson investigator. Hell, you helped write the official guide that came out of the University of Florida in the 90's."

"I was a student then."

"Still, we know you had input, not to mention you're trained and did your arson internship in the HCFD. Eve specifically asked for you."

Ryan knew Eve Woodward Callahan from when she came to Hidden Cove to investigate the fire chief and not only proved his innocence but fell in love with him. They got hitched and even had a kid.

Erickson nodded to the computer. "With Allen taking on our budget, we can't afford to hire someone else."

Fascinated, Ryan wondered what she'd do. She had a rep of being pretty by-the-book, something he was not, so he bet she'd go along.

"All right. But please, Chief, just this one case."

"I promise. This one time. Head on over to the library now. Eve's still there."

Cal made pleasantries then left.

"You really don't want to do this?" Ryan asked as she closed down her computer.

"I found arson work intellectually challenging. But I missed the buzz of fighting fires. Investigation's not for me."

"I know. I feel that way about rising in the ranks of the police department. I didn't want to go off the streets. Besides, the special assignments are great."

"Yeah, I get it."

"Why'd you agree to help Eve?"

"I believe in pitching in." She stretched her arms over her head. Her shirt pulled up revealing a patch of skin and Ryan did a double take. He recalled seeing her with Derek Dennison the night of the gala. She looked hot all dressed up, wearing something gold and shimmery. And clingy. After that, he'd had a couple of dreams about her that he forgot about until right now.

"But mostly, it's because of Brody," Felicia continued. "I'm pissed as hell that he was hurt by an arsonist."

"Thanks, I appreciate that." Ryan's phone rang, the tone indicating it was his Captain. "I gotta take this. It's my boss. He's probably calling about the time off I requested. Hey, Cap. What's up?"

"Hi, Ryan. I have another special assignment for you."

"I, um, told you I need a week off."

"Yeah, but you're gonna want to do this. You've been requested by Eve Callahan to be the police liaison for the arson where your brother got hurt."

"Ah. I'm with Felicia White and she's been summoned too."

She looked up quickly from the computer case she'd been zipping up.

"I see. This okay with you?"

"Yeah, sure. I need tomorrow with Brody, though."

"I guess it would be okay if you go over to the library now. Eve wants to see you both tonight."

"All right." Emma could stay with Brody so he guessed it was okay to leave his twin for a few hours. Besides he really wanted to catch whoever put Brody in the hospital.

When he clicked off, Felicia frowned. "You too?"

"Yeah. I've had experience, like you, with arson investigations."

"I'm surprised he asked you."

"Don't think I can handle the job, Lieutenant?"

"It's not that. But you're personally involved."

"So are you."

"Maybe. Anyway, it's a *fait accompli*."

"Yeah, looks like we're going to be working together."

Her face gave away nothing. He sensed she didn't like him and from a few things Brody let slip, he had reason to believe it was true. And she always razzed him about women and his *playboy* status. But that was okay. He didn't much like her either. He preferred his women blond, built and beautiful. The lieutenant was brown haired, slender, ordinary looking and cold. Not his type.

Well, except in those few dreams he'd had of her after the gala.

• • •

FELICIA ENTERED THE charred building with Ryan O'Malley at her side. He was bigger than she realized, and he had a…male presence that made her jittery. She stepped a bit away.

"Ick. It smells like shit in here."

"Lay people have no idea how much a fire stinks."

The space was still dark, but in the back where the explosion went off, huge lights had been set up for Captain Callahan's study of the site. Stepping over wet books, fallen shelves and displaced furniture, they made their way across the room.

Eve pivoted when they reached her. Dressed in a jacket which read, Anderson County Fire Investigation on the back, she looked healthy and rested even at this time of night. "Hi, Felicia. Thanks for coming on board."

"You're welcome. I want to help."

"You must be Ryan O'Malley. You look like your brother."

"Twins."

"I know. I got a twin, too." Her smile was golden, despite the gravity of the situation. "So," she said checking her notes. "Let's get started. I have people following up on who called in the fire, insurance information, cars in the lot—which weren't many as the library closed at five today—and my people have interviewed witnesses." She smiled at Felicia. "Your group, except for you, Felicia. We'll do that before you leave."

"You've gotten a lot accomplished. So what do we do?"

"Because you're both experienced, I want you to collect the evidence from the scene. The burn pattern suggests the fire started forty feet away from where Rescue 7 was working in one of the stacks."

Felicia frowned. "What about the explosion?"

Eve shook her head. "Several stacks of books were doused with gasoline and once the fire started spreading they caught on fire. One of them exploded."

"Fuck!" Felicia said.

"I know. Very intentional. They wanted firefighters to get hurt. Come on," she said leading the way. "The point of origin of the blaze is over here. Photograph everything then take some of the containers from my vehicle and put the evidence in them."

The evidence consisted of dirty rags doused in gasoline, a gasoline can left behind but no ignition devices.

"He wasn't very subtle, was he?" Ryan asked.

"Nope. It's like the torch wanted us to know what he did. And though most arsonists are men, we can't rule out a woman."

"Why the library?" Ryan asked. "Somebody got her card yanked and is pissed off?"

Eve smiled but Felicia didn't think Ryan O'Malley was funny. For some reason, being around him now was irritating her.

"As you know, there are several reasons for arson and we can't dismiss any of them yet. The mechanism used is simple so it might indicate a juvenile." The group which set the most incendiary fires. Other motives were vandalism, insurance fraud, revenge, and to cover up a crime.

"My money's on a female. They tend to buy books more."

Felicia turned to him. "Do you know that for a fact, Sergeant?"

His gaze narrowed on her. "I do. I've read a lot of the stats on books published and readership because I dated a female author once."

"Of course you did."

"Maybe a woman has revenge issues toward the library because of a man who works there." Felicia's tone was challenging.

Eve coughed. "In any case, let's get the evidence. Will it insult you if I tell you to make sure everything is labeled clearly so the lab can identify it and to be careful that every piece of it is uncontaminated? I'll take care of the chain of custody." So she could testify the results hadn't been tampered with.

Both Ryan and Felicia smiled at Eve's cunning in transmitting elementary procedure.

They worked pretty much in silence; when they finished, they had several pieces of physical evidence: a variety of rags, the gas container and smaller cans that probably held more accelerant. Then they took photos of where the perpetrator entered—wood splinters were found on a window which had been left ajar. They also took pictures of the footprints outside. They determined the depths of charred items, tracked and documented the flow and damage patterns.

It was three a.m. when they finished.

Eve sighed. "Good job, guys. I'd like to interview you now, Felicia, so Ryan, you can go home." She checked her watch. "Get some sleep and we'll meet at noon to determine what's next."

"I have a request." Ryan had turned serious. "I know it's not protocol, but can we meet at my house? I share a duplex with Brody, and even though Emma will be there taking care of him after he comes home from the hospital, I'd feel better if I was next door."

"Fine by me," Eve said easily. "I'd do the same for Ian."

"I guess." Felicia didn't particularly like the idea of visiting Ryan O'Malley's house. It was probably some bachelor pad, all chrome and glass and fur rugs in front of a fireplace.

"Great, thanks." Ryan nodded to Eve. "See you later, Captain." He touched Felicia's arm and she stiffened. "Lieutenant."

Felicia tried to mask her feelings of dislike.

When he left, Eve faced her. "What's going on with you and O'Malley? Are you...hooked up?"

"God, no, why would you think that?"

"There's an odd kind of tension between you. Pardon the pun, but you set off sparks on each other."

Felicia shrugged, weariness settling in her shoulders. "Not that kind. All right, I don't like the guy. He's cocky, he's a player and he's stubborn."

"Which bothers you the most?"

"Mostly his treatment of women as notches on his belt." She frowned. "Jesus, I can't believe we're talking about this."

Eve shrugged. "I'm only concerned if it's going to hinder the investigation."

"No, it'll probably keep us sharper."

"All right, that's what I need to hear." She grinned. "But off the record, I think he's super hot. And don't tell Noah I said that."

Felicia laughed and they started out. They met up with Engine 4 firefighters entering the front of the library. Ed Snyder, a lieutenant on the group, spoke to them. "Captain, we're here for the shitty job of salvage and overhaul." That meant they'd clean up the scene. Ordinarily, the trucks called in initially would check in the walls to make sure the fire was out and remove the debris, but Quint 7 had gone back the house. Salvage and overhaul was also usually done right after any fire was doused, too, but in the case of arson suspicion, they'd waited and called in the night shift from House 4.

"Yes, Lieutenant," Eve said, "go ahead. We're done collecting evidence."

Ed Snyder gave Eve a sour look.

The two women walked out of the building. "What's the burr up his ass?" Eve asked.

"Women firefighters make him cranky. He left our firehouse when Casey Malvaso came on board. Women as *officers* in the fire department, which includes us, must drive him nuts."

"Ah, and here we are running the fire scene." She chuckled and held up a hand to high five Felicia. "Girls rock!"

Felicia slapped her palm. "Yeah girls rock!"

# CHAPTER 3

BRODY SMILED CHEERFULLY as Ryan waited on him hand and foot. Emma had gone out to get food and he was in charge of his twin's needs.

"You look like shit," Brody said, half-joking.

"I was up all night."

His brother grinned. "I remember those days."

"Not what you think. I know you were interviewed at the hospital about what you saw at the fire, but I was called in to work on the case with Eve Callahan."

"You're handling the police side?"

"Actually, Felicia White and I are working together."

"That's right. She had all that training then decided against going into investigative work." Brody sighed. "How you getting along?"

"Like oil and water. I don't know why she dislikes me so much, being that I'm so charming and everything."

"It's *because* you're so charming and everything. I like Licia a lot, but she's a private person. When I was having trouble with Emma she said she almost got engaged once, but they split because she was so removed."

"Yeah, I hate cold women."

"I didn't say she was cold. I've seen passion in her plenty of times, but not for a guy. I guess she's immune."

Ryan thought about that a minute, then dismissed the notion. No woman was immune to the right guy.

His brother's face lit. "And, speaking of passion, here's my woman."

Emma came through the bedroom door carrying daffodils and looking like one herself in yellow and green. "These are to bring spring into your room." Leaning over she kissed his cheek. He grabbed her for a bigger, fuller one.

"I'd tell you two to get a room, but I'm in it." Ryan stood and glanced at his watch. "I'm going next door to shower and catch an hour's worth of sleep."

"I'm making lunch. I'll bring you some."

"Let yourself in and if I'm still sleeping, wake me up. I have a meeting at noon."

"She isn't going anywhere near your bedroom."

Ryan didn't take offense. "I like to nap on the couch in the porch." He kissed Emma's cheek. "Make him relax."

Brody linked his hands behind his head and grinned. "I'm relaxing. I got my girl for a whole day unexpectedly, the headache's gone and balmy air is drifting in from outside. What more could I want?"

Ryan left the two lovebirds and let himself out. Once again, he was struck by feelings of envy. Hell, what was happening to him? Maybe he was tired. He entered his house and made his way upstairs feeling a funk descending upon him.

• • •

LATE MARCH TURNED warm so Felicia eschewed a coat and settled for jeans and a summer sweater made of peacock blue with a teddy beneath it. She'd washed and curled her hair, put on some blush and lipstick, like she always did on her days off, and drove early to the duplex Ryan O'Malley shared with his brother; she hoped to get a chance to say hi to Brody. When she pulled up to the front of their home, she was surprised to see the place wasn't what she expected. Sided in sage green with black shutters, the two storey was located on a family oriented side street. The structure had a two bay garage—with cars in it, presumably Brody's jeep and a cute little Mazda that she knew from last night belonged to Ryan. Colorful crocuses and daffodils bloomed beneath the mailbox, around the lamppost and between two flowering crab apple trees. Jeez, who would have thought?

She parked in the driveway next to Emma's Civic and headed to the front of the house as one of the doors opened. Emma exited, carrying paper bags. She looked about twelve in jeans and simple white blouse. "Hi, there, Licia."

She'd picked up the nickname from Brody. "Hi, Emma. Need some help?"

"Um, yeah, maybe. I'm made lunch for Ryan."

"Oh."

"I have enough for three because he said he was having a meeting here." Her freckled face frowned. "Arson. I can't believe somebody hurt Brody intentionally."

"I know." She took one bag from Emma, while Emma produced a key. "Rye said to wake him if he wasn't up. But, um, I thought your meeting was at twelve."

"It is. I wanted to say hi to Brody."

"Ah, maybe later. He's asleep."

"What, do they sleep on the same schedule too?"

"You know, I think they might." She shook her head. "They're spooky sometimes."

"Brody told me when Ryan was hurt, he got a bad pain in his spine before he discovered his brother on the ground behind the building."

Emma smiled. "Same thing happened to Rye when the bookcases fell on Brody."

Instead of ringing the bell, Emma let herself into the other half of house. The entryway was big, with wooden moldings and trim, a table, some kind of stand in matching wood. She followed Emma back to the kitchen but stopped to admire the living room off the left, paneled in oak wood, broken up by built in bookshelves, classic art prints, and lamps and tables. Emma stopped, too, and smiled at Felicia. "It's amazing, isn't it? The whole house is done in antiques."

"Who would have thought Ryan would go for old?"

"He's got a depth to him most people don't see."

Felicia certainly didn't but she let a snide comment die in her throat.

The kitchen had been modernized but was accented in beautiful old pieces, too. A dining room sprawled out to the left, and French doors opened to another spacious area.

"What's that?" Felicia asked.

"The guys have a glassed-in porch in common. They built it themselves." Emma went to the open doorway, then whispered, "Ryan's asleep on the couch. I'll wake him."

"No, don't. Eve isn't coming for an hour. I'll entertain myself. I have a laptop in the car."

"Yeah?" Her brows arched mischievously. "So you can work on the blog? I love it, by the way."

Felicia allowed herself a half-smile as they walked back to the foyer. "I can't believe how the thing caught on."

"You know I knew Parker Allen in college. I can't fathom why she has this vendetta."

They talked more about the blog and then Emma left.

Felicia retrieved her laptop but before she settled at the dining room table, she crossed to the French doors. The sunroom was beautiful, all cedar wood, a cathedral ceiling, a swirling antique brass fan that stirred the March air and large comfortable furniture made of various shades of brown microfiber.

And on one couch was a sleeping Ryan.

Despite telling herself not to, she stared at the man before her. He wore loose fitting jeans that looked comfortable. Bare feet. A navy blue long sleeved T-shirt that outlined muscles she'd never noticed he had. His hair was tousled and damp, and his arm was raised over his head. She took a step closer, noticing the sculpted chin, the nice lips and thick dark eye lashes.

And for a moment, Felicia reacted. Jesus, her stomach clutched and her breasts felt tight. Just from freaking looking at the guy! Immediately, she turned on her heel and snuck out of the porch. She meant to go right to work, but curiosity got the better of her. She'd take a peek upstairs, that was all.

The railing was again made of oak wood and was obviously hand crafted. At the end of the hallway at the top, there was an open space which housed a chair next to a window looking out the front of the house. Off to the right was a bath and next to it another room with its door closed. The door was open to the final room so she approached that one.

Ah, here was the playboy's lair — a large space with high ceilings made of wood and windows fanning out behind a lake-size bed. All the accents were oak — a headboard, a huge wardrobe, a wall unit with stereo, TV and books facing the bed. She could see a large bathroom open up to the left.

Crossing to the bed, she stared down at the patterned quilt which covered it in masculine hues of brown and gold. Then she sniffed, and inhaled a male scent that brought back her reaction on the porch. It was so strong she dropped to the mattress for a minute. Then, she heard a chuckle. Her head snapped up and she saw Ryan lounged in the doorway, arm raised against the jamb, a sleepy, sexy expression on his face. "Well, darlin', I have to admit, I never thought I'd get you in my bed."

• • •

"I DIDN'T EXPECT lunch, but this is too good to pass up." Eve Callahan grinned down at the Panini sandwiches of Italian meat Emma had fixed, along with spicy pasta salad.

"Hmm," Felicia managed, keeping her gaze averted to the food.

Ryan bit back a grin. Felicia White had been so embarrassed by being caught snooping, she sputtered something about looking for the bathroom and fled downstairs just as the doorbell rang. He hadn't had time to razz her about it. Instead, he ate with gusto and kept trying to catch her gaze; she studiously avoided his.

After lunch, they got down to business. Eve laid out the information gathered. They reviewed the evidence they'd gathered. Then they examined the photos taken by the assistant of the parking lot and bystanders.

"We ran the plates and nothing popped." Eve was frowning.

Ryan scowled. "That would have been too easy."

"A few firefighters heard on their scanners that the Rescue Squad fell victim to a torch and it got around that

Brody was hurt. Later, we needed a specialty team for salvage and overhaul."

"Hmm." Ryan sighed. "Arson by disgruntled firefighters happens."

Next to him, he felt Felicia bristle. "I can't believe one of our people would do this."

"Didn't know you were so naïve, Lieutenant."

His comment didn't fluster her. "Yeah, well, I'm older and wiser than you, Sergeant, so I know what I'm talking about."

She was older? Man she didn't look it. Today especially, with her hair down and those denims revealing long, luscious legs. The vee of her sweater with the lacy thing underneath was enticing.

Eve nodded knowingly. "We do have to consider all the angles, Felicia. And believe me, I know what it's like to have to implicate a colleague."

Knowing her history, Ryan totally didn't understand how Eve could fall so in love with a guy that she'd risk her reputation and transfer up here. Leave a job for romance? Never.

"We need to study the crime scene photos carefully. Then we'll comb the statements of the firefighters at the scene. Why don't we split it up–" Eve's phone buzzed and she fished it out of her pocket. "I'm sorry, I have to take this. My brother and his wife are watching Sabby as Noah's out of town at a conference."

She left the room and Ryan grinned. "So, which do you want to start with?"

Felicia flushed probably because now would be the first opportunity he'd have to rub her face in her snooping. He was about to tease her, but she seemed really embarrassed.

Reaching over he touched her hand. "Look, Felicia, if it's any comfort, I would have checked out your bedroom, too. No big deal."

Her eyes widened. They were more amber today in the sunlight streaming through the windows. "I...why are you being nice about this?"

"For professional reasons. Can't have us distracted." Which was sort of true. But not wholly. The other reasons he didn't want to examine.

In moments, Eve returned with a worried expression on her face. "I'm sorry. I have to leave. Sabby's running a fever and Ian thinks we should take her to the doctor. I'm meeting them at the pediatrician's office."

Ryan nodded. "Sorry about your kid."

"Listen, do you think you can keep working on this? I'll come back after I'm done."

"Why don't we wait–" Felicia began.

But Ryan interrupted her. "You bet. Felicia and I are gonna make a great team." He winked at the lieutenant then glanced back to Eve. "Go take care of your kid."

Felicia had gathered her composure by the time Eve left. And they did have serious business. So for a few hours, they made lists, checked them against witness statements, parking lot data and personnel–fire, police and lay people.

At about four, Eve phoned and said Sabby had an ear infection but screamed when Eve tried to leave her. She apologized and said she'd be back in touch.

"Let's take a break," Ryan suggested. "I'm gonna have a beer. Want one?"

"We're working."

"Hey, live a little."

"No thanks. I'll take a soda though."

She followed him to the kitchen, went out onto the porch then outside. He brought their drinks to the yard. "Nice backyard," she said from where she was staring into their woods.

"Yeah, we like it."

"Don't you get...I don't know, hemmed in by living so close to your brother?"

"Not at all. Maybe because we're twins." He shrugged a shoulder and leaned against a stone wall he and Brody had put in. "I like having him close." He sipped his beer. "Do you have siblings?"

"A brother in Colorado."

"It must be hard having him so far away."

"We're not close now. We used to be." Her face softened. "Then we drifted apart."

"I can't imagine that. Even being separated from my other brothers would be hard."

She focused on him then. Her eyes held a kind of longing he'd seen in his own mirror. "Yeah, I watched all your brothers with each other when you got hurt."

"Isn't it great?"

"I wouldn't be comfortable with that kind of closeness."

Hmm. For some reason, he wanted to rattle her. "What kind of closeness are you comfortable with?"

Tension stiffened her shoulders. "That's a little personal, don't you think?"

"Aw, come on. Open up some."

Tiny lines marred her forehead. "I'm close to my squad."

"Yeah, that's family."

"And I used to do things with Rachel Wellington, but not since..." She trailed off. "How'd we get on to this, anyway?"

He ignored her question. "You don't like that she hooked up with Gabe?"

"It gives us female firefighters a bad rep. Wait till Parker Allen gets hold of that one."

"The bitch. Brody really hates her."

A small smile flirted with Felicia's lips. "I think of her attack as a challenge."

"You're having fun thwarting her, aren't you?"

"I guess."

"What else do you do for fun, Felicia?"

"What do you mean?"

"Activities."

"Now that the weather's nicer, I like to hike in the hills around Hidden Cove."

"Hey, me, too. Maybe we can do it together sometime."

"Hardly."

Her clear distaste irritated him. For one thing, he wasn't used to not charming a woman immediately. Second, he'd never done anything to her personally. "You got a boyfriend, Lieutenant?"

"I'm a little old for a boyfriend."

That was the second time she alluded to her age. "All right then, a friend with benefits? I saw you with Derek Dennison at the New Year's Eve thing."

"Isn't bragging about conquests your thing, O'Malley?"

"I never brag about them!" Purposely, he arched a lascivious brow. "Though there are legions." He pushed away from the ledge more irritated than he let on. "But you're right about one thing. This is a bit too personal. Let's go finish our tasks."

He went inside ahead of her so she couldn't tell by his face that he was upset by her barbs, though he couldn't freaking figure out why. He'd opened the conversation to see what made her tick and realized more than ever that he didn't like the woman.

She was too cold and withholding for his taste.

# CHAPTER 4

SATURDAY WAS A work day at Hale's Haven, a camp for the children of slain firefighters and police officers of Hidden Cove. Three years ago, Megan Hale and Mitch Malvaso had gotten the place running, and the whole endeavor had grown exponentially after they extended invitations for neighboring departments to participate. This year, they were roofing the sixth cabin, which would bring the tally to three units for boys and three for girls. There was also a boathouse and a patio home for Mitch and Megan who'd subsequently married and lived on site during the summer months. Both took unpaid furlough from their individual departments for July and August so they could keep the camp going.

When Felicia arrived, the sun was so bright she had to shade her eyes to check out the scene. She'd overslept because she'd been working hard on the arson case for three days and that meant spending time with Ryan O'Malley. Which made her edgy. He'd managed to do what no other man had been able to: get under her skin.

So she was glad to be working outside today. She took in the scent of the lake, the clatter of hammers and the buzz of saws amidst the shouts and chatter of workers, all of which put her at ease. She reached Gabe Malvaso, who held a clipboard in a group of about six; he nodded to her.

"Okay, we've got three people up there already. Anybody have roofing experience?"

Felicia raised her hand. "I do. Last year, when we put shingles on the second girls' cabin."

"Good, head on up then. You'll work on the right."

Dressed in olive green shorts, boots and a light green shirt with a tank beneath it, she headed to the ladder and climbed up to the top. Two people were working in tandem to the left but the sun bounced off the shingles and she couldn't tell who they were. Same with the guy to the right, whom she edged toward carefully because of the steep pitch of the roof. "I'm here to help," she called out.

The guy's naked back was already sweaty and gleamed in the sun. It was a nice back which narrowed to a trim waist. "See anything you like, darlin'?" he asked over his shoulder.

Shit. She'd been caught ogling Ryan O'Malley. No way, though, would she let him upset her today. "Just checking to see if you're getting sunburned. What can I do?"

"Come here and help me."

She edged her way up to him. When she was close enough to see the expression on his face, he said, "Didn't know it was me, did you?"

"Well, I have to admit I didn't. We work together enough, don't you think?"

"It's fine by me." He dropped down on his butt on the roof, braced his feet on the slant and held out some shingles. "You nail, I'll hand. I been at this a while." Half of their side was done.

She liked that he didn't try to put her in a passive role.

Someone set up a CD player down below and Roy Orbison blasted out with *Pretty Woman*. Ryan sipped some water from the bottle he unsnapped from a work belt, then started to sing along. Of course, he was good. But at least the tunes occupied his mouth. They'd finished several rows when he said, "Okay. I'm rested, I'll do the nailing now."

"No thanks. Keep exercising your vocal cords."

After another half-hour, he insisted. And she *was* tired so she sat, took a water out of her own belt and drank as she handed him some nails and shingles. They finished another row. She, however, didn't sing. When the sun continued to rise, she took off her over shirt, exposing the tank.

Ryan glanced at her. "Trying to make me fall off this roof, Licia?" The nickname his brother sometimes called her.

"Shut up and keep pounding."

At noon, the lunch break was called. Below them people scattered but she and Ryan finished a few more rows. They'd quit to eat when from the other side, someone screamed.

"Oh, Jesus, what? Hey, *somebody*..." Rachel Wellington had lost her footing, fallen face down and slid toward the edge of the roof. Felicia started over with Ryan behind her.

She reached Rachel just as the woman slipped over the side. Her hands gripped the edge of the roof but she wouldn't be able to hold on for long. Felicia went down on her belly, and felt Ryan immediately grab onto her legs. Thank God. She managed to get hold of the Rachel's forearms. "I got you, Rach."

"Good, 'cause it's a long drop." Though her words were lighthearted, there was fear in her brown eyes when she looked up.

Straining all her muscles to stay in place, Felicia heard Ryan ask, "Can you get her over?" he asked. "Or should I try?"

"I can, but don't let go of me."

"I won't. I'm squatting down and my feet are braced."

Felicia pulled on Rachel's arms as Ryan held tight. Her own muscles screamed. The woman was heavier than she looked. "I'm gonna have to back up on my stomach. Ryan, help drag me back."

"You'll get scraped to hell," he said.

"No choice. I've done it before."

"Yeah, with a harness and proper clothing. But you're right. We got no choice."

Inch by painful inch, Ryan drew Felicia back. She tracked her progress by Rachel's body parts coming onto the roof: her wrists, her forearms, then elbows and finally her chest. When half of Rachel was braced, Felicia said, "Ryan, let go of me and help her the rest of the way so she doesn't go back down. My arms are saturated."

Edging down beside her, Ryan grabbed onto Rachel. Felicia collapsed into the roof. She watched him help the other woman to safety. From her vantage point, she saw Rachel lay back, breathing hard.

Ryan was sidled over to Felicia and eased her to a sitting position. "How badly are you scraped?"

"I don't know. The heat of the shingles was the worst."

They heard from below, "Hey, what's going on up there?" Gabe Malvaso stood on the ground staring up at them, unaware of the danger the woman he loved had been in.

• • •

A CROWD HAD gathered around them as Ryan knelt beside Felicia, where she lay under a tree in the cool grass. The scrapes and burns on her arms and legs looked painful.

He'd had to pick her up and descend the ladder with her over his shoulder because she was too hurt to get down by herself. "Shouldn't she go to the hospital?" Ryan asked, his voice as shaky as he felt inside.

Zach Malvaso checked her pulse and heartbeat as Casey, his wife, both paramedics, set out antiseptic, gauze and salve. "I don't know yet," Casey told him. "I've got to clean the wounds." To Felicia, she said, "Want a shot of painkiller?"

"No, just fix me up."

"Shit, Felicia, take the shot." This from Gabe who hovered over her, a stunned expression on his face, holding Rachel's hand. Ryan had never seen the captain so visibly shaken.

"I don't need a shot."

Gabe growled, "Give her the shot, Malvaso. My orders."

As the analgesic took effect, Casey shooed everybody away, including Ryan; he hadn't realized he was holding Felicia's hand. Backing off, he watched the process.

When her wounds were cleaned, he realized the scrapes were not as bad as he thought they'd be. But her knees were scarlet. Together, Casey and Zach treated everything. Ryan's heart was still beating fast.

"Hey, your forearms need some salve," someone said from behind him. He turned to see Grady O'Connor holding a first aid kit.

Ryan looked down. There were red blotches all over his arms, too. "Yeah, I guess."

"What the hell happened?" Grady asked as he pulled Ryan to a picnic table nearby and began doctoring him.

"Rachel lost her footing and Felicia got to her first. I braced Licia while she dragged Rachel back up. It was a sight, I'll tell you."

"Licia's pretty banged up."

"I know. She was unbelievably brave. She didn't even hesitate putting herself in harm's way."

"None of us would. You guys either," he said referring to the police department.

"I guess." In his mind, he could see Felicia's muscles bulge, hear her grunts as she saved Rachel from certain broken bones, if not worse.

Since Felicia refused to go to the hospital, they brought her into the house Mitch and his wife shared, placed her on the couch, and sent everybody back to work. "I'll stay with her," Ryan volunteered. "I can't go to the roof either because of my arms."

"I'll hang here, too," Rachel offered. Her face was still bloodless and her eyes concerned. Otherwise, she wasn't even scraped.

"No, you're coming with me." Gabe stood behind Rachel with his hands on her shoulders. His face was ragged. "For a bit."

Megan directed Ryan to water and food, and finally the house cleared out. Felicia lay with her eyes closed, and Ryan stretched out on the other couch, watching her.

"I'm not asleep," she said, her words a bit slurred.

"Want something?"

"I want to have worn jeans and kept on my long sleeved shirt today."

"Ditto."

She opened her eyes. "You hurt?"

"Just my arms."

"Thanks for helping us."

"Thanks for saving Rachel."

"…am mad at her."

He chuckled. "I know. It didn't seem to matter. You were very brave, you know that?"

"Come'ere." Ah, the painkiller must be really working if she wanted him closer.

Stiffly, he rose and crossed to the couch, which was wide. She patted the side. "Sit."

When he did, she placed her hands on his pecs. His muscles leapt and he regretted putting on an HCPD shirt.

"I like your chest."

Uh-oh. "You do?"

"Yep."

Well, he was only human. "What else do you like, Licia?"

"...hair...nice legs..."

"That's my line."

Her eyelids drooped. "...can see why..."

"You can see why what?"

"The women. Why they flock." She sighed and took his hand, brought it to her breasts.

Then she went out cold.

Ryan couldn't help but grin. So the aloof lieutenant liked his looks? Cool.

Returning to the couch, he stretched out and for a while stared over at her. Even with the bandages, he thought she was attractive. More, really. Sexy. Funny, he'd never viewed her as more than passable.

Huh? he thought, a bit confused. He certainly hadn't seen this one coming!

# CHAPTER 5

FOUR DAYS AFTER the roof incident, Felicia drove to Noah Callahan's office. She was healing fine and would return to work tomorrow. While she was off the line, she'd met with Eve and Ryan O'Malley and they'd finished documenting their evidence, did some analysis on their own and the findings were to be presented to the chief today. Profiling and further investigation would be the responsibility of the arson team so she was done with the assignment today. She only hoped they'd catch the bastard who set the fire where Brody got hurt.

An odd thing had happened those days she was off, too, and she thought about it on the drive. Rachel Wellington had come to see her...

On Felicia's doorstep, Rachel held up a wicker picnic basket. She looked young and fragile in a way Felicia had never seen her before. "Hi. I brought you lunch."

Her offer made Felicia uncomfortable because they'd been estranged—her decision—since Rachel and Gabe broke all department rules and became a couple. Since Rachel transferred to another house, Felicia hadn't had to deal with her former friend.

At Felicia's silence, Rachel cleared her throat. "Look, if you don't want me here, I understand. I know how you feel about Gabe and me. Let me say thank you for saving me from the roof fall, and take this." She held up the basket. "It's your favorite stuff. Quiche Lorraine, salad with pine nuts, and crusty bread."

Rachel remembered—hell knew—all her favorites? Suddenly Felicia felt foolish. They'd been friends since Rachel came on the force and truthfully, Felicia was beginning to feel petty for ostracizing the woman. "They're your favorites, too."

The woman's pretty hazel eyes sparked. "They are."

"I don't suppose there's any Pinot Grigio in there?"

"Chilled and ready to drink."

"Come in and have lunch with me. I, um, miss you, Rach."

"I miss you, too."

They'd had a great time and Rachel honestly explained how she simply couldn't control her feelings for Gabe. Never having experienced anything like that about a man, Felicia listened and they'd come to a truce…

Still bemused by the encounter, she reached the Academy—the chief had one at headquarters, too-exited the car and walked into reception. The Academy was a three storey building made of glass and chrome with a slate floored reception area. The woman at the desk told her Noah was waiting for her. She went through a door and down a corridor painted blue with white trim and firefighter photos graced the walls. She found Ryan O'Malley leaning against one of those walls, his arms crossed over his chest. Was he waiting for her?

And, damn, she was a sucker for men in uniform–his navy blues were dynamite on him. He looked scrumptious. Hell, she didn't even like that she had the *thought*, but in her down time, she'd admitted she was attracted to him.

Not that she'd ever do anything about it. Getting mixed up with a womanizing younger man was not her idea of smart. Avoiding temptation was another reason she was glad she was off the arson case.

He gave her a killer smile when she reached him.

"What are you doing out here?" she asked neutrally.

He put his finger to his lips and angled his chin. "Look inside."

Felicia peered through the crack in the door. Noah sat in his chair, hands crossed over his chest, staring up at Eve, his wife, who leaned her butt on the edge of his desk. Felicia gave out a tiny gasp at the expression on the chief's face. If any look could say *madly in love,* his did.

Pushing away from the wall, Ryan drew her down the hall a ways. "It's something, isn't it?"

"Yeah. So intimate. Wow!"

For a moment, he studied her, his blue gaze intense. "Do you want that in your life, Felicia?"

Fat chance she would confide in him about anything. "Nah. When I'm in a relationship, it's for the hot sex." Hell, why had she said that to *him*? She hoped she wasn't blushing.

"That works for me." His grin was brilliant. Today his sandy colored hair caught the overhead lights. She'd never noticed the golden highlights in it.

"Besides, your reputation tells me you're nothing like that." She pointed to the chief's office.

"Maybe I'm a new man since I got hurt."

She couldn't help but smile.

"How you doing with the bruises?"

"Good, I'm back at work tomorrow."

"Hmm."

"Your knees okay?"

"Uh-huh. That was nothing compared to how hurt you got." Reaching out, he grasped her forearm. "I want to say again that what you did was very brave. Heroic even."

Her brows knitted. "You would have done the same thing if you got to her first."

"That doesn't make what I said any less true."

Felicia wondered when they'd gotten to this level of understanding of each other. Not liking it, she stepped back and he was forced to drop his hand.

"Hey, there."

Turning, Felicia saw the two junior assistants to Eve had approached them. "Hi, Tom. Martin."

Martin said, "No one's here yet?"

"Yeah, everybody now." Ryan nodded. "Me and Licia were chatting. Let's go inside."

Ryan went ahead of Felicia and the rest of them trailed behind him. He knocked loudly on the door, and heard, "Come in."

He noted that Eve Callahan was seated in a chair, acting all prim and proper now, but he saw what he saw—a passion, a love so deep on Noah's face it had made him wait outside for fear of interrupting the honesty. Damn, he wished he had that!

*Nah. When I'm in a relationship, it's for the sex.*

Recalling Felicia's retort, he pictured her in the sack. With him.

"Hello, everybody." Noah greeted them from his chair. The chief didn't stand on formalities and Ryan liked that. "Take a seat, guys."

They found a place to sit and Ryan noticed Felicia dropped down into the farthest chair away from him.

"Before we start, I want to thank you, Lieutenant White, for what you did at the camp last week. Not only is Rachel Wellington a valued member of this department, we all like her. Again, thanks, Felicia."

Hmm, must be he wasn't pissed at Gabe and Rachel falling in love. Then again, the chief and Eve had done the same thing.

"You're welcome."

"She was something to watch," Ryan put in. "Don't get on her bad side. She's got more muscles than me."

The group laughed and he winked at Felicia. She looked away quickly. Ryan grinned inwardly. He didn't know exactly when he started thinking of her as a woman—a sexy woman—but now that she'd confessed in her painkiller haze she was attracted to him, too, he'd decided to use that to his advantage and ask her for a date. He also decided not to tease her about what she admitted in the Malvaso's home. For one thing it would alienate her. But it also didn't seem fair. He wasn't above capitalizing on what he knew, though.

In clear concise language, Eve explained their preliminary findings. The fire was definitely incendiary, Ryan and Felicia had collected and bagged the evidence, photographed the scene, then Eve released the site for salvage and overhaul.

"Incidentally, the team from Engine 4 wasn't happy about the cleanup job."

Noah nodded and glanced at Eve. Ryan bet the chief didn't like the lieutenant at Engine 4 who Brody absolutely hated.

Eve handed him a folder. "In there are the reports from the lieutenant and sergeant, along with a diagram of the site.

The file also contains Tom's and Martin's external investigation of the 911 call, the insurance on the building, hospital checks, and interviews from firefighters."

They discussed what the last of the reports indicated.

Eve added, "There was evidence of forced entry, and the fire was set after the library closed. We have no internal prints or any on the window, but we did get shoe imprints on the ground below. Only a handful of people were outside and there were a few cars in the parking lot, but they weren't much help."

This didn't come as news to Noah. "So, we aren't very far along, are we?"

Eve shook her head. "My team and I are going to do some profiling and analyze the evidence again in terms of targeting the torch, but as I told you before, we don't have much."

"Not for a lack of a thorough investigation," he said kindly.

"No, not for that."

Ryan had read that not even ten percent of arson cases were ever solved.

"Then I'll wait for your final report." His gaze swept Ryan and Felicia. "Thanks for pitching in here. Your expertise was greatly appreciated."

"Just doing our jobs."

"Above and beyond."

Felicia and Ryan left the investigators with the chief. They were walking out to their cars together when Gabe Malvaso's truck swerved into the lot. He exited it like a man with a mission and approached them. Today, he looked a lot better than when Ryan had last seen him at the camp and Rachel's life had been endangered.

"Hi, Cap."

"Gabe."

"Eve let it drop that you were meeting with Noah today, so I came over to find you both." He held out two letter-size envelopes. "These are for you. Open them now."

From the inside, Ryan pulled out a hundred dollar gift certificate for the Lakeside Restaurant. "What's this all about?"

Gabe's expression turned profound. "It's out of my pocket. I can't thank you enough for what you two did for Rachel. If something had happened to her…" He glanced away, clearly emotional. When he looked back to them, he gave them a weak smile. "Go have fun, each of you. Take a date."

"This isn't necessary, Cap," Felicia said.

"It is to me." He said goodbye and headed to his car.

Staring at Gabe's retreating back, Felicia shrugged. "That was nice of him."

Ryan was moved by Gabe's naked emotion for Rachel. So he asked, "You gonna bring a date there?"

"And that would concern you why?"

Casually, he shrugged a shoulder. "I thought, um, well, I wondered if you'd want to have dinner with me at Lakeside. With two of these, we could get an expensive bottle of Cabernet, lobster and crab, and still cover the tip."

She smiled, he guessed, against her will. "I love all those things. It sounds tempting, but…"

"It wouldn't be like a date," he added coaxingly.

Felicia stared hard at him.

"I thought maybe working with me made you like me a little better."

Now she laughed. "Actually, it did. Oh, all right, if you're sure it's not a date."

"Scouts honor. When?"

"My social calendar isn't exactly full. You're the one with women falling all over you."

"Not the right ones. How about tonight?"

"Fine by me. I'm off till tomorrow. I'll meet you there." She shook her head. "Oh, wait, I can't. I'm dropping my car off today at the garage. I won't have it tonight. Let's do a rain check."

No way was he giving her time to reconsider. "Felicia, I can pick you up."

Her glare seemed false. "This isn't a date."

"I promise, I'll remember that."

"I guess it's okay. What time?"

"Seven."

"I live at…"

He grinned. "I'm a cop. I'll find out."

When she walked to her car, Ryan watched the gentle sway of her hips in the skinny black pants she wore and how the breeze blew her hair askew. She hadn't fought too hard against going to dinner with him.

He wondered if convincing her to do other things with him might be this easy.

# CHAPTER 6

STANDING IN FRONT of her mirror, Felicia shook her head in disgust and yelled at herself. "Damn it, what the hell are you doing?"

This was the third outfit she'd put on. After she'd done her hair and makeup. She had to admit she looked good. Her curls were fluffy, the mascara accented her eyes and this dress, a little black one with three-quarter sleeves to cover most of the scrapes from the roof incident, also had a low neckline and gathered at the waist with a flared skirt. Felicia liked clothes, probably because she wore a uniform in her job. She splurged on both dressy and casual outfits, and enjoyed herself. Sometimes she and Rachel had gone shopping together. And she missed that. Maybe after her friend's visit the other day, they could go out again.

She'd just spritzed on some perfume when the doorbell rang, preventing her from changing her mind again about her appearance. She grabbed a bag, headed downstairs and drew open the door.

Damn, he was even more gorgeous dressed up. She'd forgotten that after she'd seen him clubbing. Or maybe she hadn't noticed then. He wore dark slacks, a dark shirt and a taupe blazer with a jaunty little handkerchief in the pocket. His hair was mussed beautifully from the slight breeze.

Something jolted inside Felicia; it took her a minute to recognize the kick as desire—even stronger than what she'd felt as she watched him sleep that day on his porch.

"Hi, there." He drew his hand from behind his back and held out a bouquet to her. Petty little roses, a couple of dozen of them, stuck their heads out from green tissue paper.

She didn't take them, instead eyed the bouquet suspiciously. "This isn't a date, Ryan."

"Hey, a woman who risked life and limb this week to save someone deserves a few buds, don't you think?"

The desire inside her shifted to an emotion she didn't normally feel for people. Tenderness. "I guess. Come on in."

He followed her into the foyer. "You look terrific."

"Thanks. Thought I'd dress up. I don't get much of a chance to do it."

The condo was big and spacious with an entryway leading directly to a great room overlooking forever wild, a kitchen with a big dining area open to that, and bedrooms at either end.

As she fished out a vase from a kitchen cabinet, she sensed Ryan looking around. "Very nice."

"A lot different from your place."

"I like all kinds of décor."

"How'd you get interested in antiques?"

"My aunt and uncle. We used to stay with them a lot. Their house was full of antiques because they owned a store which sold them. They taught me about antiques and when I earned enough money to furnish my own place, I decided to buy some for myself."

As she set the vase of flowers on the island, her computer pinged from the desk across the room. "Damn it."

"What was that?"

"I get an automatic alert every time Parker Allen posts about the fire department."

"Ah, the woman on all our *Most Hated* lists."

"You got that right. Mind if I check?"

"Go ahead. Cops don't cotton her any better than you guys do."

Having a bad feeling about this one, Felicia sat down at the desk and called up Allen's blog. Ryan stood close behind her and she got a whiff of his cologne. Oh, man! Her fingers slipped on the keys.

But all thoughts of Ryan O'Malley fled when she read the heading of the post. The Good, the Bad and The Beautiful. There was a short paragraph where Allen wrote that she'd captured some video of America's Bravest and Finest.

From behind her, Ryan startled when images of him and Felicia came on screen. They were on the roof at Hale's Haven, Felicia was flat out on her stomach grasping onto Rachel arms. "Ouch," she said aloud.

"Yeah, ouch. But look at those muscles." Ryan touched her shoulder and squeezed. "You go girl."

Then the camera zeroed in on Ryan holding onto her.

"Uh-oh. I didn't realize my hands strayed into private territory." They were grasping her bare thighs. "Did I bruise you? I'm hanging on tight."

The thought that the marks on the inside of her thighs were from O'Malley's fingers dismayed her. She hadn't realized that. "No big deal."

A voice over came on. "This is the good and although I've taken on excess spending and the free time of firefighters, here's one of them managing a feat of undiluted courage. Hats off to Lieutenant Felicia White for her actions to save sister firefighter, Rachel Wellington. That's the good in this story."

"What next?" Felicia asked.

"Notice the hottie holding onto her. He's one of America's Finest." The shot cut out to, what the hell? — her and Ryan at the arson scene. "These two work together. Which is still okay."

Another clip. This one from the inside of Mitch and Megan's house at the camp. "But here they are later in, let's say, a tender moment."

The screen showed Felicia, bruised and battered — and drugged — lying on the couch, with Ryan seated next to her. She took his hand and held it to her chest. She spoke and he gazed down at her enrapt. Then he brushed her hair back in a very sweet gesture. The narration continued. "Is this taking camaraderie to an extreme? It also begs the question, what happens in those firehouses?"

"Fucking shit!" Felicia was infuriated.

"Yeah, fucking shit." He shook his head. "You know what? I've had it with that woman. I stopped myself from doing something out of respect for free speech but I'm sick of how she's slanting things."

Felicia looked up at him. His blue eyes sparked like flames: hot and angry. "What do you mean?"

"I'm going to investigate her."

"Ryan, we already did a Google search on the woman. We have the normal stuff: where she's from, her schooling, an engagement announcement, some early jobs. There were a lot of missing pieces."

"Yeah, well I bet I can find more on her. There has to be a reason for her vendetta." He crossed his arms over his chest. "How hungry are you?"

"What do you mean?"

"I can do it tonight. From here."

"Do what?"

"Access police data bases. See what it turns up."

Felicia knew her face lit up. "I'm all in."

He grinned. "Though it's a shame to waste that beautiful dress."

"Hell, we'll spend the gift certificates another time. I'll order pizza, cancel our reservations and get out some beer."

"A girl after my own heart."

And for a second, Felicia thought maybe she'd like to be. Especially since he was willing to give up a fancy dinner to get information so they could figure out why Parker Allen had a mafia-like grudge against fire and police workers. The situation had become very important to her.

And apparently to him, which, unfortunately, made him even more attractive.

• • •

RYAN STARTED WITH a search for Parker Allen in the police data bases. Vaguely, he was aware of Felicia behind him. As he waited for the data to come through, he stared at the screen but thought about the woman he was with. The way she looked in that dress made him hard as soon as he saw her. And that probably wasn't good, though she did admit this afternoon that she liked him a little.

After ten minutes, he got the results of his search. "I thought so."

From the kitchen island, Felicia asked, "What is it?"

"This shows no illegal activities,"

"Damn. Where do we go from here?"

"To check relatives for criminal activities."

"There have to be tons of Allens in the criminal system."

"Uh-huh, but we'll go to her home town first and find out her parents' or siblings' names."

"Or we can do a genealogy chart."

"Hey, that's a great idea."

"It'll take a while to process."

He stood then and faced her. "Aw, shucks, the dress is gone." Instead, she wore lightweight gray sweats which outlined her curves.

"Another time." She nodded to his outfit. "I wish you could get more comfortable."

It was on the tip of his tongue to flirt, to suggest he'd be more comfortable in bed with her in the interim but he checked himself. He was enjoying her company and didn't want to ruin their time together. Instead, he took off his suit coat and rolled up the sleeves of his black shirt. He noticed she was staring at his bare forearms. Well, that was good. "There, I'm more comfortable."

Her eyes raised to his. He caught the flicker of female interest in them, how she swallowed hard. Ryan was mesmerized by the expression on her face.

The doorbell rang. Hell of a time for the pizza to arrive. While she did the genealogy chart, he got the pie and put it and beer on the coffee table. He sat on one of the wide, stuffed couches and finally she joined him.

"All done. Now we wait."

"Speaking of genealogy, tell me about your family," he said when they both dug in. "You know all about mine."

"Not much to tell. My parents came from a typical middle class background in Binghamton. My father worked in a factory, my mother was a nurse. My brother's older."

"You mentioned him before. What does he do?"

"He's a smoke jumper in Colorado."

Ryan whistled. "Pretty dangerous job. What did your parents think of you two going into risky professions?"

She scrunched her nose. Even that expression was cute on her. "Stereotypical reaction. It was okay for Garth but not me. Honestly, I can't believe people think that way."

"How'd you get so liberated then?"

"I had a great English teacher. She started this elective called Women in Society. She changed my thinking, though unconsciously I always believed I was capable of doing what a man could. Still, I did what my parents asked. I went to college and took every gender studies class I could. As soon as I graduated, I took the firefighter test and got a job here in Hidden Cove." She seemed sad. "My parents died when I was a junior in college, so they never had to see me become a firefighter."

"I'm sorry you weren't more supported. My parents are unbelievable, I guess."

"Yeah, Ryan, they are."

"Did your brother back you?"

"Uh-huh." She bit into another slice and took a big slug of beer. "He came to my probationary class graduation, and after that we talked several times a month. We grew apart when he got married. He's divorced now." She frowned.

"What?"

"I don't think too much about how close we were. It kind of makes me sad now." She watched him. "Especially having contact with your tight knit family."

"It isn't too late to get in touch with him."

The computer pinged again and they both stood quickly, both started out together and bumped into each other. He grasped onto her arms and stared at her face. She was at least a head shorter than he, but solid and firm. And supple.

She wore a bit of makeup that enhanced her features, especially with her hair down and fluffy. He longed to touch it... and more. How had he once thought this woman was plain?

She bit her lip and the gesture made his gut clench.

"Licia, I–"

At first, she froze, then she stepped back. "We need to check the computer."

It was awkward, but he let the moment go, allowed her to precede him and sit in front of the screen. He pulled over a dining room chair and hovered next to her so their shoulders were almost touching. He didn't think he'd ever been more aware of a woman. "Here's her family tree. I'll start right before with her grandparents." She clicked on the leaves. Maternal grandparent information showed both Sara and Thomas Allen came from wealth. A lot of it. Then onto parents. Mother, Patrice Allen, was a housewife and active in charity work. She clicked onto the green leaf of the father. And came up as Nigel Larson, a birth date and not much else.

"She doesn't have his last name," Felicia noted. "What does that mean?"

"I'm not sure. But with his full name and date of birth we can find out."

When Felicia switched places with him, their bodies brushed. He noticed her small intake of breath and wanted to touch her badly. Instead, he sat while she retrieved their beers. Ryan typed in information. They waited ten minutes, making small talk about Allen, and eventually a data base came up. "Holy cow, it says he's at Menard Penitentiary in Illinois."

"Can you get more information?"

"Sure." He called up yet another data base. "I got a good feeling about this."

"Me, too. Thanks for helping me find out about her, Rye. I really appreciate it."

He clicked keys, then when it was time to wait, he placed his hand over hers. Squeezed it. "My pleasure. I want to stop her, too." Awkward now, as she looked away. But she didn't remove her hand.

Another ping.

Ryan and she skimmed the screen together. Nigel Anthony Larson had been imprisoned for the crime of setting an incendiary fire on a huge complex of warehouses he owned. Several people were killed. He was convicted on the belief that the business was floundering and he'd make millions in insurance. Despite the fact of his wife's wealth, the motive was considered valid, along with physical evidence: footprints at the scene, DNA on the window, and witnesses who testified to his suspicious behavior.

"Christ." They read on. "Oh, man," Ryan said. "Look at that."

"Damn." The man was cleared ten years later when another arsonist confessed. But the damage to the family's lives had been done.

Felicia frowned. "I wonder why this wasn't in local papers."

"It probably was but because the last name was different and nobody who searched connected the two. Besides, Chicago is a big city." Ryan sat back, folded his arms over his chest and stared at the screen. "This is a hell of a thing." He gave a soft *huh*. "It almost makes me feel sorry for her."

"Almost. She's done a lot of damage to both our departments, Rye."

He grinned over at her. "I like when you call me that."

She shook her head. "Anyway, we should get this to Noah and Will Rossettie."

"I agree. When?"

"ASAP."

Now that their tasks were done, they both stood. "Want more pizza?" she asked.

The last thing he wanted was food. He watched her for a minute. Her cheeks were flushed, her eyes flashing with the pleasure of success. How to proceed? He didn't want to scare her off but he couldn't walk away. So he stepped closer.

She surprised him in not stepping back. She did put a hand on his chest and his heart leapt at that simple touch. "What are you doing?" Her tone wasn't belligerent or angry. Curious, maybe. And her eyes held...interest.

"What I've wanted to do all night." He grasped her biceps gently. Rubbed her arms up and down. "For a while now."

Hazel eyes narrowed. "This is not a good idea, Ryan."

"I think it is." He tipped her chin. "Come on, one kiss."

She stared at his mouth.

He took that as agreement. Slowly he lowered his head. Her sexy scent filled his head. The zing he felt as soon as his lips touched hers was strong. And unusual for him. Must be for her, too, because she leaned into the kiss, slid her hand around his neck and exerted pressure of her own. His arms banded around her then and drew her close. She melded into him. Fireballs of desire shot through him as he deepened the kiss. Lifted her up a bit. Her hands clamped at his neck, and he opened her mouth with his tongue. Her whimper broke the last of his restraint. He devoured, consumed, took. So did she.

Soon it wasn't enough.

He dragged his mouth away. "Where's the bedroom?"

She looked as dazed as he felt. She blinked a couple of times and then seemed...skeptical.

He threaded his hands through her hair and kept her in place. "Licia, please."

It was an interminable wait, but finally she said, "Down the hall to the left."

• • •

SHE TRIED, SHE really did, not to rip his clothes off, they were so nice. But still she popped a few buttons and tore at his belt after he'd stripped her bare in her bedroom.

"Hurry," he said in a gravelly voice.

"I am. Oh, hell! I can't get the snap."

He pushed her back, barked, "Let me," and got himself naked in seconds.

"I can't wait."

"Me, neither." He started for the bed.

"No, here."

"Honey, we need protection."

She swore like a sailor, grabbed his hand and dragged him to the bed, pushed him down. He chuckled as she rummaged for condoms in her dresser drawer, tossed those on the bed, too, took one and sheathed him.

Then she was on her back. "My turn. Again, he dug his hands through her hair and ravaged her mouth. She squirmed, shifted, tried to get him to come inside her but he wouldn't be deterred. He left her lips and attacked her breast next. She bucked off the mattress, afraid she was going to come just from that action. "Please, Rye, now. I can't wait."

With one last suckle, he leaned back, took her legs and draped them over his shoulders and plunged into her. She spiraled out of control.

Afterward, she was sweaty, sore and…embarrassed. She'd seen stars, heard music, felt the earth move, every single cliché ever invented. And now, she loved the weight of him on her, the scent of musk surrounding her.

He lifted himself up and braced his arms on either side of her. "Wow!" he said.

She opened her eyes to his chagrined look.

"You came, right?"

Felicia laughed out loud. "I was about to ask you the same thing."

He laughed, too, a husky sound that burrowed out of his chest. "What happened?"

"I lost it."

"Me, too." He looked so cute with his hair damp and mussed, his face red with his own embarrassment. "I thought the top of my head came off."

Tenderly he brushed the hair from her face. Uh-oh. She wanted passion, not this. But he held her pinned to the mattress. "I, um, it's been a while for me."

"Same for me." The words were out before she could censor them.

"Oh, good." He rolled off her, sank into a pillow, dragged her close. "I knew we'd be hot together but this was combustion."

She tried not to cuddle into him but her body, her face had other ideas. "Who would have thought?"

"Actually, I've been thinking about this since the incident at the camp."

"Really, why?"

"I wasn't going to tell you this to save your pride, but since we've...gone this far...in the video clip Parker Allen showed, you told me you were attracted to me."

She felt cold. "Shit. Is that what prompted this?"

"Hardly. I told you, I lost my head." Easing up on his elbow, he watched her a minute. "I like you, too, Licia. A lot."

She shook her head vehemently to dim the effect he was having on her. "No, Ryan, I don't want that. I mean, sure, we can be friends, but nothing romantic."

"Hmm. To me what we did was romance novel romantic."

"It was some crazy hot sex. Truthfully, I'd take more of this, but nothing, you know, relationship-wise."

Ryan knew better than to argue with her. He'd been surprised she was so willing the first time, and he was going to have to bide his time with her. Because one thing he knew–this wasn't just physical for him.

Of course, he'd take the sex but wait for more. Rising from the mattress, he disposed of the condom and scooped her off the bed.

"What are you doing?"

"Shower sex. We're covered in sweat."

Her approving smile was answer enough. He carried her to a big bathroom and set her on her feet. She leaned into his back as he turned on the faucet, then gently drew her inside.

"Turn around."

"Why?"

"You'll see."

He washed her back and then slid soapy hands around front to her breasts. "These are fuller than I expected. Nice, round, firm."

"Hmm. Your hands feel good."

He played with her for a while. Then he went lower. It didn't take much for her to come again and he felt a sense of satisfaction so great he almost let her know about it. After she was done, she turned around. Kissed him. And slid to her knees. He leaned back against the tile and let her caress him. After a minute, he put her hands in her wet hair. "Now."

She made him come in convulsions so strong, he was rocked by them.

Later, he slipped on his boxers and T-shirt, she donned a robe and they ate cold pizza and drank more beer and talked about Parker Allen. Then, sated with food and sex, he smiled over at her. "I suppose I have to leave."

She arched a brow. "Not if you have anything more in you."

He popped up off the couch. "Ah, sweetheart, I do."

"Good, cause I'm ready again."

So was he, and as he led her to the bedroom, he wondered briefly if he'd ever get enough of Lieutenant Felicia White.

# CHAPTER 7

FELICIA LIKED THE ambience of the Hidden Cove police station. She entered the free standing building in the center of town with a smile on her face. She was thrilled they found something to use against Parker Allen. That was why she was so happy. Not because of the hot sex last night with a certain police officer who exited a glassed-in office as she reached the reception desk. He approached her in long, masculine strides. "Hey, there. I was looking for you."

If she was an ordinary woman, and they were an ordinary couple, he'd kiss her on the cheek. Maybe even the lips. She touched hers, for a second remembering what had happened between her and this man.

Ryan's intense blue gaze focused on her mouth and his expression told her he was recalling the same thing. Today, it seemed as if his uniform fit him better, his muscles bulging in his bare arms and biceps. She'd draw the Superman analogy if it wasn't so lame.

He cleared his throat. "I'll show you the way to the chief's office, Lieutenant."

Falling in step next to him, she didn't say anything more and neither did he until they got to a small alcove and he pulled her out of the corridor and into it. "Don't–"

"Shh, I won't touch you." He gave her a lopsided grin and she noticed a small nick on the underside of his jaw he must have gotten from shaving. "I gotta know, do you regret last night?"

Did she? Yes, no, how could she? It had been wonderful. "No, I don't." A moment of panic. "Do you?"

"What? Regret the best sex I've had in my life?"

"Really?" Hell, she sounded like a teenage girl.

"Yeah, really." He arched a brow that was shades darker than his sandy colored hair.

"Okay, for me, too." She frowned. "But don't get ideas about anything more."

"Who me, the playboy of the western world? The womanizer you hate? The guy who–"

"All right! I get it. Just so we're on the same page."

"Same book, same chapter, same page, beautiful."

"Watch what you call me."

"In public I will." He leaned in. "But in private, I get to call you, do anything I want to you."

Jesus, her knees went weak, like the time she rappelled too fast off a bridge. The aftershave he'd put on was doing it to her.

"There you are." Will Rossettie stopped across from them in the hallway. A big burly guy with white hair and a no nonsense attitude, he asked, "What are you doin' out here? Noah said he saw Felicia's car pull in."

"Catching up," Ryan said easily. "We were heading in."

When they settled in Will's office, Felicia spoke. "We discovered some things about Parker Allen that sheds light on why she's out for the departments."

"There's a reason other than she's a stone cold bitch?" Noah asked.

Ryan nodded. "You tell them, Felicia."

As concisely as she could, she filled them in on Parker Allen and her father. When she finished, Will lasered a gaze on Ryan. "Do I want to know how you got this information?"

She rushed in to say, "No."

"Yes." Ryan leaned forward. "I tapped into the police department data bases to get it."

Rossettie scowled. "Sergeant O'Malley, now that I *know*, I have to say you're not allowed use our data bases unless it's for genuine police work."

"It *was* for genuine police work. Allen's making such a stink that job cuts have caused us to be in more danger than normal."

"The force would have been down sized with or without her harangue," Will said, but gently. "The entire New York State budget is a mess."

Felicia jumped in. "By endangering the reputation of police and firefighters, she's putting all of us in harm's way. The community won't trust us, our school education presentations won't be as effective. We–"

Will held up his hand. "Okay, okay, I get it."

"So," Felicia asked, "Can we use the information to shut her up?"

"I'm not sure." Will looked to Noah.

"Me, either. We have to analyze a move on her from all sides. A direct hit might not be in our best interest."

Rossettie nodded. "Noah and I will talk it through. We'll let you know in a few days."

Felicia was surprised and she'd seen the same emotion on Ryan's face. They both stood.

"And O'Malley," Will said gruffly, "No reprimand but you skirted the edges of protocol."

"I don't see it that way, sir, but I'll remember what you said."

When they were far enough away from the open door of the chief's office, Felicia stopped this time. "Why were you so honest? We could have been evasive about how we got the information. Will and Noah would have let you off the hook."

Cocking his head, Ryan held her gaze intently. "Because lying always comes back to bite you in the ass. Besides, I don't like hiding things."

"So, you're an open book?"

"Book, chapter and page," he repeated. "You remember that."

Charmed, in spite of her vow not to be, Felicia left Ryan at his office and headed out of the police station. She'd have to be careful around that much…charisma. Even though she was sleeping with him, she couldn't afford to fall for the guy.

• • •

"COME ON, SWEETHEART. Sock it to me." Gabe Malvaso stood at home plate while his cousin's wife wound up with the softball on the pitcher's mound. The early evening sun was warm and Ryan was already sweating.

Megan Hale Malvaso threw a fast one at the captain, Gabe connected and the ball grounded to third. Ryan scooped it up and bulleted it to first base, where his colleague in the department tagged Gabe out. Megan turned and stuck her tongue out at Gabe. One reason Ryan liked playing in this softball league comprised of cops and firefighters was because they were all friends but competed like sworn enemies.

He was distracted when another firefighter strode to the plate. Dressed in tight bike shorts and the team's dark green jersey, she wore a cap to match. So he couldn't see the amber color of her eyes, the little mole she had next to her ear or the way her nose scrunched when she didn't like something. He knew Felicia's reactions, her body and, he thought, her whole outlook by now. They'd first been together ten days ago, and since then had four non-dates. All were steamy encounters with more talk than she liked. She was trying to keep the relationship solely about sex and he was trying to establish a deeper bond.

So he cupped his hands and yelled, "Easy out."

When she turned her head, he imagined her eyes taking a bead on him. God, he loved making them spark with fire, now and in bed.

The ball flew toward her, she got a good crack at it and the thing arced to right field. She raced to first where Brody signaled her to keep going. She took second on her own but the ball was retrieved and heading right to Ryan so she had to slide into third. He tried to tag her but tumbled to the ground instead, their legs entangling.

The ref, Will Rossettie, yelled, "Safe!"

"What the hell? She was out by a foot."

The police chief shook his head. "Sorry, boy."

Felicia rolled to her feet but Ryan stayed down and moaned. "What's a matter, pretty boy, I hurt you?"

*No, but you could.* The thought popped into his mind before he could stop it. Damn, if the notion wasn't true. He reached out a hand as an excuse to touch her. She angled her head but helped him up. He held on too long, and she finally murmured, "Watch it."

He grinned.

"So," he said as the batter at the plate walked. "Can we hook up after Badges?"

Clearing her throat, she hesitated. She did that every time he asked to see her. "We were together last night."

"Yeah, baby. I remember." It had been a particularly *energetic* time and he could still hear their grunts and groans, feel their slick skin against each other's. "I didn't get enough."

She snorted. "Okay. Just be circumspect."

"You mean like not leave the bar with you? God forbid."

Whirling around, she growled, "If this isn't working for you…"

"It's working just fine." He nodded to the plate. "Now pay attention to the game."

The batter had been tip fouling so the play was at a standstill.

"Why wouldn't it be all right?" he asked when the guy got yet another foul ball. Ryan was pushing the issue but couldn't stop himself.

"I don't know. Sometimes you…never mind."

She had to be sensing he wanted more. Because she was right, *he* had to be careful or he was going to lose his shot with her altogether.

The firefighter finally walked and Ramirez came to bat. He yelled, "Get ready, Licia," and hit one over the fence.

The police department lost 9-5.

At Badges, the cops took a razzing. Ryan was leaning against the juke box next to the door, sipping a beer when Parker Allen walked in. She was dressed in jeans, boots and a tight white shirt set off by hair that cascaded down her back. Briefly he recalled how she tried to seduce his brother, so he ignored her.

She sidled up beside him. "Hi, handsome."

"What are you doing here?" His comment was rude and his Mama would skin him alive if she heard him speak to a woman that way, but he wanted nothing to do with this one.

"I came to see the boys and girls at play."

"Bring your camera?"

"No. Observing this time. I did get some shots of you at the camp."

Man, she had balls.

Before he could respond, someone approached them. Ryan turned to see Felicia slipping money out of her pocket. "Move over, O'Malley. You got shit for taste in music."

Ryan gave Allen his back. "Yeah, what are *you* playing?"

Taking the hint, the reporter left and Ryan touched her arm. "Thanks for the rescue. I thought she was gonna eat me alive."

"Yeah, you looked like you could use some help." She chuckled. "We call her Parker the Piranha."

Ryan tracked Allen and saw her approach Ed Snyder. Hmm, that couldn't be good. She appeared to be introducing herself to him, and he wondered if she heard about how nobody in either department liked him.

Beside Ryan, Felicia chose music while he sipped his beer. "I kinda feel sorry for her."

"Why? Callahan and Rossettie decided not to use what we found out about her to dilute the blog."

The chiefs didn't want to stoop to Allen's level. And, they believed, it would look like they were bullying her. Besides, Ryan knew both men had integrity, and slandering a woman because she was calling things like she saw them wasn't in their genes.

"Maybe. She seems…alone."

Ramirez wandered over to them. "Hey, guys."

"Tony." Felicia glanced around. "Where's Sophia? I saw her at the game." His beautiful wife was quiet on the sidelines though. Usually, she cheered like a banshee.

The guy's handsome features tightened. A lot. "She went home. We, um, shit, we had a fight."

"Oh, dear." Felicia put a hand on his shoulder. She knew Ramirez's family meant the world to him. "Want to go sit somewhere and talk about it?"

"No, it's old stuff. Now move your pretty little ass while I play something." When he gave them his back, *they* took that hint and walked away.

"Huh!" Felicia said.

"What?"

"I thought the Ramirez's had a match made in heaven."

"All couples fight."

"And you'd know this how?"

"I been in a relationship before."

She poked him in the ribs. "I heard you live by the Rule of Six."

Ryan sputtered his beer all over his red jersey. "Holy, shit, I don't even...how did you...who told you about that?"

"I overheard it at the firehouse. Pretty sucky, O'Malley, if you ask me."

"I don't do that anymore."

She counted on her fingers. "Well, we passed the six day mark."

"Really, Licia, it was mostly a joke."

Arching a brow, she said, "You're 34. Nothing's stuck."

He gave her his best sexy smile. "Not yet."

"Don't get carried away."

"Wouldn't think of it, babe."

"I'm going to find my own kind." She started away, then turned back. "Um, what time? You know…to leave?"

Ah, that was a very good sign. She was anxious to be alone with him. "Fifteen minutes."

As he watched her go, he mumbled in his beer bottle, "As I said, not nothing's stuck, sweetheart. *Yet!*"

# CHAPTER 8

THE TEXT READ: *We're gonna mix it up. Tonight. Seven. The Hidden Cove Hideaway.*

She typed into her phone: *What room?*

His response: *21. See you then.*

Felicia sighed from the kitchen of the firehouse where she sat at the table. She'd been the first to finish her chores and was waiting for the hour until training. Confined space. That was a tough one.

Brody straggled in. Ever since he came back to work and she caught a glimpse of him, she was startled by how much he and Ryan looked alike. "Hey, Licia. How's it going?"

"Great." She put the phone away. As far as she knew, Ryan hadn't told Brody about their assignations. He'd promised he wouldn't but still, they were twins. And anyway, Felicia didn't trust men to keep their promises.

Her former fiancé, Tim, had promised he could handle her job and deal with the stress of being in love with a firefighter. It took him six months but eventually he confessed he couldn't cope with the fear and loneliness.

"You coming tonight?" Brody asked.

She cocked her head.

"The get-together at my place. It's a thank you to everybody for taking care of me with food and visits when I got hurt."

"Um, no. I forgot the date. I have plans."

"Oh."

"Yeah, I'm sorry, I can't change them." She didn't want to.

"Huh. Rye has plans, too, that he can't get out of."

Uh-oh. "A hot date for Mr. I'm-Too-Sexy?"

Leaning back and propping his feet up on another chair, Brody chuckled. "Yeah. I think so. He's been happy lately so I know he's getting some. He doesn't want to talk about it, which weirds me out. Ryan never keeps his conquests to himself."

*...must be getting some.*

*...never keeps his conquests to himself.*

The phrases bothered Felicia, even when the training started. The drill was to crawl through a three-foot-by-three foot circular pipe with the entrance and exit covered after the trainee got inside. The exercise wasn't easy. Sydney Sands particularly had trouble with completing it. Last year, she got trapped in a well and hadn't been able to navigate the pipe since then.

"Who wants to go first?" Gabe asked.

Sydney stepped forward. "I might as well get my humiliation over with."

"That's no attitude to have, girl." Ramirez stepped up to her and pulled her aside. He whispered in her ear and she giggled.

At the opening of the pipe, she dropped to her knees and shimmied her shoulders into the sphere.

There were shouts of encouragement. Gabe dropped the curtains at both ends.

"Go, girl."

"Come on, babe."

Felicia called out between cupped hands, "Women can do this, Sydney. Don't let us down."

Ramirez headed to the other end of the pipe and talked her halfway. Three quarters. And low and behold, the young firefighter poked her head out the other end. Tony helped her up and hugged her. So did the rest of them. Her face wreathed in smiles, Syd was glowing with the big accomplishment.

It wasn't until Felicia was halfway through the pipe that she realized why she was bothered by Brody's comments. Though she'd asked for that—to keep their relationship on the level of *getting some*—the cheapness of the statements made her uncomfortable. Fuck, she couldn't change her mind about them together. She just couldn't. Like being midway through the pipe, you had to keep going and hoped you got through.

• • •

RYAN OPENED THE door to suite 21 at the Hidden Cove Hideaway on the end of the lake. He loved this little inn with tons of privacy and a lot of amenities-like the roomy balcony off the suite with a hot tub, the dining alcove in a set of bay windows set for an intimate dinner and the huge bed against the wall with mirrored ceilings. He lit a few of the many candles he placed all over the room and inhaled the scent of vanilla. This was a perfect place for a seduction. Only he wasn't here for the same kind of seduction as other people who booked suites.

Over the past few weeks, Ryan had become certain he wanted a real relationship with Felicia. Not just sex. And he'd decided to convince her to go along with it tonight. He planned to bathe her in tenderness, gentle courtship and poignant lovemaking. As he finished with the final touches, there was a knock on the door.

When he opened it, she stood before him in a pretty dress of purple and green with tan sandals on her feet. "You look like a bunch of violets."

Her face reddened. Then she said, "Don't get carried away, O'Malley."

Kissing her nose first, he led her inside. In the entrance, her eyes widened. "What's all this?" She waved to take in the candles placed all over the room, alongside fresh cut daisies and daffodils.

"I've got spring on the brain."

"Looks like you're setting the mood for seduction." Turning to him, she looped her arms around his neck. "I gotta tell you, lover boy, you don't have to seduce me. That's what I'm here for."

Sliding his arms around her waist, he tugged her close. "Humor me."

She sighed. "Whatever. I'm starved."

There was another knock on the door. "Good, because that's room service."

A waiter pushed a cart full of food inside and rolled it next to the table in the bay. When he left, Felicia sniffed. "The food smells heavenly. What is it?"

"Lobster, crab, asparagus, and a great bottle of Cab."

She grinned. "We never did get that dinner at the Lakeside."

"That night was better the way we spent it, no?"

"Um, yeah."

"And we have the exact food now."

As they ate, the seafood was succulent, the vegetable *al denté* and the wine dry. But mostly, Felicia looked beautiful sitting across from him in the candle light, her eyes sparkling. Her cheeks flushed. Her whole body relaxed.

He lifted his glass. "Shall we take this out on the patio?"

"It might be cold for the end of April on the lake."

He grabbed fuzzy blankets off a table by the sliding glass doors. "We'll cuddle. There's a chaise."

Mellow now with the wine, Felicia agreed. They snuggled on the big padded lounge-for-two, sipped wine and talked. He got her to tell him about college, and he shared his own exploits. He was surprised that she was editor of their literary magazine and voted most valuable player of the tennis team her senior year. Running his hand down her arm, testing her muscles, he whispered, "You certainly are competent in a lot of sports." He leaned in closer. "Especially the one played on a king size bed."

His knuckles grazed her cheek. He traced the scoop of her dress with his finger. But when she lifted her mouth to his, he avoided a kiss—he knew it would lead them to bed. Instead he drew her closer and cherished the feel of her tucked into his chest. He told her about his and Brody's college forays: the time they doubled dated identical twins, when they initiated a panty raid on a girls' dorm down the road, the surprisingly rigorous training at John Jay. After a while, he thrust off the blankets, stood and pulled her up. "Time for a bath before you go to bed, little girl."

"Hmm."

His fingers found the zipper at her back and slowly released it. He slid the dress off her shoulders and it fell to the ground, revealing a black thong and a why-bother bra that had her breasts spilling out of it. "Oh, I must have been a very good boy. Leave them on in the Jacuzzi."

She tugged at the buttons of his gauzy shirt, yanked it out of his pants and removed it. He kicked off his shoes and slacks and underwear and stood naked before her. The air was chilled but Ryan felt the heat rise in him. He took a moment to toss their clothes inside, then he scooped her up, brought her to the tub, and carefully walked in with her.

When he sat, he kept her settled her on his lap, making sure her upper body was submerged. He traced the curve of her jaw with his lips, massaged her shoulder, and rubbed her waist gently below the water. It was hot and bubbly and he could feel her relax in his arms.

Until he began to arouse her. Slowly. Light brushes on her breasts, her abdomen, his big hand cupping her mound. Then he slid a finger inside her thong and teased her. He took his time, exploring, rubbing. She tried for more — contact, pressure, activity. But he kept it subdued.

"Ryan, please, let's go inside."

"Stay here, then." He sat her on the bench, got out of the tub and returned carrying a fluffy white robe and wearing one. When she stood, he helped her out and surrounded her with it. "Oh, dear Lord in heaven, it's warm."

"There's a heat light in the bathroom for them."

Carefully, he led her into the room to their bed. They disrobed and slid under the covers together.

And then he began step three of his plan. He started with kisses all over. She squirmed.

He trailed gentle fingers to all the intimate places on her body. She shivered.

He turned her over, massaged her whole back this time. Kissed her butt, behind her knees.

By the time he finished, she was mush. Only then did put on a condom and slip inside her, once again gently, drawing out the sensations of each thrust. Finally, nature overcame nurture and he began to move faster. She orgasmed immediately. Screamed his name. Swore. He held on and began again. After her second climax, he followed her into oblivion.

• • •

AT THREE IN the morning, Felicia awoke with a start. She was in the middle of a nightmare–Ryan was holding her prisoner and she wore velvet handcuffs and a fluffy robe. He kept saying, "You're mine now."

Frowning, she lay back on the pillow, trying to figure out where the awful images had come from. As her eyes focused in the dark, she could make out the table where they'd eaten, see the chair on the deck where they'd lain together. She heard the water in the hot tub bubble and blip. The vanilla candles still scented the air.

What had he done to her last night? Quietly, she slid of bed, grabbed her clothes from the chair and headed for the bathroom. Turning on a small light, she stared at herself in the mirror. *Oh, no!* Her hand covered her heart. *No, please, not this.* She couldn't, wouldn't, please dear God, not *this*.

But no matter how much she protested, she couldn't lie as she stared at herself in the glass. She'd made the huge, *huge* mistake of falling for Ryan O'Malley.

She shook herself. That wouldn't do. It simply wouldn't. So as quickly as she could, she dressed, slipped out of the bathroom, and headed for the door only to realize she wasn't wearing shoes. Retracing in her mind the path they took last night she figured her sandals were on his side of the bed.

Deftly she retrieved them, but when she turned, she got a glimpse of Ryan splayed out on the mattress. The moonbeams highlighted his hair, and she could see the broad expanse of his naked back, his biceps and hands that could be so gentle.

Her heart ached so bad she was afraid she might be having an attack. But still, whispering a quiet, "Goodbye, Ryan," she fled the room, the inn and the proximity of a man she promised herself she would never, ever allow herself to love.

# CHAPTER 9

A BREEZE WAFTED off the lake as Ryan sat at a picnic table and waited for Felicia to show up at Rachel's condo. She and Gabe were getting married—a decision made in part because of Rachel's accident. They said they didn't want to waste their time together.

Which Felicia had done for seven days running. Ryan had been totally shocked when he woke in the cozy little inn and found her gone. And she'd refused to talk to him all week. He'd texted her, phoned her and even stopped over to her house. No luck. He didn't even know if she was coming to the wedding. He could have gone to the firehouse when she was working, but he had to respect her wish that no one in the department know about them—even though she was giving him the brush off.

As if he'd let her.

Brody came up to the table and dropped down on the top of it. They were wearing similar outfits—khaki shorts and polo shirts—though Ryan wore blue and Brody green. Everyone in attendance was told to dress casually. The bride sported a pretty white gauzy dress that hit above her knees, her sister a peach one. Gabe was in linen pants and shirt, and his best man, Mitch, in similar garb. May had turned hot with the sun blazing above so Ryan welcomed the cool of the shade where he sat. There were two tents set up for food and drink, and umbrellas tables spread over the lawn and deck.

He and Brody made small talk and Ryan kept a weather eye on the side of the house. When Felicia finally arrived, his heart soared.

Then nosedived. What the hell? She brought a date? He was too dumfounded to do anything but stare with his mouth open.

"See a ghost?" Brody asked.

"No, no ghost." His voice was hoarse with emotion.

Brody tracked his gaze. "Ah, it must be on again."

His head snapped around to his brother. "What?"

"Licia and Derek. They've been together on and off for years."

"Like sleeping together?"

"No, I think they play tiddlie winks."

"Very funny."

His twin frowned. "Where's Shelly? I thought you'd bring her."

Hmm. He covered fast. "She wasn't sure she could make it but she was going to try." And, he thought as he watched Dennison slide his hand around Felicia's waist and whisper intimately in her ear, maybe he'd call his own on-again-off-again to see if she might be able to sneak over to the wedding.

Shit, he wasn't going to sit by and take this! So when Brody left to find Emma, Ryan stood and approached the couple where they'd disappeared into the drink tent. Felicia was alone by the wall of canvas and Dennison was at the bar. Stalking over, he grabbed her arm none too gently. "What the hell do you think you're doing?"

Her pretty hazel eyes widened. She had on a yellow sundress that made her skin golden. "What do you mean?"

At least her voice was shaky. He felt as if his stomach was going to cave in on itself.

"You know damn well what I mean. Why would you bring a date here?"

She seemed to regain her cool. "The invitation said to bring guests."

His heart lurched at her dismissiveness. "I thought we'd come to this wedding together."

Doubt flickered in her eyes. "Why? We're not dating, O'Malley."

Streams of anger rolled through him now. "Like hell we're not."

Her eyes widened. "We had an agreement."

"That lasted six weeks with neither of us dating others." His chest got tight. "You weren't like…you weren't sleeping with Dennison while you were with me, were you?"

"No, of course no!"

At least her expression was disgusted at the thought.

"Here you go, Licia." Dennison looked to Ryan. "O'Malley, right? You're Brody's cop brother."

"Right." The guy held out his hand to shake, which Ryan forced himself to do.

"Nice crowd here for only inviting family and dates. You close to the couple?"

"Yeah, with Gabe."

"Ryan fraternizes with all his brother's firefighter friends."

Now that made him mad. They'd more than *fraternized*. Much, much more.

From outside, Gabe called for attention, asking everyone to be seated down by the water.

"If you'll excuse us," Felicia said as if he meant nothing to her. "Derek, we need to sit."

Still in shock, Ryan found a place next to Emma and Brody. His heart felt as if somebody had ripped it out of his chest and stomped on it. He barely registered the happy couple taking their vows, the exchange of rings, the clapping. He kept his gaze four rows down, staring at Felicia letting another man touch her.

After the ceremony, people began to mingle. An hour later, Ryan caught sight of Felicia heading into the house. He made a beeline for the same doorway and followed her when she went down the hall, tried one bathroom, then disappeared into a bedroom. He stepped into it too, just as an inside door closed. Leaning up against the wall, he folded his arms over his chest and waited. She wasn't getting out of this room until he had some answers.

• • •

FELICIA WAS BARELY keeping it together. In the bathroom, she stared at herself almost losing it. Her hands were shaking and her face flushed. "Breathe deep," she ordered the image in the mirror. "Like you do when you're scared in a fire."

Ryan had thrown her by his confrontation out in the open, in front of everyone else. She didn't think he'd do something so blatant. But then, he didn't play fair. Like killing her with gentleness and sweet talk the last time they were together. Still, she couldn't believe her own reaction to his anger, his nearness, his hurt. She splashed water on her face and then took in more fresh air through the open window. After a while, she felt better and opened the bathroom door, stepped out into the bedroom and...Jesus Christ, there he was.

"What are you doing here?"

"I followed you inside. I want some answers." His tone was angry, but it was the shock in those beautiful blue eyes that got to her.

Pretending to be cool, though her heart was galloping in her chest, she said, "All right, ask away."

"Why did you leave the inn last week so abruptly? Why wouldn't you answer my texts and phone messages?"

How much to say? "I didn't like how you acted that night at the Hideaway."

"You could have fooled me. You seemed to like it fine."

"You were too...clingy."

He laughed. "Boy, I really got to you, didn't I?"

Nerves jittered inside her. "What do you mean?"

"We were close that night. Hell, we've been getting close for six weeks."

"It wasn't just sex that night. You changed the rules."

"Because I care about you! I want a real relationship with you."

She began to shake her head wildly. "I don't want one with you. We're done, O'Malley. We had an agreement, you reneged and I don't want to play the game anymore."

He puffed out a big breath, ran a hand through his hair. "Licia, please. Let's talk about his calmly."

"I am calm. Look, I know this has to be a first, a woman ditching you, but you'll get over it, O'Malley."

Now he swallowed hard, his expression bleak. "I can't believe you're saying this me. After all we..." He broke off as if he couldn't continue.

She felt tears well in her eyes, but she couldn't show any weakness, so she battled them back. "I'm sorry, Ryan, truly I am, but the thing between us wasn't working for me anymore. Now please, let me get back to my date."

*Please,* she thought weakly, *let me out of here before I make another big mistake.*

Thank God he stepped aside. She reached for the door handle but he stayed her arm. "Don't sleep with him, Felicia. We won't be able to work through this if you do."

He had no idea he was giving her a way out of his trap.

"If I want to sleep with Derek or any other man, Ryan, I will. But it won't be you."

She made it out of the door, stumbled into the other bathroom and dropped down onto the toilet seat, horrified that she'd done this awful thing to him. But deep in her heart, she knew why she behaved so badly. Protection, pure and simple. She'd protected herself all her life by not making commitments after the bad experience with Tim. By not getting close to anyone. But more so, Ryan O'Malley was a player and there was no reason to think he'd change. Nope, it was better to be the dumper than the dumpee.

Still, none of that rationalization prevented Felicia from quietly crying into her hands.

• • •

TWO HOURS LATER, after Ryan made a phone call, he was dancing with Shelley, semi-drunk and still simmering. Especially when he watched Felicia snuggle up to Dennison on the improvised patio dance floor.

"I'd like to leave," Ryan told Shelley.

"Yeah, where to?"

He winked at her. "For a smart girl, that's a very dumb question."

She raised blond brows. "I haven't heard from you in weeks."

"I got caught up in something." He glanced over her shoulder at the woman he...never mind. He gave Shelly his killer grin. "So, my place or yours?"

"Yours."

Twenty minutes later he led her upstairs to his bedroom. He wouldn't think about finding Felicia here that day snooping. Or all the times they'd made love on that bed.

He turned to Shelley, grasped the hem of his shirt and yanked it over his head. Then his hands went to his pants.

"Let me," she said. She already had her top off.

"Be my guest, dollface, be my guest."

• • •

ACROSS TOWN, FELICIA took Derek's hand and led him down the hallway to her bedroom. She felt like crying, screaming, swearing. Instead, she gave him a sexy smile. "I'm glad you came home with me," she lied.

"I was wondering where you disappeared to all these weeks."

"Doesn't matter." Her hands went to the buttons on his shirt. "I'm here now."

• • •

HE WAS SICK and sweating when he woke up, but Ryan bounded out of bed. He took the quickest shower on record, and without even stopping for coffee, he drove the distance to Felicia's house. Bolting out of his car, he hurried to the front steps, his heart beating at a clip. He only hoped she'd done what he'd done last night. And had the same revelation. Ringing the bell, he waited. No answer. He rang again. On the third try, she pulled open the door. And he had hope. She'd obviously been crying. Her hair was a mess, her eyes puffy, her face blotchy.

"Ryan? Oh, my God."

"I'm not giving up. And by the looks of you, you don't want to either. I'm in love with you Felicia, and I'm ready for a commitment. I promise I won't let you down."

Her eyes widened. In fear?

"There's nothing to be afraid of. I went home with Shelley and I was gonna make love with her but I couldn't so I asked her to leave."

She stared up at him. "Oh, Ryan, I feel the same way about you. I know that now. But–"

"But nothing. That's all I need to hear." He reached for her.

Again she shook her head.

He was distracted by something behind her. When he realized what it was, his whole world turned dim.

Derek Dennison stood a few inches away in unbuttoned slacks, no shirt and barefoot.

Apparently, Felicia *hadn't* done what he had. Instead, she fucked somebody else. Amidst the shock and sourness in his gut, Ryan was struck with the realization there was no future for him and Felicia.

# CHAPTER 10

IN EARLY JUNE, the sun was high and the water calm for the first camp of the summer at Hale's Haven. Felicia stood by the entrance to the lake front property on Hidden Cove waiting for the campers to arrive. She tried to cancel out on being a counselor for the week but two other volunteers had been unable to come so Felicia didn't feel right about letting the kids down. She hoped she could get through the week without any confrontations with Ryan.

While the rest of the counselors talked in small groups, she sat down on the grassy incline and looked out over the camp. Would she have to watch him reach and dive for balls on that baseball field or the tennis court? See him climb the ropes and hurdle all the obstacles on the beams course? Dance in the big open pavilion where group activities were held? She glanced further out at the cabins, the boats and swimming areas and shook her head. It would be impossible not to run into him. Though she'd gotten stronger in the last four weeks, and resigned herself to their split, she hadn't had to see him. Not once had he come to the firehouse, gone to Badges or shown up at a fire scene or accident site she was called to. He must be keeping track of her schedule. But any minute he'd pop up at the camp. Hell, she'd just have to be strong.

"Hey, there, why so glum?"

Felicia looked up at Jenn O'Connor and smiled genuinely. Her shoulder length dark hair was damp from the heat and her face had a glow to it.

"Hi, Jenn." They hugged, awkwardly because Felicia was sitting down, then Jenn dropped to the grass, too. "I'm excited about chaperoning the seven-to-ten cabin with you."

"Same here. I've been so busy between my job and Angel and Grady." She rolled her eyes and placed her hand on her stomach. "And it's only going to get worse."

Simultaneously Felicia felt joy and envy. She picked at the grass to have time to rein in her emotions. "You're having another one?"

"Two. It's twins."

Felicia swallowed hard at the reminder of Ryan and Brody.

"There's a lot of twins among us."

"Yeah, I heard you worked with Eve Callahan for a while. Was it cool? She's so good at what she does. They're thinking of letting me assist her since I'm off the line now, though I can't go to fire sites."

"There's a lot of other arson work to do." Jenn elbowed her arm. "Now tell me why you look so sad."

*Because I slept with one man when I was in love with someone else. Even though he told me if I did it was over.*

"I guess all these weddings, babies, that kind of thing are making me melancholy."

"The campers are here," Mitch yelled through a bull horn.

Sure enough they heard the squeal of the yellow busses marked with Hidden Cove School District making their way toward the camp. *Good*, Felicia thought. Now she wouldn't have to dwell on how she'd made the biggest mistake of her life. How she'd cried right after she did it, so hard, she'd vomited. And how she'd taken three days furlough to try to get herself together after Ryan ditched her for good; she'd been readily given the time because she'd never asked for a spontaneous furlough in her seventeen year career as a smoke eater.

"We'll talk more later," Jenn said rising.

She and Felicia reached the bus area before they parked. Felicia tried to keep her gaze straight ahead so she wouldn't spot Ryan, but she heard his husky, male laugh off to the right and her whole body tensed. It was, of course, accompanied by female laughter tinkling through the air. Had he found someone here already? A week's diversion? He wouldn't have to worry about his Rule of Six, as camp was only five days.

*Not fair. You know it. He'd changed.*

But it had been too late for Felicia, too late before she realized he really did care about her enough to make a commitment. Way, way too late.

She heard hers and Jenn's name called and saw a group of little girls looking a bit lost, huddled together with sleeping bags and backpacks. "Let's go," she said to Jenn. "I think we have our work cut out for us."

Thankfully, Felicia managed to get away from the arrival sight without laying eyes on Ryan. She couldn't avoid him for long, but this was some respite. She'd have to take one day at a time as she recovered from her Ryan O'Malley addiction.

• • •

THEY GATHERED UNDER the picnic pavilion and Ryan sat amidst his assigned fourteen-to-seventeen year olds.

From beside him, his brother said, "Rye, Juan asked you a question."

"Oh. Sorry. What did you say, Juan?"

Ryan had finished telling the boy that no, during the course of his job, he'd never had anyone die on him. At least not literally. But personally, four weeks ago he'd experienced a loss so great it had leveled him as much as death could. He'd been so shocked when he found Felicia with another man. He'd really thought she'd send Dennison packing after Gabe's wedding, maybe even come and see him. Instead, she'd fucked him. Ryan could never forgive her.

"Hello, campers," Megan called through the bull horn.

The kids and counselors responded.

"I'm going to give you a few rules, and then I won't have to use this thing…" she held up the bullhorn "…again."

Trying hard to focus on Megan Hale, Ryan listened to her tell the kids three rules that were important at the camp: when a leader raised her hand in a group meeting, all campers were to stop talking and raise *their* hands. This was how order would be maintained. Second, the campers couldn't go anywhere without adult accompaniment. Finally—and here the counselors joined in and yelled *"A clean camp is a happy camp!"* Ryan knew from past volunteering that keeping the eating areas and cabins clean was a must in order to handle nearly eighty people on the grounds.

"We're going to conduct an opening service up on the hill, and then our food will be ready for dinner. So follow your counselors to the outdoor chapel."

Ryan put on a happy face. But as soon as he stood, he caught sight of Felicia, and like he feared, just seeing her poleaxed him. She looked okay in white shorts and a red camp shirt emblazoned with *Hale's Haven, Three Years and Counting*. But she didn't fill the clothes out well. She must have lost fifteen pounds in the last month. Pounds she didn't need to lose. And though she was laughing at something one of the kids said, when she turned and her face came right into his line of vision, he saw the ravages of what had happened between them etched out on every feature. For a minute she stared at him, then gave him her back and started up the hill.

"I told you she looked like shit," Brody said, placing his hand on Ryan's shoulder.

Ryan had been on a slippery slope right after he found Felicia with another man and realized what that meant, so he'd told Brody everything. His brother had been pissed Ryan hadn't confided in him earlier, but knew how raw Ryan was and never reamed him out. Lately, though, Brody had been making noise about forgiveness.

Which totally wasn't going to happen.

"Yeah, she does look like shit. Her own fault."

As they began the hike up the hill, the sun beat down on them mercilessly, making Ryan even more uncomfortable. One thing about having older campers, though, they didn't have to hold hands with the counselors and could be trusted to wander within sight. Problems came in getting that age group to sleep at night.

Brody picked up the topic as he fell into stride next to Ryan. "I guess you could look at it that Licia got what she deserved. In any case, she hasn't been herself since May."

"Can we rule her out as conversation this week?" he asked as nicely as he could.

"Yeah, after I ask you this. What are you going to do when you have to talk to her?"

"I'll avoid her."

"You might not be able to."

"I will. Now, let's catch up to the boys."

. . .

THE FIRST NIGHT ended early and when the kids were ready for bed, one cabin was chosen to do Tuck-Ins. This was a routine where all campers settled down, then one cabin of kids would visit each of the other five and say goodnight-with a hug. The scent of the lake wafted into Felicia's and Jenn's cabin, but it was stifling in the small space. Still, everybody loved this activity. Waiting in line, Felicia hoped that Ryan's group wouldn't be doing the drill but that was dashed when she saw Brody walk through the door. Damn. What was she going to do? Could she duck out? She looked around wildly. There were people packed in here and there was little room to move. A lot of other counselors who weren't assigned cabins milled about. Damn, she'd have to grin and bear it.

And maybe that wasn't so bad. They'd have their first confrontation in front of everybody and be done with it. Still she started to sweat and her heart triple timed in her chest.

Each camper came down the row. The hugs were awkward at first even though her girls were little and the boys big. Brody led the way, with Ryan taking up the rear. She watched Brody lean down and speak to one of her girls, the homesick one. He got her to smile and hugged her fiercely.

"Hey, thanks for that," she said when he reached her.

"No problem." He enveloped Felicia in a big embrace. "Be strong, honey," he whispered, shocking her.

Brody had told her right after the night of Gabe and Rachel's wedding that he knew what happened between her and Rye, he wished he could help her out, but his brother would always be his first priority. He also said he was sorry they were both hurting so badly.

Too soon, the line wound down. Ryan inched closer. Closer. Closer still until he stood in front of her.

She was stunned by his physical presence: how he towered over her, his scent of man and musk and sweat, how he hadn't shaved and his beard flecked on his jaw. Which was clenched. "Goodnight," he said stiffly. He slid his arms around her. Expecting a weak embrace, she got it.

When he drew back, he couldn't even look at her. Felicia lifted her chin and didn't move.

Unfortunately, she dreamed about that hug and his stony expression all night long.

• • •

AFTER A POLAR swim, where kids got up at six and dipped their feet—not often their bodies—in the shallow end of the lake, everybody headed for breakfast. Kids shouted and squealed their way through the meal because they were excited and more familiar with the camp. Afterward, Megan got up to announce what activities were planned for that morning.

"We'll break up into groups and you get to choose what you want to do with these counselors: basketball with me, Mitch and Zach, Kelly and Tamara." The other four waved. Ryan knew Kelly Long from work and she'd flirted with him last night. "Next, there'll be an acting studio headed by our own Broadway star, Lisel Loring."

The beautiful woman also waved.

Jenn O'Grady was assigned to crafts, others to a variety of physical and non-physical activities. Ryan began to worry when he and Felicia hadn't been called for anything. Rightfully so because finally Megan said, "Last will be our hiking adventure. You'll be going on a hike in the woods at the end of the lake with Ryan and Felicia. You'll be back for lunch."

Son of a bitch. He remembered now he and Licia had shared a conversation about hiking. They must have both put the interest down on their interview sheets. He approached Brody immediately. "Hey, bro, you need to change activities with me."

"Can't," Brody said. "Emma's coming out to look around and after lunch she's doing a reading hour with the little kids. I'm helping." He cocked his head. "You know, maybe you should talk to her."

All his muscles hardened. "Over my dead body."

Eight kids volunteered to hike — five boys and three girls who all surrounded Felicia. She kept darting glances at him and Brody. Finally, he threw in the towel and approached the group. He noticed one camper from his cabin, Mikey, who was a pistol, in the crowd. Tamping down thoughts of the woman in the middle of the kids, he made a note of keeping an eye on the boy.

They all piled into the camp van and rode it to the end of the lake; the whole time, Ryan managed to look right through Felicia. She sat in front with the driver, Nick, a full time jack-of-all-trades for the camp, who flirted with her the entire trip. She didn't say much back. When they got out of the van, they headed to the bottom of the trail. Felicia caught Ryan's gaze and arched a brow.

He crossed to her. "Do you want to lead or take up the rear?" Other than goodnight, those were the first words he'd spoken to her in four weeks.

"I'd rather lead."

Figures. He wondered if she led in bed with Dennison. Sometimes she did with him. And he loved it. Fuck!

"Okay, guys, fall into line, whatever order you want."

A young girl approached Felicia. "Will you hold my hand?"

"Sure, honey."

Ryan pulled out a sheet of printed instructions Megan had given him. "You each get a bottle of water. If you drink it all and have to go to the bathroom, I'm afraid there's only the woods."

The kids giggled.

"Stay on the trail. Do not wander off."

He gave a few more warnings and they started up.

Felicia went slowly, then picked up the pace. The sun was beaming down on them and he yelled to the kids to put on the caps they'd been given in their camp-provided backpacks. He noticed Felicia didn't don one. The delicate skin of her face already showed some red. Not that he cared.

Halfway up the trail, Ryan called for a break because some boys had to pee. "I'll go with them," he called to Felicia and she grunted without looking at him.

From his post several feet away, he told the kids to do their business and tried not to think about how Felicia looked holding the young camper's hand. She was good with kids, but she'd never have children of her own. He'd thought at one time...

"Ryan, Ryan, help!"

Ryan bolted through the woods and found Mikey had gone past a sign that read, "Danger, keep out." Ryan darted around the meager fencing, raced forward. And stopped short when he came to a pit in the ground. Hell. He took out the walkie talkie they'd been given and spoke into it. "Felicia, you need to come into the woods with the girls. Mikey's in trouble."

• • •

"IT'S NOT VERY deep," Felicia said, clicking into firefighter mode. She was glad to be distracted from Ryan's presence and not too worried about Mikey, who appeared unharmed.

"Too deep for us to pull him up." Ryan's tone was dry.

"I'm scared," the boy yelled up.

"It's okay, buddy. We're gonna get you out." He turned and drew Felicia off to the side. A soft breeze had picked up and played peek-a-boo with her hair. "Any ideas?"

"Yeah. I'll go get him. The pit is sloped with gravel sides so I can ease down on my butt. Then I'll boost him up on my shoulders. I'm five seven, the kid's about five feet, so you should be able to drag him out."

"What about you?"

"I'll dig holes in the gravel. Let's hope I can climb five feet then you can pull me the rest of the way."

"That sounds precarious, Felicia."

"I've done worse."

"Yeah, so I've seen."

Glancing around to see who was near—nobody—she turned on him. Her face was red and her eyes flaming. "Look, I know how you feel about me. You're going to have to put that aside so we can help this kid."

"No problem. I hardly think about you anymore."

She took the emotional jab square on the chin, swallowed hard and crossed to the shaft.

Ryan shooed the other kids back ten feet in case something went wrong and put the oldest in charge.

Back at the lip of the shaft, he watched Felicia scale down the gravelly side. Her legs were going to get scraped again. Her descent was going well until she lost her footing and tumbled down the last five feet.

Though he could see she was unhurt, his heartbeat escalated. "You okay?"

She looked up at him. "Yeah, my pride's dented and my rear's sore, is all."

Damn it all to hell!

She explained the procedure to Mikey and squatted down. By bracing himself on the side of the pit, the boy was able to get up on her shoulders. Then Felicia slowly stood. Ryan could picture her calf muscles bulging. God, that had to hurt. But she only grunted. Squatting, Ryan was able to grab Mikey's arms and pull the kid out. Just from that small exertion, he was breathing hard and his muscles hurt. What must she be feeling?

After Mikey was safely with the others, Felicia yelled, "I'm ready, unless you need a rest." Was that a challenge?

"Nope." He stretched out on his squatted again as he had on the roof weeks ago and leaned over the edge of the shaft. "Come on up."

She made her way slowly, finding purchase at odd angles. Two feet. After three she slipped and swore.

Four feet. She was at five when he said, "Give me your hands."

She lifted one arm at a time; he grabbed onto her and pulled her to the top of the shaft, got her head and shoulders out. Then he grabbed her waist, and with her help and footing, yanked her all the way out.

Then fell backwards and she landed on top of him. Without thinking, his arms went around her. When he realized what he was doing, he couldn't let go for a second. He locked a hand at her neck while his other arm banded around her waist. God, her curves felt familiar. Good. Wonderful.

Felicia sank into him and buried her face in his neck. And for one moment, he held her close to his heart.

• • •

RYAN WAS MAD at himself because he couldn't let go of Felicia yesterday when he'd pulled her out of the shaft. He'd made a point of staying away from her all morning and at midday he and Brody were down at the lake showing some kids how to fish in the shallow part of the lake. It was blessedly cool with the water lapping at his ankles, and in the shade of a few trees, so he was trying to enjoy the morning.

"Sounds like yesterday was exciting," his brother said casually.

He grunted.

"I heard the guys talking last night. They said you pulled *this broad* out of the pit and you were all over her afterwards."

Now he looked up from the hook he was baiting. "We fell to the ground together. No big deal."

"Still it sucks. Since you hate her so much."

Ryan stalked down the shore leaving Brody with the guys. He didn't want to talk about Felicia, think about or see her. Which was too freaking bad because from this vantage point he caught sight of her on a sailboat with five other counselors preparing for a morning sail. The sun cast her in halos. She shouldn't be working so hard after her ordeal yesterday. The nurse had said to lay low for a day, which she probably thought she was doing. The woman needed somebody to take care of her!

Turning back to his fishing gear, he shook his head. *Don't think about her. Just don't.*

After a few minutes, a shout rent the air. "Felicia, watch out!"

Ryan pivoted in time to see the jib swing around and catch Felicia on the head. She went over the side of the boat.

Dropping the pole, he raced to her. In seconds, all the counselors were in the water—it was shallow—and had Felicia standing, so he stopped about ten feet away.

"Are you okay, sweetheart?" Nick asked. The jerk had been flirting nonstop with her since they got here. Now his hands were way too close to her breasts.

Dripping with water, she pushed her hair off her face, revealing a purple bruise at her temple. "My head and back hurt."

Nick touched her back, neck to waist. Ryan's hands fisted at the thought of this man touching her. Then, an image of another man four weeks ago swam before him.

When she looked up and saw him, she seemed startled. But before he walked away, he saw the bleak expression on her face. Good, let her remember he wasn't going to forget that she'd callously been with someone else!

• • •

TWO DAYS LATER, Felicia's scrapes from the hiking incident had healed, the bruise on her head turned yellow and she could participate in physical activities again. She was looking forward to *doing something* because being sidelined only gave her time to think about Ryan and how he'd held her after the pit rescue. She tried to block his accusing expression when she'd fallen into the lake and Nick had touched her. She *knew* what Ryan was thinking.

From where she stood with a group of kids at the go carts, she caught sight of him heading to the ropes and beams course. His strides were long and purposeful, his head down so that his honey colored hair ruffled in the breeze. Stark pain shot through her so she turned her attention to the track–it was small but contained a few dips and turns appropriate for little kids.

"You go first, Felicia," one girl suggested. Her name was Millie and her mom had been a police officer over in Camden Cove who was killed in a drug bust.

"Sure." She stuffed her legs into the cart, put on the head gear and started down the track. The rumble of the car was low and throaty. It went moderately fast and was kind of cool. In her peripheral vision, she saw something flying toward her; it hit her helmeted head with enough impact to knock her out of the cart and onto the grass. She wasn't hurt though her skull reverberated from the impact. The girls raced to her and surrounded her. "I'm okay," she said taking off the helmet. "Don't worry."

Each of them frowned.

Pushing herself up, she met their gazes. "We're going to ride these. It was the football that knocked me off." At their doubting faces she said, "Go back to the starting point. I'll be right up." She wanted a minute to collect herself. Before she could stand, a shadow came over her. She knew immediately who created it because the wind caught his scent—so Ryan—and wafted it to her.

Kneeling down, he asked, "Are you all right?"

"Yeah. Sure. No harm done."

His eyes were...angry. What the hell? "Jesus, first the shaft, then the sailboat and now this. What are you trying to do, get yourself killed?"

"None of those things were my fault."

Still close to her, he snorted. "You're going to be bruised all over before the week's done."

Okay, she was sick of his shit. Lifting her chin, she spat out, "What do you care anyway if I get hurt? You never talk to me. You look right through me when you pass me by."

Out of nowhere, he grabbed her wrist roughly. "What do you expect me to do after you broke my heart?"

She deflated. What *did* she expect? What did she want? "I don't expect anything. I *want* you to forgive me."

He stood abruptly. "Not a chance, Felicia."

• • •

HE AND THE kids were in the pool and Ryan was having a hard time keeping his eyes off Felicia as she walked around the cement lifeguarding. Occasionally, she'd blow a whistle to keep a kid in line, or she'd stop to talk to one of the little ones. The gold in her hair caught in the sunlight.

Ryan was playing volleyball on a team mixed with other counselors and campers. A ball came right at him and he missed it.

"Heck, Rye, what are you doin'?" This from Zach Malvaso.

"Sorry." He'd been watching a sleek black bathing suit filled with all woman parading before him. "I'm gonna take a break."

"Me, too," Kelly said.

They met at a big plastic tub filled with towels and she threw one at him. "Catch, handsome."

"Thanks."

Drying off, she stretched and her two piece suit rode up a bit, revealing an un-tanned patch of skin around her top.

And it did nothing for him. *She* did nothing for him. Damn it.

"Want a soda?" he asked. "I'm getting one."

"Sure." She sank down on a chaise and tugged at his hand. "Come sit with me after."

He smiled. Maybe he *could* be interested. There was no harm in trying. On his way to the snack bar, someone grabbed his arm and pulled him off the cement over to the chain link fence. It was Felicia, with fire in her eyes. "What are you doing, trying to make me feel even worse?"

He was so incensed, he opened the fence and dragged her out and over to a tree for privacy. He wanted to push her against it, take her mouth and kiss her till he didn't hurt anymore. But instead, he faced her with his whole body, making her back up against it. "I think you got that backwards, sweetheart."

Her eyes welled. Now that threw him. "I haven't been able to eat. To sleep. And now I have to watch you flirt with everybody in a skinny suit."

"Nothing less than you deserve."

"When did you get so cruel, Ryan?"

"When you fucked somebody else after I told you I loved you. That I wanted a commitment."

She stilled and her wet eyes widened. "You didn't tell me you loved me until the morning after."

He grabbed her arm. "Why did you do it to us, Felicia?"

Lifting her chin, she looked like she was facing down dragons. "Because I was scared."

"Of my feelings for you?"

"No, of *my* feelings for you."

He stepped back. "I don't believe you."

"It's true." A few tears fell. "Damn you," she said, broke away from him and fled down the banked lawn. She stopped to say something to another woman, who went inside the fence, presumably to lifeguard and then she disappeared beyond the road.

"Good," he told himself as he approached the soda. Now he didn't have to deal with her.

But all afternoon he was unable to forget the sight of her tears. He'd never seen her cry before.

# CHAPTER 11

ON THE LAST night of camp, a dance was held in the pavilion. People had dolled up and most of the counselors wore sundresses or nice pants and shirts. Ryan was in a foul mood as he approached the gathering place with his brother.

"Sorry you had such a bad week," Brody commented. "We should have tried to switch time frames."

Ryan said, "Yeah, we should have."

"Why didn't we, Rye?"

"What do you mean?"

"Well, you knew Felicia was going to be here and still you didn't ask to be reassigned."

He shrugged a shoulder, but his mind whirled with the question. "We're not supposed to juggle the schedule. It gums up the works."

"Still, we could have tried to find replacements and subbed for them at the station houses. Why didn't we?"

"I don't know why."

"I do."

Ryan stopped, ready to take his frustration out on the nearest target. "Then enlighten me, wise guy."

Brody's eyes flared. "Don't get on me. I'm trying to help even though you're being an asshole."

"I what?"

"You came this week because you wanted to see Felicia. Unconsciously, maybe."

"You make a lousy psychiatrist."

"I don't need to be one to see what's going on. You're miserable, you've *been* miserable for four weeks and you're not getting any better. Plus, you've acted like a shit to her and she's taken it because you've made her feel like a slut."

"She is a slut."

"Jesus Christ. What's wrong with you? Felicia is a good woman who made a mistake, by her own admission, because she was afraid of what you two had together."

"Then answer me this, Freud. If Emma had slept with Mark Adams while you were together, would you be so understanding?"

Brody bristled. "For one thing, you two weren't exclusive when she did this. And second, the answer to your question is, yes, I would have forgiven her, especially knowing what I know now."

He felt himself weakening. "What do you mean?"

"I'd forgive Emma anything if I knew I could have what I have now with her. And I'd be very sorry if I let my pride prevent me from making a life with her."

"It's not pride. I'm hurt, Brody!"

"Yeah, well, welcome to the world of relationships. Get over your hurt. She's the right woman for you and you should be grown up enough to admit it." With that Brody stalked away, up the rest of the hill into the pavilion.

Ryan dropped down on a bench off to the side and stared up at the starry sky. Was Brody right? He'd never even given Felicia a chance after what she did. He went back over the chain of events. Should he have kicked Dennison out that morning and stayed. Instead, he'd told her he loved her then slammed the door in her face.

*I didn't do it after you told me you loved me.*

Well, hell, that didn't matter. She knew how he felt. Didn't she?

• • •

THE MUSIC OF a local rock band filled the pavilion, and people danced on a gym-size wooden floor. Felicia wore a peach sundress and a phony smile and was talking to Nick. He was flirting and she had to tell him to stop. She'd been bruised and battered both physically and emotionally all week, and she couldn't handle any more stress.

So when he asked her to dance and pulled her close, she blurted out, "Nick, don't flirt with me anymore. I'm coming off a bad breakup and I can't handle it."

"Oh, geez, I'm sorry. I like you Felicia, but sure, I'll back off. Let's finish this dance."

She expected to feel awkward but Nick amused her by telling her all the reasons he was a good catch and if she ever got over the other guy, to give him a call. By the end of the song, she was smiling.

And then she saw Ryan, standing stone still by the door, watching them. She hoped he left her alone; she didn't need any more drama. He'd been horrible to her all week and she couldn't take any more of that either. Especially after she begged him to forgive her.

She watched as he turned away, walked over to Kelly and drew her to the dance floor. The woman draped herself over him and he smiled down at her intimately.

A golf ball size of emotion lodged in her throat. This was it! She was giving up. She couldn't take the pain he doled out every time she saw him. Crossing to Megan and Mitch, Felicia asked if she could speak to Megan outside.

• • •

IT WAS THE last Tuck-In of the camp and Ryan knew Felicia's girls were the visitors tonight. For the last two hours, after Brody reamed him out, he'd been thinking about what he'd done and what he wanted for his life. And as hard as it was to swallow, he'd decided losing Felicia wasn't going to cut it. He wasn't sure if they could make a go of it, but he was going to have a long—and kind—talk with her.

They were lined up and waiting for the girls to come in and already he felt lighter. Happier. More expectant. The kids trundled through the door led by Jenn. Felicia must be last. Good, he'd grab her and take her out of the cabin right now. Talk to her tonight.

But when the line filed down, he saw Megan taking up the rear. When she got to him, hugged him, he said, "Where's Felicia?"

"She's sick. She left camp about two hours ago."

• • •

ONCE AGAIN, FELICIA did something totally unprofessional. But she had to get her act together. So she told Mitch and Megan she was ill, left camp and got out of Dodge. On Sunday, she called in sick for her next tour, and on a whim, she'd flown out to Colorado and surprised her brother, Garth, with a visit. He'd been overwhelmed, and off duty for a week, so they were able to get reacquainted. They'd talked on his beautiful deck with its panoramic view of the mountains, drank wine and walked the streets of his artsy town. She'd had a good time here, and it made her feel as if she wasn't so alone in the world. Sad, but not so despondent, she was in his spare bedroom packing, ready to face the world again, when she heard a skirmish out in the living area of her brother's home.

Male voices. Loud.

Making her way out of the room and down to the foyer, she found Ryan and Garth in each other's faces. Ryan's was flushed, but it was Garth who had his hands fisted in Ryan's navy shirt. "I'm not letting you anywhere near my sister after what you've done to her. She came to me broken emotionally and battered physically. And now *you*, the cause of all this, want to see her? Well, you'll have to go through me to get to her."

Uh-oh. She'd shared with Garth what had happened in her life the last few years. He said he'd been shy of relationships, too, because smoke jumpers typically feared getting close to someone. But he'd found love in a cute little nurse and Felicia would, too.

"I wouldn't exactly say I was the cause of her battered appearance. She had a series of misfortunate events at–"

Garth backed him up to the door. "Don't give me shit, O'Malley. I won't let you hurt her again."

Instead of fuming or responding physically, Ryan sank against the door and said simply, "I won't. I promise."

Felicia came fully into the foyer. "Garth, it's okay. I'll talk to him. I'm stronger now."

It took a while but she got her brother to back off and led Ryan out to the wide expanse of deck. The sun was shining down on the landscape, but Felicia couldn't appreciate the stunning view. Turning, she faced Ryan.

Man, he didn't look good. Oh, sure, he had the O'Malley male presence still, but his eyes were bloodshot and his posture slumped. "Why are you here?" she asked.

He drew in a deep breath. "I've been a shit. I treated you badly and I shouldn't have, no matter what you did."

"Water under the bridge, Ryan."

"In any case, I'm sorry." He moved in closer.

She held out her hand to stop him. "No, don't. I'm better now, and I think I can get over you, but I don't want to test it right now."

"I don't want you to."

"Well, good. You can leave."

"No, I meant I don't want you to get over me."

Her heart twisted in her chest. "Now that's just plain mean."

"I want you to love me and try to work things out with me."

"What?" Her eyes welled. "No, no, Ryan. We're done. We both have to face it. I have."

This time he stepped closer and didn't stop. He took her mouth and kissed her, a long devouring kiss that she fully participated in. Which was why Ryan was shocked when he drew back to find Felicia crying again.

"Oh, baby, don't cry. We need to give ourselves another shot at this relationship. I care too much to let you go without a fight."

"B-but what…" Hiccups "What if it doesn't work?"

He shrugged a shoulder. "I can't guarantee it will, but I think it's worth the risk. Please, forgive me for being stubborn and cruel. Please, consider giving us a second chance."

For a moment, she simply stood there and watched him. He thought he might be too late, that he might have hurt her too much. Then she threw herself into his arms. "All right, I'll do it. I'll take the risk that we can work this out."

He kissed her again, this time allowing the passion he'd kept at bay for weeks to surface. Finally, he dragged his mouth back. "Damn it, why are we hundreds of miles from our beds?"

"Speaking of which, how did you find me?"

"No one knew where you were. So I went onto the police website and tracked your cell phone."

"Uh-oh, Will Rossettie said not to use those sites for anything that wasn't police business."

He chuckled and cupped her cheeks. "It was a matter of survival of one of his sergeants. I'm sure Will would understand."

Her face bloomed like flowers in the sun. "Do you really mean that?"

"I do." And right there on the spot, Ryan knew he was a changed man and he would try his hardest not to do anything to make her go away again.

What he didn't know was Felicia was promising herself the same thing!

• • •

# EL BOMBERO

Novella number four in the
AMERICA'S BRAVEST SERIES

**KATHRYN SHAY**

# PROLOGUE

"I NOW PRONOUNCE you husband and wife." The Catholic priest said the words with a frown on his face. The scent of incense lingered in the church, and candles flickered, but neither soothed fifteen-year-old Tony Ramirez, who'd never been so scared in his life. But he'd be damned if he'd let his new bride know. It was bad enough that her mother was crying in the back of the church. At lease Louisa Cruz had come to the wedding. His own family hadn't, though his mom had signed the consent form, needed because of his age.

Sophia gave him a watery smile. Her thick black hair curled below her waist, her black eyes were somber and he thought she'd never looked more beautiful than in the simple white dress. She was ecstatic to be marrying him but not at having a baby so soon. Before this mess had happened, she was planning to go to nursing school after she graduated — she was really smart. Tony swore he'd get her there, like he promised himself he'd get into the firefighter program offered at the high school next year. Their marriage and a baby coming weren't going to ruin their lives!

He leaned over and kissed her. Then he whispered, "I love you, Sophia. Nothing means more to me than you, and we're gonna have a great life."

Now her smile was more genuine, and her eyes sparkled. "I love you, too, Tony. And I'll do anything to make you happy."

As they clasped hands, Tony knew they both intended to keep those private vows.

# CHAPTER 1

*Nineteen years later*

BREATHLESS, TONY ROLLED away from his wife Sophia and stared up at the ceiling in their big bedroom, watching the fan whir, hearing the crickets chirp in the September night.

Sophia eased up from the bed and draped herself over him. She was so beautiful, sometimes it hurt to look at her. "For a man who just got laid—twice—you don't seem very happy."

He grunted but ran his hand down those still-long, thick, black locks that felt like silk.

"Antonio, talk to me."

Because that was part of the problem, he tried. "I'm bummed about not sleeping in this bed anymore."

Her features tensed. "We agreed it would be best if you moved out."

*No,* he thought, angrily, she *demanded he leave the home he loved.* He guessed he should consider himself lucky to still be making love with her. But physical contact wasn't enough. He wanted his family back. Instead of telling her, he said, "It tears me up, *querida.*"

She mumbled something in Spanish, which he couldn't make out, slid off him and stood. Not bothering with clothes—why would she, her body was perfect—she crossed to the dresser and pulled out... *Dios Mio*, what the hell? "Why did you start that? We haven't smoked since our twenties." They were now both thirty-four.

"I don't know." She lit up and the acrid smell of tobacco filled the spaced around him. As a firefighter, he was used to the stink of it but not in his own bedroom.

"You don't do this when the kids are home, right?"

She whirled on him, her hair swinging around her like a cloak. "Of course I don't. And never in the bedroom. You've upset me."

*He'd* upset *her*. Oh, that was rich. "I'm sorry, I didn't mean to. But when we're together like this, I want everything back."

"So do I, *hombre*."

He pulled himself up to a sitting position and leaned against the headboard. "Then let me move back in. We'll work all this out from here." God, he hated that he had to beg.

"Not until you decide."

Bolting off the bed, he crossed to her and grasped her shoulders gently, always gently, no matter how angry he was. "You make me crazy, Sophia. How can I pick you or the fire department? Both are my life."

Her face crumpled and tears sprang to her eyes. "I know I'm not being fair. I can't live with the danger anymore. First there was 9/11..." the anniversary of the day had recently passed "...then Sinco four years ago..." where four Hidden Cove firefighters died "...and then a woman with two kids the same age as ours died six months ago in Camden Cove." Because Tony had known her, they'd gone to the funeral and Sophia had cried the whole time. "Fuck it, Tony, now there's an arsonist on the loose."

Damn the torch who was targeting the fire department! He'd lit two more incendiary blazes, sending Sophia into a tailspin. And this month, a veteran firefighter, Ed Snyder from Engine 4, had been trapped and suffered from smoke inhalation and first degree burns that kept him off the line. He was forced to help out at the Fire Academy. But to Tony, the worst involved Sydney, his closest friend in the department, who had gotten a shoulder injury in one of the blazes that was purposely set.

No doubt about it, there was more danger these days in the profession than when he started at eighteen.

But it was a profession he loved almost as much as the woman before him.

"I know the arson thing is a problem." He kissed her shoulder, then nodded to the cigarettes. "Give me one of those."

They put on robes and went outside to a patio right off their bedroom. He and his group at Firehouse 7 had built this area and a couple of decks that sprawled off the home he and Sophia had bought ten years ago when Miguel came along.

For some reason, he thought about another baby who had never been born. Sophia had experienced a lot of loss in her thirty-four years, but none had been as devastating as the stillbirth of their first child. Though they'd had two more, the tragedy scarred her.

Among other things.

They sat at a teak table he'd refinished right before he left the house and smoked in silence. The cigarette tasted like shit but it calmed him. She butted hers out. "Look, can we keep trying? You only moved out two weeks ago."

Into Brody O'Malley's side of the duplex he'd shared with his brother Ryan. Brody had been living with the love of his life, Emma, for a while now. "I know it hasn't been very long. So *I'll* keep trying to figure things out. What about you?"

"Me?"

"Have you given any thought to seeing a counselor?"

She shook her head. "I don't need counseling, Tony. I need to come home from work and know you're safe. I need you to not miss birthdays and anniversaries. I need you to talk to me like you talk to Sydney. Or the guys."

This was new. "Where the hell did that all come from?"

"I've been writing in a journal. The other things sort of came out."

"*Jesús*, I never knew you resented my crew. The team thinks you're the best wife a firefighter could have."

"I've been playacting at that. At a lot of things."

*Well,* he thought, *join the club.* He'd been pretending all his life, first with his mother, then Sophia and the kids, even at work. Nobody, not even this woman, who he'd loved since he was fourteen, knew the real Antonio Ramirez.

He wasn't even sure who that guy was anymore.

• • •

"I MISS DADDY." Marianna, their eight-year-old daughter, got teary as she pushed away the oatmeal Sophia had made for breakfast. Petite with pretty waist-length hair, sometimes she cried at night for her father.

"I know, *niña*. I do, too."

Miguel scowled like his dad. He was the spitting image of Tony — dark hair clipped short, black eyes, beautiful olive skin. And he was almost taller than her. "Then why isn't he living at home? I heard him here last night."

From the counter, Sophia finished packing lunches. "We told you both, sometimes adults have to spend time apart to figure things out."

"What are you figuring out?" Miguel persisted.

"It's personal stuff, baby."

He looked like he was going to argue more, so she said, "Hurry up, now. The bus is coming soon."

After she bade them good-bye at the curb, she slid into her little red Civic and headed toward Hidden Cove Hospital. She longed for a cigarette but had promised herself she'd only smoke when she was home alone and stressed. Or lonely. Damn, what a mess things were. She and Tony had spent so long, worked so hard, building a good life together, and now she was blowing it. For what?

*They're called panic attacks, Sophia,* a colleague at the hospital had said to her. *My guess is something in your life isn't being dealt with.*

Of course it was the fear, the deep wrenching fear of losing Tony. Sometimes, though, with the separation, she felt like he was slipping away from her anyway.

Glad to have arrived at the hospital, which treated patients from all the surrounding areas, she parked, hurried inside, stored her lunch and went to the big, white board in the surgery wing where the schedule was posted. Though most people hated the atmosphere of hospitals, the PA crackling, the phones ringing incessantly and the smell of ammonia, it all brought Sophia peace because she'd wanted to work in medicine all her life. As a pediatric surgical nurse, she was scheduled for two surgeries today. A few post ops. A lot of charts.

Noting the surgeon whose staff she was assigned to, she was glad to be working with Brock Carrington. He was a stellar cardiologist, well liked, happily married. Maybe. Who knew? Everyone thought she and Tony had iconic wedded bliss.

She was in the scrub room soaping her hands — the scent of harsh soap and antiseptic stung her nostrils — when Brock came in. "Sophia. You're looking lovely today."

"Considering I have a paisley cap on my head, that's hard to believe."

His blue eyes twinkled. "Entitled to my own opinion."

"Does Susan know you're such a flirt?"

"How do you think I got her?"

They chuckled, then turned serious. He began to scrub as he talked. "This case is a tough one."

"Open heart surgery always is."

"The child's only three."

"Ah." She stared down at her nails, which she was cleaning with a stiff brush. "Young."

"You ever going to have another?" he asked. His wife gave birth two months ago to her third girl.

"No, we're all set."

"I always wanted three."

*I would have had three,* she thought, banishing the notion as soon as it came. She hated thinking about the loss of so long ago, which could be accessed by the most trivial thing.

Five hours later, when they left the OR, she was dripping wet under her gown and scrubs and her knees were weak. She didn't know which she wanted first, food or a shower.

"Nice job, doctor."

"The kid's going to be fine." He gave her a long look. "Have lunch with me? After we shower?"

She startled.

He grinned. "No invitation intended. I meant separately."

"Of course you did. And I brought my lunch."

"Bring it along. Meet you in the cafeteria in twenty." With that he walked down the hall.

She was staring at his retreating back when Isabel, her sister, came up to her. "He's a lot of gorgeous man, isn't he?"

Sophia turned. "Is he?"

"You don't even notice because you have your own gorgeous one at home. I wish I did."

Isabel was divorced and having a hard time with being a single woman again. Sophia was glad she lived in town as their two brothers had shocked everybody and had gone to work in Puerto Rico.

"Tell you what, Izzy. Why don't you go pick your kids up at Mama's when you get off and we'll have dinner at my place."

"Tony's not home?"

"Um, no, he's on nights."

After Isabel left, Sophia let out a heavy breath. She hadn't told anyone but her mother, not even Izzy, who she was close to, about hers and Tony's separation. Because she hoped it wasn't permanent. She hoped it ended soon. She hoped Tony would either quit the fire department or transfer to the Academy. Somewhere he was safe.

With that unfortunately dim hope, Sophia headed to the showers.

• • •

TONY WAS IN a lousy mood today, anyway, but when they got the call for a fire in an elementary school, his state of mind got even worse. Little kids freaked out at fire and often did something stupid.

When the rig arrived at the scene, the students were still exiting the building. Quint and Midi 7, the other two trucks in his firehouse, pulled in behind them. Engine 6 was also on site. Gabe hopped off the truck, said, "Ramirez come with me," and headed to Incident Command. Chief Erikson had already set up a computer on his truck.

Erikson looked up worriedly. "Gabe, your team's going to do search and rescue as soon as we get water on the blaze. Right now it's confined to the back of the building, where the cafeteria is. The kitchen's a concern, so we need to be careful."

"Are all the kids out?" Tony asked.

"We're getting a head count now. Classroom teachers are responsible for keeping track of their students."

Just then a worried looking woman strode toward them. Her hair was wild and she had smudges on her face. "I'm Sara Jensen, the principal. One child's missing. A first grader. Her teacher didn't see where she went."

"What's her name?" Tony asked.

"Carrie."

The chief checked the progress of laying hose and slapping water on the fire. "As soon as Engine 6 gets their water on the front, go in with your guys, Malvaso."

Tony and Gabe hurried to the rescue rig. "Don full gear," Gabe told all of them. "We can head inside in a few minutes. One kid, a little girl named Carrie, is missing."

Amidst the cacophony of sounds at the fire ground — the pump of the water, the shout of orders, the running rigs — they tightened their turnout coats, put on their Nomex hoods and situated their air masks. They were inside the building in minutes.

"Ramirez, you and Sands take the left wing," Gabe ordered. "White, go with O'Malley to the right. I'll wait for the other crew to get inside and go back with the men."

Smoke had reached the front of the building; it was black and noxious, which was worse than gray or white. The color meant whatever was burning was bad. At the entrance to the left wing, Tony said to Sands, "We'll each search a room that's across from the other so we'll be in proximity." Contrary to what was portrayed on TV shows, firefighters worked in pairs. He was usually with Sands, who had good skills even though she was only twenty-four. They'd both come out of a city high school program that trained students to enter the fire academy right after graduation.

Tony entered room one, Sands went into two. Thankfully, the teachers had followed procedure and shut the windows, unlocked the doors and closed them. He searched under the teacher's desk, in closets, then left the room, meeting Sands in the hall. "Nothing?"

"No. Geez, she's only five." Her voice was tinny through her face mask but he could hear her concerns. Briefly, he squeezed her arm.

They checked four more rooms, all the while calling out Carrie's name. And, all the while, the smoke was thickening. One room was left, so he told Sands to go inside. As he stood in the hall, Tony's neck itched. He had a hunch, which made him go to the very end of the corridor where he found, off to the right, a small cubby hole with a drinking fountain. Beneath it, he could barely make out the silhouette of a little girl.

Closing the short distance between them, Tony knelt and touched her arm. She was whimpering and shaking.

"Shh, sweetheart I'm a firefighter and I'm going to get you out."

She uncurled herself and hurtled her small body into his arms, getting him into a stranglehold. Standing, he held her in one arm and took off his mask. The air smelled vile. "Don't be afraid. I'm going to give you air," he said, inserting the mask in between her body and his. "It's like a Halloween mask that you breathe from."

"Don't want to."

"You have to, *carina*."

Sands came out of the room. "You got her!"

"Alert the others. My hands are full."

He started out, gently forcing the air hose into the girl's mouth. Once he got her to breathe, she relaxed her hold on him. They strode fast down the hall and Tony started coughing.

"It's getting worse instead of better," Sands said, as they reached the front entrance.

Tony choked when he tried to say something. But soon he was at the door and finally outside. O'Malley dashed over to him. He took the kid and Tony dropped to his knees on the blacktop. Vaguely, he registered TV crews on site. Someone handed him oxygen and he sucked it in. His lungs burned like a thousand tiny pinpricks. A person knelt next to him. He felt a hand on his shoulder and managed to look over.

Lieutenant Felicia White smiled. "Great job, Tony."

"Thanks, Licia." He coughed. "We weren't inside very long, but the kid…"

"I know. We all felt the terror."

Again, he choked up phlegm and spat onto the blacktop, then heard her say, "Uh-oh."

He glanced up. Through watery eyes he saw the press descend on them. "Head them off, will you Licia? I don't want to talk to them. I don't want anyone to know what I did."

"Too late for that, *bombero*. They filmed everything. You're the hero of the day. It'll be all over television in a matter of minutes."

Shit, he'd never have enough time to get in touch with Sophia before the rescue hit the news. About the last thing they needed as a couple was for her to watch him running in and out of a burning building.

Tony didn't feel much like a hero. Instead, he felt like a failure as a husband.

# CHAPTER 2

"HEY, SOPH, TERRIFIC TV coverage."

"Sophia, great guy you got there."

"Go, Tony!"

As she walked toward the nurse's station, Sophia acknowledged the comments, but the people who said them were rushing by so she couldn't ask what they were referring to. It was about her husband, for sure. And immediately, she felt her stomach coil. *Oh, no, here it comes again.* She told herself he was okay, because of the tone of people's remarks, but the cramps continued until she got to the doctor's lounge and ducked inside.

Brock greeted her. "Have you seen the TV?" he asked easily.

"No. I don't even know what happened."

"Another daring save by your hero husband."

Her throat got tight.

"Come on over, they're showing it again."

He sipped his coffee as she joined him in front of a television; they both stared at the screen.

A clean-cut, good-looking guy read from a prompter as he faced the camera. "With some recent criticism in the news of the local fire departments about their hours, free time and salary, one firefighter earned his pay today when Martin Luther King Elementary School caught fire in the kitchen."

A picture of the structure came on screen. "The building was enveloped in smoke when America's Bravest rolled onto the scene to save the day."

A close-up came on of Tony's rescue rig as he jumped off along with the others. For a moment, Sophia appreciated his muscular six-foot frame, that confident stride that sucked her in when she was in junior high—and still did.

The camera cut back to the school and showed him hurrying in with his crew. Well, that wasn't too bad. This was something he did every day. Still her pulse sped up. Especially when the camera panned to the inside of the building, filled with smoke thick enough to obscure the rooms and people in them. Suddenly, Tony came on screen at the front door carrying out, oh *Dios*, a child about Marianna's age. The little girl head-locked Tony while he held his air hose on her mouth.

Another shot of him on his knees. Coughing, choking, unable to stand. She felt her own knees turn to gel.

"Sophia?" Brock grasped her arm and brought her to the couch. He eased her down. Got her a glass of water.

"I can't or I'll throw up."

"What on earth... Jesus, put your head between your knees."

She bent over. Her pulse calmed and she could breathe again. When she felt well enough, she sat up.

"Soph, what happened?" When she looked at him, his features were taut and his eyes held concern.

"I've... God, I hate this. I've been having reactions to Tony's job lately."

"What? For how long?"

"A year, maybe. It's worse around 9/11 and other anniversaries."

"Are you getting treatment?"

She frowned. "What do you mean?"

"Psychological help in dealing with these episodes."

"I don't need help," she blurted out. "*He* needs to quit his job."

Brock's brows arched. "I had no idea."

Before she responded, Sophia breathed in deeply, then out again. "I've kept it from everyone. But I can't do it anymore, Brock. He's been a firefighter for fifteen years and it's always been tough for me."

Squeezing her arm, he picked up the water. "Here, drink this now. I think you can handle something in your stomach."

The water soothed her parched throat. "Thanks. I—"

The cell phone in her pocket rang. "Sorry I have to get this. It's my personal line." She checked the ID then clicked on. "Mama, what's wrong?"

Louisa's unsettled voice came across the lines. "It's Mari. She saw the TV when she got home from school. She's crying"—now Sophia could hear her little girl in the background—"and wants her father."

"I'll be right there."

"Should I call him?"

"No, his shift doesn't end till five. I'll take care of this." She stood and pocketed the phone.

"The kids?"

"Marianna. She's upset because she saw the damned news on television. I've got to get someone to cover the last hour of my shift."

"Go. I'll find another nurse for you."

Doctors never made that kind of offer. "Really? Thanks so much."

"We'll talk more later."

"Okay."

Sophia hurried out of the lounge to get her stuff, thoughts of Brock's kindness, Tony's *heroism* fleeing from her mind.

She had to get to her daughter because she knew exactly how Mari felt.

• • •

CELEBRATION TEMPORARILY REPLACED anxiety and it felt good. Tony was sick of worrying about his wife, so he turned his attentions to his crew. They'd cleaned up, and everybody's face was bright with victory.

"Hero of the day, *bombero*," Gabe said, toasting Tony with his coffee mug.

"*De nada.*" But it *was* something. It was the greatest feeling in the world and about the only time he felt...capable. Like he was enough.

Felicia smiled. Because she lived in the O'Malley duplex, she and Brody were the only ones so far who knew he was living apart from his family. "It *is* a big deal, Tony. And I'm gonna exploit your success."

"With Parker Allen?" Brody asked. His face was alight with confidence. A save made everybody feel like Supermen—and women.

"Uh-huh." Felicia was practically dancing around the table. "I'm gonna write one hell of a blog on this, complete with you puking your guts out afterward."

"Up to no good again?" The voice came from behind and Tony looked over to see Ryan O'Malley, Brody's twin and Felicia's guy.

Without reserve, Ryan approached Felicia and kissed her cheek. She eased away from him. "Not here," she hissed.

"Oh, yeah, I forgot. Sorry." His eyes shone with mischief and negated his apology. He stood close to her, too. "Hey bro," he said to Brody. Then he crossed to Tony, clapped him on the back and smiled. "Great job, Ramirez. Amazing, really."

"Tony?"

Ryan stepped to the side and Tony saw his wife, still in her scrubs, in the doorway of the kitchen. Holding Marianna's hand. His daughter's tear-stained face and frown alarmed him.

"Soph? What...?"

Marianna broke away from her mother and dashed toward him. He stood in time to catch her. He swooped her up and she got a stranglehold on his neck, not unlike the little girl he'd saved; her legs clamped around him.

"*Carina*, what's wrong?"

She buried her face in his shoulder. And started to quietly cry. His heart beating at a clip, he looked to his wife.

"I'm sorry to bring her here," Sophia said wearily to him, then scanned the guys. "But she wouldn't calm down and I didn't know what else to do. She saw the TV segment of your rescue."

"*Dios mio.*"

As he murmured to his daughter, Tony saw Gabe cross to Sophia and slip his arm around her shoulders. "No problem, Soph. I hope you feel free to come here anytime. And if there's an emergency at home, we can get immediate coverage for Tony in the event of a call. Any officer can sub in a pinch."

His wife seemed embarrassed. Her dark complexion reddened. "I know." She shrugged. Tony couldn't tell if she was trying to control her own fear and anger, or if she meant what she said.

One by one, the group started to wander off to give his family privacy. Sydney stopped to squeeze Sophia's arm while Tony sat down and settled Mari on his lap. "Can you let go of my neck, sweetheart?"

His little one nodded, then gradually eased her arms from around him. She looked up at him and her tearful expression almost broke his heart.

Fuck, maybe he *should* quit this job. Maybe being on the line *wasn't* worth causing his daughter this kind of trauma.

• • •

"THANKS FOR COMING, Mr. and Mrs. Ramirez." Miguel's teacher, Anna Pearl, smiled from across the table from where Sophia and Tony sat. Sophia glanced around the room at the brightly colored bulletin boards sporting student work, maps and pictures on the wall. She didn't feel good about being here, though. They should have been home with Mari, but this visit couldn't be helped. Tony had kept their daughter with him until his shift was over, taken her home, eaten chicken in paprika sauce, one of Tony's favorites, which Louisa had prepared, and by the time they left, their little girl was excited to be watching an old copy of *Finding Nemo* with her grandmother. Miguel had been in his room.

"Of course, we'd come," Tony said, always polite, always respectful to teachers. Even though his job was tough, he believed teaching was one of the most important professions in society. "You said you wanted to talk about Miguel."

"Yes. His grades are slipping."

"Miguel's grades?" Tony's shock was evident. "He's a straight-A student. And he loves school."

Mrs. Pearl frowned. She was one of the good, new teachers who was devoted to the job and had implemented a lot of creative techniques into her instruction that Sophia appreciated. "That's why I'm concerned. Something's bothering him. He's not causing trouble, but he's aloof. He doesn't play at recess—he loses himself in a book instead—and his mind seems somewhere else. I don't mean to pry, but usually when things turn around for a good kid like Miguel, something's going on at home. Is that the case?"

Sophia gripped Tony's hand.

Tony squeezed her fingers, guessing she'd feel guilty for causing Miguel's issues. She was the one who insisted on the separation. "His mother and I are having some difficulties. I've moved out for a while."

"Ah, I see. And I'm surprised. Miguel has painted his family as indestructible. But that's none of my business. I assume he's talking about this."

"Not much to us. We've tried to get him to open up." Sophia's voice was tinny even to her own ears.

"Maybe he should see a counselor."

Sophia stiffened. She was against outsiders' invasion of their privacy. Besides, there were other reasons she wouldn't get professional help, no matter how trusted or kind the counselor seemed to be. "We don't believe in that kind of thing."

Her husband didn't agree, she knew, but went along because he was aware of what had happened to her as a child. So she was shocked when he said, "*Querida*, maybe we should consider it for the boy. This is so not him."

"We have a wonderful psychologist here at school. Bonnie Campbell. She loves kids and works well with them."

"How old is she?" Sophia asked.

The teacher's brow furrowed. "I'm not sure. But she's got grandbabies. Mostly, though, she's good with students. She does workshops in our classes about difficult topics, and Miguel seems to like her."

"I read the note she sent home when she gave a presentation on the meaning of terrorism because the kids kept hearing the term on TV," Tony said. "It seems like a good program." He faced his wife. "What do you think?"

"Can we have some time to discuss this?"

Mrs. Pearl tried to hide her surprise. "Of course. But I wouldn't wait too long. Miguel's floundering."

"We'll let you know soon." Tony stood along with Sophia. "Thank you for caring about my son."

"And his family. I hope you two work this out. In the few times we've met, you four have always seemed so close."

They left the school holding hands. Sophia marveled at how connected she and Tony could be amidst this mess, and the teacher had picked up on it. As they approached the parking lot, the night air was cool and darkness had settled around them. Stars dotted the sky, but Sophia couldn't take pleasure in them.

"Want to go home?" he asked. "Or we could get a drink and talk."

"Not home. Mama's staying all night because I have an early surgery. Let's go for a drive. Park a while and talk."

They drove to Hale's Haven, closed now for the fall and winter. Like most firefighters and cops, Tony loved the camp for the kids of slain firefighters and police officers, and he and Sophia volunteered here when their kids went to summer camps of their own. They parked the car down by the water and Tony turned the motor off.

Silence. Then she heard him sigh next to her. So she said, "I know he needs help."

"So do you, Soph."

That pissed her off. She felt her blood pressure rise, and the rhythm of her heart pick up. "This isn't only my problem, Antonio."

"I know. Let's talk about Miguel." He turned to her in the dimness of the car and grasped on to a lock of her hair. It was long and straight but curled on the ends, the way he always liked it.

"I want what's best for him, Tony. But a *school* counselor…"

"Baby, what happened to you was criminal. I know. I was there to pick up the pieces."

Though she tried not to think about the awful incident, Tony had resurrected the memory. She envisioned herself finding out she was pregnant, telling Tony and their parents, then being sent to see her beloved school counselor in order to get into the program for mothers and their babies. The man had assaulted her and she'd gone to Tony with the story.

"This woman comes highly recommended," Tony continued. "And we can take precautions. Ask Miguel questions about her behavior in the sessions without telling him why."

"I guess." His calm assurance, his reasoning, his gentle concern for her brought on an overwhelming sense of loss. She couldn't remember a time when they weren't together — or foresee one when they weren't.

"What's wrong?"

She leaned over and buried her face in his shirt. "I'm so sorry about all this. I wish I was stronger. I practically fell apart when I saw you on TV. And in front of Brock."

"Who's Brock?"

"Dr. Carrington. He was in the lounge where there's a TV, and he was watching the news when I went inside."

"And what did Brock do to comfort you, Sophia?"

Damn it. In some ways Tony was typical Puerto Rican male, with the possessiveness and jealousy of one. "Nothing, *hombre*. You know how much I love you. *Tenecisito*."

His anger abated at her profession. "I need you, too. And I miss you."

Swamped by sadness, Sophia felt physical need well up inside her. She raised her mouth and pressed her lips against his. He responded by tugging her closer. The kiss was tender at first, comforting. Then desire took over and the contact turned hot. His hands roamed her back, covered her breasts; his mouth traveled to her neck. He mumbled words of love, as did she, but she was filling up with fire and was about to explode. Images of him in danger today conflated with images of a young boy defending her honor, standing by her, marrying her at fifteen.

And when she lost the baby who caused the hasty marriage... No she wouldn't think about that. Instead, she let her feelings take over. "Put your seat down," she demanded hoarsely. When he did, she came up on her knees, lifted herself over the gear shift and straddled him. She was barely aware of ripping at his belt, raising herself so his big hand could slide beneath her skirt. He ripped off her panties, then he freed his penis.

In an instant, she impaled herself on him.

"Slow down, *mi amore*," he said against her mouth.

"No, no slowing down. Hurry. I… *Dios Mio*."

Soon oblivion overtook her.

Afterward, after she'd come and he'd practically exploded inside her, she lay limp against his chest. They were almost prone and she could feel his heart beat a wild tattoo. His hand brushed down her hair. The scents of their lovemaking filled the confines of the car.

Neither spoke for a long time. Finally, he said, "We always do this to make things better. I'm not sure it's helping our situation."

"I don't care," she mumbled against his sweaty skin. "I don't care. I need you. I need to be connected to you. Please, don't take this away from us, too."

"I won't."

"Promise?"

"I promise."

# CHAPTER 3

BATTALION CHIEF IAN Woodward stood in front of the class of seasoned firefighters and smiled sardonically. "Welcome to the Academy. I know you're all dying to be here for training."

As usual, Mitch Malvaso took the lead. "We are, Chief. Right, ladies and gentlemen?"

All forty-five seasoned firefighters cheered. Their enthusiasm was a sham—basically the group hated classroom days—but they also revered Ian, who'd been a victim of the 9/11 terrorist attacks and was now in a wheelchair. He'd told them teaching antiterrorism techniques made him feel like he was paying the enemy back. Most of the multi-house guys here today were willing students because of him.

Sitting next to Tony, Sydney yawned. She looked tired today. He wrote on a paper, "You okay?" then slid it to her.

She scribbled back, "Daisy's having nightmares. I slept in her bed."

He grinned, remembering those days. Longing for them in some ways, he mused, thinking of Miguel. That problem was yet to be solved.

Ian began again. "So this class covers bomb threats from terrorists and techniques to handle them. How many of you have had training on bomb search and rescue and diffusion?"

Gabe had done a few things in their house, so his group raised their hands. Ian asked Gabe to explain.

After Gabe's summary, a big, beefy man with a permanent scowl on his face raised his hand and began to speak. "No offense, Chief, but we got the Hazmat Team housed at Engine 4 for things like this. Why do we all need training?"

He heard someone mumble under her breath, "Asshole."

From three seats down, Casey Malvaso had made the comment. Her husband Zach gave her a small smile. It was common knowledge that the complainer, Ed Snyder, had transferred out of Firehouse 7 when Casey came on board because he hated working with women. He'd been called on the carpet a couple of times for his misogynist attitude.

With the expertise of a diplomat, Ian said easily, "Ed, calls come in all the time and we have no idea Hazmat's needed. Your group will go and you won't know what you're walking into. Everybody needs training in what to do until specialty teams get there—and afterward."

Snyder grunted but shut up.

And Tony realized that this training meant another responsibility for firefighters that would be another thing for Sophia to worry about. Pushing thoughts of his wife from his mind, he watched as Ian called up a chart on the screen in a Power Point presentation, then rolled aside to give them a clear view. "This is in your packet, too, so no need to take notes."

The chart consisted of introductory material in two columns. He began to read.

"'The definition of a terrorist attack is defined by the FBI as an unlawful act of force or violence against a person or property with the intent to coerce or intimidate a government or people for political and social purposes.'" Ian sighed. "In the past, the objective was to bring attention to a political or social cause. Today, the objective is to kill."

Gasps from a few people who probably hadn't trained with Ian before and weren't used to his candid language. "I know that's stark, but it's reality. And they'd just as soon kill America's Bravest because we're highly visible due to our activity at Ground Zero."

Dead silence.

"Aw, shit, don't go all quiet on me when I mention 9/11. I'm in this thing" — he pounded the arm of the wheelchair — "because of them, but I'm helping to stop them, too. I don't have a thin skin about it" — here he gave a big smile — "though I used to."

Next, he defined the difference between IED's — improvised explosive devices — and bombs. "Basically, an IED is more homemade and could be stuffed into a bag, pipe, bottle, can, backpack, package, or fifty-five gallon drum. They're easy to make and you're more likely to encounter *them*."

"So, how do we protect ourselves?" a woman Tony didn't know asked.

"I've got the information here." Ian put up another slide.

Tony slipped his copy out of the folder in front of him so he could read along and take notes. He followed as Ian read the list aloud.

1. *When the truck arrives, park it in a safe location and stay there until you get instruction from Incident Command. The rig should be upwind and shielded if possible.*

2. *Turn off cells and radios — as these can trigger explosive devices.*

3. *Don't listen to politicians, even the mayor or building owners, who tell you to go in the building, approach a vehicle etc., until the fire officer gives orders.*

*4. Know it could be a dirty bomb. Stay upwind of the device in case it explodes, wear protective defensive gear used by Hazmat, don't expose yourself for too long to the contamination if it explodes and, if it does, get far away if you can.*

*5. If there are no lives in danger, let the fire burn. Water or foam can spread the contamination faster than letting it burn itself out.*

Ian rolled in front of the screen again. "I imagine you have a lot of points to make."

A lively discussion ensued.

"My wife will flip if she hears about us dealing with this kind of thing."

"Honestly, Chief, don't you think this is above and beyond the call of duty?"

"I know I didn't sign up for this."

A few more comments resonated. Ian let them go and then made a few remarks. "I agree with all of you about the continual extension of a firefighter's duty. But it is what it is. You're gonna have to live with it. Like a lot of things."

Grumbles this time.

"What else?" Ian asked.

"Will protective equipment be standard on all trucks?" This from Grady O'Connor, who was smart and thoughtful.

"I'll let Battalion Chief Erikson answer. What's going on in that area, Cal?"

From a seat in the corner, Erikson shook his head. "We've petitioned to get the suits on all trucks. But you know what's going on in the state budgets these days. *Cutback* is our new mantra. I wouldn't plan on them anytime soon."

"Especially with Allen on our backs." This from Felicia. "Parker the Piranha would have a field day if we spent money on suits we didn't use often."

Very unflattering remarks about the news reporter who'd made their lives hell were made all around. Tony didn't like what Allen was doing to them, but he hated the way everybody dissed her in public.

The session wound down at lunchtime when Ian closed the morning. Sydney leaned over and said, "I brought a picnic. Want to go outside with me and eat?"

Training days were usually opportunities for smoke eaters from different houses to mingle. They rarely ate with their own groups. But Tony didn't feel like pretending everything was okay or answering questions about his family.

Besides, he really cared about Sydney. She was only twenty-four but she was very wise in the ways of the world because of her difficult past. He also guessed she wanted to talk to him.

They made their way out of the room and stopped in the Academy cafeteria where Syd had stored some cold stuff. After she grabbed it, they headed outside.

The day was still warm for September, so they set out food on a picnic table under a tree. The sun shone, but didn't beat down on them and a breeze filtered through the trees.

"When'd you have time to do this?" he asked, noting the spread of cheeses, crusty bread, salads and lemonade.

She shrugged. "Daisy finally slept, but I couldn't. I stayed up, got some things together and baked." She held up a plastic bag. "Chocolate chips."

They dug in. After a few mouthfuls, Tony asked, "So you got a problem you need to talk about, kid?"

Downing some lemonade, she set her glass on the table and zeroed in on him with an intense gaze. "No, but you do."

"What do you mean, *bonita*?"

She smiled at the affectionate term he often used for her. She had no sisters or brothers and seemed to like it.

"Tony, it's me. Syd. The one you got through several messes. You need to let me in as an adult in our relationship. You don't have to take care of me all the time. I wanna know why you look like you've lost your best friend these last weeks."

Suddenly the cheese he'd been eating tasted like cardboard. He set it down and drew in a heavy breath. "Because I have, in a sense. Sophia and I are separated. I kept the situation from all of you because Sophia wanted privacy, but truthfully, I'm tired of pretending everything's all right."

Genuine concern filled her light brown eyes. She reached across the table to touch his arm. "I'm so sorry. And also shocked. You have—"

"The ideal marriage. I know, everybody thinks that." He pounded his fist on the table. "And in some ways, that's caused our issues."

"I don't understand."

He found himself spilling everything except the intimate details of what his life had become.

"Man, that's a big secret to keep." She raked a hand through her short dark hair. "I'm glad you told me."

"Why? It won't help our situation."

"True, I can't give you advice, because I've never been married. But you need to unload. And give yourself a break from all this. You can spend time with Daisy and me and Mama if you get lonely. As a matter of fact, why don't you come to dinner tonight?"

"Yeah, that would be nice."

"And I know I'm not as old as you, *concho*, but for what it's worth, don't try to become someone you're not for another person. I did it, Tony, and it only causes heartache."

"Daisy's father? You hardly ever talk about him."

"Yeah. My relationship with him was a disaster."

All Tony knew about the circumstances of her pregnancy was that the guy had been married. When they became close, Syd had asked him and Sophia not to probe into that dark period in her life.

"Then I'm glad you're out of the relationship."

They talked some more about Sophia's concerns and then Sydney checked her watch. "I gotta call Mama to see how the baby is. I'll meet you inside."

"I'll clean this up. Go ahead."

Tony finished packing their leftovers and headed back into the building. After he put the remains of their lunch in the fridge, he went looking for a bulletin board he'd noticed, where Academy business was posted. He found it at the end of the hall, next to Jack Harrison's office. The guy was coming out as Tony reached it. Tall, muscular, with a full head of dark hair, the forty-something psychologist smiled at him. "Hi, Tony."

He wondered how Harrison remembered people's names. They'd met, of course, but it had been a while ago and they hadn't seen each other much around the department.

"Hey, Jack."

"How's it going?"

"Great."

He nodded to the bulletin board. "Looking for anything special?"

"Nope. Passing time until our training starts."

The man shrugged a shoulder. "If you need anything, let me know."

*Jesús*, did the guy have ESP? "Will do."

Studying the board, Tony scanned information about Academy training, an indoor volleyball league that was forming, support groups offered, recent department news, and then he came upon Job Opportunities. There were four positions open for trainers to join the Academy staff.

He remembered Sophia's tearful plea...

*Why can't you work at the Academy training firefighters? At least you'd be safe and you'd still be in the field. Besides, you always said that if you weren't a firefighter, you'd be a teacher.*

Huh! Was it fate that brought him here, or had he unconsciously been looking for positions available? He could do this. Take one of those jobs and get his family back. But it almost broke his heart to think about giving up firefighting.

• • •

SOPHIA GLANCED AT Tony as they approached the huge modern structure that belonged to Brock Carrington. In the light from several outdoor lamps, her husband smiled tentatively. God, she hated the tension between them.

Reaching over, she tugged on his shirt. "You're so handsome tonight." He wore a dark gray shirt, light gray blazer and charcoal pants. Sophia's black dress with silver accents went well with his outfit.

"I like dressing up. Most firefighters do. I think because we live in grime."

*Well, there's a way out of that one*, she wanted to say but didn't because she'd spoil the evening and she'd been looking forward to tonight as a respite from what they'd been going through.

Thankfully, the door opened. Brock's wife, Susan, stood before them in a chic jewel-toned periwinkle dress. Her blond hair was perfectly coiffed, and her blue eyes stood out in a remarkably unlined face. "Sophia, hello," the woman said warmly. "I'm so glad you could come. Brock would have been very disappointed if you didn't."

"Good to see you, too." Tony moved restlessly next to her.

"This is my husband. Tony, Susan Carrington."

"Nice to meet you." She perused them. "What an attractive couple you make."

"Thank you, ma'am."

"Please, call me Susan."

"What time is Brock getting here?" Sophia asked.

"In a half hour." She stepped aside and invited them into a foyer made of marble, glass and chrome. A huge, probably real, crystal chandelier descended gracefully from a high ceiling. "Come back and get a drink."

About fifty people were in the rear of the house, mingling in a great room that opened to a porch, which gave way to a deck. A warm breeze drifted inside. Sophia scanned the guests; she recognized about half of them, as they were from the hospital. Brock was involved in a lot of charity work, held positions on the board of directors at various agencies and belonged to a golf club, so he had many friends and acquaintances.

Susan showed them to the bar and Tony ordered them both Cosmopolitans, which they drank when they were out for a night.

"Some digs," he said without rancor. One of the many things she loved about her husband was the absence of any kind of jealousy in his makeup. Sophia herself could covet this kind of house if she let herself.

"It's beautiful."

A group of nurses approached them, her sister, Isabel, among them. "Hey guys, nice to see you." She kissed Tony's cheek. "Especially you, handsome. You're never home when I come over."

He shot Sophia a *she-doesn't-know?* look. Subtly, Sophia shook her head.

"Duty calls." He slugged back some of the drink.

"Can you believe Brock's forty?" Izzy continued. "Honestly, he's so young looking."

"Oh, yeah, forty's old," another nurse, in her fifties, commented. "Just wait."

Tony was pulled aside by someone he knew, and Isabel studied Sophia's face. "Hey, girlfriend. Is everything all right?"

Suddenly, she wanted to confide in her sister. "Not exactly. Maybe we can get together sometime."

"Sure, honey. I'll call you tomorrow."

They made small talk with the rest of the crowd from work until the guest of honor arrived. Brock was surprised and pleased by his lovely wife's party. He mingled and eventually made his way to Sophia. She was out on the patio getting some air, and Tony had found a guy he knew from church, so he was off somewhere. Brock approached her. "There you are."

She turned. "Happy birthday."

"Thanks." Leaning over, he kissed her cheek. At her startled response, he said, "A birthday kiss, right?"

"Oh, sure. You, um, have a lovely house."

"Do we? Sometimes I don't even notice. Comes from growing up with money."

"Hmm."

"I hope that wasn't crass. I know you didn't have much when you were younger, and I have to say I really admire what you've done on your own, without help."

"Oh, I had help. Tony and I made our way together."

Brock scanned the others around them. "He didn't come tonight?"

"He's here, mingling."

Glancing behind and to the side, he pulled her farther away from the crowd. "We haven't had a chance to talk about what happened three days ago in the lounge."

She tossed back her hair. "When I had a meltdown? Please, let's forget it."

"No, I don't want to. You had a full-blown panic attack. What's going on?"

"What I told you that day. Worry." She smiled to distract him. "Look, let's talk about something else. This topic depresses me. Am I going to get to see the new baby and the other girls tonight?"

"Yes, the nanny's bringing them down. Let me say, if you ever need a shoulder to cry on, Sophia"—here he touched her arm—"know I'm available."

*Uh-oh*, she thought. *Is he hitting on me?*

• • •

TONY STOOD AT the end of the patio watching the guest of honor hitting on his wife. It stunned him so much, he simply stood there as the guy kissed her cheek, leaned into her personal space, touched her several times.

*Dios mio*, he thought. Was something going on here he didn't know about? Was Sophia using his job as an excuse for that? Hell, could his wife be cheating on him?

# CHAPTER 4

DRESSED IN CIVILIAN clothes of jeans and a light red sweater, Rachel Wellington Malvaso stopped into Firehouse 7 on the way back from an appointment. Tony caught sight of her as Gabe started to read a joke from the Joke Jar. They read the stupid things routinely to brighten up the days.

"'The captain went to see his priest.' Jeez, why are there so many captain jokes these days?"

"Come on, read man." This from Brody.

Gabe read on. "The priest asked, 'What's wrong?'

"The captain said, 'My wife's poisoning me.'

"Shocked, the priest shook his head. 'How can that be?'

"The man then pleads, 'I'm telling you, I'm positive she's poisoning me! What should I do?'

"'Let me talk to her,' the priest offers. 'I'll see what I can find out.'

"A week later, the priest calls the man and says, 'I spoke to your wife for three hours on the phone. You want my advice?'

"'Yeah, sure.'

"The priest replied, 'Take the poison.'"

From behind and unnoticed, Rachel said, "As a newly married woman, I have to say I resent that joke. Who's is it? O'Malley's, I'll bet."

"Nope," Brody said, "I think Gabe put it in there himself."

"That'll be the day." Gabe went to Rachel and slid his arm around her. The look that passed between them was hot. Tony turned away from the sight, feeling the familiar pit in his stomach that his marriage was crumbling.

"How was your dental appointment?" Gabe asked.

"Good. No problems. With that anyway."

Felicia looked up from where she was preparing lunch at the huge gas stove. "Something else wrong?"

"It's Parker Allen again, I'm sorry to say. Have you seen today's post in the *Herald*?"

"No, we've had calls all morning." Felicia rolled her eyes at Gabe. "Besides we're not supposed to be doing personal stuff on the computer, thanks to her."

Rachael's soft features sharpened. "This *is* business."

Producing her computer from its case under the table, Felicia clicked some keys and scanned the screen, her face reddening as her gaze scrolled the page. "Son of a bitch!"

"What is it?" Gabe asked.

"She has the training materials from three days ago. How the fuck is she getting so close to us?"

Gabe's scowl was fierce. "Read what the blog says."

Felicia cleared her throat. "The heading is *Heroes or Hiders?* 'On September 24 about fifty area firefighters attended training at the Anderson County Fire Academy. They were instructed by Battalion Chief Ian Woodward, who suffered the loss of his legs in 9/11. The thrust of the content begs the question, Why would he put out material like this?'"

"What the hell is she talking about?" Sydney asked, her own face flushed.

"Listen. 'The topic was first responders' reaction to calls involving bombs. Good material was given about evacuation of *civilians, differentiating bomb types, etc. but then this little treasure was in there.'* Oh, shit."

"*Felicia!*" This from Gabe again.

"It's the list the captain gave us for protecting ourselves. Going to a safe spot and waiting for instructions. Using shields, special protective gear, minimizing time in contamination danger areas. That must be what she meant by hiding."

Chief Erikson burst into the kitchen, his face red, his shoulders tense. He noted the computer in front of Felicia. "I assume that's Allen's blog. Goddamn it, somebody gave her the material from our training."

Tony was steamed, too. "Why did she skew it that way?"

"She's after blood and I'm sick of it. White, get your guy on the phone. See if you two can meet with Noah and Will and me after work to discuss what you found out about her. We may have to use it after all."

"Yes, sir."

Erikson stalked off.

Gabe whistled softly. "I don't think I've ever seen him this mad."

"Is this about Allen's background?" Tony asked. He'd been in agreement to keep the stuff with her father and fiancé out of their public feud.

"I guess. I'm gonna go call Ryan."

Brody shouted after her, "No phone sex."

"Bite me," Felicia retorted.

"I gotta get some air." Tony stood and walked out of the kitchen into the firehouse yard. Sitting on the bench near the blacktop that held the basketball hoop, he sighed. He hadn't told Sophia about the training content. Contrary to Ian's suggestion that they show the list to their families, he feared it would only give her more ammunition to use against him.

God, when had he started looking at her like the enemy?

• • •

SOPHIA WALKED AROUND Brody O'Malley's half of a house, noting the comfortable leather furniture, the plush rugs over hardwood floors and the unusual sunken conversation pit he'd put in. She was glad Tony had someplace nice to live. She wanted the best for him, and of course, pleasant surroundings assuaged her guilt. Making her way through the porch he shared with Ryan, she went out into the backyard and took a seat on the patio. The wind was swirling at five o'clock, and clouds were superimposed over the formerly sunny day. The atmosphere matched her mood.

She shivered, thinking of Parker Allen's blog today. And Tony hadn't told her any of it—about the training, that the fire department got those kind of calls, that they were in even more danger than she'd realized. *Jesús!* How was any woman expected to withstand this?

*You used to be able to take it.*

She used to be young and foolish, too. Besides, 9/11 hadn't happened then. Or Sinco. Or Teddy Thompson's death.

She heard from the porch, "Sophia, there you are. Come on inside, it's going to storm."

Once on the porch, she noted he was still dressed in his uniform. Lines of fatigue etched his face and he seemed sad.

*Of course he's sad. You kicked him out, and despite how nice this place is, it's hard for him to be separated from the family that means everything to him.*

He asked, "Did something happen?"

From her purse, she fished out a copy of the blog. She noticed her hands were shaking and she tried to still them. "Why didn't you tell me what the training last week was about?"

"Take a wild guess." His words were sharp, disgusted almost. "I need a beer. Want one?"

"Yeah."

When he returned and gave her the drink, he took a chair opposite where she sat on the rattan couch, not next to her. They always used to sit as close as possible when in a room together.

*What did you expect? He's going to get tired of this.*

Suddenly, the thought of what he might do while they were separated turned her stomach. Everybody always said he was the most gorgeous man they ever met. Women flirted with him even when Sophia was with him. Did he consider himself free now?

"I was afraid to tell you, of course."

"I guessed." She glanced down at the nasty words. "Have you ever been called to a suspected terrorist attack?"

"Not the dirty bomb kind. Usually, Hazmat gets right on that."

"Usually. Okay, what about the rest? Have you been in buildings during search and rescue when there was danger?"

"There's always danger on a fire call, Sophia."

"Don't hedge. Damn it, Tony." She held up the paper. "This is even more reason to get a safe position in the department."

He ran his hand through his hair, and his eyes glistened with frustration. "I don't know what to say to you. You knew when you married me that I had a dangerous job."

"I thought I could handle it."

"You *did* handle it."

At his vehement, angry tone, she gave an impulsive little gasp.

He stood, then, and came to sit next to her. Sliding his arm around her, he drew her close.

Nosing into him, she grasped his shirt. They must have had a fire today, because his clothes smelled of smoke. "I can't fathom a life without you."

He kissed her head. "You don't have to. Nothing's going to happen to me."

"I wish you wouldn't mouth those platitudes. They're insulting."

She felt him stiffen, swear under his breath. "I'm sure you could find somebody else, Sophia. You're a beautiful woman."

Abhorred by his comment, she yanked herself away and glared at him. "What a horrible thing to say."

"Not after watching Brock Carrington drool all over you last weekend."

Because she knew she was being unfair to him with her demands, she attacked. "He was not. There is nothing personal between us."

"Yet."

"You're picking a fight because you're wrong about this whole thing."

"Fuck it, Soph, there's no right or wrong here. It's simply a shitty situation."

"I don't want to be a widow!"

"How about a divorcée, then? Because that's the kind of wedge you're driving between us."

"Oh, is someone waiting in the wings for you?"

His face totally blanked. "Of course not."

"Give me a break, Tony. Women have been falling at your feet since you were fourteen."

Now his whole body coiled with anger. "And what did I ever, once, do about that?"

She deflated. He was right, of course. Tears welled in her eyes and she moved away so he wouldn't see them. With her husband, crying wasn't fighting fair.

He knew, anyway. Reaching over, he encompassed her from behind. She leaned back against him, feeling the play of his muscles against her body and wondering again what she would do without this man in her life.

She forgot all those thoughts, though, when he stood, scooped her into a carry and brought her upstairs, where they made breathless love.

For a while, it was enough.

• • •

TONY WOKE FROM a sound sleep when the PA system blared into the bunk room. "Fire at Green Ridge Lodge. Quint, Midi 7, Rescue 7, go into service."

Eleven firefighters bounded out of bed, donned uniform trousers over boxers and T-shirts and rushed out to the rig. As they jumped into boots and turnout pants, grabbed their coats and hustled to the rig, Brody swore. "Emma loves that place."

"Green Ridge Lodge?" Sydney asked. She didn't get out much.

"Un-huh. That historic building right on the outskirts of town. It was built in 1856. Emma likes old. We had dinner there not too long ago."

Luckily, when they arrived—first in—the building was not fully involved. Erikson set up Incident Command and summoned the blueprints. The guys on the Quint laid hose to mount an exterior attack, and as soon as they got the stream going, Gabe gave the order for his crew to head inside. The structure was a restaurant so it should be empty at this hour of the morning, but they had to search the inside, top to bottom. Brody used the rabbit tool to pop the locked front door, and the alarm went off. Hell of a thing. Amidst some godawful blaring, they entered the foyer.

"A lot of smoke, Cap," Tony commented into his mic.

"I know. Too much." With an arsonist on the loose, every detail had to be noticed. "Stay alert."

Because of the intense heat, they dropped to their knees and crawled to the center of the room. "Ramirez and Sands, go to the attic. The three of us will cover the first floor." He ordered two guys from Quint 7 to take the second floor and two more to the basement.

They fanned out. Tony led the way for his assignment. As he and Syd crept up the stairway, Tony's spine pricked. Something wasn't right. He could feel it when he opened the heavy door to the attic.

There was another short flight of steps; he and Syd mounted them and shined their lights on the interior. The heat was suffocating up here, though there was no smoke yet. The attic space had one window, but it was black. Going over to inspect it, he saw the glass was boarded up from the outside. That was odd. Too odd.

"Syd, turn around and go back down the steps." Into his radio he said, "Gabe, something's not right in the attic. We're coming back."

No response. Quickly, he followed Sydney's path down the stairs. At the bottom of them, she stood wide-eyed. "It's locked."

"What?"

"The door to the attic's locked. I tried to jimmy it."

"Let me take a shot." He wriggled the doorknob, pushed, then he slammed his body against the heavy wood. Nothing. Hell. He thought about Sydney being squeamish since she was trapped in the well six months ago. "Don't panic."

"I'm not." But her voice was shaky.

Into his radio again, he said, "Mayday, Mayday, Firefighters Sands and Ramirez are trapped in the attic. The door's stuck. Window's boarded up from the outside. We need help."

Still, there was no answer.

He and Sydney stared at each other and he saw a flicker of fear in her eyes. He wondered if his revealed the same emotion.

• • •

"WHAT DO YOU mean, he's gone?"

At five in the morning., Sophia spoke to her mother over the phone. Louisa routinely stayed over when Tony was on nights and Sophia was on call at the hospital. She'd just finished an emergency surgery and had been filling in a chart at the nurse's station.

Her mom's voice was trembling. "Mari had a nightmare. I went in to see what was wrong and noticed Miguel's door open a little. It was closed when I went to bed. He's not there."

"Did you check downstairs?"

"Yes. He never gets up this early. I'm worried."

"So am I. I'll be right home."

Her heart thumping in her chest so loud she could practically hear it, Sophia clicked off, turned and bumped right into Brock. "Hey, what's the hurry? It's the middle of the night."

For some reason, she clutched at his shoulders. "Miguel's gone. My mother called." She pulled off her scrub cap, sending her hair down her back. "I have to leave." She started for the elevator.

Brock called out, "Sophia, you need your purse with the keys."

"Hell." Turning back around, she circled the big desk, got her purse out of a locked drawer, then went back to the elevator, where Brock waited. He pressed the button. "I'm going with you. You're too shaky to drive."

"I—" She looked down. Her hands were unsteady. "Okay."

When they reached her car, he asked for the keys, then they slid inside. The twenty-minute drive to her house was nerve-wracking. She tried Tony's cell and it clicked into voicemail. "He must be on a call."

"That's all right, I'm here to help. You're not alone." He used his calm, reassuring doctor's voice and it comforted her.

"No, I need T—" She stopped herself. "You're right, I can do this."

Bolting out of the car as soon as they pulled into her driveway, she ran into the house through the garage door. It was still dark out and she tripped on a bike. Pain shot up her leg, but she ignored it. Louisa met her in the kitchen. "*Dios mio*, what has happened to him?"

Sophia put her hand on her mother's shoulder. "I'll call his friends." She was dimly aware of Brock coming in behind her as she approached the phone. Four very sleepy friends later, Sophia started to panic. "He's nowhere. *Nowhere*."

Brock, who her mother had served coffee to, came to her and took her hands. "He has to be somewhere."

"We argued before bed," Louisa said. "He was mad at me."

Again, she touched her mother's shoulder. "He's mad at everybody these days, Mama."

"Where does he usually go when he's angry?" Brock asked.

"To Antonio." This from Louisa. Her mom had not been in favor of Tony moving out, but she's supported Sophia anyway.

"Yes!" Sophia said, grabbing her husband's house keys from the drawer.

"You're still stressed," Brock said, following her out. "I'm driving."

"Whatever. Let's go. Mama, keep calling Miguel's cell."

The streets were deserted on the drive to Tony's, with only a few cars passing them. The eerie time before dawn chilled her. Brock was silent for a while, then he asked, "He's not living at home?"

"No."

"For how long?"

"Two weeks or so. But, Brock, I don't want to talk about my problems with Tony."

When they reached Brody O'Malley's street, then his house, Sophia gasped.

On the porch stoop, under a dim light, sat Miguel.

# CHAPTER 5

"THANKS FOR SEEING me, Chief. On such short notice." Tony tried to keep the weariness out of his voice, the fear, but he wasn't sure he succeeded. His shoulders were heavy with fatigue and his heart about crushed by his mission here.

From behind his office desk, Noah Callahan smiled kindly at Tony. "Of course I'd see you. You're a valued member of this department."

Now, that hurt. *Jesús*, the guy never told him that directly before. "Thanks."

"Can I get you coffee?"

The scent hovered around Tony, but it turned his stomach. He shook his head.

"Are you here about this morning's fire? I know you and Syd were trapped in an attic and the blaze was incendiary. If I were you, I'd be pissed as hell that somebody deliberately set you up."

The incident *had* scared the shit out of him and not merely because it took so long to be rescued. The fire had gotten worse and not better. But Sydney had been really scared, and he was shocked. She was always so tough. The remnants of the well-rescue-gone-awry were still with her.

"It was a bitch all around, and yeah, I'm pissed. But nobody was hurt and I think they got more information on the torch. I'm here, to..." he looked down at the floor, toeing the leg of Noah's desk. At the thought of what he was about to do, his gut clenched and his heart twisted in his chest. But this was no time for recriminations. What choice did he have after all that had happened? If he wanted to save his family, he had to do this.

"...to apply for an instructor's position at the Academy."

Literally, the chief's mouth dropped. "This is a surprise. I thought you liked being on the line."

"I do. There are reasons to transfer."

The chief frowned. "I have to ask. Are they physical?"

"What? Oh, no. I'm healthy as a horse."

Sitting back, Noah steepled his fingers. "Can you tell me why you made this decision?"

How specific should he be? He couldn't tell the chief how, when he'd gone to Brody's duplex after the nightmarish call, he'd found his wife clinging to another man and his son shivering on his front steps. Though he'd been sick at the thought of Sophia turning to Carrington, Miguel had been his primary concern.

"My family. They're not doing well with my job."

"I'm sorry. The hours are better at the Academy and you can get time off more easily."

"It's more than that, Chief, but truthfully, I can't talk about it."

The man he respected a lot watched him. "I see. Well, then..." He took out a folder and opened it. "We've filled two spots for training the recruit class, so two more are open. You'd be a real asset to them, having recently come off the line."

"When does it start?"

"October seventh."

"So soon?"

Setting down the folder, the chief's gaze narrowed. "Tony, don't you want to make this move?"

Tony glanced out the window, where the wind had picked up and was blowing the trees. Finally, he answered. "I got no choice, Chief. I'll take the position if you'll have me."

"Of course I will." The chief was thoughtful. "On one condition."

Not more demands. Tony wasn't sure if he could take much more. "What is it?"

Callahan leaned over the desk. "Look, I can see you're conflicted by this choice. And I know a lot about conflict. In the job and in relationships and how the two clash sometimes. Often when we're in the middle of things, we can't always see our way clear. You can have the job, but I want you to talk to Jack Harrison at some point about what's going on with you."

Tony was going to object but kept his mouth shut. It'd probably help to be able to be honest with somebody, totally honest and totally selfish. "Yeah, okay. That sounds like a good idea."

The chief nodded. "Then, glad to have you on board. And remember, this is for the recruit class that lasts four months. We can decide what will happen permanently in February."

Tony scowled. "What about my position on Rescue 7? That'll have to be filled."

"Actually, I have some officers I'd like to rotate in and out of the Rescue Squad for the experience. We can cover for you for the time the class runs."

He'd never expected this. And he wasn't sure the gift made his move easier or harder to accept. In any case, his part was done. He stood and so did the chief.

"Stop by HR on your way out. I'll call down."

"Thanks, Chief. I really appreciate you shuffling the schedule around for me."

"People care about you in the department, Tony. And want you to be happy."

He swallowed hard and couldn't respond. Instead, he started out. At the door, he turned back. "Can I tell my group myself? We're off for four days, but I can get them together."

"Sure, go ahead."

After wading through the paperwork, Tony left the Academy and got in his truck. But he just sat there, on this beautiful Indian Summer day, feeling like thunderclouds had descended on his life. He couldn't believe he'd given up the job he'd loved since he was eighteen. It hurt so bad he started to choke on the grief. So, he made himself think back to last night....

"What's going on here?" he'd asked, his fists curling at his sides at the sight of his wife standing so close to Carrington. He hadn't known then that Miguel had run away.

Sophia raised her chin, but her lips were trembling. "Miguel came here after they all went to bed."

"Here, *hijo*? You knew I was working nights."

Miguel glanced away. Tony looked to Sophia. She shook her head, indicating she didn't know what was going on, either. So he dropped down next to his son on the porch. For a minute, Miguel sat there, staring at the ground, then he pivoted and threw himself into Tony's arms. "I gotta be with you, Dad. It's not right you live alone. I wanna move in with you."

"Aw, son," he whispered, clasping on to the boy. "Shh. I'll make everything all right again. I promise...."

The memory of why he was going off the line gave him strength. He sat up straight in the car and turned on the engine. He'd done the right thing for his family, and that's all that mattered.

• • •

LATE MORNING OF the day after Miguel had run away, Sophia paced the garden at their home. Marianna had gone to school, and her mother had taken Miguel to her house to sleep so she and Tony could talk. They'd taken a nap, but he was gone when she awoke. As Sophia had waited for him to return, she'd made the mistake of turning on the news. Damn it. He'd been caught in the arson's trap, as she feared would happen, and this time, he almost didn't get out. She'd known a terror so great it immobilized her. So she came out here hoping the fresh air would make it easier to breathe. But today she couldn't appreciate the fall chrysanthemums, the blue mist shrubs or the tinge of fall in the air.

"Soph?"

Turning to the house, she saw him in the doorway, holding a mug of the coffee she'd made. She said, "Hi. I was worried."

"Now, that's an understatement, isn't it?"

She couldn't read his mood. When he came out onto the deck, she saw that his face was ravaged and for once, he didn't look good. There was the bleakest expression in his eyes—one she'd seen only once before. Not when they were fifteen and she'd told him she was pregnant. But when she'd lost their baby. "Tony, what is it?"

"We have to talk."

"I know about the arson. It was all over the news."

Wearily, he settled in a chair under one of the umbrella tables. She dropped down adjacent to him and picked up his hand. It was really cold. "I'm so sorry about Miguel."

"That's not your fault, *carina.*"

"Yes, it is. I was the one who insisted you leave. I keep making decisions based on my fears and I'm hurting everybody I love."

"It doesn't matter anymore."

"What do you mean?"

He stared ahead.

"Oh, no, Tony, if you want a divorce, I swear I won't give you one. I'll fight for you."

That brought a sardonic smile to his lips. "No, no divorce. I'm going off the line," he said, his voice cracking on the last word. "I took a job this morning at the Anderson County Fire Academy."

"What? Why didn't you discuss this with me before you made your final decision?"

"*Querida,* we've been discussing this forever. After Miguel, after getting trapped, after…never mind that.… We couldn't go on this way."

"Oh, Tony."

"It's okay. I'll be teaching a recruit class that starts next week." He tried to smile. "It'll be fun. Like I said, teaching's the job I would have picked if I wasn't a firefighter."

Forcefully, she quelled any tears. *He* was the one suffering now. "I—I know this isn't what you want."

"I *want* my family back. Quitting the line is the only way to get it."

She couldn't speak because of the lump around her throat.

He stared at her. Finally, he said, "It'll work out. I promise." He stood. "I'm whipped. I couldn't sleep when you did. If I don't get some zees, I'm gonna collapse."

She asked, "Want me to come?"

"No, love, really, I gotta sleep."

With shoulders slumped, his gate uneven, Tony made his way into the house. Sophia sat on the deck, staring after him, thinking that for a woman who'd gotten what she wanted, she was absolutely miserable.

• • •

HIS GROUP DROPPED everything to meet Tony later that afternoon. Which only made the task at hand harder. Syd had to get a sitter, the O'Malley boys and their women were taking their parents' boat out of the water for the winter and Gabe had planned a day with Rachel. Still they came through the door of Badges willingly.

"Hey, *hombre*, you okay?" Gabe's tone was concerned, though he looked relaxed and happy. "You said you were, but you sounded 'off' on the phone."

Bleakly, Tony wondered how long he would be *off*.

"Nope, I'm fine. But I gotta tell you all something and I wanted to do it together and not in the firehouse."

After O'Malley slapped him on the back, and Syd kissed his cheek, they ordered a pitcher of beer and snagged a table. He must look like shit, but nobody teased him and they were unusually subdued. Tony prayed to God he could get through this without breaking down. These people were his family, too, and he was giving them up for Sophia and the kids. He placed a hand over his heart which pulsed with angina-like pain.

"Thanks for coming. I, um…" *Jesús,* his eyes welled and he battled the emotion back. "I'm taking a position at the Fire Academy, effective next tour."

Gabe recoiled. "Why would you do that? You're one of the best line firefighters I've ever worked with."

Syd, next to him, put her hand on his arm and squeezed. Her face was glum despite the bright red sweatshirt she wore. "What made you decide?"

"Sophia and I have been separated for almost a month, Gabe. I didn't tell you because you're my officer and I didn't want you to worry about my performance."

"Damn it, Tony. I thought we were friends. And as captain, I didn't worry when O'Malley went off the deep end for Emma, when Felicia had to take a leave because of Ryan. Hell, I was a basket case over Rachel myself." He drew in a breath to calm himself. "But let's table that for now. Why are you separated?"

"After Teddy Thompson over in Camden Cove died in that fire last year, Sophia wigged out. She got all worried and nervous like she did after 9/11 and then Sinco. Only this time, the worry didn't go away. She has anxiety attacks over my job."

"I'm sorry to hear that." Gabe's tone was genuine.

"I've been living at Brody's place, so him and Licia know. And I confessed to Syd the day we trained at the Academy."

"Tony, you didn't do anything wrong to *confess.*" Felicia's eyes were warm and supportive. "You're in a no-win position."

"I was, but there's more to why."

He explained about Miguel.

Brody rolled his eyes. "Tough, brother, when it hits your kids that way. Wives sign on for the job. Children don't."

"Then I got trapped and it scared the shit out of me, not because of my safety, but I was terrified of what would happen to Sophia and the kids if I died that night. That's no way to do my job."

"You did your job better than I did at Green Ridge." Sydney was still touching him. "But I can see why you quit the line."

"There wasn't another way out."

"What are you gonna do at the Academy?" Brody asked.

"Work with the new recruit class."

*That* they did tease him about.

Then things got quiet.

"Okay, I gotta say it." This from Felicia. "Are you positive this is the right thing to do, Tony?"

He averted his gaze for a minute. Then nodded.

"I'm not sure I'd do it for Ryan."

"I'd do it for Emma," Brody put in. "If she was in Sophia's spot. No offense guys, but she's more important to me than you are." He zeroed in on Felicia. "And you can say all you want you wouldn't do it for Rye, but it's because you know you'll never have to. He's in his own dangerous job. Same goes for you, Cap, because Rachel's a firefighter, too."

"I suppose."

Tony let them debate that until they wound down. He took a few sips of beer, gripping the mug tightly. When they were done, he said simply, "I'm gonna miss you guys."

They all protested....

"Hey, we'll still get together."

"We'll make time."

"We're not lettin' you go that easy."

Tony scanned the faces of his brothers and sisters. "I know you mean all that. But, if nothing else, we live in the real world. It'll never be the same."

"Never?" Syd asked, her voice hoarse. "What about when the class is over?"

*Fuck*, he thought they understood he wouldn't be coming back. "Things won't have changed with Sophia, so, yeah, never. Though Callahan did say he was gonna sub people in for me until the class was done. But this is my final decision." He stood, unable to contain the swell of emotion inside him. "I gotta go."

"Want some company?" Now Syd sounded desperate.

"No, I need to be alone." He reached for his wallet.

Gabe stayed his hand. "Don't insult us."

Again, he nodded.

Tony made it to the car, out of the parking lot and down to a nearby church where he pulled in. He drove to the end where it was deserted and turned off the engine.

Then he put his head down on the steering wheel and lost it.

# CHAPTER 6

"THIS IS SO cool," Miguel said as he approached the roller coaster where screeches and hollering practically drowned out his words. "Will you come on with me, Dad?"

Tony rolled his eyes at Sophia, who was carrying Mari's cotton candy. They both knew he hated roller coasters. So she jumped in. "I'll go, *hijo*."

"I want Dad."

Miguel had been clingy since the night a week ago when he'd run away to Tony's then-dwelling. Her husband had been living at home for seven days and everybody was happier. But the boy's behavior had been different around his father.

Interrupting the disturbing thought, Gabe's son Joey came running to them, followed by Gabe and Lilliana. Joey pointed to the ride. "Wanna go on the Beast, Miguel?" He peered at Gabe. "We can go alone, right?"

"I think so." Gabe's eyes twinkled. "I'll come with you and watch."

Tony stood. "No, I will." Sophia noticed he'd shunned his buddies today at the annual HFCD Fall Family Day at an amusement park outside of Hidden Cove.

After the guys left, Mari said, "Mommy, Lily and I wanna go on the teacups."

When Sophia stood, Gabe slid his arm around her. "Let's go chaperone."

They passed clowns, a child's race car ride and a stand selling fried dough — which smelled heavenly — to get to the teacups. She sat on the bench with Gabe. It was a beautiful day, but despite the warm sun, Sophia was glad for the black jeans and light cotton sweater she wore with tennis shoes.

Finally, she broached the subject on both their minds. "This is awkward," she said.

Gabe shook his head. "It doesn't have to be. For what it's worth, if Rachel asked me to quit my job, I would."

For some reason, emotion clogged her throat. "Thanks for telling me that."

She watched the teacups spin in their peacock blue and bright pink splendor and then confessed, "I'd fix this if there was another way, Gabe."

"I know you would. Nobody blames you."

"I doubt that."

"No, really, we're all family. We want what's best for both of you. Tony can survive not being on the line, but he could never make it without you, Soph." He smiled sardonically. "I'm beginning to understand that feeling."

She socked his arm. "Madly in love, aren't you, guy?"

"Yeah." His face reddened. "I can't believe how much."

"Speak of the devil." Sophia watched Gabe's wife come toward them, cute in simple blue pants and a white cotton T-shirt. When she shot a glance at Gabe, the expression on his face moved Sophia. Briefly, she wondered if Tony would keep looking at her the way Gabe looked at his wife, now that she'd deprived him of something so sacred to him. She'd been having that thought a lot lately.

The three adults chatted until the rides ended and they hooked up with the boys.

"We want to go on the flume ride next."

Gabe shook his head. "Great. We'll get wet." He faced Tony. "Come on, *bombero*, let's take the boys on it."

Tony's face blanked. Then he said, "Can't. I promised Mari I'd go on the baby coaster with her. I think I can handle that one. We'll take Lily with us. Set up a meet time with Sophia."

Then he was off.

Gabe turned to Sophia. "What's that all about?"

She bit her lip. "I think it's too hard being with you all right now."

Rachel leaned over and slid her arm around Sophia's shoulder. "I'm sorry, Soph. But it'll all work out in the end."

*Would it?* she wondered briefly. Or had she made the biggest mistake of her life by forcing her husband to leave his beloved job?

• • •

"THE FIRE DEPARTMENT is a paramilitary organization." Battalion Chief Jeb Caruso, who ran the show at the Academy, stood before the fifteen men and women of the 2011 Recruit Class at the Anderson County Fire Academy, which serviced all surrounding area fire departments. "You should view your time here as boot camp."

All newbies stood stone still, staring ahead, dressed in fatigue uniforms: long-sleeved light blue shirts, navy pants, black ties and hats with wide brims covering their eyes.

Caruso continued. "First, you need to know that this training will be one of the most significant sixteen weeks of your life. You measure up and you're a career firefighter. If you don't, you're out and miss the chance of a lifetime."

A few of the young men and women shifted from foot to foot. Though there were often second career recruits in their late thirties or even forties, this group appeared to be in their twenties. A lot of hopes were going to be realized or dashed in the next four months. Tony remembered his own Academy days when he'd excelled at everything. Funny, he didn't feel that *good* at life lately, though things were better at home.

Jeb continued speaking. "I'm going to introduce the head of this recruit class, Battalion Chief Olive Hennessy, who will be in charge of your training."

Tony smiled at the choice of a woman for this big job. Noah Callahan really did believe in equality. Though some guys hated having women in authority, Tony didn't. And he knew Olive, having worked with her on Engine 3 in the early years of their careers. She was a top-notch firefighter and a good person.

Tall and confident, Olive approached the podium and didn't smile; she addressed the recruits soberly. "Your days at the Academy will simulate an average firehouse's routine. We arrive at promptly 0700 hours, check the rigs and start all the equipment, like the trucks, power and pry tools. Roll call is at eight. Make sure you're dressed correctly or you'll receive demerits."

She went on to outline the rest of their duties: several hours of classes, cooking lunch or dinner, training with all kinds of equipment and cleaning up the rooms used. The Academy consisted of the huge gym, where they were now, several fitness training stations, a stage, a maze, lockers, a kitchen, classrooms, the EMS office, administrative offices and bays. There was also a four-storey tower in back of the parking lot, where fires were simulated with white mist, which could blind you as much as real smoke. Recruits, as well as veteran firefighters and specialty teams, all used the grounds for training.

Then Olive introduced the officers in charge of various areas—curriculum, Hazmat, EMS—the trainer from the high school recruitment division, of which Tony had once been a member, and then the line guys. She gave a bit more information, convened roll call and started an inspection.

Ed Snyder joined Tony from where he'd stood off to the side. "Wanna go pick on some of the cherries with me, Ramirez?"

"Nope."

"Why not? We're supposed to."

Tony eyed the lieutenant from Engine 4 who gave everybody grief. Tony didn't understand how he'd ever become an officer. "I didn't realize you were still here."

Snyder's craggy face scowled. "Smoke inhalation and burns from the fucking torch take a long time to heal." His eyes narrowed. "I wasn't lucky like O'Malley to get time off when I got hurt."

"Brody was banged up good."

"Yeah, yeah. You rescue guys got the juice."

He didn't ask Tony why he was there, which was good. Snyder would probably spread it around that Tony was pussy whipped. An unwanted question popped into his mind: Was he?

Tony lagged behind Snyder going down the rows. He complimented the recruits, gently tipped hats to indicate the right set on the head and casually straightened a collar, while Snyder insulted their shoe polish jobs and how their ties were knotted.

After inspection, the group headed to their lockers to change for fitness class.

The staff gathered around Olive. "Hi, all. Sorry I didn't get to greet you in orientation, but I had a family emergency."

Snyder mumbled something about women under his breath.

"But anyway, welcome to those of you here by choice and those drafted."

Some good-natured joking. Training recruits was not a plum assignment. Tony had given up something most of the HCFD members wanted—a spot on the Rescue Squad—for it.

Olive handed out a sheet of paper. "Here are your assignments for this week. I tried to accommodate your preferences on where to work, but know you'll be pitching in where needed."

Tony's name was under "physical fitness."

That was good. At least he could run off some of the pent up feelings he had at the thought of no real firefighting coming his way today—or ever again.

• • •

"I LOVE YOU so much, *mi amore*," Sophia said as Tony thrust inside her.

"Not as much as I love you."

She heard the words, wanted to say no, she loved him as much, but she didn't. Instead, she closed her eyes, arched her back and lifted her hips.

Afterward, they lay together in their bed, breathing hard. She cuddled close to him, hearing his heart thump against her ear, smelling his unique scent, familiar to her since she was fourteen. She began to rub his chest. "You didn't say much about your time at the Academy."

A slight tension invaded his body. "It's okay. I got to work out a lot with the recruits, which was great."

"Hmm. Talk to me about what you do there."

"We went on our first Confidence Walk today."

"What are they?"

Absently, he brushed his fingers down her arm. "They're grueling outdoor mile walks, where the recruits have to dress in full firefighter attire, air pack included."

"That doesn't sound too bad."

"Said the woman who never wore sixty pounds of gear. It's in the middle of the day, so they get hot, though not as hot as in a fire. Today we kept them on an even slope, but next week it'll be hills. We also go up and down the four flights of stairs in the training tower several times."

"How'd they do?"

"Only nine out of twenty made it through the entire exercise."

"I—"

The phone by the bedside rang, jarring them both. Tony grabbed for it, as both kids were at overnights with their friends. "Hello." A pause. "What's wrong, Gabe? *Jesús!* Of course I'll come." He was already climbing out of bed. "I'll be right there."

"What is it?" Sophia asked when he clicked off.

"My team was in a church fire tonight and Sydney got hurt." He grabbed the clothes he'd dropped on the floor. "She's asking for me."

"How hurt is she?"

"They don't know. She's on her way to the hospital in an ambulance."

"Oh, Tony, I'm sorry. Do you want me to come with you? I know she's like a sister to you."

Grabbing his phone and keys, he said, "No, I'll go alone. Shit, I partnered with her for a year and we depended on each other. I should've been there to protect her."

"Tony, you can't—" But she was speaking to his retreating back.

Sighing heavily, Sophia laid down, taking his condemning words to heart.

• • •

TONY ENTERED THE ER treatment room to find Sydney sitting up in bed, bruises on her right temple and some bandages on her hands. Battling back the abject fear roiling inside him, he said from the doorway, "Hey, kiddo."

Her eyes filled with emotion when she saw him. "Thanks for coming."

Tony watched her, trying to downplay his reaction. "You don't look too bad. I was expecting worse."

Gabe, sitting at her side, shook his head. His face, and Syd's, were still dirty from the fire. "Concussion, bruises, the temple thing isn't good, but she's okay. I should've waited to call you."

"*De nada.*" He came fully inside and approached the bed. There, he stuck his hands in his pockets. "What happened?"

The rest of the crew was against the wall. Brody's face was grim, but fire lit his eyes when he spoke. "The son of a bitch rigged the pews. He knew we'd have to crawl under them to check for people who might have gotten into the church at night. The first pew almost collapsed on her."

"Almost?"

Felicia pushed off from where she leaned against the wall. "He screwed up when he jimmied it. The seat caught on something."

The details made Tony fume. "How do you know it was jimmied?"

"Three other pews had the same tampering. We found the wires and cut marks on the wood." Gabe's face was grim. "He wasn't taking any chances."

Tony blew out a heavy breath. *"Jesús!"*

Another man he didn't know stood near the wall. "Hey, Ramirez. I'm Linc Jackson. I'm subbing for you."

*My replacement.* For a while, the guy would be a part of this crew like Tony used to be. He'd be with them when accidents like this happened. And afterward, when they consoled or celebrated with each other. Or in the middle of the night when somebody woke in a nightmare. "Nice to meet you."

Gabe stood. "Okay, let's get out of here and give the two of them some privacy." As he passed Tony, he said, "Don't know why she likes you better than us, *bombero,* but she wouldn't talk much. She made me call you."

"That's 'cause I'm better lookin'."

"We'll be back," Felicia told Syd as the four of them left.

When they were alone, Sydney peered up at him with eyes round as saucers.

"I know the real reason you wanted me to come." Gently, he sat on the side of the bed. "Come here." He held out his arms.

She threw herself into them. He held her close to him, smelling the smoke and grime on her that he used to be so familiar with. Even if you were able to get the stink out of your clothes, it lodged in your pores for days. His hand on her back, he soothed her hair with the other. Her body trembled and he heard the quiet tears. She could let down with him, and she knew it, so he didn't say anything, just allowed her to vent. She'd seen him lose it once when he couldn't save a child.

When she was done, she drew back and swiped her hands over her cheeks. "Fuck. I hate this. If the guys at other houses knew I broke down, the women in the department would never hear the end of it."

"I won't tell. Besides, *carina*, we all let go of it in our own ways."

"Yeah, well, I'd rather be smashing my fist against the wall than blubbering all over you."

"Believe me, this is better."

She rolled her eyes. "When that thing hit my head, I kept thinking, what if I die here? What will happen to Daisy?"

"Your mother would take care of her."

"She's getting on in years."

"Then make Sophia and me guardians. We already love Daisy. My kids do, too."

"Oh, Tony. Thanks. I'll think seriously about that. I guess I was wondering if Ken would…" She trailed off, her face flushing.

"Oh, no. Tell me you're not seeing him again."

Sturdy shoulders straightened. "No, of course not . But I wish he was helping to raise Daisy."

Shifting his position, he grabbed her hand. "You're a beautiful woman. You need a guy who's free, who loves you more than anything else in the world."

"Like you love Sophia."

"That's right."

She snorted. "If only there were more like you."

He gave her a half grin. "Sorry, doll, I'm one of a kind."

She laughed, as he meant her to.

"Did you ever feel this uneasy about the danger, Tony?"

"Of course, we all do. Being a firefighter is tough physically, but most people don't realize the emotional toll it takes on us."

From the doorway, he heard, "Yeah? Want to tell me about all that?"

Glancing over to the entrance, Tony saw...hell, Parker Allen? "How did you get in here?"

Her violet eyes widened and she flipped back skeins of dark hair. Tonight she was dressed in a skirt and sweater, which fit her well. "I charmed a male doctor."

"What do you want?" Tony asked.

"I thought I'd do a blog on injuries. Seems you guys have had a lot of them lately."

"I'm fine, Ms. Allen. Thanks for asking." Syd's tone was sarcastic.

For a minute, genuine emotion crossed Allen's face. Tony wondered briefly if there was more to this woman than they all thought. "Oh, sorry. Glad you're fine. I heard the pews were rigged."

"How on earth could you know that?" A crazy idea hit Tony and all concern for Allen fled. "Unless...you did it."

Her face scrunched up. "What are you talking about?"

Tony stood. "There's an arsonist on the loose. You seem to have quite a few details about tonight's fire that couldn't possibly have been made public."

She gave him a haughty look. "Boy, are you guys desperate. I must be really getting under your skin."

"You are, and you know it." Tony felt anger build and flow over. "Maybe if we'd had another firefighter on duty tonight, Syd would have been safer. But thanks to your blog, the crew got cut from six to five."

Something that looked like regret flashed briefly in her eyes. "The mayor was going to do that anyway. I facilitated the process. You're looking for reasons why I'm taking you on."

"We don't need to look," Syd blurted out. "We know plenty of reasons."

"What does that mean?"

"We'll let you wonder."

"I'm glad you're all right. I'll include your views in tomorrow's blog if you talk to me tonight."

Tony stepped close to Syd. "Over my dead body."

Syd sat up straighter. "I wouldn't do it anyway. Now, get out of here."

"Your loss," Allen said shrugging. With that she turned and swaggered out.

Concerned, Tony looked to Syd. "You think she might be the torch?"

"I wouldn't put anything past that woman. We know why she has a grudge against us. Who knows how her background screwed her up?"

"Yeah, but she'd have needed help to pull off some of these things. She wouldn't be physically able to rig the pews tonight, I don't think."

"Maybe she's in cahoots with the torch."

He sat back down and Syd took his hand this time. "Distract me. How you doing over at the Academy?"

"I like it enough. It's more challenging than I thought it would be. But I hate these reviews we have to give the recruits every Friday. All the teachers get together and rank them on appearance, performance, attitude, knowledge of material and EMS. The other staff aren't always nice."

She squeezed his hands. "You must really miss it."

"What?"

"Being on the line. You know. With us. Come on, Tony, you can tell me."

He waited a long time before he admitted, "I do. Like I'd miss my right arm if I lost it."

"I'm so sorry, buddy."

"Yeah, me too."

Mostly because Tony had learned something tonight. He'd never been on the other end of worrying about one of the crew. It simply didn't happen when they were all working together. But now that he was away from the actual firefighting, he'd been scared shitless that something worse had happened to Sydney. That was how Sophia must have felt for years. And for the first time, Tony admitted he was truly done with line work; he couldn't keep putting his wife through what he'd just experienced.

# CHAPTER 7

ON EDGE, SOPHIA had asked Isabel to take a coffee break with her and they sat in a secluded corner of the cafeteria, sipping the hot brew.

"Tell me what's wrong," her sister said. "I know something is."

"Tony quit the line."

"Excuse me?"

"I made him quit the line. He's working at the Fire Academy."

"Why would you take something he loved so much away from him?" Isabel's total shock—and accusatory tone—ripped into her already fragile composure.

Sophia started to cry. "I'm a horrible person. I did it for selfish reasons."

"You're one of the most unselfish people I know."

"Not in this. I'm afraid, Izzy, all the time for him. I can't deal with risks he takes."

Her sister sat back and watched her. "Have you tried counseling?"

"No, and I won't. Look," she said defensively, "it's solved. He's off the line."

"Oh, honey, this is far from solved."

Sophia left the cafeteria feeling worse than she had before she confided in her sister. She worked hard all morning, trying to shake off her sadness, but it clung to her like a shroud. At noon, she headed to the hospital gym to work out instead of eating. It was small in comparison to most exercise facilities but was big enough for the medical staff to run around the track, use the aerobic and weight machines and sit in a whirlpool. Once on the treadmill, she started slow as she watched the TV announcer talk about the president's new job initiative. But her thoughts were with her husband. In some ways, she knew Isabel was right. Sophia would never forget the bleak expression on his face when he'd found out Sydney had been hurt.

*I should've been there to protect her.*

Sophia hadn't known that her husband felt so protective of the young girl. Or was it his grief over losing his position on the line? His attempts at hiding his real feelings were heartbreaking.

Last night, she'd tried to wait up for him but fell asleep. At three, though, she'd awoken and his side of the bed was empty, so she got up to check to see if his car was in the garage. And found him instead, sitting outside in the cold October air, smoking a cigarette....

She put on a robe and went to join him. "Tony?" she asked. "Are you okay?" Oh, God. "Is it Syd?"

The moon cast him in shadows. But she knew what she'd see if she could look into his eyes. "Syd's okay. Concussion, bruises."

"Oh, good. Mind if I sit?"

"No, don't do that. Go back to bed. I'll be right in."

Instead she took a chair. Grasped his free hand. "I'm sorry she was hurt."

"Me, too. Part of the job," he said. "Of course, you know that."

"Still, I feel bad. For her and you. I know you're hurting over taking the Academy position. Talk to me about it."

The moon cast his face in harsh planes and shadows. "I found something out tonight."

"What?"

"That I'm never going back on the line." He laced their fingers together. "Willingly."

"What do you mean?"

For a long time, he explained to her how terrified he was for his friend, how he'd never felt that way before when he'd worked with Syd and the others, and how it was a cold slap in the face when he experienced exactly what she'd been going through all these years.

But instead of making her feel better, she ached for him. "Oh, baby, I'm so sorry."

He shook his head. "No, *carina*, I'm sorry for all I put you through. My change in jobs will be good for us."

That was hard to believe then, when she'd gone back to bed alone because he'd wanted to stay up by himself for a while, and now, in the pale light of day.

"Hey, exercise is supposed to release endorphins. You look like you're in pain." Brock, dressed in a slick sweat suit, had come into the machine room and took the treadmill next to her. He seemed rested and fit and happy, compared to her husband, who'd been exhausted and haggard last night. Briefly, she wondered how Brock's wife dealt with the long hours and his focus on medicine. Maybe Susan Carrington was simply stronger than Sophia was.

They made small talk and Sophia was winding down her workout when something on the TV caught her attention. The newscaster's voice came over a clip of the fire last night.

"And in local news, firefighters were called to the scene of a church fire at one o'clock this morning. Search and rescue teams were sent in to check for trapped victims. Captain Eve Callahan is here to explain why."

The TV panned to Eve. Lines of fatigue etched her pretty face, but she sat erect and alert. "Protocol demands the fire department search the premises after a fire regardless of the assumption that the church was empty. For example, a homeless person might have found access and fallen asleep in the pews. Our people comb the scene no matter what the time or circumstances."

"And you're involved in this case, why?" the newscaster asked.

"The fire was found to be incendiary."

Sophia stopped walking on the machine.

"What does that mean?" Brock asked.

"It's arson."

"Ah."

"Somebody set the fire in the sanctuary," Eve clarified.

"And a firefighter was hurt."

Anger sparked in Eve Callahan's eyes. "Yes, Firefighter Sydney Sands was injured when a pew collapsed on top of her. She was taken to Hidden Cove Hospital and released this morning."

The newscaster frowned. "There have been an unusual number of arson-related fires recently, haven't there, Captain Callahan? Do you believe they're connected?"

"I do. But I can't give any details."

The program went to a commercial, and Sophia sighed heavily as she stepped off the machine.

"Was it Tony's crew?" Brock asked. He'd stopped his walk, too.

"Uh-huh."

"Then his decision to go off the line was good. It could have been him trapped under the pew."

Sophia swallowed hard. "You're right; his decision is good."

Now, if she could only convince herself of that.

• • •

"WHO KNOWS WHAT this is?" Olive Hennessy asked as she stood before a five foot high, fifteen foot long structure.

A very bright, very eager recruit who Tony had come to like in the two weeks he'd been at the Academy raised his hand.

"Kyle, go ahead."

"It's a training maze. It's built like a house, with stairs and doorways and a roof."

"That's correct. The goal of this exercise is to find your way through it...blindfolded." Grumbles through the crowd. Tony remembered his own first experience in the maze. To him it had been a challenge, which he'd aced, like everything else in the Academy.

She held up a black strip of cloth. "Who can tell me why we cover your eyes?"

A female recruit with excellent physical skills answered. "Because the smoke in a fire can get so thick it's *like* being blindfolded."

"Good. Oh," Olive said as if it was an afterthought, "One more thing. Certain barriers have been put up, like those you'll invariably encounter in a real-life situation at some point. So you might find a wall blocking your way or missing steps. You have to use your ingenuity to get around any obstacles and make your way to the other side." She glanced over at Tony. "Firefighter Ramirez will set you up and get you ready to go in. Good luck."

Tony found himself looking forward to today. He liked helping newbies with their training. It was enough. It *was*. After last week's arson fire, he was sure he'd made the right decision to change jobs. He could picture Sydney bruised and battered in that hospital bed. This time, he'd been in the loved one's position. He'd felt a fear so great, he hadn't known what to do with it. He shuddered to think of Sophia routinely living with that kind of terror.

Banishing the thought, Tony crossed to the structure, which had been built off the gym, and picked up a blindfold as the recruits gathered around him. They'd suited up in their full turnout gear, then gotten in line. "A few pointers. Feel your way through this, like you learned in your training manuals. You won't be able to stand up because the ceilings aren't high enough, but that's okay. We crawl in most fires. Who knows why?"

"Because it's cooler on the floor. Heat rises." The recruit hadn't raised his hand, but these kids were nervous, so he let it go.

He lifted a sample air mask. "Second, breathe as easy as you can. If you run out of air, you lose points." He was grading each recruit on his performance, and this training would count heavily on the evaluations they were given each week.

Some of them shifted from one foot to the other.

"Finally, you'll get another chance at this if you screw it up."

Audible exhales in the room.

Of course, John Kyle volunteered to go first.

Tony walked with him to the doorway of the house. "Any problems I should know about, Recruit Kyle? Claustrophobia, fear of confined spaces or heights?"

"No, sir."

"Then, go. Good luck."

The first five recruits—three young women and two guys—went through the maze successfully. He gave them each a perfect ten. But the sixth ran into trouble. After a reasonable length of time, he crossed to the doorway. "Recruit Smith, you okay in there?"

No answer.

"Smith?"

Still, nothing.

"Damn it," he said under his breath. He stepped inside the maze. It was tight in here, stale smelling, with a hint of sweat. Dropping to his knees, he made his way to the first barrier easily because he wasn't blindfolded. There, he found Recruit Smith huddled up in a ball beside a wall. "Smith, you okay?"

The girl said nothing.

"Take off your air mask." When she did, he removed the blindfold. And got a good look at her. Dark haired, with big eyes, she reminded him of Syd, who also had a fear of confined spaces.

"Get scared, Smith?"

She nodded.

"It's okay, not everybody makes it on the first try."

Her eyes welled. Hell!

"Honest. I got a friend on my old crew and she's been a firefighter for five years. She finally made it through a pipe-crawl training for the first time."

"Really?" There was so much hope on Smith's young face, he had to smile.

"If you like, I'm sure she could talk to you about how she beats her fear."

"That'd be great." She hesitated. "Firefighter Ramirez, how come you're not as mean as some of the other instructors? Lieutenant Snyder would have reamed me out for getting stuck. He threatened to kick Bobby Schaefer out of the class because he couldn't make it up the ropes."

"I don't know about the nice part. But you're learning. And teachers don't have to be stern. Now follow me out."

Later that day, Tony was in the training office, and Olive Hennessy came inside. She scanned the area and then closed the door.

"Got a minute, Tony?"

"Yeah, sure."

"I heard what happened in the training maze today with Smith." Her face was inscrutable.

Hell, had he done something wrong already? "Yeah?"

"The kids were buzzing that you didn't yell at her."

"Yelling's really not my style."

A smile flirted with her lips and she edged her hip on the corner of the desk. "None of the recruits after her failed the maze. Why do you think that is?"

"I have no idea."

"I do. They were relaxed. They knew they weren't going to get their heads bitten off if they couldn't succeed on the first try."

"What are you saying, Olive?"

"That there's a difference between strictness and jumping all over the recruits. Some of the line guys come out here and behave like assholes."

He grinned. "They're assholes on the line, too."

She stood. "I always liked you, Tony. But I never figured you'd be such a good teacher. I hope you're here to stay."

"I am, and thanks for the compliment."

After she left, Tony stared down at the picture of Sophia, Miguel and Marianna on his desk. Huh! Maybe this wasn't going to be so bad after all.

• • •

SOPHIA AND TONY sat in the dining room of the Hidden Cove Hideaway while soft piano music drifted around them. Her husband was drop-dead handsome tonight in a gray suit and tie, his dark hair black in the lights from above and his eyes, for once, not bleak. She'd been shocked when she got home from work today and he said he'd made arrangements for Miguel and Mari to stay overnight with Gabe and Rachel and their kids, and for her to get dressed up. He wouldn't tell her where they were going.

"This is so much fun, Tony." She tasted the tart Chardonnay he ordered for her. He was having a beer. "We haven't done this kind of thing in a long time."

"Ryan O'Malley recommended this place. He brought Felicia here once before they…really got together, I guess."

She took pleasure in the muted music, the lights twinkling dimly from the corners, the fire blazing off to the side. "It's gorgeous."

They'd ordered dessert when Whitney Houston's "I Will Always Love You" began to play. "Oh, Tony. Remember this song? We loved it when we first got together."

"Want to dance?"

"Of course."

They fell into each other's arms on the small dance floor. Suddenly, Sophia felt like she was young again, floating around with her boyfriend. Often, when she thought back to those days, she wondered who those people ever were.

As he held her close, she could smell his scent. "Hmm, is that new aftershave?"

"Uh-huh. I figured now that I don't stink of smoke anymore, I could buy some good stuff. It was expensive."

"But worth it."

Drawing her even closer, he put his lips to her hair. "I always loved how *your* hair smelled."

After the song ended, they went back to the table and were greeted by a different scent—chocolate lava cake."

Sophia tasted hers. "Oh, my God, this is so sweet and rich, it's orgasmic."

"Hold off on that, will you? I'll give you orgasmic later."

The sexy banter was fun. It had been a while since they'd engaged in it. Purposely, she put the spoon to her mouth and licked. "I know a little bit about giving orgasms myself, *hombre.*"

"I know you do, babe." He reached in his pocket and drew something out, handed it to her.

"What's this key card for?"

"Room 21. Ryan said to ask for that one."

"We're staying *here* tonight?"

"We are."

"Oh, Tony, this is so cool."

"*Te amore, querida.*"

"I love you, too."

"Now, hurry up and finish that cake. I'm as hard as a rock watching you eat it."

"Oh, goodie."

Twenty minutes later, they stumbled into the room. He slammed the door shut and pressed her against the heavy wood. "*Dios mio,* I can't wait to get inside you."

She grabbed his crotch. It was like granite. "Don't wait. I'm ready."

Yanking up the skirt of her black dress, he ripped off her panties. Thank God she hadn't worn hose. She loosened his belt, tore it off, yanked open his zipper, releasing his hard length. He lifted her up, and she banded her legs around him. He moved in. And…

Nothing.

For a minute, she didn't know what happened. Then she felt the soft flesh against her belly. "Tony?"

He leaned his head on her forehead. "Fuck!"

"What…?" She placed her hand on his neck. "It's okay. This has happened before."

When he was so exhausted from being up with a colicky Mari during the night. When he'd broken his leg. When he was worried sick about where their next meal was coming from.

"Yeah, maybe three times." His voice was hoarse. "*Jesús,* I was so ready."

"Um, let's take a Jacuzzi, relax and try again."

"Yeah, okay, sure."

They did that. And other things, but nothing worked.

Despite their best efforts, that night, Tony was unable to make love to his wife.

# CHAPTER 8

JACK HARRISON'S OFFICE was painted a slate blue, with Berber carpeting on the floor, like he and Sophia had put in their basement. He imagined Jack's space got a lot of traffic, given the rigors of firefighting, and needed a durable rug.

The man stood and shook his hand. "Good to see you, Tony." A friendly smile. "I was wondering when you were going to make it down here."

He cocked his head.

"No one was talking out of turn. Noah Callahan mentioned it was a condition of you taking the instructor's job. He didn't say why, though."

*To keep tabs on me.*

"I see." At Jack's request, Tony sat on a cushiony chair and clasped his hands together. He knew he'd done harder things in his life, but this ranked right up there. "I, um..." He looked down at his feet. "I don't know where to start." After a moment, he looked up. "Can you help me with that?"

"Tell me why you took the job at the Academy. From what I hear, you're one of the best line firefighters in the department."

They were going to jump right in. He *hated* this. But suddenly, he was besieged by the memory of having Sophia up against the door—could anything be more sexy?—Friday night and going flat on her. Only an idiot wouldn't relate it to the changes he'd made in his life.

*Just say it,* hombre.

"After Teddy Thompson died over in Camden Cove, my wife wasn't handling the danger I was in on the line."

"Define *handling the danger.*"

"She started to worry all the time. Have panic attacks over it."

"How long have you been married, Tony?"

"Eighteen years."

Harrison's brows cocked as he checked the information sheet Tony had filled out this morning in preparation for this visit. "And you're only thirty-four."

"Me and Sophia have been sweethearts since middle school. I know it sounds silly, but we knew then we'd be together forever."

"It doesn't sound silly. And you were right."

"I got her pregnant at fifteen and we got married."

Again, he checked the record. "It doesn't say you have an eighteen-year-old child."

Tony swallowed hard and he felt everything drain out of him. Even after all these years, it still hurt. "She had him stillborn. It was a nightmare for us, and I don't think Sophia ever got over it."

"Did she talk to anybody at the time?"

He shook his head. "But we did great. I was in the fire department's pilot program for training guys in high school. We both worked two jobs until I was out and into the Academy. She went to school to get her nursing degree and, later, her certification to be a pediatric surgery nurse."

"I'm impressed at how far you've come."

"We're happy. Or we were, until 9/11. She freaked out then, too, and again when Sinco happened. But it was the female firefighter who died that turned the tide for us."

Jack shook his head. "Yeah, I was pretty busy after Teddy's death."

"I bet."

"So what are you saying, Tony? You left the line for her?"

His eyes widened. "Yeah. I did. And don't tell me I shouldn't have done it. I'd do anything for her."

Harrison waited a beat. "First off, I'm not going to tell you to *do* anything. I'm here for you to talk, to frame things, to maybe see things in a different light. But I have to know one thing. Are you in my office today only because Noah made it a requirement?"

Tony shook his head.

"What is it you want from me?"

His eyes welled. *Jesús.* He pressed the lids with his thumb and forefinger. "It's so embarrassing."

The psychologist chuckled. "If you only knew the things guys come in here and tell me."

*Just fucking do it!* "I can't get it up anymore. I can't make love to my wife."

"Hmm. I've heard that hundreds of times in twenty years, so don't worry, you've got company among the ranks. Have you ever had this problem before?"

"Yeah, of course, all guys do." When Jack said nothing, Tony asked, "Don't they?"

"Absolutely. So, what's the issue?"

"It's been a week. It never lasted a week. And in the past, it only happened when I was tired, when the babies could burst out crying any minute, when my mother died."

"Again, all normal. So?"

He swallowed hard. "I read the papers, magazines, and I've gone on line, about, you know, *it*."

"Impotence."

"Oh, God." Again he sighed. "The reports say its cause could be emasculation by women. But I don't understand, Jack. I love Sophia. I don't feel emasculated. She's always made me feel like a god. Especially in bed."

"You've had a good sex life?"

"Man, the best. Even when we were separated."

"You separated over your job?"

"Uh-huh. But I'm back home now."

"Why?"

He told the counselor about Miguel. About his own fear when Sydney was hurt. He didn't mention Brock Carrington. This was enough humiliation for one day.

"Are things good at home?"

"They're great. The kids are happy. Sophia loves having me work regular hours."

"What about you? Do you like being here at the Academy?"

"You know, I didn't at first. It was like being in an alien universe. But after a few weeks, I do. I'm different from the other instructors."

"How?"

"I'm nice, for one thing."

Now Harrison laughed aloud, making Tony smile, too.

"But I'm good at transmitting knowledge. Seeing weaknesses and how to correct them. Right before this happened, I was pretty psyched by how good teaching felt."

"Then you couldn't get it up."

Tony nodded.

Harrison watched him.

"You think there's a connection between the two things?"

"I told you I won't tell you those kinds of things."

"No, give me your opinion. You think the fact that I'm beginning to enjoy working at the Academy might be connected to not being...to impotence?"

"It could be, Tony. It could be."

• • •

OVERWROUGHT AT THE end of her shift, Sophia drove out to the lake and sat on the bench at the public beach. She watched the waves lap and recede, and though it was chilly, breathed in the cool, soothing air.

*Be careful what you wish for,* her mother used to say. Sophia shook her head. She'd gotten exactly what she wanted from her husband, and still, she was miserable.

And afraid in a different way.

One of things that had always been great between her and Tony was sex. They'd learned and experimented together, gotten books and videos when they were older, but mostly, they'd always been so close, the chemistry simply exploded between them. Had she destroyed that by her fear and cowardliness?

This morning, he'd said he had an appointment with Jack Harrison, the fire department psychologist.

And Sophia admitted to herself that *she* was the one who should be going to therapy. Not him. But she couldn't; she just couldn't.

Pulling her coat tighter around her, Sophia closed her eyes and tried to relax. Despite the bracing breeze, she couldn't stay in the present. Her mind drifted back...

Fifteen-year-old Sophia walked into her guidance counselor's office and smiled at Mr. Brady. She adored him because he'd been so kind to her for her two years at the high school, and was very understanding when she told him she was pregnant. Sophia trusted him more than any other adult in her life. And he was the one the school required she see to be accepted into their mother-to-be program, which serviced area city schools.

"Hello, Sophia. Have a seat." Geez he looked big today, even sitting behind his desk. He picked up her file and read it. Frowned. "So, you want to keep the baby?"

"Yeah. I don't believe in abortion. The Catholic Church forbids it."

"The Catholic Church says premarital sex is a sin, too." His tone was sort of mean.

She didn't expect this from him. Her mother had already made her confess to their priest and he hadn't been this way before.

"I'm keeping him."

"Then what, Sophia?"

"Tony and I are getting our parents' permission to marry as soon as we turn sixteen."

His expression was almost...disgusted. "Do you know how hard it'll be for two young kids like you to make it? The odds are against you."

"I don't care," she blurted out. "I love Tony."

"All the girls who come in here in your condition say the same thing about the losers who got them pregnant."

Though she was scared of him now, and totally embarrassed by her circumstances, she lifted her chin and pretended not to be. "I'm different. We're different."

He leaned back in his chair and she didn't like the way her was watching her. "You're a beautiful girl, Sophia. You'll be a gorgeous, sexy woman. Are you sure you want to tie yourself down to some deadbeat boy?"

"Tony's not a deadbeat. He's going into the firefighter program junior year. He's gonna be one and support us."

"He's not even a man yet."

Sophia swallowed hard. Despite the fact that she thought she could trust this man, she wasn't going to let him put Tony down. "I won't listen to you talk about him this way."

"You'll listen to anything I have to say or you won't get into Hope Hall. You'll have to drop out of school."

She bit her tongue. They needed this. She still had dreams of being a nurse, and Tony promised he'd help make that dream come true.

The counselor stood then, circled the desk and, uh-oh, locked the door. He came to stand in front of her, towered over her really, so she was facing his belt buckle. He traced his fingers along the metal. She was afraid to look up. Then he knelt before her. She tried to inch back in the seat. He raised his hand and traced the cross that laid in the vee of her blouse.

"W-what are you doing?"

"Being nice. Like I've always been to you, sweetheart. Now that I know you're not one of those boring *good* girls, I could show you" — he cupped her very full breast— "what it's like to be with a man."

"No, don't. I don't want you to."

"Maybe *I* do." His hand fisted on the neckline of her blouse and he yanked. Hard. The material ripped down the side. *Oh my God.*

Fueled by fear and anger, Sophia pushed him back and he fell on his ass. "What the...?"

Tony had taught her some things because he said she was so pretty, some guy was bound to try to force himself on her. So before Mr. Brady could finish, she kicked him in the balls.

While he was groaning on the floor, she fled the office.

Later, at Hope Hall, she heard that he'd put the moves on other pregnant girls but they were too afraid to tell, and she didn't plan to, either. But Tony knew something was wrong, and so she'd told him. He'd never trusted the guy anyway, and when she told him what Mr. Brady did, he found the guidance counselor alone, punched him out good and told him if he kept Sophia out of the program or reported to anybody that Tony had hit him, Tony and Sophia would tell the principal what he did and get all the other girls to back them up....

The slap of the wind brought her back to the present; her feet were like ice and her hands red and roughened. Shaky from the awful memory, she stood and walked back to her car.

If anything, she was more miserable than when she'd come out here.

• • •

IT WAS TAKE Your Child to Work day at the middle school, and for the first time ever, Tony could bring one of his kids with him. Miguel happily missed school, dressed in navy pants and light blue shirt so he looked like a miniature firefighter. They entered the Academy gym together. He was proud of his kid, and he wanted everybody to meet the boy.

Olive Hennessy approached them. She addressed Miguel. "Welcome, Miguel. We have four kids here today. I'm Battalion Chief Hennessy, and those guys over there" — she pointed to a group of staff — "are the other teachers here."

"Like my dad."

She smiled at Tony. "Don't tell anybody, but he's worked here the shortest period of time and he's the best teacher I've got on staff."

"Thanks, Chief."

Straightening, Olive nodded, then strode to the front of the group where the recruits were lined up. They went through the roll call, though after a month, the corrections were few and the recruits less nervous.

Olive gave them the rundown for the day. "Today, you'll be in the 'firehouse,' aka the Academy, going about your routine and you'll have to respond to a call. I'm going to let the four kids visiting us today ride the fire truck from the Academy to the tower, then back again, so you'll need to stuff yourselves in."

The "call" came right while the recruits were cooking lunch, which often happened and line guys hated. Once they'd received a call during Thanksgiving dinner at the firehouse where families were in attendance. The guys Tony was working with said their spouses were pissed off, but Sophia took it like a trooper, as she always did. Until now.

Tony got a kick out of watching the recruits and kids arrive at the tower when the rigs swerved into a tight space. There were three trucks—one Ladder, one Quint and one Pumper. Already Tony had forgotten the noise of the trucks when they came screeching to a halt, sirens blaring. Even after they arrived, loud beeping and simply the motors running hurt his ears. He wondered how Miguel was doing.

Soon, his boy descended from the truck—one of the recruits helped him down—and Tony noted somebody had put a helmet on him and a turnout coat that was only about one size too big. The probies positioned the aerial ladder, the mechanical one that could reach the entire four stories of the training tower. For today's exercise, the recruits would operate the aerial by themselves, place it at a window on the second floor, then climb through the opening. They'd go inside and do a simple maneuver.

Hennessy approached him. "Miguel wants to go up. Kyle's taken a liking to him, so he'll be right behind him. We won't let him inside, of course."

Tony grinned, proud of his son. "Yeah, sure."

It was fun watching Miguel mount the aerial. As far as he knew, the boy didn't have any vertigo. When he reached the top, he turned and raised a fist to his dad. Tony raised his back.

Afterward, Miguel couldn't stop bubbling about the fun he had that morning. Tony had enjoyed the drill, too. He got off on seeing his kid participate and helping with the training exercise.

*Good thing, Ramirez, 'cause you're not getting off any other way.* Shit, for a brief respite, he hadn't thought about his problems. He'd seen Harrison twice more and still nothing had improved in the bedroom. It made Tony so mad, he couldn't contain the anger sometimes.

He ate with the other staff members while Miguel sat with the recruits, who were doting on all four visitors. He noticed Smith, the girl Tony had helped in the maze, was particularly attentive. He ate the spaghetti they'd cooked—heated up but still good—and chatted easily with the staff.

After they finished, Miguel even helped clean up and joined Tony only after they were given a half-hour break.

The kid bubbled with excitement. "That was so cool, Dad. Did you see me? I didn't even get scared. And these guys are great. The girls, too."

"I'm glad you're having fun, *hijo*."

Miguel looked thoughtful. "Can I ask you something, Dad?"

"Sure. Anything."

"Don't you miss those kinds of runs?"

He swallowed hard. Out of the mouths of babes. "Yeah, I do."

"You like teaching here?"

"Yeah, son, I do. But nothing's ever a hundred percent in life. It's full of choices, and often, each of the alternatives has drawbacks."

"I know. So how come Mom isn't happy now?"

"Mom?"

"Yeah, you know, because you're not in danger anymore."

*Huh!* They'd only told the kids he was switching jobs.

"How do you know she feels that way?"

Miguel rolled his eyes like Sophia did when she was thinking, *puh-lease*. "I heard you two talking."

"Were you eavesdropping?"

"No. You were fighting and I heard stuff. More than once."

"Why didn't you ask me about all this?"

"I was afraid. All me and Mari want is for you to be happy. And for Mom not to be so sad."

That was food for thought.

"So, why's she still moping around if you're safe now?"

He looked at Miguel and wondered what he should tell his son. Finally, he said, "I don't know, buddy, I really don't know."

Sophia picked Miguel up at three so he could go to basketball practice. She seemed fine to Tony. Of course, he knew she was feeling shitty about the whole sex thing, but he didn't know she was as sad as before. An hour later, he was in Harrison's office wanting to talk to Jack about this.

"What's going on?" the counselor asked.

He told Jack about Miguel coming to work with him, about the boy's question.

The guy sank back in his chair. "How does that make you feel, Tony? That she's still not happy."

"Sad, I guess."

"You're not pissed? Don't answer right away. Think about it."

He did. And here, in the safe confines, he let emotion rise in him. "Yeah, I am pissed. What do I have to do to make her happy?"

"Interesting question. But I'm not sure it's the right one. You know, we've never talked about therapy for *her*."

"Not a chance."

"Why?"

"Um, it's so private, Jack. We...we never told anybody else."

"You can tell me. Everything's confidential here."

After relating the whole sad story, Jack was visibly upset. "Did the asshole keep working at the school?"

"No, after we grew up and thought about what happened, I checked. He got fired right after we graduated. No reason given. That's a laugh."

"I'm glad he was away from kids."

"I wish he was dead."

"Why?"

"That episode did so much harm to Sophia. She'd never go for counseling after we lost the baby or after 9/11 or now. But I don't blame her."

Jack waited a minute. Tony liked that he was reflective in these sessions. "I could talk to her."

"She'd never agree."

"You could come with her."

"I used that argument before, and still no."

Harrison watched him. Now the guy looked like he was making a decision. "I've been thinking about something for a while now. We have support groups here at the Academy."

"What kinds do you have?"

"One for PTSD, for example."

"Sophia doesn't have that."

"I agree. But I've been getting some calls and had some clients who talk about how their families have a hard time with their jobs, especially on the anniversary of September eleventh. I've been toying with the idea of starting a group for the families of firefighters who have issues with the job."

"That's a great idea, Jack. But I don't think Sophia would come. It's still therapy."

"With the safety net of other people around."

"I doubt it. The scars go deep."

"You know what, Tony? When we started talking, I said I wouldn't tell you to do anything, but I'm going to say something now that might contradict that. For your own good, since you're my patient and not Sophia."

"Don't say anything against her."

"I won't. But you have rights in your marriage, too. You've given up a lot for her. Maybe it's time she does something for you."

Jack's suggestion wasn't a new thought, but Tony was still bothered by it.

# CHAPTER 9

THEY TRIED AGAIN to make love, and it was still a no go. Sophia didn't think she'd ever seen anybody as frustrated—and angry—as her husband was. Bolting out of bed, he strode to the bathroom and slammed the door shut.

She sat back against the headboard, closing her eyes, knowing, *knowing*, she was at fault for his impotence. She was a nurse, for God's sake, and it didn't take Freud to figure out this one. Though Brock Carrington had helped.

She'd been sitting in the cafeteria, playing with some chicken salad when he came up to her...

"Want some company?"

"Yeah, sure."

He smiled as he sat. Once again, she wondered if he and Susan had a good marriage.

"You look so sad," he said after he unwrapped a BLT. I thought things would be better now that Tony's given up firefighting."

"In some ways they are. In others not."

His blue gaze held hers. "Look, I wasn't going to say anything, but I can't stand watching you suffer like this. You need help, Sophia. I can recommend a good psychiatrist."

"I don't like the idea of counseling."

"You've alluded to that before, but something's gotta give. And as long as I'm in this deep, I might as well say if Susan asked me to give up my career as a surgeon, I'm not sure I'd do it. I'd feel, I don't know, less of a man. In my book, Tony's more of a man than I'll ever be, but he has his limits...."

Shit, shit, shit. She stared at the closed bathroom door. Getting off the bed, she walked to it, knocked, then opened it. He was standing in front of the mirror, his arms braced on the sink. His muscles bulged, his shoulders were stiff and his face impossibly taut. "Do I make you feel like less of a man, Tony?"

His eyes widened when he caught her gaze in the mirror. He shook his head, but she interpreted the emotion in his eyes.

"Is that what you've been thinking?" she prodded.

Still facing her in the glass, he shook his head. "I didn't think so initially, but I did some research, and Harrison mentioned it today."

"You didn't say anything about your meeting with him."

"I..." Now his face got bleaker. "I know. I was afraid to."

"You were afraid to tell me something? Oh, God, I hate all this between us. And I feel like I've caused the breach."

Turning, he tugged her close and held her against his bare chest. "You can't help what your mind wants, Soph. It's not your fault."

"I guess you can't help what your body's saying, either. You can't make love to me because of something psychological. We need to face that."

He sighed. And didn't contradict her.

"That's what Jack Harrison thinks, right?"

Waiting a long time, holding her so close she could feel his breathing escalate, he finally murmured, "Yeah. He does."

• • •

IT WAS THE halfway mark for the recruits at the Academy and Tony was glad the course work was finished. The probies were in shape, and the rest of the time would be spent on practical application, like now, learning how to use a K-12 saw. Ed Snyder was demonstrating the technique, and immediately Tony knew what the guy was doing wrong. Inwardly, Tony smiled. He was a good teacher, better than most of the staff, as Olive had told Miguel.

She approached him. "Boy, I like it when we get to this point. Now the training's all hands-on."

"I was thinking the same thing."

They watched the recruits fumble, unable to start the monstrous saw. She asked, "Can I ask you something?"

"Sure."

"You gonna stay after February, at the Academy, I mean?"

"I'm planning to."

"Why, Tony? You're a top-notch firefighter. Like I said before, you're the best teacher I've ever seen from the line, but this doesn't seem...you."

"It's a long, and very unpleasant, story."

"Okay, but if you ever wanna talk, I'm here. For now, I'm gonna count on you for staffing next year."

After Olive left, his heart ached so bad, he thought maybe he was having an angina attack. He told one of the other line guys he'd be right back, and hurried into the building. As he walked, he got more and more upset, more and more in pain. Had he really thought, in that unconscious Harrison talked about, that things would get better and he could go back on the line? If so, it wasn't happening. Things weren't better, they were worse. *Jesús,* he thought, what was he going to do?

Maybe Harrison could relieve the awful pressure in his chest, he thought as he reached the office. Before he could knock, the door opened. Out came Harrison and…Sophia? What the hell?

When she raised her head, she wasn't crying. She wasn't having a panic attack. She looked…better.

"Hey," he said, kissing her cheek. "What are you doing here? Oh, God, Jack didn't call you, did he?"

"No, of course not. After you told me what he said about the counseling and the support group, I decided to come see him today."

"Alone?"

"Yeah. I'm thirty-four years old, Tony, and I can't be afraid like I am. Of the counseling." She sidled in close. "For your safety."

Jack was right behind her, smiling serenely. "I've got the support group in place for two weeks from today. Seven women and two men are attending."

"Eight women," Sophia said, holding Tony's gaze.

"Really?"

"Really. I promise, Tony, I'm going to fix myself."

He hugged her tight and said, "Don't fix yourself too much. I like the woman you are."

She smiled.

Jack smiled.

And the pressure in Tony's chest was gone.

• • •

THE INTRODUCTIONS ABOUT why they were all here came wrenchingly, but the reasons needed to be exorcised. Sophia was grateful she was last in the circle where the nine other family members of the HCFD sat in a conference room of the Academy.

"I worry about her all the time," one guy said. "She's not safe walking into burning buildings. I was doing okay with it until we had kids. Now it's hard to explain why Mommy risks her life every day."

"I feel left out," a woman commented. "He's so close to his buddies on the line. They're a second family and I'm not good at hiding how jealous I am."

Another woman shook her head. "For me, it's not the physical danger. It's what he sets himself up for every single day. He willingly puts himself in a position to feel so much pain and loss. People die in fires. When it's a kid, he's destroyed for days. Why would anybody willingly subject himself to that kind of emotional torture?"

When Sophia's turn came, she stuck out her chin. "I made my husband quit the line."

There were a few gasps.

"My fear and anxiety were too much to handle. It's hurt us a lot. I hate how I feel, what I've done. I want to get over it, and I want him to go back to firefighting."

As she scanned the faces of the others, she realized she was probably the only person in this room who wanted that. "I'll give you a word of advice, all of you. If he or she quits the line because of you, it isn't the end of your problems. It could be just the beginning."

• • •

CHRISTMAS EVE

Every year, Tony and Sophia sat near the tree decorated with lopsided reindeer, knitted Santa faces, cardboard candy canes and other homemade decorations. Tiny lights twinkled from the branches and the scent of evergreen created a cocoon of security around them. They were both at peace, surprising after such a tough autumn.

"The kids are so excited," Sophia said. "I hope they sleep tonight."

He locked his hand on her neck, leaned over and kissed her. "We took the edge off that by letting them open one present."

"They loved the Wii."

"We'll have fun with it too, *carina*." He smiled at his lovely wife. Tonight she wore pink satin pajamas, and her hair curled down past her breasts. But best of all, she seemed happier than he'd seen her in a long time. "So, do you want to open our presents to each other now?"

She sipped her eggnog. "You go first." Picking up a small package, she handed it to him.

"No, you." He pulled an even smaller one from his bathrobe pocket, gave it to her and watched her tear the paper off the jewelry box. Her smile was super bright. God, he loved being able to put that on her face again. But it dimmed when she opened the box, which held a gold heart locket. On the front he'd engraved, *Wife, Mother, Friend.*

"Open it," he said.

She pried open the locket and saw that he'd put in pictures of the kids. When she glanced up, she still wasn't elated, as he'd thought she would be, about the expensive gift. But there was something else in her eyes. "Um, this is lovely but…"

"What's wrong?"

"Nothing. Well…" she shrugged. "Maybe you'd better open your gift."

"I don't understand. I thought you'd be happy."

"Oh, I am happy, but"—she shoved her present into his chest—"just open this."

He tore off the bright silver bow, then the red paper. The box said, "Carter." What the hell was Carter? And why didn't she like her present?

Inside he found...doll clothes? He looked up at her. "Did you mix up the presents? Is this for Mari's new doll?"

She shook her head.

He took the clothing out. It was a tiny undershirt. I don't...oh, *Dios mio*." He grasped on to her arms. *"Oh, mi amore!"*

"It must have happened right after Thanksgiving."

"That was the first time we…"

"Made love after that horrible drought. And if you recall, we were in so much hurry, we didn't use any protection."

"Oh, yeah, *carina*, I recall. Are you sure, though? That was only a few weeks ago."

"I'm sure." She moved closer and placed his hand on her stomach. "We're having another baby, *hombre*. But I'm afraid your beautiful locket won't be big enough now."

"Tell you what, we'll put our pictures in it."

"Are you glad about the baby?"

"Of course I am. Sure, of course, but I...never mind."

She grabbed his hand. "Antonio Ramirez. Don't you dare clam up on me. Haven't we learned our lesson?"

The support group was instrumental in Sophia's change in outlook, but just as beneficial were their couples meetings with Harrison. He'd told them they both had to stop protecting each other and be honest about their feelings.

"Yeah, we have. I don't want the new baby to make us backtrack. Make you worry when I go back on the line in February."

"He or she won't. I promise. I think we should look at this little miracle as a new beginning."

He grinned like the boy he'd been when she'd told him the first time that she was accidentally pregnant. They'd started out on shaky ground, but now, the earth had firmed under their feet. And when it went rocky, as it was bound to, they'd be honest with each other and get help if they needed it.

Standing, he crossed to the pocket doors of the living room, slid them shut and locked them.

"What are you doing?"

"Insuring our privacy. I want to make love to you here, in front of the tree, to celebrate our own Christmas baby."

She laughed aloud and held her hands out to him.

Tony took them, knelt in front of her. While still on his knees, he said a silent prayer of thanks for all he'd been given.

And he swore the angels were smiling down on them.

• • •

# RESCUE ME

Novella number five in the
AMERICA'S BRAVEST SERIES

KATHRYN SHAY

# CHAPTER 1

RESCUE 7 SCREECHED to a halt in front of the small office building in a strip mall in the center of town, and all five firefighters tumbled out of the rig. The Quint and Midi followed behind them, and the Battalion Chief's vehicle stopped on a dime. Cal Erikson exited his Jeep, his stance erect, his movements quick. "Get the lights on first and I'll set up Incident Command, but know we're going in fast. Malvaso, come with me."

The April wind had picked up, fighting Sydney as she tugged on her turnout coat and put her SCBA in place, ready to pull it over her face. Quint and Midi crews unloaded the huge halogen lamps and switched them on, slicing light through the darkness. She glanced over and saw the chief set up his computer on the hood of the Jeep. Gabe returned to the truck and called for their attention. "We'll wait till the Quint gets water on the fire, but be ready. This is the chief's best friend's office building."

That news had come from dispatch on the ride over. Thankfully, it was eleven at night, so Max Delinsky, local businessman, more than likely wasn't inside. The small building's windows were dark, too, which was good.

Quickly, water was slapped on the fire and Gabe led his team to the chief. Erikson faced them; his expression was bleak. "Max isn't home. I can't reach him by cell." He glanced worriedly at the structure. "I'm afraid he's inside. He works late sometimes."

"If he's in there, we'll find him, Chief," Gabe said, squeezing Erikson's arm. "I promise."

"Fuck it. Give me your gear, Malvaso. I'm going in with your guys. You take over out here."

"Cal, that's a very bad idea. You're personally involved."

He was already whipping off his HCFD windbreaker. "What if your cousin was in there?"

Waiting a beat, Gabe finally nodded. "I hear ya."

Erikson donned the turnout coat, Nomex hood and face mask while the rest of them checked the layout of the building on the computer. He handed Gabe his cell phone. "Speed dial four. Keep calling him."

The chief lead the way to the front of the building. Sydney had taken the rabbit tool, so she popped the lock on the heavy door. No alarm. Not a good sign for Delinsky; if he hadn't turned it on, the chances went up of him being inside. Adrenaline began to pump through Sydney's veins.

"Ramirez and Sands, come with me back to his office," the chief ordered. "White and O'Malley check out the left. There's a kitchen, lavatory and a break room down there."

Sydney and Tony followed the chief to the right. Thick, gray smoke filled the foyer and the corridor as they made their way to Delinsky's office. "It's behind that door." A fire door, which might be good for the chief's friend.

"I got it." Again, Sydney situated the tool and sprung that door. She stepped into a five-by-five hall space in front of an office.

Suddenly, an explosion rattled the building and the fire door slammed shut. Sydney looked down. She held the pry tool in her hand. And neither man had had the chance to step in behind her.

Over her radio, she heard, "Sands, you okay?"

"Yeah, chief, but I got the rabbit."

"Try it from the inside."

She set the pry mechanism in position but couldn't get purchase this way. She told the chief.

"Some of the fire doors are like that. Ramirez is going for another tool. Sit tight."

Glancing over her shoulder, Sydney frowned. "Why, Chief? Your friend's office is right in front of me. I can get in there."

"Wait for us."

"Yes, sir." *Not.*

She remembered a lesson she'd had at the Academy from Zach Malvaso, who confessed that he thought there were times when a firefighter had to follow his own instincts even if it meant disobeying a direct order. Her gut told her this was one of those instances, so she approached the door labeled *President*. Through the glass she saw a lot of smoke. Hell, if Delinsky was inside, he didn't have much time left. Smoke inhalation was the leading cause of death in fires. Removing her glove, she found the knob hot to the touch; she slid her hand back into the Nomex and tried the handle. It opened.

Once in the office, Sydney dropped to her knees. She could see absolutely nothing, so she tried to picture where the desk might be. Straight ahead, she guessed. She crawled forward. Bumped into a chair. Swore. Moved to the left.

"Sands, you okay?" The chief's voice sounded worried.

"Yeah, I'm fine."

Raising her hand, she felt the edge of something. A leg of the desk. Feeling her way upward along the wood, she stood, met a flat surface and felt around. She moved along the edge, encountered what might be a computer, papers, then...human flesh.

"Sands!" she heard through the radio. The chief's voice was more panicky than she'd ever heard it. "The horn blew. We have to evacuate. The burst in the back was a stove blowing. The building's fully involved. We're on our way out and will head around the side. Go into the office and stand near the big windows. Don't open them though, or it could make things worse."

"I, um, Chief, I'm *in* the office. Your friend *is* here. I found him collapsed over the desk."

"What the...?" He swore. "Is he alive?"

Taking off her glove again, she felt his neck. "Still has a pulse. Thready but strong."

"Stay calm and give him some of your air."

As if she didn't know what to do. But Gabe had said on the way over that Erikson and Delinsky were like brothers so she understood the chief's concern.

"You have to stay with him and give him air. Don't try to get him out. We'll be right there and come in as soon as we get the order that the place is ventilated."

"Okay, buddy," she told Max Delinsky as she pulled the chair back, eased him out—he was heavy—and slid to the floor with him. He was unconscious, but she spoke to him anyway. "Here take this." She removed her mouthpiece and as soon as she got a gulp of smoke started to cough. There was nothing like breathing in this shit—and Delinsky had been in it a while.

*Please don't let me be too late,* she prayed.

After several seconds of air, Max came awake, took in more oxygen and finally started to cough, signaling his lungs were working.

Relief swept through Sydney, making her weak. Thank God, she thought as she shoved the air piece back into her mouth. She'd hate to kill the chief's best friend.

• • •

PAIN FILLED MAX'S chest as consciousness dawned. Suddenly, air flowed into his lungs. When he came fully awake, he realized he was stretched out on the floor, a warm body was behind him and the person was stuffing something in his mouth. Disoriented, he couldn't remember what had happened. He opened his eyes to total blackness and a thousand needle pricks stinging them. Then the mouthpiece was removed and he started to cough as his lungs refilled with—Jesus, smoke. A minute of the panic and pain again, then the air hose was placed back in.

The owner of the body said, "Mr. Delinsky, I'm Firefighter Sands from Cal Erikson's division. We're in your office. A fire broke out in the building. I'm the only one who made it back here, so we have to sit tight and share the air until the others get us out. Can you do that?"

"Yeah. What happened?"

"Let's not talk. Lay back against me. I'm leaning on the wall so I can hold your weight." He did as she asked, her presence calming. He took in her air, then went to pull the hose out of his mouth. "No. Wait at least sixty seconds."

"I can't see my watch."

"Don't joke either." But he felt her chest rumble.

As they switched the hose back and forth, a thousand thoughts crossed his mind. Was he going to die? What would that do to his daughter Amber? To calm himself, he thought about the woman risking her welfare for his. Did she have a husband who worried about her? A child she didn't want to leave an orphan? How old was she?

Vaguely, he heard her radio go on and off, heard Cal's voice, though Max was light-headed and couldn't make out the words well.

The air came back to him. She said, "It's taking longer than they thought, Mr. Delinsky. Before we break the windows in here, they have to ventilate from above so we don't go into backdraft."

After he breathed in air, he handed the nozzle back to her. "Make it Max."

"What?"

"Max. What's your first name, Firefighter Sands?"

"Sydney."

"Thanks, Sydney."

Seconds crawled by as the woman shared her breath with him. At last, the sound of glass shattering; he heard bodies come into the room. He was lifted up off the floor by big, strong arms that were probably Cal's. Dragged to the window. Handed out.

He hoped Sydney Sands was right behind him. He wouldn't be able to live with something happening to his guardian angel in order to save him.

• • •

"HI, MAX. WE'RE over here." Chief Erikson called to his friend, who they'd rescued five days ago. Max was recovered enough to want to meet the group who'd saved his life, and suggested he buy them drinks at Badges. Sydney had changed out of her uniform into jeans and simple white blouse, and the others were dressed in civilian clothes, too. Even the chief.

A tall, broad-shouldered guy approached them. Hmm, he was a nice specimen. As he got closer, she could see his hair was sandy colored, and his eyes a piercing green. They locked with hers immediately. The warmth and gratitude in them warmed her. "Well, there she is."

She wondered how he knew she'd been the one with him? They all got credit for the rescue, of course. "Hello, Mr. Delinsky."

He grasped her hand and held it between both of his. Big masculine palms caressed her. "We're on a first name basis. *That* I do remember." Smiling, he tugged her close and gave her a hug. Sydney wasn't used to the affections of strangers, but she *had* held this man in her arms and let him breathe her air. So she hugged back. Besides, people usually got sappy after you saved their lives.

"Yeah," she said easily as she drew away. "We're more than acquainted. How you doing, Max?"

"Very well, thanks to you." He kept staring at her, and his intense gaze made her nervous. "You're a little young to be executing a solo rescue, aren't you?"

The chief clapped him on the back. "Yes, she is. Syd's been with us since she was eighteen. And she's an excellent firefighter which is why she got on the Rescue Squad so soon. But, I'll have you know, she went against my orders to go into your office alone."

His eyes widened. "Seriously? You got in trouble?"

"Not exactly." The chief was smiling and Sydney enjoyed seeing him in the role of friend and not boss. "Protocol demanded a letter in her file, but I worded it so she's shown as a hero. Come on, you can buy me a drink and meet the rest of the group."

Max smiled again at her. "You're staying around, right? I'd like to talk to you some."

"Sure, okay."

Tony approached her, handsome as sin in jeans and a purple shirt nobody else could wear. "Only had eyes for you, kiddo."

"What?"

"He's taken with you."

"'Cause I was with him. Gave him my air. We all conduct the rescue."

"Maybe. But you're a beautiful woman, Syd. Men are attracted to you. It probably surprised the hell out of him to see somebody like you in the role as savior."

"Give me a break. Now, you, *you're* married to a beautiful woman."

His grin was infectious and his dark eyes lit from within. "Yeah, and she's even prettier with that big belly." Sophia was due to give birth at the end of the summer. Sydney had had dinner at their home a few nights ago, and Sophia looked stunning with a cute, rounded belly.

Unlike Sydney, who'd blown up like a balloon early in her pregnancy. She'd had a difficult time with Daisy all around, but she loved her almost four-year-old to distraction.

She talked with Tony and finished her beer. "I gotta go," she said after a while. "My mother's watching Daisy, but I don't like to take advantage of her time when I'm not working."

Tony kissed her on the cheek. "See you tomorrow."

On her way to the door, she stopped at the bar where Gabe was talking to Max. "Sorry to interrupt, but I have to leave and wanted to say good-bye."

Soft brown brows scowled. "I wanted to talk to you." He set down his drink. "Let me walk you to your car."

"Um, okay."

They left Badges and as Sydney strode beside him, she felt...small. He was big and muscular, but still, she was no weakling at five eight, a hundred and forty pounds. The notion discomfited her. At her battered Jeep, she stopped. "This really isn't necessary."

He stuck his hands in his pockets. "Saving my life isn't a big deal?"

"We all saved your life."

"Not in my book. You did."

"Well, in any case, you're welcome."

He pulled a card out of the pocket of his jeans and handed it to her. "My daughter Amber sent this."

"Oh." She slid open the note and scanned it. *Thanks for saving my dad, Firefighter Sands. It's just me and him and I don't know what I'd do if I lost him. He says you have a little kid and I'm offering free babysitting whenever you need it. I'm thirteen, btw.*

She looked up. "This is so sweet."

"Her mother died three years ago. Amber's possessive of me because we're close. She got hysterical when I was hurt, but after she calmed down, her first thought was to do something nice for you."

"Amber sounds like a doll." She leaned against the car. They were under some trees, but the April air was warm. "I'm sorry about your wife."

His expression was bleak. "Yeah, cancer. I don't know what I would have done without Cal."

She cocked her head.

"His ex-wife, Laura, was Annette's best friend. We spent a lot of time together as a foursome and, at the end, Laura was a godsend for Amber." A bleaker look.

"What's wrong with that?"

"I kind of blame myself for the Erikson's divorce. Laura freaked after Annette died." He rolled his eyes. "I don't know why I'm going into all this. I want to know about you." He nodded to a bench off in the grass. "Can you stay for a minute?"

She checked her watch, knowing she should get home, but drawn, somehow, to this man. "For a bit." They crossed to the bench and sat. The trees swayed above them and birds chirped. God, she loved spring. "But you seem to know about me already."

"I confess. I asked Cal. Then my daughter showed me your picture on the blog the women in the department write. It's a great PR tactic."

"Thanks. Self-defense, mostly. The reporter, Parker Allen, has it out for us."

"Yeah, Cal talks about that all the time." He sat back, stretched out his legs and linked his hands behind his head. "So, tell me what makes Sydney Sands tick."

She thought for a minute. "My kid. And firefighting."

"Why did you choose firefighting? It isn't the most common job for a woman. Especially a mom."

"*My* mother would agree with you. She's lives with me and helps out a ton, but she doesn't like the danger I'm in."

"Danger lurks everywhere for everybody. There are no guarantees in life. Annette was a teacher and was *safe*. Still, she's gone."

"That's a great philosophy to live by."

"So, what made you go into the profession?"

"I had a tough childhood. I grew up in a bad part of New York City. When the Anderson County Fire Academy set up a firefighter class for inner city kids at my school, I went to it as a way to escape a very bleak future. Right after

I graduated, we moved to Hidden Cove because I automatically got in the recruit class here."

"So it wasn't firefighting itself? It was just a way to get out?"

"Actually, no. I was attracted to the job because the FDNY had a station house near us. The guys were friendly and did a lot of work with the community." She smiled.

"What?"

"I go back there every once in a while. They can't believe a bad kid like me is one of them now."

"What about the rest? Personally?"

Suddenly, she didn't want to tell him about other parts her life. Not only was her history seedy, but she hated talking about her failures. So she checked her watch again and stood. "I have to go. I need to relieve my mom."

"Oh." He seemed disappointed. "Sure." He rose, too. "Thanks again for what you did for me. But I'm afraid I have another favor to ask."

Her brows arched.

"Can you give Amber a shot at babysitting? She's very determined and I know she'll pester me until you let her try it at least once. I'd provide rides for her back and forth."

Suddenly, Sydney got a funny feeling in her stomach at the thought of seeing this man again.

"She's a great kid. Everybody loves her. And she'd had experience with my brother-in-law's kids."

"I'd have to meet her first. See how Daisy likes her. But, yeah, sure."

"Can we set up a time?"

"All right. How about my next shift off? My mother works part time at her sister's restaurant when I'm not due at the firehouse."

They set the date, and when they walked to her car, once again he hugged her. This time she noticed his woodsy scent—cedar with a hint of citrus—and how strong his arms were. When he stepped back, she was off-kilter.

Wow. It had been a long time since her pulse rate sped up and her heart started to beat faster from a man—and a stranger. A very male stranger, but still...

# CHAPTER 2

"WHAT'S SHE LIKE, Dad?" Amber sat on the deck of their house, computer on her lap, and didn't even greet him when he returned home. All she wanted, all she *had* wanted, was to know about the woman who'd saved his life.

"Hello to you, too!"

She gave him Annette's patronizing look and kissed his cheek when he leaned over. Sometimes, especially when she affected one of his wife's mannerisms, she looked so much like her mother with her blond hair and blue eyes that his heart clutched. "Hey, Dad."

Dropping down onto the chaise opposite her, he smiled. "She's very nice." But not what he expected. For one thing, she was *young*. But maybe that's because he felt ancient these days, even though he was only thirty-eight.

"How old?"

"Somewhere in her twenties."

"Is she pretty?"

He wouldn't say that about her. She was tall and sort of tough-looking, but there was a womanliness about her that was appealing. And she had beautiful, light brown eyes.

Huh! This was the first time he'd had a thought like that about a female in a very long time.

"She's attractive. Dark brown hair and brown eyes. She looks like a female firefighter."

"She butch?"

"Honey, where did you get that term?"

"Da-ad. I'm thirteen."

"She's more feminine than butch." Time to distract his daughter from Sydney Sands' attractiveness. "She also said you can babysit if you and her child hit it off."

"Cool. I'm old enough to do that."

"I know, honey. You've babysat for Bobby's boys." Bobby was Annette's brother, who missed her almost as much as Max did and loved spending time with Amber. His wife's parents coveted his daughter's visits, too.

"Yeah, but he's family. This'll be more real."

"I set up a time next week to go over and meet her and Daisy, so we can see how it goes."

"Awesome."

He glanced at her lap. "What are you doing on the computer?" He worried all the time about the sites she might visit and the predators she might encounter. And he wouldn't let her have a Facebook page, either, which made her mad. They'd had a discussion about the Internet, and he'd put some parental controls on her laptop but still he was concerned.

"Reading the women's firefighter blog. Somebody name Felicia posted today that an arsonist is targeting the department. She says she wants everybody to know what they're up against." Her blue eyes darkened. "Dad, the fire at our business wasn't arson, was it?"

"They don't think so."

She nodded to the computer. "Sydney's posting tomorrow."

"Ms. Sands, honey."

"She saved your life. She's practically family."

At first he'd thought his daughter's preoccupation with the woman was cute, but after four days of her harping on Sydney, he worried. Amber tended to get obsessed with things, and Annette had been effective at dealing with her excessive enthusiasm. He was not the good parent his wife was. "Baby, we don't even know Sydney. You shouldn't get too enamored with the fact that she saved my life."

"We're gonna know her. I'm gonna babysit for them."

"Maybe. If you get along with her kid."

"I will. I love kids. Uncle Bobby says I'm a natural."

"Don't get carried away." He stood. "I'm going to do some work now." He was running his business from home until they moved into other offices, and his three employees were doing the same. "Be good."

"Yeah, I'll only hit one or two porno sites."

"Brat." He ruffled her hair, walked into the house and down to the den. These days, his large colonial, with four bedrooms, three baths, a finished basement and more rooms than they used on the first floor, seemed empty. He and Annette had planned to fill the space up with kids, but that had never happened.

In his big office with huge floor-to-ceiling windows, he sat down at his desk and booted up his computer. But instead of going to his profit-and-loss sheets for his quarterly, *The Heart of Hidden Cove*, the magazine he ran, focusing on the good things in their picturesque town, he clicked into the HCFD site and then the women's blog. He told himself he only wanted to see what Amber was reading, but in reality, he wanted to peruse the back blogs to learn more about Sydney Sands. God knew why, but he had the urge and followed it.

• • •

DAISY STUCK HER fingers in her mouth and stared over at Max Delinsky and his daughter, Amber. The teenager was gorgeous with thick blond hair, blue eyes and a just-becoming-feminine body. She remembered that stage in her own life and how awkward it was. Her mother had tried to help, but Amber didn't even have that solace. Was Max good with girl things?

"Daisy, this is Mr. Delinsky and Amber."

Her child, the love of her life, with her own blond locks and gray eyes, stared at the girl. "Hi, Ambs," she said. She was talking pretty well but often shortened names.

"That's right." Amber's eyes shone when she got up and crossed to the child. Immediately, Daisy lifted her arms for Amber to pick her up. "You can call me Ambs. It's cute."

The girl was gentle when she scooped Daisy into her arms and straightened. She was also grinning so broadly, it made Sydney smile. Glancing over, she saw the same expression on Max's face. When he smiled, he looked young and happy. At other times, there was a sadness in his eyes that added years to his nice features.

"You're pretty." Daisy hugged Amber.

"See, Dad," Amber was saying. "She likes me."

"I see, Princess."

A pang shot through Sydney. Daisy didn't have a father to call her nicknames.

Sitting on the floor, Amber picked up the rings for the holder. "Want to play with the building blocks, Daisy?"

In answer, Daisy took one and tossed it across the room. "Play fetch."

Max laughed and said, "Maybe we can leave them alone here for a while. Let Amber have some time with Daisy. We could sit on the porch."

"Great idea, Pops."

Sydney stood. "Go on outside, Max. I'll get the girls and us something."

"Juicy," Daisy bubbled. "And cookies."

"Juice and cookies it is, baby." She smiled at Max. "Coffee or iced tea?"

"Iced tea would be terrific."

They separated at the foyer of the house she'd scraped to buy a year ago. Thanks to her crew at the firehouse, much of it had been renovated, and Tony and Sophia had given her Adirondack chairs for the front.

After bringing drinks, she dropped down in a chair next to Max. "Amber's a doll, Max."

"The love of my life."

"Funny, I was thinking the same about Daisy."

"Kids get to you, don't they?"

"Uh-huh."

He lounged back in the chair, full of masculine grace. He seemed so comfortable with his body. She liked the way his shoulders looked in a pinstriped oxford-cloth shirt matching them with pressed jeans. On his feet were Dockers. Actually, he dressed like Daisy's father, Ken, a thought she *didn't* like at all.

"So, Amber was on the blog again yesterday. I took a cue from her and read it." His eyes twinkled. "You were fascinating."

No one, to Sydney's knowledge, had ever called her fascinating. "Really? Which blog entry did you like best?"

"I guess the one on being a mother. If that didn't affect the public's impression of firefighters, I don't know of anything that would."

"It was mixed, actually. Some people wrote in that I shouldn't be on the line with a three- going on four-year-old." She snorted. "They'd never say that about my male colleagues."

Taking a swing of his tea, he smiled. "Cal says your department is more liberated than most."

"Thanks to officers like him. And I'm lucky my mom lives with us, so night shifts aren't a problem."

He glanced out at the lawn with its big oak tree in front, the quiet street with a few cars parked on either side. "Both my parents are dead. No siblings. Annette's family is in town, though."

Sydney was an only child, too. Her mother always said she couldn't handle more than one. In truth, Sydney had been *more* than she could handle.

"What are your wife's parents like?"

"They're great. They live in the same area of Hidden Cove as we do and pitch in whenever I need to travel. They'd like even more time with Amber than they have."

"That's sweet."

This time, he sighed. "They were destroyed when Annette died."

"You too, huh?"

"Yep. Oh, we had our problems like any couple. But we were really close. I never thought I'd get over her death."

Thinking of Ken, she said, "It's hard to lose love."

For a moment, he looked at her questioningly. To cut off any personal inquiry, she spoke again. "Tell me about *The Heart of Hidden Cove*. I've seen the magazine around the firehouse. It's really good."

He described his baby, the project that had been his salvation after Annette died. All of the articles were upbeat.

And, some thought, superficial. But his subscriptions both in print and online were huge.

"I started it when Annette got sick. She loved Hidden Cove. Her family goes back to the founding fathers. So that was my gift to her before she died. It's become very popular in the last three years."

"That is so cool. What did you do before the magazine?"

"I was an engineer for computer software. I, um" — here he blushed — "I invented a chip for airplane computers and it made me a lot of money — still does. I worked long hours in those days." His expression was faraway. "Because it was so successful, I was able to quit when Annette got sick. After she died, I stuck with the magazine so I could be around to raise Amber myself. We aren't rich, but we get by." He smiled over her. "And that's probably more information than you wanted."

"Not at all. I liked the story. I'm afraid I'm a klutz on computers. When I write something, I erase it without realizing what I did. Sometimes, things disappear and I don't know how to get them back."

"How about I give you some basics?" He glanced at his watch. "I could do it now."

"That'd be great."

As they stood, Amber came to the door, holding Daisy. "Can we go out back, Sydney?"

"I like the sandbox," Daisy said.

"Fine by me. I'll get her a sweater."

Amber looked to Max for approval, too.

"It's okay, honey. I'm going to give Sydney some lessons on the computer."

His daughter rolled her eyes. "Good luck. Once he gets into his geek stuff, you're committed for hours."

Sydney smiled over at him. God, he looked good. Right now, hours with him didn't sound too bad to her.

• • •

LIKE THEY DID three mornings a week, Max met Cal at the diner in town at six in the morning to run. They took to the streets in companionable silence and jogged over to a park in the center of Hidden Cove. The end of April had turned warm, but there was a slight chill in the air, so both wore light sweatshirts over their shorts and T-shirts.

"You sure you're up to this?" Cal asked.

"Uh-huh. It's been three weeks since the fire. I'm perfectly recovered."

"Not a long time, after sucking black smoke into your lungs. We'll never know how much time elapsed after the fire and while you were in there before Sydney got to you."

Max noted Cal's phrasing about the fire department. He always spoke in terms of *we* and *us*, and at times, Max was jealous of that camaraderie. At least he had Cal.

"We'll go slow." They took an easy pace, which made talking manageable. Sometimes they raced each other, sometimes they sprinted. He couldn't remember how many years they'd been running together.

"So, did Amber get to babysit for Sydney?" Cal asked.

"Yeah." He thought of dark brown hair and the glow on her face when she talked about her kid. "That toddler's a doll."

"So is Sydney. She's one of the most competent young firefighters we have. When an opening came up on the Rescue Squad last year, she was the first one to come to mind when we wanted to include a rookie."

"A rookie? At her age?"

Cal shot him a puzzled look. "She's twenty-four."

Shit. He'd guessed late twenties. He did some calculations in his head. "Huh. So she got pregnant when she was twenty?"

"Yes. She'd been a firefighter for two years. She took a desk job, had Daisy and came right back to the line. She got on the Rescue Squad a year ago. She's the youngest there, hence the rookie status."

He was dying to know about Daisy's father. "Is, um, Daisy's father in the picture?"

"Not that I know of. I try to stay out of the personal lives of my squads. Her application does say she isn't married."

"I'm surprised. She doesn't seem the type."

Cal snorted. "Well, you and I know there's no typecasting women."

The same sinking feeling Max always got about this subject hit him in the stomach with more force than usual. For a while, they ran in silence. "I'm looking forward to tonight," he finally said.

"So is Group 3. It's nice of you to throw a party for them."

"They saved my life. By the way, there was no arson involved in the fire at my business, was there?"

"No reason to suspect it. Best we can tell, sparks in the basement caught the boxes you had stored there. The fire started right below your office. You'll be getting an official report, along with the building owner and the insurance company. Meanwhile, while you renovate, have the electrical utility check everything."

"I'm not renovating. I'm scouting for a new place. But it looks like we'll all be working from home for a while."

"Do the others mind?"

"No. It's a change for all of us. Can't say I enjoy being by myself all day long while Amber's in school."

They ran a block before Cal spoke again. "Annette's been dead three years. You haven't even dated. Maybe it's time to think about seeing someone again."

A vision of light brown eyes with full, wavy hair came to his mind. Nah, he thought as he picked up speed. She was fourteen years younger than him. That was a gap too wide to bridge.

Wasn't it?

# CHAPTER 3

SYDNEY'S GROUP ARRIVED almost together for the party Max was throwing tonight for them. As she watched Gabe and Rachel enter holding hands, Brody and Emma, arms around each other's waists, Felicia and Ryan bumping shoulders, and Tony and Sophia, attached at the hip, a pang of loneliness shot through Sydney. Would she ever find the kind of love each of those couples had?

"Do you need a drink?" Max came up behind her. He'd brought Amber over to babysit, as he'd promised, and picked up Sydney to drive her back to his house. Then he'd reverse the process at the end of the night. She liked being chauffeured.

She held up a bottle of Molson's. "No, I got a beer."

He tracked her gaze into the family room, where conversation buzzed and laughter rung out. "I have to say, your group are some of the happiest people I've ever seen."

"You know, they are. And they're lucky to have found each other."

"I know the feeling." Sadness drifted into his eyes again.

"I'm sorry. You must miss your wife at times like these."

"I do." He faced her. "How about you?" Every time he watched her with those startling green eyes, something shifted inside her.

"I'd like to have somebody to share my life with."

"You're still plenty young."

"Not a lot of men are interested in three-year-olds." *Even their own.*

Leaning against the table in front of the big window in the living room, where they were talking, he focused on her. "Any guy who wouldn't appreciate Daisy isn't worth his salt. She's such a treasure." He winked at her. "And you."

Startled at the flirting, her heart kicked in her chest. "Think you'll find someone else, Max?"

"I don't know. I have my work and Amber. Maybe that's enough."

"At thirty—what are you anyway?"

"Thirty-eight."

"Wow, an old man!" *Not.* Especially tonight. Dressed up a bit, he wore knife-pressed slacks and a long-sleeved, green shirt that made his eyes the color of the grass. She'd gone the extra mile, too, and put on a fitted, royal-blue dress. She'd noticed the others from her crew looked especially nice, too.

"I *am* old. And you're a young thing."

"I'm older than my years."

Cal Erikson, without a date, crossed in front of the window and Max straightened. "Excuse me." He headed to the door, but Cal opened it without ringing. Suddenly, Sydney felt another kind of loneliness. She didn't have a girlfriend who would walk inside her house without knocking. She wondered what Max and the chief talked about. Sydney had always found her boss a bit intimidating.

After Cal got a drink and some food, Max asked everyone to head into the family room and take seats. Dark wood tables and comfortable furniture graced this area, but it felt...heavy in here. Maybe because of the thick drapes on the windows.

Max raised his glass and smiled. "I'd like to propose a toast to the men and women of Rescue Squad 7. Thanks for saving my life." He turned to Sydney and bored her with an intense gaze; she had to force herself not to squirm. "And especially to Firefighter Sands who broke the rules and kept me alive."

Joking and toasts all around.

"And I plan to pay it forward. America's Bravest has taken it on the chin the last few months from the *Hidden Cove Herald* and I'm going to counteract their articles and blogs. The November issue of *The Heart of Hidden Cove* is going to feature the fire department."

Ryan O'Malley said. "That is super cool."

Others agreed.

"I've drafted some preliminary things I'd like to cover." Bending down, he picked up sheets of paper and passed them around. Sydney took one and began to read along with him.

"First, I plan to do an article on my rescue. I need to talk to all of you about what I don't remember. Know that I'll include my heartfelt thanks and praise. Second, I want to interview Noah Callahan and some battalion chiefs about the good things happening in the department, including programs and other information from your blog. I'm particularly interested in the Affirmative Action you've got going on."

"Oh, brother," Brody O'Malley teased. "Why does everybody like these chicks so much?"

"Because we're so adorable," Felicia returned.

Max grinned, and Sydney's stomach clenched. "I'm also going to feature cameo bios on all of you, along with photos. Since the issue won't come out until November, I won't include anything about the arsonist, since I'm sure he'll be caught by then."

Max explained a few more aspects of his plan for the magazine, then smiled. "Last, I'd like to put Sydney on the cover."

"Oh, no," she said immediately. "Not just me. Our whole group, maybe, but not just me." And she meant it. She hated being the center of attention. Though the guys agreed with Max, she would fight against that.

"All right, we'll put the cover on hold for a while."

The crew cheered when he finished and clapped him on the back when they milled around, got more food or drink. Sydney waited until he was alone, then approached him. "You sure do know how to impress a girl."

His eyes twinkled. "In more ways than one, I'll have you know." The suggestive remark was cute coming from him, not sleazy.

"I love it all, except the cover part."

"Even if we put you and Daisy on it?"

"No, really, I want the whole group."

His cell phone rang and he fished it out of his pocket. "It's Amber.... Hello, Princess. Everything okay?" He smiled at Sydney. "It is. Want to talk to her?"

"Yes." She spoke briefly to Amber, who was checking in, then she mingled with the others and ended up in the kitchen. The scents of dough, marinated meat and beer comforted her. Glasses and dishes had piled up, so she filled the sink with soapy water began to wash them. This was a beautiful Colonial but not her taste, which ran to modern. Sydney didn't care much about material things, except putting a good roof over her daughter's and mother's heads.

She easily found the spots to put the glass and dishware away, because of the glass-front cabinets. To reach the soffits, where platters were stored, she pulled a chair over to the cupboards, kicked off her shoes and climbed up.

Reaching down, she lifted a stack of the oblong dishes. In a pile, they were too heavy and she lost her balance.

"Hey, be careful there!"

The sound startled her, and the platters tumbled out of her hands, crashing to the tile. Sydney fell, too, but strong male arms caught her; instead of hitting the floor, she landed right on Max's chest. For one brief second, she leaned into him, her heart thundering. From the near fall or from Max Delinsky? Then there was a flurry of noise, and several people came running into the kitchen. Looking up at him, she saw an expression in Max's eyes.

Pure male interest.

• • •

MAX TOOK CARE of his sexual needs himself, but what he felt when Sydney Sands plunged into his arms earlier in the night was different. And wonderful! The zinging need for sex had shot through him, and that intense physical response to a woman hadn't happened in three years. Really, four, given how sick Annette had been. As they drove to Sydney's place at midnight, he was still semi-hard.

*Best remember she's only twenty-four.*

Though she looked *very* womanly in that dress that clung in all the right places, especially now that she was seated close with her legs crossed. Her *nice* legs. Very nice legs. And he'd felt her curves, intimately, when she'd tumbled from the chair.

"Amber said things were fine when I called at eleven." Sydney spoke into the softness of the night. "I told her to make sure all the doors were locked and she could lie down on the twin bed in Daisy's room if she got tired."

"That's nice. She goes to sleep around eleven on weekends."

"Max, I'm really sorry for breaking your platters." There had been china pieces everywhere that Tony insisted on cleaning up.

"No problem. They're old."

They talked about normal things but the atmosphere in the front seat of the car practically crackled. She had to feel it, too. And the scent of her sexy perfume drifted over to him; he found himself inhaling surreptitiously.

"The party was great."

"Catered food, though I don't like to have paid help serving."

"Did you entertain a lot with your wife?"

"Yes, we both liked it. How about you?"

"My time and circumstances don't exactly foster entertaining."

"What do you do for fun, Sydney?"

She shrugged a shoulder and stared out at the road "I work out every day. I play with Daisy. I spend time with my mother. She loves old movies." Sydney shrugged. "I really like to dance."

He waited a beat. What the hell, he might as well ask. "I imagine you have scads of dates to take you dancing at clubs."

"Wow, you're great for my ego."

"I'm not lying." Though the thought of her arousing those phantom men like she had aroused Max so easily tonight didn't sit well. "So, do you?"

"Hardly time for that."

They arrived at her house and he pulled into the small driveway. When he shut off the engine, she went for the handle on the door.

"Wait a sec, it sticks. I have to bring the car to the dealership." Leaning over, he reached out to jimmy the handle to un-stick it, and his arm brushed her breasts. Combined with her scent, the touch hit him square in the groin. He heard her slight intake of breath, and he was no longer *semi*-hard. He couldn't draw back for a minute, and in the light from the porch when he did, he saw her staring at him.

Jesus. Like a woman.

Straightening, he said, "I, um, I'm sorry."

"Sure, no problem." She fussed with her skirt. "It was an accident."

Not thinking about what he was doing, he grasped her arms gently, which turned her to face him. He stared at her directly. "Actually, I lied. I'm not sorry."

Again, a little gasp, then she chuckled. "I lied, too. It is a problem." She licked her lips. "A nice one. I'm…"

"Turned on? Me, too."

She leaned forward and so did he. His mouth came down on hers forcefully. She met his with equal enthusiasm.

And for Max, all thought fled.

• • •

"PUT THE SEAT back." He left her mouth to bark the words, then took it again. Took, claimed, devoured.

Still kissing him, she sprung the seat mechanism and went down flat on her back. Reaching over the gearshift, he slid his hand under her dress, caressed her thighs, tugged at her panties. She murmured, "Hurry. Take them off."

Yanking the dress up around her waist, he dragged the scraps of lace from her, then lifted himself over the console separating them. His weight came down on her and she basked in the feel of the hard planes of his body aligned with her curves. They kept kissing, and Sydney couldn't get enough of him.

When he eased to the side, she protested.

"I have to get my damned zipper down."

"Hurry," she repeated.

He managed to free himself; to accommodate him, she bent and spread her legs. Then he settled between them.

She said, "Now," and he said, "Yes, now," and plunged inside her. She was wet and ready and he was hard as a rock.

One thrust...

Two...

"Oh, my God, oh God." On the third push she felt the spasms begin. Closing her eyes, she saw only color, light and brightness.

Max tried to hold off, tried to endure her pleasure, take joy in it, but being inside her was too much for him. He jerked forward, pushed himself in even farther, and exploded.

Afterward, he lay heavily on top of her, but couldn't move. Couldn't catch his breath. Then he became aware of his surroundings. He was covered in sweat and was nearly gasping for breath.

Finally, he was able to raise himself up on his elbows. What he saw socked him in the gut. Her hair was damp, her skin sweaty and her cheeks rosy. Her sleepy-eyed gaze held his, and a smile broached full and swollen lips. Had he ever seen a lovelier sight?

"You pack quite a punch, Max Delinsky."

"Me? You blew me away." He grinned and kissed her nose. "It was fantastic."

Her eyes closed, she arched and aftershocks went through them both. "Hmm. Me too."

He laughed and shook his head. She caught the gesture. "What?"

"I have no idea what happened here. This so isn't me."

"Me, either. For several years, anyway."

Silence, while he brushed the hair from her eyes. "We should talk."

"All right."

Max swore twice trying to maneuver himself up and get back to the driver's side of the car. Feeling like a horny teenager, he tried to right his clothes. When he glanced to the right, she was sitting up, her dress—unfortunately—pulled over her thighs.

Tenderly, he took her hand in his, brought it to his mouth and kissed her knuckles. "I guess this showed I haven't had sex in years."

She was quiet. In the light from the moon, he saw her expression was full of feeling. "I haven't either, Max."

"No, kidding?"

"No kidding."

Sliding his hand to her neck, he caressed her there. He couldn't seem to stop touching her. "Are you sorry? About this?"

"No. I feel too good to have second thoughts."

Sexual satisfaction singed the air. He luxuriated in the once-familiar feeling, absent from his life for so long. Too long.

Finally, she spoke. "Why do you think this happened, Max?"

"Well, that dress for one thing. I haven't been able to take my eyes off it all night."

She ran her hand through his hair. "So many happy couples there tonight, too. I felt almost bad being by myself."

"Loneliness. For us both, it seems."

Laughter bubbled up in her. "Hell of a way to break a fast."

Tenderly, he cupped her cheek.

"Maybe it's because I saved your life."

"Yeah, then what's your excuse?"

Again, more laughter.

He sobered. "Sydney, I'm fourteen years older than you."

She let her hand drift down and over his crotch. "Couldn't prove it by me."

"Arrgh." Then, "Seriously, do you think this was a good idea?"

"It wasn't an idea, Max. It was a volcano. A force of nature."

He leaned his forehead against hers. "What do we do about it?"

"Nothing, probably. We live completely different lives. I have a toddler. Your best friend is my boss."

"Not to mention the fourteen years."

She drew away again and watched him. He seemed thoughtful, like he was making a decision. Finally, he said, "What if I wanted to do it again?"

"It was really a showstopper, so if you want an encore, I'm game." Boldly, she placed her hand over his groin. "Oh. I guess you are, too."

"I do. But I meant, maybe it doesn't have to end tonight. We could see where this goes between us."

"Maybe. We should give it some thought, though. Be practical. Figure out the angles."

"I suppose we should be adult about jumping into anything."

Sydney moved in closer. "Let's not talk anymore about it tonight, okay?"

"Fine by me. Your turn to climb over the gearshift."

# CHAPTER 4

THE NEXT MORNING, after he awoke in the bed he'd shared with Annette, Max tried to open himself up to recriminations. He thought he'd feel at least vaguely guilty. But instead, his body stirred at the memory of being with Sydney in the car last night and their *volcanic* response to each other. They'd been foolish, because anyone could have come up to the car and seen them. And because they'd been careless. Hell, she could be pregnant. What possessed him to have sex without condoms?

*You haven't bought any in years.* He wondered if she'd had any with her. After Daisy, did she carry them? That thought unnerved him, and he didn't want to think about her past, what she'd done with other guys. It wasn't any of his business; it wasn't part of *now*. Was it?

He heard Amber stirring, so he got up—he was hard again—took a shower (cold) and dressed. He spent more time on his appearance, picking out his favorite casual shirt of white gauzy material and pressed blue jeans. On his feet he wore Docksiders.

"Hi, Dad." His daughter greeted him in the bright sunny kitchen, which smelled like pancakes. She was still in pajamas, not the pink polka dots he used to love, but a T-shirt and pj bottoms. His little girl was growing up.

"Hey, Princess."

She eyed him with teenage scrutiny. "You okay?"

"Yeah, great, why?"

She sniffed. "You got on that mag aftershave I like."

"No crime in that."

"And you look better than usual. Not so...sad, I guess."

*I'm not sad.* "I'm looking forward to interviewing the firefighters this morning. I have to be downtown by eight."

Amber's blue eyes twinkled. "You seeing Sydney today? She is so cool, Dad."

He'd have chosen the opposite of cool—*hot, very, very hot*—but he smiled at his daughter. Best to get his mind off Sydney, though, so he asked her about her day. "What time are you going over to Millie's?"

She took a gulp of orange juice. "Late this morning."

After pouring coffee, he took a seat adjacent to her. "Do you need a ride?"

"No, Janie's mother is picking me up. You can drive us home, though."

"Just give me a time."

His pleasant breakfast with his child enhanced his mood and he drove to House 7 feeling lighter than he had in years. When he reached the big, brick building, he turned off the engine and stared ahead. He'd see her in a few minutes. Be close enough to smell her. Was he up to it? "Bad, bad choice of words, Delinsky."

Amused with the reaction of his body, he got out of his car and headed to the side door. It was ajar, welcoming the fresh air, so he walked inside and followed the scent of coffee to the kitchen. He'd been here before, of course. For one thing, Cal was a captain in this house years ago and now, as battalion chief, had his office in the building. But the interior looked brighter with a new coat of paint and some updated stainless steel appliances.

The crew was subdued, sitting around a scarred oak table, engaged in various activities. Brody O'Malley was texting, probably to his lovely girl, Emma. Felicia White sat in front of a laptop computer, most likely working on the blog. Tony Ramirez, the big guy with an even bigger smile, read the newspaper. Gabe Malvaso had a *Firehouse* magazine in front of him.

Max left Sydney till last. She was staring at what he recognized as the latest edition of *The Heart of Hidden Cove*. Her dark brown hair was tucked behind her ears, and little earrings, the ones he'd nibbled on last night, still pierced the lobes. From beneath her light blue uniform shirt peeked a navy blue tee.

He cleared his throat. "Good morning. The door was open, so I came in."

Glancing up, Sydney's eyes glowed with pure delight when she saw he had arrived. There was no regret in her expression, which was what he'd dreaded she'd feel. "Hey, Max." Her voice was husky. "Great party last night." Now her eyes danced with mischief.

Others chimed in about the evening. Then Brody stood. "You a coffee drinker?"

"Yeah. High test. Black."

"Take my seat next to Syd. For some reason, she's in a great mood today."

She smiled at Max when he sat. "Daisy slept soundly through the night. Amber must have tired her out."

He wanted to ask how she'd slept. Had she pictured them together in her dreams and when she awoke? Had she thought about his suggestion that they start seeing each other? "Amber loved staying with Daisy. Though she said she found several gift cards for iTunes in her purse. The babysitting was supposed to be free."

"It was. Those were exactly what they're advertised as—gifts."

Gabe leaned over in his chair. "So, what's first today, Max? The chief took us out of service for ninety minutes so we could get the information for your magazine issue rolling."

Max removed a small laptop from the case he carried and woke it from sleep. "I'd like to get everyone's impression of the rescue. I already wrote mine out right afterward, so now I need you to fill in the gaps."

"First off," Gabe started, "your buddy Cal stole my gear so he could go in."

Max's brows shot up. "He didn't tell me that."

"We're not broadcasting it. His actions weren't protocol. So don't use the information. I just thought you'd like to know."

"I won't use it. I won't use anything that would reflect badly on you guys." He grinned at Sydney. "And girls."

"Cal took Syd and Tony with him toward your office." Gabe spoke of thick, black smoke, which, having gotten a taste of it, Max knew was noxious.

Tony reported how they'd popped the fire door, and Syd went ahead.

"Who decides which firefighter carries what tool?" Max asked.

"Usually, we grab them arbitrarily," Felicia put in. "But if these guys start getting macho on us, Syd and I ream them out."

Brody recounted how pissed they were when the evacuation horn sounded and they couldn't get inside the fire door to Sydney.

That disturbed him. A lot. He faced her. "You were trapped because of me?"

"No, I was doing my job."

"You did it really well."

"Thanks." Geez, she actually blushed.

He'd finished recording all the details of his rescue and had gone on to other saves when he heard the PA go off. "Call on Lexington and Cameron. House fire."

All five firefighters bolted up. Sydney turned before she left. "Sorry, Max. Our time must be up."

"The hell it is. I got permission for a ride-along. I'm coming to see you in action." Leaving the computer, he slid a small camera out of his case, along with a tape recorder, and followed America's Bravest out to the bay.

He had to admit he got a kick out of watching Sydney dress in her turnout gear. Not as much, though, as he'd enjoy watching her *un*dress what was underneath.

• • •

HE MANEUVERED TO sit right next to her in the back of the truck, Sydney thought. The driver and cap took the front row, of course, but Max could have sat with Felicia and Brody in the second seat, where there was room. Instead, he climbed over them to get into the back with her. His presence unnerved her right away. She swore she could smell his aftershave, even in the stuffy cab of the rig with gear that still reeked of smoke.

"Put your seatbelt on," she said.

He looked at her. "You're not." He nodded to the front. "No one is."

"Do it," Felicia called back. "Ride-alongs are rare and we don't want you hurt."

Thankfully, Max obeyed. Sydney slipped hers on, too, because she knew what was coming. When they turned the first corner, the horn blaring and the siren running, she swayed right into him. With no belts she'd probably be in his lap.

Where she'd had the most incredible sex last night.

All morning long, she'd thought about them together and how, well, simply wonderful, it had been. He wanted to keep seeing her. In her heart so did she, but she had a lot of reservations. Ugh...she shouldn't be thinking about this at work.

"Quint 9 is already there," Gabe told them. "We're second in."

"Which might mean not a lot of action," she said to Max.

Gabe gave them a rundown on who was in the building, the fact that no victims had fled the house—not good—and how they'd wait to see what they could do to help. Seven minutes later, they arrived at the scene.

When they leaped out of the rig, the cacophony of noise must have surprised Max, because he startled at the still-arriving trucks and their sirens, the loud hum of the rigs already there and shouts as equipment was set up.

Gabe hurried to Incident Command as the rest of them approached their own truck and pulled out some kind of funny-looking axes. Again, Sydney explained, "Halligans. We never approach a scene without tools."

Max waited with them only a few minutes until Gabe returned. "We got roof ventilation. Sydney, take the K-12 saw."

"Why her? She's a rookie," O'Malley said to jab her.

"It's my turn." She lifted her chin. "And I've done it before."

The cap rolled his eyes. "You can help. O'Malley, bring the saw to the roof ahead of her to conserve her strength. Nine's getting the ladder up." Gabe faced Syd. "Wait for my signal to cut, and mine only."

She nodded.

They dragged the huge saw out of the back of the rig where a myriad of tools were stored. Brody started it as a test run, and a teeth-gritting sound rent the air. He turned it off and he and Sydney approached the ladder. She felt self-conscious about Max watching her, but as soon as she was up top, thoughts of him fled.

For now at least.

• • •

AS MAX SPOKE into the tape recorder, an April wind carried the scent of smoke, reminding him of when he was trapped. "Four members of Group 7 are ascending the ladder. It sways with their weight and the heftiness of the saw, which is huge.... Up on the roof, below which, fire can be seen in the windows, they creep into position. They've removed their turnout coats, I assume for better maneuverability.... As if it's a toy, Sydney lifts the apparatus into the air."

Max caught that with the camera—her muscles bulging and the sun sparkling down on her hair. Another shot as Brody stood close behind her, ready to help. "Jesus, she slips and O'Malley grabs her waist while she rights herself. The angle of the roof, the awkwardness of the saw, is precarious. *This* is dangerous. But also fascinating. No one seems to care or even notice that a fire's blazing below them." He reminded himself to check how hot it was up there.

Gabe Malvaso left the command post and hurried to the building. "From below," Max added to the record, "the officer shouts, 'Now, Sands.' The saw is started again. She positions the blade on the roof and cuts. And cuts. Layers, it looks like. Other crew members peel back shingles. On the final cut, the firefighters fall back."

Max could see why. Holy shit, flames ratcheted up through the ceiling, then calmed down again. He guessed this was ventilation. Hard sweaty work, then acute danger when the saw cuts through.

And what did it say about Max, that his heart was pounding and his palms were damp, because Sydney slicing through the roof like it was butter was about the sexiest thing he'd ever seen a woman do?

• • •

MAX SAT ON a chair in an upscale motel on the outskirts of town, removing his shoes. The room was spacious with beautiful furniture and a down coverlet on the bed. He had good taste.

Sydney watched him from the doorway. "I can't believe we're doing this."

His expression was wry. "What, lying to my daughter and your mother?"

She laughed as she unbuttoned her shirt. "I feel like a kid."

"You make me feel like one, too." He picked up a bag he'd brought in before she arrived. "I stopped and got condoms this time." Standing as he removed his shirt, he said, "I'm a bit worried about the consequences of last night. We didn't use anything—twice."

She couldn't decipher his tone and she was a little uneasy about his comment. "I'm on a pill, Max. Most female firefighters take it to lighten their period and make them regular. It'll be fine."

"Then how did you get..." He reddened. "None of my business."

She stopped undoing her shirt. "How did I get pregnant? I didn't know about these pills then. Apparently, the condoms we used didn't work. After I had the baby, Rachel and Felicia talked to me." She smiled. "Can't say I wish they had earlier, though. I wouldn't have my girl. She was worth all that I went through."

He didn't say anything.

Still trying to figure out her behavior, she continued, "I've never been promiscuous, though. Something happened with you. I was easy, I guess."

"Well, if you were, then so was I."

Her face softened. "What a nice thing to say."

"So we don't need these? Since we both haven't been with anybody..." A wary expression crossed his face. "That was true, right?"

Her insides tightened and she stopped removing her clothes. "Of course it was. But, Max, if you don't believe me about something like that, maybe we *shouldn't* be doing this. We really don't know each other very well. And we haven't even discussed taking this further."

He bolted from the chair, crossed to her and grasped her shoulders. "No, I want to do this again. I know we were both still considering a relationship. But truthfully, Ms. Firefighter, after watching you up there on that roof, I knew I had to have you again. Forgive my clumsiness. I never did date much." He rolled his eyes. "I got married right out of college, and Annette and I were together for most of those four years."

"I'm acting weird, too. With you. Sorry."

He reached for the hem of her shirt. "Let me. I haven't even seen you naked. I dreamed about us together last night, though."

"Same here." She ran her hands over his chest. "Let's see if you live up to expectations." She slid his shirt off his shoulders and it fell to the floor. He had beautiful skin, not too light for a sandy-haired guy, with the right sprinkling of hair. His chest was sculpted, too. He must work out. "Hmm. I'd say you live up to them just fine." She leaned over and kissed his breastbone.

His hand went to her neck and pulled her face to his chest in a gesture so tender it made her weak inside. Then he eased her back and drew off her T-shirt. She wore a sports bra, which he also removed. When her breasts spilled into his hands, he murmured, "Damn, you are so beautiful." He stared hard at her. "So lovely, Sydney, so, so lovely."

Bending over, he began to suckle her.

Sydney closed her eyes and basked in the pull of his mouth, the scrape of his teeth.

Who cared that they hadn't made a real decision to see each other or that they were practically strangers? She decided to enjoy the two hours they'd bought themselves with lies.

• • •

"I'M SO EXCITED about babysitting for Sydney tonight." Amber made the statement from the kitchen counter, where she helped her grandmother prepare lunch.

"Yeah, baby, I'm excited about it, too." Which was a complete understatement. Max hadn't been able to go to the firehouse today because he and Amber always spent Sundays with his in-laws. Right now, Barbara Collins was showing Amber how to make BLT wraps and Mitch, Annette's father, was doing a crossword puzzle at the table.

Barbara looked over. "Are you sure Amber should be babysitting on a school night?"

"Syd said only for a couple of hours. She has a meeting."

*With me*, Max thought. He couldn't wait to get his hands on her again, even though it had been only twenty-four hours. Yep, they were definitely acting like kids, and it felt so damn good.

"I think your offer of free babysitting is great, pumpkin." Mitch sipped one of the beers he'd gotten for himself and Max. Grinning fondly at his wife, Mitch rolled his eyes at Max. "Barbie, you're being overprotective again." He only used the name when he wanted to tease.

"Yeah, well, I'm entitled. I'm the only grandmother she's got. And she's the only…" Barbara trailed off. Max saw her bite her lip, so he stood, crossed to the counter and set his hands on his mother-in-law's shoulders. "I miss Annette, too. Barb. It's okay to show it when we're together."

She sniffed. "I can't believe I'm still doing this. It's been three years."

"Showing you loved someone and miss her is never wrong."

After a pleasant afternoon with Annette's parents, Max drove Amber to Sydney's house. They arrived at five, and Daisy was on the porch sitting in Sydney's lap. Amber burst out of the car and went running over. "Hi, baby. Ambs is here."

"Ambs, Ambs." Daisy slid off her mother's lap and raced over to Amber. His daughter scooped her up. The child hugged Amber's neck. "Play dolls with me, Ambs."

"Thanks for letting me do this again, Sydney."

Max had followed his daughter to the porch. Sydney said, "The pleasure's all mine."

He smiled lecherously over Amber's head. "Not exactly," he said. The words were rife with innuendo.

• • •

"OH, MAN, SYDNEY, I can't wait."

"Don't."

"Are you ready?"

"Are you kidding? Jesus, come inside me."

"Yes, ma'am."

On their sides, he lifted her leg and slung it over his. She loved this position because she could see his eyes go liquid when he came. If she could last that long. He thrust powerfully into her.

She arched back. He gritted his teeth trying to control himself, to make it last between them.

"Don't." She kissed him hard. "Don't hold back."

Her words broke his restraint. Grunts encompassed the room and he let go in a series of wrenching groans.

After she came, twice, he cuddled her close. "Jesus."

"I know." She nuzzled into him. She felt safe like this, with their skin touching, a direct opposite of the wild abandon she'd experienced a few moments ago. "We're great together."

"Even if we are sneaking around your mother and my daughter."

"Hey, we took them on a picnic yesterday." They'd been seeing each other only two weeks, but it seemed longer, and they took every opportunity to be together.

"It was fun." Almost like a family outing. Now that scared her. They were getting way ahead of themselves.

She played with his chest hair. His heart beat a slow tattoo next to hers and he tugged her even closer. He asked, "We never really made a decision to start seeing each other."

"I know. We kind of fell into it."

He palmed her ass. "I couldn't resist you. And things seem okay. About our ages."

She laughed out loud and ran her hand down his stomach to his groin. "As I said before, you keep up with me pretty good, old man."

He chuckled.

"What about the chief? You'll have to tell him."

"I know."

Turning, she braced her arms on his chest so she could look at him. "Before we go any further, Max, I need to tell you something. This thing between us, it isn't just sex for me. But if it is for you, tell me. I'll be okay with it."

"Hell, no. I like you Sydney, a lot. And I admire you."

"Oh, thanks. Though we don't know each other very well."

"We should stay out of bed long enough to talk more."

She pulled up the covers. "I got a better idea. Let's talk here, cuddled up."

"All right. Tell me how you grew up?"

She stiffened. "Can we start with something easier?"

His hand grazed her biceps. "Why is that hard?"

"I told you I lived in the city. In a rough neighborhood. I, um, did some things I'm ashamed of."

"Honey, that was a long time ago. We all did foolish things in our lives."

"Oh, yeah, you probably broke your curfew by a half hour once and I...slept around. Not for very long, just until I got into the firefighter program."

He was quiet a minute. "Again, you were young and foolish. Though I hate the thought of some other man's hands on you."

"Don't think about it then."

"Do you have brothers and sisters?"

"None. It's me and Mom. She was a single mother." Sydney pulled away and ran her hand through her hair.

"What is it?"

"Jesus, we sound so low class. We were poor, sure, but saying it aloud makes us appear to be...white trash."

Easing her over onto her back, he said, "Think of it this way. You overcame great odds, both you and your mom, to become the wonderful women you are. Me, I had everything given to me. Growing up in the suburbs, Ivy League College, all paid for. I said earlier that I admire you, and I do. Even more now."

"Max, you're so sweet. You give me such confidence. Thank you."

He started to kiss his way down her body. "I can think of another way you can thank me."

"Don't you have that backward?"

He stopped at her navel. "Nope, sweetheart, I don't."

# CHAPTER 5

SYDNEY PUSHED DAISY in the stroller along the blacktopped pavement of the Public Market after having just enough time to go home, pick up her daughter and mom and head back downtown. Though most of the market's fresh produce and baked goods were bought in the morning by bargain hunters, now, at around five, even greater sales of anything left were in abundance. They'd also started a fair of sorts for kids on Saturdays—stands set up selling hotdogs, clowns doing face painting and some arts and crafts booths. Sydney often saw young mothers here with their kids or single dads. Today, she'd agreed to meet a certain single dad and his daughter. The picture of him in her head made her smile. Though tonight would be family time, her skin still sizzled when she thought about them together.

"How was work today?" her mom asked as Daisy squealed, "Flowers!" with delight at the colorful bouquets they passed. No money for that, though.

"Busy. A car fire before our shift ended, a flooded basement and a house fire early this morning." She didn't tell her mother that she was the one to climb into the car and extricate a small child. The save had given her an adrenaline rush like no other. Well, almost no other, she thought, remembering her and Max again. Geez, she was getting smitten and he'd only come into her life five weeks ago.

The early May evening was comfortable, with a warm breeze that ruffled Daisy's caramel-colored hair. "Is Max Delinsky still visiting the firehouse for his magazine?"

Oh, yeah. Dressed in a black-and-white checked shirt and black jeans, he'd looked like a million bucks. And smelled heavenly. And he contended watching her work today turned him on. Though surprised, Sydney was pleased about his attitude big-time because she couldn't handle someone who worried about her on the line, the problem Sophia had with Tony.

They wandered through the stalls buying vegetables, pastries and fresh bread—that smelled so good she wanted to break off a piece and eat it right then. She was leaning over the stroller, handing a chocolate chip cookie to Daisy, when she heard behind her, "Dad, there they are!"

Her pulse rate escalated in anticipation of seeing Max again; turning, she watched him and Amber saunter toward them. He wore the same clothes tonight as he'd had on during the day, and his hair was tousled a bit in the spring wind. She remembered its coarse texture and how she'd been surprised by its thickness. "Fancy meeting you here," he said easily. He looked to her mother. "Hello, Mrs. Sands."

"Linda, please. I think we know each other well enough to be on a first-name basis now." Her mother was beginning to like Max. Too much. Was the same true for Sydney? She'd taken a nosedive into this relationship without considering much how she could get hurt.

Daisy's face lit. "Ambs. Gimme a kiss."

Amber bent down and kissed Daisy's cheek, then spoke to her mother. "Hi, Mrs. Sands."

Noticing a little butterfly on Amber's cheek, Sydney lightly swiped a finger around it. "What's this?"

"Face painting." She looked down. "Hey, can we get one for Daisy?"

"I be like Ambs, Mommy."

"Oh, honey, I don't know...."

"The paint's washable and allergy free," Max put in. "I think a little decoration on Daisy's cheek would be all right."

"I'll take them," Linda offered, "and you two can chat. Relax."

"Thanks, Linda."

"There's tables under that canopy." Sydney's mother pointed to the left. "Have something to drink."

The three took off and Sydney gave Max a delighted smile. Though they couldn't touch, it would be fun to hang with him.

Crossing to the table groupings, Sydney dropped down on a wrought iron chair; Max asked what she'd like and approached a nearby stand for coffee. She saw a clown go by, probably to the face painting, and heard a vendor calling out for cheap tomatoes, but she only had eyes for Max's cute ass, his broad shoulders and how his hair curled at his neck.

When he returned, he sat and stretched out his long legs, so his feet were in touching distance of hers. "And how are you tonight, Firefighter Sands?" His green eyes twinkled like emeralds. God, she loved putting that look there.

"I'm well. You?"

"I'm good now that I get to see you." He stared straight ahead and sipped his java. "Wish I could kiss you though." Instead he leaned over and picked up her hand. "And do a lot more. I gotta stop watching you work. It makes me crazy."

All her insides warmed. "I was just thinking about that. Why, Max?"

"Do you have any idea how competent, healthy, strong you looked up there on the roof? I wanted to ravish you."

"Most men would worry."

He shrugged. "I'm a little surprised at myself. I was very overprotective of Annette. And Amber, too."

She didn't know whether that was a compliment or not. Or if she liked the notion or not. She was so busy pondering his words that she didn't notice the man that came up to them. But when she did, her whole body froze. He was with two little girls. His blond hair was longer than the last time she'd seen him. But he still had those gray eyes, sculpted features and lanky build.

"I thought that was you. Hello, Syd." Leaning over, he kissed her cheek. "Nice to see you again."

Her jaw dropped at his public display of affection. He looked to Max. Max stood.

"I'm Max Delinsky. A friend of Sydney's."

Ken studied him. "Ken Kessler. I'm a friend of hers, too. An old, old one."

His twelve-year-old, Megan, tugged on his arm. "Did you know her before or after you and mommy got divorced?"

Well, this was news to Sydney. She'd had no idea Daisy's father was a free man.

# CHAPTER 6

IT WAS LIKE getting hit with a blast of cold water from one of her fire hoses. Had Sydney had an affair with a married man? Images of her juxtaposed with Annette and Max couldn't separate them.

He glanced at Kessler's daughters. They looked to be twelve and maybe ten. The girls moved back a little as if they sensed the charged air, too.

Still, if she'd had an affair, Sydney had been young.

Still, she should have known better.

"What have you been up to?" the guy asked silkily. Max hated him on sight.

"Working at the fire department. I'm on the Rescue Squad now."

"Ah, the elite group you used to talk about. Congratulations."

Max shifted uneasily on his feet. He hated seeing this little reunion. Thankfully, his own daughter and Sydney's family were coming toward him.

The three of them reached the table and Amber was all bubbly. "Daddy, look at what Daisy has on her face. She picked out the one she wanted. She knew the connection to her name."

Automatically he looked down. Daisy had a tiny yellow daisy on her face. She also had the same gray eyes and hair color as Kessler, who turned, looked down, and practically stumbled backward into his daughters. His gaze flew from Daisy to Sydney. His whole body tensed and his hands fisted.

Oh, dear God in heaven. Daisy was his child. Max knew it intuitively.

"Who is this, Sydney?" Kessler asked carefully.

What? He didn't *know* he had a daughter with her?

Sydney raised her chin in a gesture of defiance Max already recognized. "My daughter, Daisy."

One of his little girls came forward and squatted down. She didn't even know she was taking her sister's hand. "Oh, Dad, she's adorable."

"Yes, she is." His voice was clipped. Cold. "How old is she?"

Linda Sands stepped forward. "Almost four. Hello, again, Mr. Kessler." Ice dripped from the woman's voice.

"Mrs. Sands." He shoved his hands in his pockets. But Max could tell he was struggling.

Hopefully the little girls didn't know what was going on.

Finally, Max said, "Daisy looks adorable, honey." Reaching out, he took Amber's hand. "How about you and I go get something to eat?"

Amber's face fell. "Oh, I thought maybe we could eat with Sydney and Daisy and Mrs. Sands."

"We don't want to horn in on her and her friends. Besides, I have to drop you off at your Grandma's for your overnight. We shouldn't keep them waiting for you." He turned to her mother. "Thanks for watching Amber." Then to Sydney, "Have a nice night." He scanned the rest of them. "Good-bye, all."

They walked away, Amber sulking about his abrupt decision. He'd been hoping for the same thing his daughter had expected—to spend the evening with the Sands. Not now, though. Now, he had a whole lot of thinking to do.

• • •

AFTER HE BROUGHT Amber to the Collins', Max went straight home. He was drawn to the informal den, a spacious area with floor-to-ceiling bookshelves and windows. Five years ago, his entire life had changed in this room. He closed his eyes, remembering.

Annette had been diagnosed with breast cancer three months before and, abhorred by the notion that he might lose her, Max had thrown himself into his work at the computer firm—and drank some to cope. But that fateful day, reality had hit him. He needed to get his act together to be there for his wife, so he'd left work at two and came home. It had been an afternoon much like today, with the warm May sunshine drifting into the room.

He found her on the couch, but she wasn't alone. She was cuddled up, literally, into another man's chest. Nausea roiled in Max's stomach as he took in the scene. The guy was bald, he wore jeans and a shirt that was too big, and he had a tattoo on his arm. Annette had always hated tattoos. Max couldn't determine how old he was. Purposely, Max didn't make his presence known....

"It's okay, Annette. You'll get used to this."

"It's been several weeks of chemo, Tim. I'm never going to get used to it."

The guy tipped her chin—and fuck!—kissed her nose. "I did. And you will, too." He smiled down at her, then clasped the back of her head—she wore a scarf because she'd also lost her hair—as she nuzzled back into him.

Max gripped the doorjamb so hard his knuckles got white. He couldn't believe what he was seeing with his own eyes.

Unnoticed, he walked out, too upset to even confront them. He waited in the backyard, seated in the sunshine, feeling like clouds had dumped a downpour on him. After the guy left, Annette must have noticed him or his car in the driveway. She'd come to the deck....

"Max? What are you doing home in the middle of the day?"

He looked up at her thin face. There wasn't a trace of guilt on it. "I wanted to talk to you. I'd had some...revelations." He angled his head in the direction of the den. "But you were busy."

"Oh, honey, I'm sorry you saw that."

"Sorry that I saw or that you did it?"

Her chin came up. "I haven't done anything wrong."

"Don't lie to me. I saw him kiss you. Hold you. You were hanging on to him like a lifeline."

She was very quiet, then she said, "He's *been* a lifeline for me, Max."

It turned out she'd met this Tim the first week of chemo; they were both on the same schedule and they'd gotten closer during every treatment. "I'm not denying we're close. But we aren't having an affair."

"The hell you aren't."

"We're friends."

"Do you love him?"

"Yes, as a friend."

Max's world dimmed. He threw back the chair and stood. "Even if I believed you weren't sleeping together, you've betrayed me emotionally. That's even worse."

She'd clapped her hand over her mouth and began to weep. "I...I never saw it that way."

"Why, Annette? We've always been so in tune. So *together*."

"I *needed* someone."

"You had me."

"I don't want to hurt you, Max, really I don't. But I didn't have you. You withdrew when I got sick. You worked all the time. When we were together, you didn't want to talk about what I was feeling. If it wasn't for Laura Erikson and Tim, I never would have made it this far."

All his anger diminished with her accusation. Deep inside, he knew her words were true. "I couldn't bear to think about your illness, let alone talk about it."

"We all deal with this in our own way. I'm sorry. But as I said, I needed someone."

Because Max loved her, because she was sick and because she was right, he drew in a deep breath and tried to calm down, tried to see things from her perspective....

Eventually he had. But he'd never forgotten what he still considered her infidelity. Years later, he and Cal had talked about what was worse—Annette's emotional cheating or Laura's physical unfaithfulness. They never came up with an answer and decided both were equally painful.

Now, Max went farther into the room and brushed his hand across the colorful afghan Annette had knitted. No wonder he'd reacted so badly to tonight's revelation about Daisy. He just hadn't realized he'd already gotten so involved with Sydney. Jesus, he was really hurt and needed to step back.

• • •

AT TEN O'CLOCK, Sydney lost the battle with her more sensible side and now sat in her car in front of Max's house, staring at the three-storey showplace. She didn't belong here, she knew she didn't, but she couldn't stand the idea of what had happened earlier going unexplained. She and Max had been so close for weeks and she'd come to like him—a lot. She thought he'd reciprocated her feelings, but today he seemed repulsed by her.

*Still, you don't owe him any explanations.*

"I know," she said aloud. But she exited the car anyway, pulled her light cotton sweater tighter around her and marched down the front bricked path past lush landscaping and budding flowers. Taking the one step up to the porch, she rang the bell, knowing Amber wasn't home so she wouldn't wake the girl. No answer. Hmm. Maybe he went out. Maybe he had a date. When the notion caused her heart to squeeze in her chest, she shook her head. What was she *doing?* Since Ken, she hadn't let any guy make her feel this way. She rang again, and again. She'd turned to leave when the door opened. Max stood in the entryway, in pajama bottoms, no shirt, his hair damp and his skin glowing. "Sydney? I was in the shower and just heard the bell. What are you doing here?"

"I came to talk to you. Can I come in?"

He hesitated. And that hurt.

"Look, I won't stay. I have a few things to say." A thought assaulted her. "Oh, unless you have company."

He shook his head. "No, Sydney. I don't have a woman here. I'm not the type to sleep around."

A good enough opening. "But now you think I am. And worse."

Without responding, he stepped aside. "Come in."

He led her back to the family room. The fireplace in the corner was dark, but she could have used its warmth. "Sit. Can I get you something?"

She dropped down onto a couch and he stood across from her. His face was granite hard and unyielding and she was having trouble reconciling him with the man she'd been with for weeks. But she was going to give this a shot. "How about an open mind?"

"Excuse me?"

"I saw your face when Ken came up to us and his daughter spilled the beans."

"Yeah? And I saw yours, too."

"I was shocked."

"So was he."

"What do you mean?"

He finally sat. "It's obvious Daisy is his and he didn't know anything about her."

Taking in a deep breath, she sat back. "That's not true. Not exactly anyway." Shit, she was just going to spit it out. "He knew I was pregnant. He—" God this was hard. "He gave me money for an abortion. I had her instead and spent the money on baby stuff."

"And never told him what you did."

"No, I didn't. Why should I, when he wanted to get rid of her?"

"Because he's her father."

"Only biologically."

Max stared past her. "Well, none of this is really my business."

That was a slap in the face.

"After what's happened between us, how can you say that?"

He focused on her and his green gaze was cold. "Maybe I don't want it to be my business."

Self-defense made her stand. "Fine. Sorry I bothered you. I thought you might want to know the whole story. That his actions before her birth might make a difference." Turning, she strode out of the family room, through the living room and had reached for the front doorknob when he grabbed her shoulder from behind. Caught off guard, she was easily whirled around.

His face was still set in hard planes and angles. "Damn it. Damn this whole situation." He shoved her against the wall and took her mouth. It was a hard, bruising kiss and tears sprang to her eyes. He was passionate in all their encounters, but tender. Always tender. Tonight he was rough and uncaring.

No, this wasn't going to happen. She wasn't going to let a man make her feel inferior and inadequate again. She pushed him away. He stumbled backward, and his face was blank. "Don't you dare kiss me like I'm some slut you can manhandle! Okay, I made a mistake when I was barely out of my teens. I came here tonight to explain things, so you wouldn't see in me in a bad light. For some fucking reason, that was important to me. But I won't be mistreated."

He still held her shoulders, but his grip on her gentled. He seemed shocked now. "Oh, God, Sydney, I'm sorry. I don't know what's come over me. I behave so out of character with you."

She tried to step back but he held her in place. "Don't worry, except for seeing you at work while you finish the articles for the magazine, I won't come near you again and throw you off your game. And I'd appreciate the same consideration. We'll work something out with Amber so she doesn't have to suffer for our mistake." This time she did yank away. "Good-bye, Max."

Sydney had done the right thing; she knew she had. She only wished she didn't hurt so much. But she was strong. She knew she could handle anything. If she could get over Ken's rejection and have a baby on her own, she could survive the loss of a man who'd only been in her life a few short weeks.

• • •

AS HE HELD a paper he'd picked from the department's Joke Jar, Brody O'Malley sat across from Max, grinning. Brody had said Max looked down since he'd come in this morning and needed some cheering up. "You'll like this one since you're friends with Chief Erikson." Brody looked at the paper and read aloud. "A fire chief died and went to heaven. When he got there, he saw a long line waiting to get in to the pearly gates. He told himself, 'I am a Fire Chief, I'm not going to wait in line.' He went to the angels guarding the gates and said, 'Let me in, I'm a Fire Chief.'

"The angels replied, 'You'll have to wait in line like everyone else, sir.'

"While waiting at the back of the line, he saw a sedan pull up with red lights flashing and a man got out wearing a white helmet that said Chief. The angels popped to attention and let the guy enter heaven.

"The waiting fire chief was really upset now and went to talk to the angels. He asked, 'Why did you let that Fire Chief go through and not me?'

"To which the angels replied, 'You have it all wrong, sir. That's *God*, he just thinks he's Fire Chief.'"

The stupid joke almost made Max laugh. If he'd slept last night, if he hadn't behaved so badly with Sydney, he would be caught up in Brody's good mood. "Don't let Cal hear that one," he replied halfheartedly. Then he glanced at his computer. "All right, we'll stay with the good stuff. Tell me something pleasant about your crew."

"We're all saps these days, even Sydney until she came in today." He frowned. "She barked at me when I asked her what was wrong."

Max ignored the last comment. "You're saps because—?" Though he knew why.

"We're in love." A slight frown. "Sorry, I know your wife's dead."

"It was a while ago. Besides, I like seeing people happy. Tell me about Emma."

"For the magazine?"

"I won't print anything bad. But I talked to Felicia and she filled me in on your brother. What's it like having them involved?"

An even broader smile. "Unbelievably good. The four of us do a lot of stuff together. Right now, we're remodeling the duplex I used to share with him until I moved into Emma's house. He and Licia bought my half from me when they got together. They're going to live there after they..."

Max raised a brow.

"Can't tell you the rest yet. It'll be public soon."

Brody went on about his life with Emma and his job as a firefighter. Max found himself envying the man's situation, as he had with Felicia. Despite their one issue, he'd loved Annette to distraction and was hoping maybe he and Sydney... What was the use in thinking about that? There was no future for them. Not after he blew it big-time. And he wasn't even over his confusion, maybe even disgust, that she'd hooked up with a married man.

Max wound down the interview with Brody just as Tony Ramirez walked through the kitchen with the woman Max couldn't stop thinking about.

"Where you two going?" Brody asked.

"Outside to play basketball. Sydney needs some exercise, she says, and she thinks she can beat me on some one-on-one today." He zeroed in on Max. "You know, you should put this in that magazine of yours. Parker Allen keeps ragging on us for our *downtime*. What she doesn't know is we stay fit and let off steam for the calls."

He noticed Sydney didn't even look at him but stared out the window, her back to them. "Let off stream?"

"Come on, Tony," Sydney said, again without turning around. "I'm restless."

"Be right there, babe."

After he made some notes on his computer, Max got coffee and headed outside. He knew he shouldn't. First of all, Sydney wouldn't want him there. Second, it wasn't good for him. He'd made a decision and should stick to it. But like before, he was drawn to her.

He didn't expect what he found on the blacktop. The weather was warm at noon in May and though they were in T-shirts, they still wore uniform pants and sneakers. Sweat glistened off Sydney's face and arms; she had the ball and dribbled around Tony. He got in front of her again and body-blocked a shot. She rammed into him hard enough to recoil back. "Hey, that was a foul." Her tone was annoyed.

"No fouls, remember. If you're not up to this, girl…"

"Shut up and play."

Tony took the ball out. Sydney jogged to the key they'd painted on the blacktop. Hands up, she shifted from side to side. He noted the play of her muscles, the healthy sheen of her skin. Slowly, Tony dribbled the ball, never taking his gaze from her face. He went right, she went left. He went left and she stole the ball. Pivoting, he tried to get it back from her and she jabbed him with her elbow. "Hey, watch it. That hurt."

She kept dribbling and went for an easy layup. Her movements were graceful, agile, and she looked...good doing them.

Leaning against the brick of the firehouse, Max was mesmerized at their rough play and at their competence. Until Ramirez stole the ball, she blocked him and he ran into her, knocking her over flat onto her back.

Max bolted across the blacktop. "Jesus Christ, Ramirez." He dropped to his knees, as did Tony, while Sydney lay prone on the blacktop.

"Hey, kiddo, you okay?" Tony asked.

Taking a deep breath, she nodded. "I got the wind knocked out of me is all."

"That's because you're playing like you're in the NBA." Max turned to Tony. "You should be more careful with her."

Tony cocked his head. He stared at Max, then looked to Sydney. She eased up to a sitting position and appeared equally nonplussed.

Tony asked, "What going on between you two?"

• • •

SYDNEY HAD SEEN Max come out to the blacktop and caught sight of him watching her. And okay, maybe she played a little harder than usual. But now, as he hovered above her, his face showing shock and concern, she thought, *Tough shit.*

Max sighed deeply. "I don't exactly know, Tony. Can I have a word with Sydney?"

The man stared him down. "I don't think so."

"Let me up." They stood and backed away. Sydney rolled to her feet. "I'll talk to him by myself."

"You sure?"

"Uh-huh. Go put some ice on your ribs."

Snorting, he walked into the firehouse, leaving them alone. Appropriately, clouds had come out, and the sun went behind them.

She plopped her hands on her hips. "What's going on with you? Last night you were horrible to me and now you're acting like a worried suitor. It's not okay."

He jammed a hand through his hair, mussing it. His face was stiff with tension. "I have no idea what's going on with me." He waited a beat. "No, that's not true. I know one thing. I behaved badly last night. I think my emotions are so conflicted that I'm acting like a jerk. If you only knew how much this wasn't me."

"I bring out the worst in you."

This time, he touched her arm with gentleness, and his eyes warmed. Still, she remembered how they'd turned glacial yesterday when she'd told him about Ken. "Actually, no. I've been in a holding pattern for years. I've controlled every reaction, every emotion I've had. I think that's why I haven't dated. Around you, I can't seem to get a grip on myself."

Shaking her head as if what he said didn't make a difference, Sydney crossed to the bench and picked up a towel she'd left there. She wiped her face with it to stall for time. What did she really want here? "There's an easy solution to all this, Max. We stay away from each other. You control yourself better when you're at the firehouse and I'll avoid you."

Brows raised, he crossed his arms over his chest and frowned. "I'm not sure that's what I want. And I'm furious with myself for last night. I'm so sorry about what I did. I don't think you're a slut and I wasn't treating you that way. I simply let out all my feelings."

She shrugged. "Whatever. All's forgiven. Now, leave me alone."

He watched her as if he was deciding his fate. "Is there a chance we can keep seeing each other. Work this out?"

"No."

"No? Just like that?" His tone was exasperated.

"I can't trust you. You're too erratic."

"Only with you."

"This has all gotten too confusing. It's not good for either of us."

His gaze narrowed. "Is it because you know Kessler's free now?"

*Damn him.* "No, it's not. It's because you'll throw those kinds of remarks in my face. I won't live waiting for you to ambush me."

His jaw hardened and he glanced away. "Maybe I'm jealous."

"I don't care, Max. Leave me alone."

"I don't think I want to give up that easily."

"*Maybe you're jealous... You don't think?* Listen to yourself. You're so wishy-washy, even to your own ears, you have to sound unsure. I don't need that in my life. Goodbye, Max."

She walked into the firehouse wondering how many times she was going to have to say those words to him? Though she'd put up a good front, she was sick inside about him and didn't want the pain.

# CHAPTER 7

"OKAY, OKAY, SWEETIE. Mommy's done." Sydney dumped the last of the hot water into the baby pool she'd assembled in her backyard. Though six at night, May had turned so hot, she'd decided the evening was good for swimming. So she dressed both herself and Daisy in pink bathing suits, tied their hair in knots on the tops of their heads and set up the plastic pool in the backyard. Crossing to Daisy's bouncy seat, she unsnapped her daughter and picked her up. The solid baby feel of her child made her content like nothing else could. This is all she needed.

"Water, water," Daisy shouted, kicking her feet.

"I know, we're going in the water. Mommy, too."

Stepping over the plastic side, she plunked down into the middle of the pool. She sat Daisy between her legs. "Hmm, feel good?"

Daisy splashed. Sydney picked up a small bucket, filled it with the warm water and poured it over Daisy's head. The little girl squealed with delight. "No sissy, are ya, babe? We're not afraid of the water."

"Looks like you're not afraid of a lot of things."

The deep male voice caused Sydney to stiffen. Inside the gate to her yard stood Ken. Dressed in a shiny brown T-shirt and khaki shorts, he looked cool and, unfortunately, confident. One thing she'd loved about him was how *in command* he always was. He closed the distance between them and towered over the pool. She had to shade her eyes to look up at him.

With her other hand, she gripped Daisy tighter. "What are you doing here?"

"I've come to see you without an audience like we had the other night."

Bravado won out. She wouldn't be cowed by this man.

"I'm Daisy," her little girl said.

Ken gazed down at his daughter. "Hello, sweetheart."

"Daisy, Mommy's getting out to talk to this man. Play by yourself for a minute." Sydney made quick work of exiting the pool and putting on a cover up. She moved out of hearing distance of her child, and he followed.

Rounding on him, she was about to speak but he said, "And I've come to see my daughter."

She said harshly, "She's the daughter you wanted to get rid of."

His face fell. Really fell, as though he was genuinely sad. "I can't tell you how much I regret that hasty decision."

"Too late."

"Obviously not." He gestured to Daisy. "Why didn't you tell me?" he asked, pitching his voice low like he had when they'd had sex.

"Oh, when? All those times you called to see how I was?"

"I told you I had to give it one more try with Diana."

Sydney didn't respond.

Ken stared at her. "She looks like me."

"Unfortunately."

"I knew she was mine right away."

"So you can count. Big deal."

"Sydney, please, can't we talk about this civilly?"

Her pulse rate sped up as anger gritted through her. "There's nothing to talk about. We went our separate ways. I'm sorry you couldn't keep your marriage together, but having affairs often gums up the works."

"*An* affair. Only with you."

"I'm honored," she said sarcastically. "This is tiresome, Ken. I have no interest in letting you into our lives."

"What if I do?"

Now she glared at him. "Why?"

"How can you ask that? I'm her father. Since I know she's...here, I want to get to know her."

"No."

He gave her his killer grin. "I'd like to see you again, too." His perusal of her from head to toe was icky. "You've grown into a lovely woman."

"Give me a break. I've grown up all right. I won't fall for your lines again."

"What we had was real."

"What we had was two nights a week. While you were supposedly playing racquetball. Jesus, I can't believe I actually helped you wet your clothes down so Diana would think you were where you said you were. How humiliating."

"You make it sound so seedy. And trite."

"It was both. We met in a bar. You said your wife didn't understand you and I fell for it."

"All that was true."

Daisy slapped the water and said, "Mommy, come back!"

Crossing to her daughter, Sydney picked her up, wrapped her in a towel and held her close. Raising her voice some, because she was upset, she said, "I'd like you to leave."

Leaning back on his heels he jutted his chin out. The sun glistened off the highlights in his hair. "I'm not going anywhere."

"Yes, you are." Again, a strong masculine voice came from the near the gate.

Sydney looked over to see Ryan and Felicia in the yard, now, too. Must be it was a night for visitors. They crossed to the pool.

"Who are you?" Ken asked.

"Uncle Ryan." Daisy held out her arms.

Ryan took Daisy and held her close to his chest. "Sergeant O'Malley. I'm a police officer. So, if I were you, I'd do what the lady asked and get out of here. Harassment's a crime."

Ken shook his head. "All right. I'll go." He turned to Sydney. "This isn't over by a long shot."

As he passed her new visitors, Felicia grabbed his arm. She was shorter than Ken, but stood on her toes to get in his face. Literally. "I'm not a cop, buddy, but I'll tell you this. You come here unannounced again and you'll answer to all of us."

"And who is that?"

"The entire Hidden Cove Fire and Police Departments."

He rolled his eyes but did indeed leave.

Ryan waited till he was gone. "Who was that, Syd?"

"Daisy's f-a-t-h-e-r." She spelled the word so Daisy wouldn't understand.

Both of their jaws dropped. She'd never shared any details of her circumstances, even with these people she cared about so much.

"What did he want?" Felicia asked softly. She could be a tyrant, but Licia was nothing if not loyal.

"It's a long and very boring story."

"Which you can tell us over ice cream. We stopped to see if you guys wanted to go with us."

"How sweet."

"Wanna go for ice cream," Daisy put in. "Brown!"

Felicia took Daisy from Ryan. "While you dress, I'll change Daisy, and we'll get some treats. Ryan can go out front to make sure Daddy of the Year is gone."

Ryan ruffled her hair. "Yes, ma'am."

Sydney grinned, said, "Yes, ma'am," and headed into the house with her friend, feeling marginally better.

• • •

MAX SAT WITH Cal at a table in the bar of the Lakeside Restaurant, stirring his scotch with a stick. Soft piano music played from the corner and the place was crowded. They met for dinner and drinks like this frequently.

Cal studied him. "You look down."

"I am." He glanced away. "And I can't talk to you about it."

"Why not? We share everything—the drag of being alone, problems at work, cheating spouses."

Now Max did snag his friend's gaze. "You know, I always felt bad for what happened with you and Laura. Annette's illness changed her. They were like sisters, and your wife fell apart when Annette got sick."

"I know that was partly the cause. But it didn't affect how I felt about her infidelity. Adultery under any circumstances is unacceptable."

Max thought about Daisy's father cheating on his wife. "I guess. But Annette and I managed."

"You know I still think her emotional involvement with another man was as bad as physical cheating."

"And I think it was worse. I forgave her only because I was partly to blame."

Briefly, Cal stared off into space. "I suppose I was, too, in mine and Laura's relationship, by working so much. And my focus on the job ruined what my son and I had."

"Have you seen Peter lately?"

"When Sally invites me over or to come to one of Tommy's games. I'd give my right arm to spend more time with my grandson. My son, too. He's still removed, distant. Now that's something I'll never forgive myself for."

"Yeah, I don't know what I'd do without Amber."

"Who's a sweetie." He took a gulp of liquor. "Hell, all that's water under the bridge. Tell me what's eating you now."

"As I said, I don't feel I can talk to you about it. You're, um, indirectly involved."

He saw the calculations tick through Cal's eyes. Few people knew how brilliant the man was. "Does this have anything to do with Sydney Sands? You two were tight at the party you threw for us."

"Yeah."

"She's pretty young."

"There is that."

"But mature and competent, too. She strikes me as a woman who knows her own mind. Is she interested in you?"

He thought of her whimpers when he was inside her. "She was initially. Now I don't know. I've already made mistakes with her that I can't seem to rectify." Max thought for a minute. But if he could... "Look, Cal, would this put you in an awkward position if I was, you know, to date her?"

"I don't think so. In any case, she might not even be under my supervision." He grinned, an unusual expression for this somber man. "I was just told something that nobody knows yet. I'm on the short list for deputy chief."

"Hey, buddy, that's great. Really great."

"Yeah, it's something I've always wanted."

"Good for you."

The waitress approached their table. Max glanced up and realized she wasn't the one who had gotten them drinks. A beautiful woman stood before them. She wore a jewel-red dress and had skeins of dark hair. And she was staring at Cal. "I thought I recognized you, Chief Erikson."

Cal's brows shot up. "Well, if it isn't Parker Allen. Our little nemesis."

Max had never heard Cal speak so condescendingly. But now that he knew who the woman was, he understood his friend's tone.

"Mind if I sit?" She was already pulling out a chair and dropping into it.

"What do you want?" Cal asked.

"Um, white wine. Thanks for asking."

Cal angled his head at Max. "Do you mind?"

"No. Not at all." He couldn't imagine what was about to unfold. "I'm Max Delinsky."

"Right. You put out *The Heart of Hidden Cove*. It's a nice little magazine, though a bit too sappy for my taste."

"And I've been reading your blog. It's a bit too brash for mine."

Tossing back her hair, Parker Allen laughed. Around her neck and at her ears were rubies. Her appearance as well as her reaction was full of sensual appeal and guys at the next table turned to look at her. "Touché."

Cal had signaled a waitress and ordered for the reporter. "Bring us another, too. I think I'm going to need one."

"So," Max said, lazing back casually. "You'll be interested to know that my magazine is doing a whole issue on the Hidden Cove Fire Department."

Her black brows rose. "I don't suppose you'll be fair."

"No fairer than you," Cal put in. "I tried to call you for a few weeks after this vendetta started and periodically since then. Why won't you talk to me?"

She leaned over giving Cal a glimpse of her cleavage. "Why do you think, Chief?"

"How the hell did you get those pictures of my crew, anyway? And the information from the training on bombs?"

"A reporter never reveals her sources, right Mr. Delinsky?"

Max held up his hands, arrest style. "Leave me out of this."

"You have to have a source in the fire department."

"I do, huh? How would that make you feel, Chief, if one of your own is feeding information to the enemy?"

Instead of answering, Cal leaned back, too, and casually crossed his ankle over his leg. Max knew this was his pre-attack mode. "You know we have you all figured out."

"Oh, I'll bet you do." Her drink arrived and she took a hefty sip. "Tell me."

"Well, for one thing, we know who Nigel Larson is."

Max had never seen color drain from someone's face so fast. When he glanced at Cal, he saw a flicker of concern in his friend's eyes, too.

Allen got her mojo back quickly, though, and raised her chin. "You bastard. You're going to regret having me investigated."

Instead of basking in his victory—he'd surely shaken her up—Cal leaned over and braced his arms on the table. "What did you expect, Parker? After how you've attacked my department."

"Humanity, maybe." Her gaze narrowed. "Why haven't you done something with the information?"

"Noah Callahan and I decided we didn't want to sink to your level and use it. Though we've been tempted over the last several months." He shook his head. "But you know what? I'm getting this close"—he made a gesture with his thumb and forefinger—"to changing my mind."

Still staring at him, she took another sip of her drink, slammed the glass down and scraped her chair back. "That sounds suspiciously like a threat, *Cal*. And I don't take to them very well." Standing, she stormed away.

Hell, he was a man, and Max noticed she looked good from the back, too. Then he turned to Cal. "Some show."

Cal rolled his eyes. "That woman drives me to distraction. I've left messages for her. Emailed her. Wrote her open letters on the blog. Nothing. Now, she flounces in here and wants a drink! Jesus." He gulped the last of his.

"I won't ask what you've got on her, but I have the same question. If you can stop her with it, why don't you?"

"It'd be cruel."

The hostess came up to them. "Your table's ready, Chief. The one by the window that you like."

"Thanks, Cindy."

Both men stood. "Feel like talking more about this?" Max asked.

"Nah. Feel like talking about Sydney?"

"Nah. Let's forget all about women tonight."

"Easier said than done, buddy."

Thinking of Sydney, Max said, "Yes, unfortunately, it is."

• • •

SYDNEY GLANCED OVER to the bleachers and saw Max, Amber and Chief Erikson sitting on the top row. Amber waved and she waved back. Max stared at her, at least seemed to, but he was wearing dark sunglasses and he could be watching anybody.

Next to her on the bench, Tony nudged her. "Who you looking at, kiddo?"

"Um, the chief is here."

Tracking her gaze, Tony said, "Hmm. And he's not alone."

Sydney jumped up and clapped when Gabe got a line drive to third and Ryan O'Malley fumbled the ball. It was a hot night and she was edgy so it felt good to move. "Way to go, Cap," she yelled through cupped hands.

Tony pulled her back down. "You can't avoid this conversation forever like you've been doing since we played basketball."

"I know. It's complicated."

"Listen, all I care about is that you're happy." He kept his voice low for privacy. "If this guy's nice enough to you, go for him."

"It's complicated," she repeated.

He let it drop and they both watched the play. Grady O'Connor was up and hit a fly ball to one of the cops in left field. When the inning ended and she headed to shortstop, she thought about how Max had respected her wishes when he was at the firehouse this week and hadn't pressed her to talk to him. He'd interview her tomorrow before they went off for four days. She should be looking forward to a respite from his nearly irresistible presence. But she wasn't. She had the absurd urge to confide in him about Ken's demands and get his advice on what she should do. Would he be sympathetic to her or would he understand a father's rights? Did Ken have rights? The question had kept her up at night.

Megan Hale grounded a ball to her. She shot it to the first baseperson for an out, then concentrated on the game. The next cop got a home run and it was all downhill from there. The police won, but they were due as the fire department was beating them regularly.

When her team returned to the dugout, Cal Erikson was waiting for them. He was out of uniform, in jeans and an HCFD polo shirt. She glanced to the stands. Max was gone. A heavy disappointment filled her chest and she chided herself for it. She'd gotten exactly what she'd asked for.

"I'm buying you guys ice cream at Abe's as a consolation prize."

Most of the team was in, and Sydney agreed to go. She needed to get away from her conflicting feelings about Max: wishing she could see him, wishing she didn't want to. Dreaming about him, then remembering his reaction to Daisy's father and subsequent treatment of her that night at his house.

Because she'd hurried out of the softball field, she arrived first at Abe's—a cute outdoor stand with several picnic tables for patrons. When she got out of her car, Amber Delinsky came running up to her. "I *hoped* you were coming. I haven't seen you in ages." She threw herself at Sydney and hugged her. "I miss you and Daisy."

"We miss you, too." The girl felt solid and right in her arms as Sydney hugged her tight. "Tell you what. I'm off, and the day after tomorrow, Daisy and I going to the beach. Want to come with us? I'll pick you up."

"Yes!" Amber said excitedly.

Taking her by the hand, the girl dragged Sydney over to where Max sat, a dish of ice cream in front of him. Amber bubbled about the invitation. He raised his brows as he looked at Sydney. She nodded.

"Sounds great," he said. "You'll have fun."

"Wanna come, Dad?"

He avoided Sydney's gaze. "No, honey, I'm busy finding a new place for our business."

Amber shrugged at his comment, not knowing the significance of it. "Sit here, Sydney. I'll go get you ice cream. Uncle Cal called and set up a tab." She asked Sydney what flavor, then headed to the line.

Max watched her go, turned and faced Sydney. "I wouldn't have come but Cal invited me and Amber, and she said yes. I couldn't disappoint her. Sorry to intrude."

"You're not intruding. I don't want Amber to suffer in all of this."

"I know. Right away, you said you didn't want to hurt her with our problems." His green eyes were full of feeling. "I can't tell you what that means to me. And what it says about you as a person."

"Kids shouldn't pay for the sins of their parents."

He ate his pistachio, and as she watched his sculpted mouth surreptitiously, Sydney was hit by a bolt of desire, so much so she could hardly speak. She didn't know what to do with all the emotion he stirred inside her.

After he checked his daughter's whereabouts, Max spoke again. "I've given you space, sweetheart, but know that I want to see you."

Before she could answer, she noticed the rest of the team had arrived and Sophia, Tony and the kids joined them at the table. There was no time to talk privately, so Sydney tried to enjoy the repartee.

"Feeling good?" Max asked Sophia when Tony went with the kids to get their treat.

"Remarkably. I never felt this good carrying a baby before."

"An untroubled pregnancy," Syd blurted out, not censoring her words because she was used to talking openly with Sophia.

The beautiful woman reached across and squeezed her hand. "How is my little Daisy? When are you going to let us have her overnight? Mari keeps asking."

"Now that you mention it, the female firefighters in the department are getting together tomorrow night. It'll be a late one. Then?"

"Great. Make arrangements with Tony."

Max asked, "What do you do when you get together?"

"Dress up fancy, go to the Lakeside and girl talk."

"Will you be trashing Parker Allen? I met her by the way. At the Lakeside, as a matter of fact." He explained the circumstances. "She was very flirty."

Sydney's pulse sped up, but she didn't comment because Amber came back with a chocolate cone for her, then left to join the other kids.

"You're an attractive man, Max." Sophia had touched his arm.

"I meant she was flirty with Cal."

Sydney almost dropped her cone. "Seriously?"

Sophia laughed. "He probably seems like an old man to you, you're such a baby. However, your battalion chief is attractive, too."

As if on cue, Cal arrived, then the kids returned, but Sydney had something else to think about. She'd seen pictures of Parker Allen. The woman was drop-dead gorgeous in a purely feminine way that Sydney would never, ever be. Watching the man across from her, she had the unpleasant image of some woman like Allen scooping him up. The notion sat heavy in her heart.

• • •

THE MORNING WAS too bright and cheery for the question Max asked. But any magazine featuring a fire department had to include their experiences on that fateful day in September. "Tell me what happened to you all on 9/11."

An eerie silence invaded the firehouse. Brody got up to get coffee, Tony swore under his breath and Sydney glanced down at the newspaper she'd been reading.

"I'll start." Gabe Malvaso was always the leader. "Mitch and I went down to Ground Zero. We'd been rookies with the FDNY and knew a lot of smoke eaters who were trapped." Here his voice got hoarse. "Most of them didn't make it out. The worst part of the recovery was finding missing body parts. Only two hundred and eighty-nine bodies were found intact and almost twenty thousand body parts were unearthed. After finding some of them, Mitch and me had to get away. When we did, we cried like babies."

Again, stone-cold silence.

Brody's face was bleak and his eyes glistened as he started out. "The brass wouldn't let me go down. I was a rookie then and the captain in my house refused to send me. He also told me if I went down on my own, I'd be suspended, maybe even kicked out of this department. I didn't know he was looking out for me. He'd heard my firefighter uncle had died in the attack, but it hadn't been confirmed, and he didn't want me" — here he glanced at Gabe — "finding what you guys found. I did some research afterward and a lot of firefighters discovered their buddies. The PTSD they experienced stayed with them a long time. But I felt so impotent. It's why I like to control things."

No one teased him about his doggedness.

"Felicia?" Max asked when no one offered to go next. "How about you?"

"I didn't know anybody in the FDNY, though I was working in Binghamton at the time. I went down to the pile, of course, as did scores of other women to work as rescue workers, nurses, police, chaplains. All we hear about are the policemen and firemen who were heroes. Hundreds of women were there, too."

"She's right," Brody added. "And she wrote a moving portrait of the three women we know of who died at Ground Zero. Captain Kathy Mazza, EMT Yamel Marino, Police Officer Moira Smith were all casualties."

"You remember their names, Brody." Felicia smiled at him. "How sweet."

"Tell us about them." Max's tone was grave.

"Kathy Mazza was a Port Authority Police Officer who ran into the towers and led groups of people down the stairs when the building began to collapse. She shot out glass windows with her sidearm, allowing them to escape. *She* wasn't so lucky." Felicia sighed. "Moira Smith was the only NYPD female officer killed, after saving hundreds of people before Tower 2 collapsed on her. And EMT Yamel Merino was working on an ambulance crew and volunteered to go inside to help the wounded. She never came out. She was only twenty-four."

Whispers of incredulity, sympathy. More silence.

"I'll go next." This from Ramirez, whose face was ravaged. "It's no secret the problems Sophia and I had this year. She couldn't let me go there because she was worried. I went anyway and didn't tell her. I carried out body parts, but when I found a kid, I lost it, too." He looked around. "I never told anybody that story."

"Thanks for sharing it with us, Tony." Max's tone was grave, befitting the admission.

Tony nodded.

"Sydney? You were very young when 9/11 happened. Do you remember anything?"

"I was Amber's age." Her beautiful eyes were bleak. "Two of the firefighters from the house I hung out at were killed. One, I…" She swallowed hard. "One I liked best. His name was Danny and he used to let me wear his helmet. He was like an older brother. I never forgot him. And it was never the same at the firehouse after that day."

Last was Chief Erikson. Somber, he pulled his wallet from his pocket and took out a yellowed-with-age paper. "Most people know about the good-bye calls the victims in the towers and on that plane made. But they don't know that a lot of the firefighters who went down to Ground Zero knew they weren't coming back. They left letters to their wives and lovers in their lockers." He stared hard at the paper. "This is from a kid who was a rookie in Hidden Cove, then joined the FDNY to roll with the big guys. I was the only person he wrote to. The letter says I was the reason he became a good firefighter. I shouldn't feel guilty that I hadn't taught him well if he died down there. He said it was because of me that he could save people." Cal bit the inside of his jaw. "Word has it he carried out ten to safety before he got crushed by a girder."

When everyone finished, the house quieted again. One by one, the firefighters of Hidden Cove got up and left the room. There was nothing more to be said.

• • •

THE FOLLOWING AFTERNOON, Max was ready to interview Sydney, or at least he thought he was, until he sat at the kitchen table once again having coffee with the group. The bell at the back door rang. Felicia, cleaning up at the stove, from where she'd cooked enough bacon and eggs for lumberjacks, said, "I'll get it," and headed out to see who was visiting at this hour of the morning. When she came back, her expression was grim.

"I had to let the first one in, Syd," she said soberly. "He's legal. This other one insisted, saying it would be best if you heard whatever they have to say from him."

Sydney's face went pale, and Max would have gone to her, but he recognized the guy as the father of her child. Much of the progress Max had made in accepting Sydney's situation weakened with Ken Kessler's physical presence. Damn it, he hated vacillating like this, but images of Annette and Tim haunted him. Still, he'd made a decision. He wanted Sydney in his life. So he sat by as she stood and crossed her arms over her chest. "What do you want?"

Instead of answering, the guy nodded to the other man. He was little and wiry with narrowed eyes. "Sydney Sands?"

Max saw Tony creep up behind Sydney and place his hands on her shoulders. "Yes."

"You've been served." He held out an envelope.

Sydney didn't take it, but Tony did. The others in her crew made a semicircle around her as the processer left and Kessler stepped forward. Max felt like he was watching a play on stage. "Read it Syd, then I'll explain."

Taking the envelope from Tony, she ripped it open. Her hand started to shake, and after Tony read over her shoulder, he lunged for Kessler. Jesus. Max catapulted out of his chair in time to catch Kessler as he was thrown back. Brody and Felicia grabbed Tony.

Gabe circled his arm around Sydney and drew her back.

"What the hell are you doing?" Kessler asked, shrugging off Max and watching Tony.

"You can't have her kid," Tony shouted.

"I don't want to take Daisy away from her."

"That's what the paper says."

"Because Sydney won't even talk to me about her. I only want visitation rights." He stared at Sydney. "And you, of course."

Max slid an arm around Kessler's chest and yanked him back. "Over my dead body."

Gabe shook his head, and the others eyed Max suspiciously.

"Who the hell are you?" Kessler asked, again freeing himself from Max, though it wasn't that easy this time.

"I'm a friend of Sydney's. You and I met the other night."

"How close a friend?"

"Yeah," Brody said, stepping up to Sydney, too. "How close?"

"Close enough to not let you hurt her, Kessler."

"I don't *want* to hurt her." He threw up his arms, then slapped his thighs. "I want another chance with her and I want to see my daughter regularly."

"You have it all planned out, don't you?" Sydney said, and for the first time ever, Max saw the sheen of tears in her eyes. Never once had he seen her cry.

"No, I don't have anything figured out. I just want a break here."

Felicia moved in close to him. From where he stood, Max could see the fire in her eyes. "You missed your chance, buddy. You abandoned a twenty-year-old girl to have a baby by herself."

"That's not the whole story."

"*I* know the whole story," Tony, who had calmed down, spat out. "And it's worse."

Sydney turned her head into Gabe's shoulder. "Just get him out of here."

"All right, I'll go. But now you'll *have* to deal with me." Casting a scathing glance at them all, he added, "Jesus, she doesn't need a posse to defend her from me."

Once again, Tony riled, but Gabe stepped in. "Enough. Leave my firehouse, Kessler."

The man stalked out. Gabe turned to Max. "I think you'd better leave, too, Max."

Right then the PA went off. "Rescue 7, Quint and Midi 7, go into service." Holy hell, there was a call for this group.

Gabe grasped Sydney's shoulders. "Are you good enough to come with us?"

Raising her chin, Sydney nodded. "Yeah. Temporary lapse."

The captain studied her a minute. "Okay, let's go." To Max, he said, "Max, you're skipping this one. I don't know what's going on with you and Syd, but we've had enough drama today. Leave now so we can lock up."

There was no time to talk to Sydney. No time to decide how he felt about the sordid scene he'd witnessed. The group was gone in a flash and they took Sydney with them. Max left the firehouse hurt, angry and more than a little concerned about her.

• • •

WHEN SYDNEY PULLED into her driveway that evening, the last thing she wanted to do was get dressed up and meet the other female firefighters for their night out. What she wanted was to get in bed and pull the covers over her head. Her mother was over at her sister's, and Daisy was with Tony's family, so Sydney would be alone. She got out of the car, thinking about what had transpired after the shift ended. Gabe had called his cousin Paulie, a lawyer, and they'd stopped at his office on the way home. Paulie had read the papers, said they were pretty straightforward and asked for her side of the story. When she finished, he gave her a reassuring smile. "I don't think you have anything to worry about. He was married to another woman, tried to pay you off, and left you alone afterward. The most he'd get is visitation."

On the way home, Gabe had asked, "Would that be so bad?"

Remembering Paulie's opinion, she felt a little better as she headed to the side door where she spotted a large envelope nestled again the wood. Whatever it was, Sydney couldn't handle much more today. She'd been embarrassed big-time about the scene with Ken, and she had a lot of explaining to do to her crew. But besides the fact that Ken wanted to see Daisy, Max had witnessed the entire ordeal. If there had ever been a chance for them, it had fled with the morning's fiasco.

Picking up the manila envelope as if it was a minefield, she went inside and plopped down at the kitchen table. In the empty house, she heard the refrigerator turn on and the batting of a tree limb against the door. The light she'd left on cast the room in an eerie glow as she stared at the envelope. Oh, hell, she couldn't resist opening it.

Inside she found a tape recorder, labeled, "Interview seven."

Huh! She was supposed to be interview seven with Max, but Gabe had kicked him out of the firehouse today. She pressed play.

"Maxwell Delinsky here." The deep baritone startled her. "Today I'm interviewing my alter ego, Max. So let's start."

Sydney's hand clapped over her mouth.

"Tell me Max, why are you acting like such a jerk these days?"

His voice was the same, of course, but held a different tone. "Because a woman has turned my life upside down."

"Who?"

A snort. "As if we both don't know. Sydney Sands."

"Ah, I like her."

"I do, too. I think...I *know* I'm in love with her."

Sydney gasped. "Oh, my God."

The tape continued, alternating egos.

"You have a hell of a way of showing that emotion."

"I agree. I've been erratic, contradictory, stupid and selfish."

A muffled sound, then, "Maybe not that bad. But you have behaved poorly."

Sydney laughed out loud at his humor.

"I never meant to hurt her."

"Why did you?"

"Because I have a hang-up about infidelity."

Well, that was news. Max had never spoken about the topic.

"Why, Max?"

"I...um, oh, God this is hard. But I'm going say it. My wife fell in love with another man."

Sydney said aloud, "No way!"

"I think you're exaggerating there, Max."

"No, I'm not. She didn't get involved physically, just emotionally. She admitted she loved the guy."

Anger rose in Sydney. But when he explained about the chemo, Max being absent, her mindset changed.

*Maxwell* echoed her thoughts. "You jerk. Couldn't you give the woman a break? Look what she was going through."

"Actually, I did give her a break. I forgave her completely, quit my job and spent all my time with her and Amber. The year before she died, we'd never been closer." His voice broke on the last word.

Tears welled in Sydney's eyes. "Oh, Max."

"I know it's no real excuse, but when I found out about Sydney's past, her situation coalesced with my past and I freaked out."

"So," his alter ego drawled, "what do you want now?"

"That's easy. Only one thing."

"Yeah? What?"

"Sydney."

• • •

SEVERAL BEAUTIFUL WOMEN entered a private room in the Lakeside Restaurant all dressed up. Blacks, reds and pinks were proudly donned, stilettos and some strappy sandals graced their feet and every woman's hair was styled and chic.

Dressed in the same blue dress she'd worn to Max's party, Sydney walked in at eight-thirty, unable to appreciate the tables set in white and black, the subtle lighting and the soft music piped in. She didn't want to be here. She'd tried to reach Max right up until she had to leave the house. Since she couldn't, she planned to stay for dinner and then head over to his place.

He loved her! Her heart rate sped up at the thought. And that explanation, oh, Lord, how hard did Annette turning to another man have to be for him? She knew what his wife meant to him. Oddly, she wasn't jealous of what they'd had together.

Felicia approached her wearing a copper-colored clingy dress with her hair spiky. "I thought maybe you weren't coming tonight. Today was pretty rough."

"No one misses these events. Besides, I wasn't going to let that man take anything else away from me." Sydney scanned the crowd. "We have extra women tonight."

"Yeah, it's a regular family affair."

Staring across the room, she said, "I recognize Jenn Malvaso. She looks great in the red one-piece thing, despite having had a second baby. Isn't that Mitch's wife with her?"

"Yeah, we invited the police."

Megan Hale Malvaso wore black and sequins. Her blond hair fell down her back and she and Jenn were laughing together.

Sydney glanced at the others. "I don't know the two women they're with. The dark-haired one and the blonde."

"I only know one. Let's go over; I'll introduce you." She touched Sydney's arm. "If you're sure you're all right."

"I'm great. I can't stay much past dinner, though."

"What's going on?"

"I'd rather wait to say, Licia, but it's good."

"That's enough for me." They headed toward the group.

Jenn was speaking. "And then Grady said if the baby pooped all over him again, he was calling my mother."

"Men!" Megan shook her head. "Mitch depends on Sabina, too, when he's with Sabby."

"Wait till you have two babies." Jenn caught sight of them. "Hey, Licia."

"You all know Sydney Sands."

The women she knew greeted her. One of the others stepped forward. "I'm Lisel Woodward."

"Oh, my God, Lisel Loring, the Broadway sensation!" Sydney was star struck.

The face that had routinely stopped shows gave a little smile. "In another life."

"Mom and I scraped for months to see *Longshot*. You deserved the Tony nomination."

Felicia nodded to the blonde, who was smiling broadly. "I'm Felicia White and this is Sydney."

The woman moved in. Up close, she had the most angelic face Sydney had ever seen. She was small, compact and absolutely lovely. "Hi, I'm Faith Ruscio. I crashed tonight because I had to get away from my twins. Lisel was over to our condo today—she lives next door—and took pity on me. I hope it's okay I tagged along."

"Sure, the more the merrier."

"Eve's here, too. Over there talking with the new female battalion chief." Lisel scowled. "She's stumped by the fact that there hasn't been another arson lately."

"We all are. We..." Megan cut off when her phone rang. Whipping it out of her clutch purse, she checked the caller. "I'm sorry. I have to take this. It's from the precinct." She stepped away.

"Faith, how's Rick doing with the twins?" Jenn asked.

"Happy as a clam. But his sisters had to come and help out tonight."

Instantly, Sydney was jealous. The woman looked happy as a clam, too.

When Megan returned, she was white-faced. "I'm sorry I have to leave. That was Ryan, Licia."

Felicia gripped Sydney's arm. "Is he all right?"

"Yes, *he* is."

All the women tensed. Most of their men were in dangerous positions. "Who isn't?" Jenn asked.

Megan faced Sydney. "Ryan said to tell you Max Delinsky's been attacked. He was checking out an office building to see if he wanted to rent space and...well, somebody attacked him."

Sydney froze. "Max? My Max?"

"Yes, honey, and it's pretty bad. He's at Hidden Cove Hospital."

"Oh, my God."

Felicia said, "I'll drive you."

"I'll meet you there." Megan was already starting off.

"Come on, Syd. Let's go."

Still she couldn't move. Something happened to Max? *No, please, not now.*

• • •

HIS HEAD POUNDED, his jaw felt like it was broken and the rest of his body ached as Max pushed himself up in the hospital bed to answer Ryan O'Malley's questions. The room was small and stuffy, housing him and Ryan and Cal, who stood by his bedside, his shoulders tense, his face hard. It had been a hell of a day.

"Let's wait till Megan gets here to start the interview," Ryan said.

"I'm here." A vision appeared in the doorway. Despite the gravity of the situation, Ryan whistled.

"You clean up good, Hale." Then his eyes widened even more. "And Lieutenant White. You make my mouth water."

"Not now, O'Malley," she quipped, but there was a small smile on her face.

Max was shocked to see another woman behind the two officers, dressed in a beautiful blue dress he'd seen before, with her hair all puffy and tons of makeup on. Were those high heels? He'd swallow his tongue if it wasn't swollen. "Oh, man!"

She rushed to Max, her heels clattering on the tile floor. Megan's brows rose as Sydney sat on the bed and took his hand. It was bruised and he winced. "Oh, Lord, I didn't realize…" She set it gently on the mattress. "I'm sorry. You must be in so much pain."

"I'm better now, thanks to modern medicine. And the fact that you're here." He glanced up. "Can I have a few minutes alone with Sydney?"

"I'm sorry, Max." This from the police captain. "We've found that if a victim answers questions right away, we get better information." She nodded to Sydney. "It won't take long."

Sydney started to rise, but Max tugged her back. "Stay."

"What happened, Max?" Ryan asked. "Cal knew you went to look at the office building but that's all."

Without thinking, Max shrugged his shoulder, making him moan. "I got a call from a realtor who worked in the office I hired to scope out rental property for my business. They'd found a perfect place for us. I didn't feel like going because" — he smiled at Sydney — "anyway, I stopped at the address on the way home. The door was ajar and so I went in. I didn't get ten feet and someone hit me over the head. When I fell, he kicked me in the stomach and ribs. Then he bent over and punched my face." Max shivered at the memory of the blinding pain.

"Was it a man or woman on the phone?" Megan asked.

"Woman. She said she was a secretary for the realtor and her boss would meet me there."

Ryan jotted that down.

"Did you get a look at the assailant?"

"I'm sorry, no. I was hit from behind first. Then I had my hands up and didn't see who it was."

"This is so horrible," Sydney whispered, her voice throaty.

"I'm okay. Nothing's broken, honey."

Again, Megan questioned him. "Did the attacker say anything?"

Frowning, Max tried to remember. "No — wait a minute. Yeah, when he bent over me. He said something about *The Heart of Hidden Cove* and to watch what stories I cover."

Cal, who'd been silent all this time, pushed off the wall. "Jesus Christ. Did he mean your fire department edition?"

"Why would anybody care about that?" Sydney asked.

"The arsonist who's been targeting the fire department might," Ryan suggested. "Maybe this is connected."

"Who else knows about the magazine issue?" Megan asked.

"The whole department." Sydney rolled her eyes. "They've been giving the Rescue Squad grief about being the focus of the November issue."

"Anybody outside of the department know?" This from Ryan.

His head aching, Max thought hard. "I didn't tell anybody."

"Yes, Max, you did." Cal shook his head. "You told Parker Allen."

Sydney gasped. "Tony's wondered all along if she's connected to the arson."

Everyone was quiet as the suggestion settled in.

"Is that all for now?" Max laid back against the pillow. "The nurse said I could go home, and I want some time alone with Sydney."

"Take all the time you want here," Cal said. "But I'm bunking at your house tonight." He looked to Sydney. "Even if she does, too. We gotta sort this out about your safety."

Megan nodded. "I'll have somebody drive by every hour."

"Is this necessary? Maybe it was a robbery I interrupted. There was a lot of office equipment there."

"We'll have to do an inventory and cross-check." Ryan shook his head. "Meanwhile, we won't take any chances."

Cal started toward the door with the others. "I'll wait in the lobby. Come out when you're discharged." As he walked by, he squeezed Sydney's arm. "Take it easy on him, will you? He's not as tough as he says he is."

"I know that now. I'll be nice. I promise."

• • •

"IS THAT WHY you came?" Max asked as soon as they were alone. Angry welts marred his handsome face, and his lips were puffy. "Because you found out I was hurt?"

"Of course I came because of that."

"Oh." He seemed disappointed.

"Don't misunderstand. I've been trying to get in touch with you since I got home from work."

His green eyes lightened. "Really?"

"I listened to the tape."

"Ahh." He sighed. "Not a nice story."

"Oh, I don't know." She wished she could touch him, but every part of him was bruised. "I think the interviewee came off looking pretty good."

"He was a jerk."

"So he said." She kissed his hair lightly. "I'm sorry for what happened with your wife. You loved her so much, you must have been devastated."

"I was. But I saw my part in what she did. It's just that we'd been together so long, I couldn't believe she'd turned to another man. It was infidelity, sweetheart. Even if she never slept with him."

"I can understand you'd see it that way."

"So I freaked about Kessler. I'm better about him now," he said. "When that clod beat me up, all I could think of was how I might not see you and Amber again. Nothing else really matters."

"Still, I'm sorry about Annette. Though I understand her, too."

"Yeah, I came to a better place about that. Luckily, I could quit my job, because I had money from the computer chip I designed. We were able to be together — really together — in the time left."

She held his gaze. "I don't know what's going to happen with Ken, but I don't care. I want you to forget about him and be with me."

"I want that, too." He brushed a hand down her hair. "I love you."

Hearing the words while he looked at her made her throat tight. "I love you, too, Max."

"Thank God." He held out his arms. "Come here."

"It'll hurt your ribs."

"I don't care. I have to hold you."

Gingerly, she nuzzled into his chest. "What a mess everything is now."

He put his chin on her head. "No, it's not. We're together. I feel like a very lucky man."

The guy was something else, Sydney thought, lying in bed, battered and beaten, saying he was lucky. And in that instant, Sydney vowed she was going to make it work with him despite outside interferences. They were both quiet with their thoughts.

Then he said, "Thanks for rescuing me."

"From that fire?"

"No, from the life I was leading."

Drawing back, she saw his face was full of love. "Then you rescued me, too."

"I did, huh? I kinda like you being the hero."

Funny thing. Sydney felt like Wonder Woman and Bat Girl all at once. Life with Max, Daisy and Amber would be great. She pictured him calling her daughter *Princess*, being there for the good and bad times of firefighting and all the great sex they had to look forward to. If she had him, she could handle anything like a superhero. Anything.

• • •

# Trial by Fire

Novella number six in the
AMERICA'S BRAVEST SERIES

### KATHRYN SHAY

# CHAPTER 1

"ABSOLUTELY NOT!" BATTALION Chief Cal Erikson raised his voice when he objected to Noah Callahan's outrageous suggestion.

Noah's brows arched and he recoiled. Cal realized what he'd done. "Sorry, Noah. I didn't mean any disrespect." The man was his boss as well as his friend.

"The hell with respect. I'm concerned about you. You've never resisted trying something without even thinking about it."

Taking a deep breath, Cal forcibly calmed himself. "You have no idea the trouble it will cause if we give Parker Allen access to the Rescue Squad, the firehouse and the calls."

"Limited access. And for a limited amount of time." Noah leaned over and braced his forearms on the desk. "Truthfully, Cal, I don't know what else to do. I can't let her diatribe go on unhindered. We're already under the gun because of the city's budget problems, and the mayor is reconsidering the brownouts I talked him out of last year."

Brownouts were the closing of one firehouse for a week while the others picked up the slack. Over in Camden Cove, where they'd tried it, they'd lost a firefighter.

"Isn't there anything else we can do to shut her up?"

"I'm open to ideas."

"We could still leak her background."

As soon as he said the words, Cal had a vision of Parker Allen's face going wide with shock when he'd intimated they could expose nasty things about her. He'd told Max it would be cruel to use what they'd found out, but wasn't that better than having the woman around the firehouse? It'd be a nightmare and the Rescue Squad would rebel.

"We've discussed this several times and always come to the same conclusion. That's not us, Cal. We're not that kind of men. I refuse to crucify her like she's doing us." He waited a beat, then added, "We're the good guys who went to Ground Zero and dug out our buddies." They'd both lost friends in 9/11 and had formed a bond over that.

"You're right, of course. Sometimes I forget what's important."

"Well, you've reminded me a time or two. We said we'd do that, too, after working at the pile."

Cal nodded, thought for a minute, then remembered something. "We're still not sure she's innocent of Max Delinsky's attack."

"We are now. Though the police suspected gangs from New York City, they discovered a footprint that matched one we found at an arson scene. It was big and probably male."

"I didn't know that."

"The report came in this morning."

"Huh. Well, White said she believed Allen could be part of the arson. Ramirez thought the same thing when she knew to come visit Sands at the hospital."

With a heavy sigh, Noah shook his head. "I just don't buy it. She'd have to have had help from somebody who's at the scenes and has knowledge of firematics, somebody who can get inside information on where we are and what we're doing. And frankly, somebody who's bigger and stronger than she is."

Unfortunately, Cal agreed. Somehow he couldn't see Allen getting her hands dirty. Though he knew for certain she spied on them. "It infuriates me to think one of ours is either the arsonist or an accomplice."

"Cal, let's just try having Allen at the firehouse and see how it goes. If it's as bad as you think, then we can stop. Deep in my heart, I believe if she gets a close-up of who we are and what we do, she'll relent."

"I doubt it." He tapped his foot on the floor. "What's the time frame?"

"Let's start with twice a tour. See how it goes."

"Okay, then. Let's give it a shot."

"I'll tell your crew."

"No. They're my responsibility. But if I end up tarred and feathered, come rescue me."

"You won't. Those guys are so in love they probably won't even notice." Noah gave a sappy smile. "It's amazing how they all found their soul mates in two years."

Cal rolled his eyes. "It's like living inside a soap opera."

The chief sat back and steepled his hands. "What about you, Cal? Any women on the horizon?"

"Sure, I date. But I think the fairy dust missed me." He stood. "Wish me luck."

"Good luck. Shall I ask Allen or do you want to?"

"I'll do it. So I can set parameters."

"Let me know what happens."

"I will. I just hope you know what you're doing."

"I do, too, buddy."

• • •

PARKER ALLEN EXITED her car and took a deep breath of the beautiful August morning. Smoothing down her summer dress with the violet, black and yellow flowers on it, she headed toward the door of the Hidden Cove Diner, her heels clicking on the blacktop as she crossed it. She'd been surprised to get Cal Erikson's email asking her to meet today for coffee because he had a proposal for her. For a minute, she recalled his overwhelming presence in the Lakeside bar last spring—he was big, broad shouldered, with a military cut to his blond hair. She was a bit startled by his chiseled features and dark green eyes when she met up with him and his buddy. He'd been intimidating, and Parker had spent years learning to stand up to men like him in her life. Still, her heart stuttered some as she opened the door.

He sat in a booth by the window, dressed in a starched white shirt with epaulets designating his rank. Parker knew a lot about the hierarchy in the fire department, as well as the difference between the trucks and the equipment. A Quint was the biggest rig, with five capacities, like hauling water and hose, carrying ladders. The Jaws of Life was a nickname for the scissor-like Hurst tool that took off the top of a car, and tours were four days on, four days off. Lucky stiffs to have that much downtime.

Briefly, she thought of 9/11 and the sacrifices fire and police personnel had made, but she pushed the notion aside. Fire departments couldn't rest on those laurels forever.

Glancing up, the chief gave her a weak wave. She couldn't imagine why he wanted to see her, but she was ready to go another round with him. They'd met only once, but his emails had kept coming and been acerbic. She never responded because it killed men when you ignored them.

He stood when she reached him. That surprised her. She didn't expect chivalry from these guys. "Thanks for meeting me, Ms. Allen." He circled around and held out a chair for her.

Uneasy with his closeness, she sat. "I wouldn't miss this for the world, Chief. I'm dying of curiosity." A waitress came over and she ordered coffee.

For a moment, he stared at her. "Noah Callahan has a proposal for you. He's asked me to talk to you about it since it involves me and one of the crews I oversee."

"A proposal? I thought maybe you wanted to lure me into a back alley and beat me up."

His gaze hardened for a minute and she didn't know why.

"So what is it?"

"We're offering you a chance to get to know the fire department on a more intimate basis."

"What does *that* mean?"

"You're invited to spend time with Rescue 7 twice a week. Come and go when they do. Watch or even participate in training. Ride along with us to calls."

Parker wasn't easily shocked. She'd carefully constructed a life where surprises were at a minimum. But she was indeed bowled over by the suggestion. "Let me get this straight. You're going to give me total access to your guys and how they spend their time?"

"Yes."

"Why?"

He leaned over, his green eyes intense. "Because Noah Callahan thinks it will change your opinion of the fire department."

"Get me off your backs, you mean."

His lips thinned, revealing his impatience. He couldn't be more than forty, but now, lines etched around his mouth. "In a sense, yes."

An adrenaline rush went through her as she considered the possibilities. "So I'd be allowed to hang out with you twice a week and...oh, wait. For how long? If it's only for one week, then you'll be on your best behavior. I won't see any warts."

"Noah was thinking two months."

"Wow. I can't believe this good fortune."

Shaking his head, he looked away briefly, then faced her again. "Can I ask you something?"

"Sure, go ahead."

"Isn't it hard living your life like you do?"

"What do you mean?"

"I've only ever been a firefighter. All I know is saving people from harm. Not destroying them. What's it like to want to hurt people?"

Parker was speechless. The gall of this man. "Look, Chief, not that it's any of your business but if you'd taken a look at my job history, as well as my sordid background, I've done plenty to champion the rights of others, to help people." But she'd be damned if she told him about the fundraising she'd done to establish a battered women's shelter back home, the reporting she'd been a part of, which had caught a serial killer, the child molester she'd exposed. She spent most of her life doing good deeds. "I believe what I'm revealing about America's Bravest and Finest is helping a community who's getting abused by the system." Delight turned to anger and she stood. "I accept your offer. When can I start?"

"I have to tell the team first."

"Oh, that'll be fun."

"I'll make sure they're courteous to you."

"I'm not worried about that. I hope they'll act naturally."

"They might not at first. That's why the plan is to have you in the firehouse for an extended period of time."

"Well, email me." Before she started away, she took in his sober expression. "This was Noah Callahan's idea, right?"

He nodded.

"Tell me, Chief Erikson, what do you think of it?"

His jaw tightened. "I think it's a very bad idea, Ms. Allen. A very bad idea."

• • •

"NO WAY!"

"Shit."

"How can you ask us to do this?"

"Maybe I'll transfer."

"You gotta be kidding me."

Though his crews were usually on good behavior around their officers, before Cal dropped the bomb today, he'd told Rescue 7 not to censor their reactions. He felt like ripping somebody a new one himself.

"Now that you got that out of your systems, I'll finish what I was saying. This is a *fait accompli*. She's coming and we just have to make the best of it."

"How can the chief do this to us?" Brody asked. "You know she'll find dirt."

Cal frowned. "We don't have anything to be ashamed of."

"Yeah, wait till she gets a look at O'Malley in the morning." God bless Tony Ramirez. Cal had hoped he'd play his usual peacemaker role.

"And smell the bathroom after you been in it, *bombero*." Brody's retort caused a reluctant chuckle among them.

Gabe waited until they were done insulting each other then asked, "Are you for this, Cal?"

"I've got my objections but I'm trying to make the best of it." He waited. "Noah reminded me that we're the kind of people who do our job even during terrorist attacks." Quiet all around. "I'm not about to let some crusading reporter cow me if Al Qaeda couldn't."

Felicia White hadn't said anything. She stared through an open window in the kitchen, which let in sun and warm summer air.

"Lieutenant, what do you think?"

Raising light brown eyes—which were troubled—to him, she shrugged. "I don't know. I'm wondering if it can get any worse with her attacks. She's got a scathing account of our inability to catch the arsonist in her blog today."

Sydney shrugged. Since she and Max got together, they'd both been walking around like fools. "Maybe it'll help to have her here. We do good work. We don't slack off. She seems to know everything about us, anyway."

"Not if she twists things around to show us in a bad light." O'Malley was on a roll.

Cal played his trump. "I know you were letting off hot air when I announced this, but if any one of you *does* want to transfer, I'll make it happen." He waited. "You won't be able to come back to Rescue 7, though. A lot of people are chomping at the bit to get assigned to this squad."

Tony said, "Hell, we're tougher than that, aren't we?"

Sands nodded. "I am."

"Oh yeah." Brody again. "You've been a cream puff since you fell in love."

"And you've been Mr. Hard Nose? Face it guys, we're all in good places in our lives. We gonna let one skinny broad scare us away?"

Gabe said, "Besides, I'll start calling you Snyder if you transfer." Snyder was a guy who transferred to another house when a woman came onto his group.

More acquiescence.

"I'm taking all this as agreement," Cal stated. "You'll do it and behave. And be respectful."

Mumbles of assent. Then Felicia asked, "When does this little party start?"

"She said she's available anytime. You're off for four days, so let's plan on her coming in the next tour."

They filed out of the kitchen one by one. Gabe stayed behind. He seemed relaxed and patient, something Cal was struggling for these days. "You did a good job with them, Cal."

"Did I? I'm biting bullets about this."

"Take to heart what you told them. We are who we are. She's gonna see some good stuff around here. I'm proud of our crew."

Cal socked him in the shoulder. "You got the love bug, too, so what do you know?"

"I know we're good people, doing good things. Screw her if she can't see that."

Gabe's words cheered Cal up. He was right. They had nothing to hide. And maybe Ms. Parker Allen had a lot to learn about him and his squad.

# CHAPTER 2

PARKER COULDN'T BELIEVE her luck. She was going to get a firsthand look at the inside of a firehouse, at how one squad operated daily. They were pretty sure of themselves to invite her in, which only confirmed what she knew to be true about firefighters. They were an arrogant lot. She remembered the arson inspector's questioning of her mother when her dad had been accused of the crime.

*Are you sure there's been no change in his behavior in the last year...? He's been losing money, you had to know that.... Come on Mrs. Larson, you had to suspect something.*

The big, burly guy had bullied her mother so much that finally her grandpa had set his lawyers on the department. Which only made her father, Nigel Larson, look guiltier. And he hadn't been. He'd rotted for ten years in prison and wasn't the same man when he finally got out.

"Can I help you?"

Parker looked up at the clerk who'd approached her in the expensive clothing shop. "What? Oh, yes. I'm looking for casual clothes with pockets." Lots of pockets, lots of places to conceal the recording device she'd bought, which was voice activated and would record for five hours. She wouldn't be able to take notes when she was at the firehouse, so she had a backup plan.

After the woman helped her find some stylish tops and pants in colors, she headed into the dressing room. And froze. Parker hated trying on clothes in stores. She ordered everything online so she could determine their fit and suitability in the privacy of her own house. But this couldn't be helped.

Consciously situating her back to the mirror, she kicked off her shoes and removed her dress. She slid on the first pair of khakis and a peach blouse that didn't tuck in. The material was soft and sensitive on her skin. Enjoying it, she pivoted around to face the mirror to see the garment from the front.

Immediately, she caught sight of the red scars on her midsection before she remembered not to look at them. And she couldn't tear her gaze away, didn't do up the buttons right away. There was no pattern to the ugly marks. They bisected, crisscrossed and sprawled jaggedly over her torso. The best plastic surgeon in the business couldn't fix her any better than this. Though they were no longer puckered and swollen, as they'd been for a long time, the obscene marks mocked her.

Parker stared at her torso and shook her head. What would her life have been like if it hadn't been for these? Would she be more sensitive, more kind, more understanding of others' flaws? Would she be married to a man who loved her and have a child?

*No sense in wallowing in it, dear,* her mother had said, *would* say if she lived in Hidden Cove and not Chicago. *What's done is done. Just go on with your life.*

And Parker had taken the advice. She'd been successful in every single endeavor she'd initiated, this job with the newspaper included. Raising her eyes, she smiled at a face one silly suitor had said could launch a thousand ships. While that was true, he was an idiot.

"Why do you always hook up with idiots?" Parker asked herself in the confines of the small quarters.

Since she'd get no answers to that question or the others she put to herself, Parker shifted her gaze away from her body, did up the shirt and concentrated on where in these new clothes she could store the recording device. Her heart quickened in anticipation of catching the men and women of the HCFD unawares while she played their game to the finish. And it was a game. Cal Erikson thought he was setting her up to be swept off her feet by America's Bravest. No way in hell. Instead, she was hoping to get an exposé on Rescue 7 to counteract Max Delinsky's flattering profile coming out in the fall, one that would supersede anything he showed about the fire department.

An image of Cal Erikson floated into her mind as he'd sat across from her in the bar last fall. She'd asked why he hadn't used the information on her father against her and his response had been *because it would be cruel.*

Well, let him have integrity. Parker knew very well how far integrity got people in life and she wasn't going to let it—or the chief—stop her.

• • •

ON ONE OF his days off, Cal walked into the Little League park with great anticipation and a heavy heart. It was always like this when he was about to see his son, Peter, and his grandson Tommy. The best and worst of worlds. Not that he blamed Peter for their estrangement. Cal was totally and fully at fault. At least Sally, Peter's wife, had convinced him to let Cal have a relationship with Tommy. Cal had heard Peter mutter once, "I hope he's better at that one."

The stands were full of excited parents so Cal stayed by the chain-link fence. He saw Peter—the spitting image of him, as was Tommy. Irony at its greatest. Sticking his hands in the pockets of his jeans, he watched Peter in his role as coach. His son smiled all the time, like he had when he was young. He ran out to the batter taking practice and gently adjusted the boy's grip on the bat. And he yelled to the pitcher every time the kid threw a good ball. When Peter came back into the dugout, Tommy went up to him and hugged him around the waist.

And Cal's heart sank. He couldn't stop the memories....

Peter at Tommy's age: "We need a coach, Dad. Can you do it?"

Cal had played ball in college. "No, son. My schedule's too erratic."

And later, Laura's curt reply: "You could do it if you wanted to. If you'd take some time away from that all-important fire department."

Peter at thirteen: "I made the JV team, Dad. Starting pitcher. My first game is in two weeks."

"I'll put it on my calendar."

That hadn't mattered. One of his men was gravely injured in a fire and Cal had spent the day in the hospital with the firefighter's family. It wasn't until ten o'clock at night that he realized he'd missed the first game his boy would play in his school baseball career.

What the hell had Cal been thinking?

The crowd cheered as Peter's team took the field. Of course, Tommy was the pitcher. He warmed up with ease and grace beyond that of a seven-year-old. The first pitch was a fast ball, the batter swung and a strike was called. "Yes!" Cal yelled and punched his fist in the air. Tommy caught sight of him, and his face lit up with smiles.

The second pitch was hit, but it was a pop fly that the first baseman caught, no problem. On the third batter, Tommy garnered a 3-2 count. Cal felt an odd kind of excitement. The kid wound up, threw the ball and it whizzed past the batter for the final strike.

Watching the rest of the game was bittersweet. He took pleasure in Tommy's success and Peter's obvious joy in coaching his son, but all the while, Cal had his face rubbed in what he'd lost. When the ninth inning ended, Cal hung around. He hadn't been asked to, but this week was Tommy's birthday and he wanted to give the boy the present he'd gotten for him. Parents and grandparents swarmed the field, but Cal stayed back. However, Tommy headed right to him after he did the end-of-the-game protocols and gave Cal a big hug. "Papa. You came! Wasn't I good?"

"You were terrific, Tom." Squatting down, he held on to the boy, savoring his young, hearty embrace.

Sally joined them. "Hi, Cal." She hugged him when he stood.

Only his son kept his distance when he approached them. "Hello, Dad."

"Peter. Great job today."

He tousled Tommy's hair. "This one did all the work."

The kid's face was bright with excitement. "We get free ice cream at Abe's" — their sponsor — "after the game if we win. Can you come, Papa?"

Awkward didn't begin to describe the mood that descended. It eclipsed the still-shining sun and hot August air.

God bless her heart, Sally intervened. "I think that would be great. I'll have company while Peter socializes with the other parents."

Cal stepped away from Peter's stony gaze. "I, um, maybe I shouldn't." Hell, he'd walked into burning buildings, once met an arsonist face-to-face and had been trapped in a car with a victim when the roof collapsed and never stuttered like this.

Peter watched him.

He saw Sally poke him in the ribs.

And Tommy said, "Why not, Papa?"

Cal waited.

His son shrugged a shoulder. "Yeah, sure, come along if you want."

And Cal's heart expanded in his chest. At one freaking offer to go for ice cream.

How pathetic.

But he'd take what he could get.

• • •

FIVE UNIFORMED FIREFIGHTERS sat around a scarred oak table in a huge kitchen with industrial-size appliances and a black-and-white linoleum floor, trying to look casual. But Parker knew their behavior was an act. She'd like to have been privy to what they'd said when the chief told them of his decision to let her get a close-up of the routine of the fire department.

Their shift started at seven in the morning and went until five so she showed up punctually and was met at the door by a sober-looking chief. "Good morning." His gaze dropped to her plain black capris, sensible shoes and simple, flowered, pink shirt. "I'm glad you dressed casually for the day."

She nodded. She'd left her hair down but brought a tie to pull it back when needed. He'd led her back here to meet the group, some of whom she'd never seen in person. Erikson introduced each of them. Tony Ramirez, thirty-four, who'd been a firefighter since he was eighteen and was about to have a brand new baby, stood. "Hello, Ms. Allen. Would you like some coffee?"

"Yes, thanks. Black."

A pretty woman, Sydney Sands, single mom and very young to be on this elite squad, also stood. "Here, take my seat."

Parker acquiesced. Sands walked over to the coffeepot and said something to Ramirez. Meanwhile, Brody O'Malley, who with his brother had been heartthrobs in their departments until, rumor had it, they met their women, nodded to her. "Morning."

Felicia White stared down at a newspaper and ignored Parker.

The captain, Gabe Malvaso, leaned forward. "Welcome to our house, Ms. Allen. As you might guess, this isn't the most comfortable thing for all of us."

Erikson, who'd gotten his own coffee and stayed on the other side of the room, shifted on his feet.

"However, we're willing to give you a chance to see who we really are in hopes of changing your mind about us."

"Thanks for your honesty, Captain."

"Want some more?" White asked, finally looking up.

"Why not?" Parker said, but thought, *Here it comes.*

"I think you're going to put your own spin on everything we do. Know, Ms. Allen, that I'll fight you tooth and nail like I've been doing if you do portray us in a biased light."

"Fair warning. And, Lieutenant White, know that I, too, will be honest and uncompromising about what I see around here."

Stepping forward, Erikson approached the table. "Well, now that that's all out of the way, let me say we've decided you should participate in our daily routine. Even the mundane. So here it is." He handed her a schedule. "This is basically what we do when we don't have calls. Obviously, a run supersedes any of what's on there."

She glanced down. The schedule read, "Arrive at 7 a.m., check the rig, start the equipment, housework at 7:30, physical exercise at 9. Lunch at noon, training at 1. Day ends about 5."

The chief added, "More than likely, some of these things won't happen. We'll be out on calls."

"I understand. I'll participate as much as I can."

"We have two other groups on with us. Quint and Midi 7. They're out on a call."

"Already?"

"Fire doesn't work on a time frame."

Gabe stood. "Here are the housework details. O'Malley's on toilet duty."

"Oh, goody."

"The Quint and Midi crew will take care of the upstairs bunkroom when they get back, unless somebody finishes early and wants to do it for them."

Grumbles all around.

"White, clean the common room. Ramirez and Sands, kitchen duty. Ms. Allen, would you like to help them?"

"Sure, I can clean. I can't cook, though."

"Neither can Sands," Ramirez teased.

"I try. Besides" —here she did a little dance step—"I have other talents."

The crew dispersed. Ramirez asked, "What do you want to do, Syd?"

"The refrigerator needs a good cleaning. I'll tackle that. Why don't you empty the dishwasher and take care of the countertops."

Ramirez faced Parker. "Would you like to sweep and mop?"

"Sure. Where are the supplies?"

As Parker glided the broom over the floor, she listened to the low drone of a radio in the corner, playing some rock music. The linoleum wasn't dirty, just needed sweeping. She said as much to the two others.

"Yeah, but it's custom," Ramirez explained. "Every morning it gets mopped. We're kind of neat freaks."

"Except O'Malley." This from Sands.

The two of them laughed and went on with their work.

"So, Sophia's only got less than a month," Sands said.

"Yeah. She's really big."

"She seems happy."

"Especially now that I talked her into taking her leave from the hospital early. She likes being home with the other two."

Companionable silence between them. Then, he asked, "How's Max?"

Parker shot a quick look at Sands. Her face had lit up. "Good. He's got Daisy today. He's taking her and Amber to the amusement park."

"That's nice. The little one adores Amber."

Parker had retrieved the mop, filled the bucket and was about to slop water on the floor when the PA crackled overhead. "Fire on Vine and First. Engine 4 and Rescue Squad 7, go into service."

The change in the atmosphere was dramatic. All teasing and camaraderie gone, the two firefighters dropped their sponges and strode out of the room. Sands looked back. "Come on, Parker, it's a call."

Parker started to put the cleaning tools away.

"No time for that. Leave everything."

Following Sands out, she made it to the bay in time to watch five firefighters go into action. Boots and pants sat waiting by the rig. Five pairs of shoes were kicked off, even that done in an orderly fashion. Once they stepped into their boots and pants, they climbed onto the truck. She'd read in her research this was called turnout gear because firefighters left it *turned out* to don quickly.

Erikson joined her and Malvaso. "You want to come with me or on the truck?"

"Um..."

"On the truck," Malvaso said. "Let her get a real feel for a call."

Taking her by the arm, Gabe led her to the rig. She stepped up onto the low-riding foot rail and looked inside. Everyone's coat and face mask were in place behind them. Malvaso gave her a little boost up. "In the back, next to Sands."

She climbed in and did up her seatbelt like everybody else, though she'd been told they didn't wear them. Hmm, they were on their best behavior for her. Glancing at her watch, she saw that it took about three minutes to get going. They headed out of the bay and rounded the corner to the street. She slid over against Sands, who gave her a quick smile. The horn blasted and they put on the siren.

"The fire started in the basement of the laundromat," Malvaso called back to them as he read from a computer printout. "It's a huge place, and at this hour was full of customers. Be prepared."

The rig sped down a street busy with people going to work. She noticed O'Malley drove carefully but quickly and didn't run any lights. Parker felt her heart beat at a clip and her palms start to sweat. She was...excited.

In a few minutes, they arrived on the scene and hopped out of the truck, coats and helmets on, masks over their heads. They looked like warriors ready for battle.

Cal Erikson parked his department Jeep a few feet over and exited with his computer. She watched the crew get tools out of the back end of the rig, then stride to the chief. He ignored her as he called up blueprints on the computer. After he scanned them, he said to Malvaso, who she hadn't noticed by his side, "The fire's here in the northeast corner. A dryer blew up." To another man, also there, he said, "Corwin, take in a hose. Malvaso, follow them in with your guys. I think people are trapped."

Malvaso jogged away as did the other guy. Erikson turned to her. "Questions?"

No longer was he the aloof, somewhat reticent man she'd met twice. Now, his face was animated, his eyes gleaming and his whole body alert. She found his demeanor oddly appealing.

Shaking off the thought, she nodded to the computer. "You have the blueprints of the entire city in there?"

"Pretty much. When we don't, it's hell to pay."

"What are they doing inside?"

"Engine 17 will slap water on the fire. The Rescue Squad goes in then to check for survivors."

Her mouth dropped. "People could be dead already?"

For a moment, he focused an intense green gaze on her. "Yeah. They could be burned or die of smoke inhalation. It doesn't take long."

Parker absorbed that fact as his gaze transferred to the front door of the laundromat, and they both watched for a few minutes. Finally, out came one of the Rescue rig guys carrying a woman in his arms. Holy hell, each member of the squad followed, carrying victims. When they were relieved by the ambulance crew she hadn't seen arrive, they went back in. Over the chief's radio, she heard, "Fire's out, Chief."

"How many more victims?"

"A few."

He turned to her. "Go up closer. Watch the crew."

"Why?"

"Rescue work takes a toll on them."

Hearing the challenge in his voice, she headed toward the people on the ground in front of the ambulance. Ten victims lay sprawled on the blacktop. Sands trudged over with another one draped over her shoulders and gently set down a woman.

"My baby. Where's my baby?"

Immediately, Sands dropped to her knee. "What did you say?"

"I had him in a carrier. By the bench. Where is he?"

"Jesus." Sands bolted up, yanked down her mask and flew back into the building. In a matter of minutes, she exited carrying a little blue bundle. Another ambulance crew member raced to her, grabbed the kid and got an oxygen mask on his mouth.

Breathing hard, Sands bent over to get more air, all the while keeping an eye on the baby.

Nothing.

Oh, God. Was Parker going to witness a child's death?

Still no sounds.

Then she heard a soft whimper.

Cheers went up, and Sands was hugged by another firefighter Parker hadn't met before. She finally let out her own breath, her entire body deflating. Full of conflicting emotions, she inched back from the scene. Her mind wasn't working right yet, so she didn't want to be asked a question or have to make a comment. She was still stunned by the miracle that had taken place.

# CHAPTER 3

CAL HAD TO hide a smile as he watched Parker Allen survey the crew at lunchtime. Saves had an effect on everybody, and she wasn't immune. Thank the good Lord for what had happened this morning and the subsequent rejoicing in the house. On top of Squad 9's successes, the Quint and Midi had done good work, which Grady O'Connor was describing to the others. "Five people were in the small apartment. Zach had to be held back to wait for the all clear." Suddenly his face reddened. He shot a worried look at Cal.

Standing off to the side by the coffeepot, Parker picked right up on it. "Zach Malvaso? Why?"

Cal intervened. He was nothing if not good at diplomacy. "Some of us are more daring than others. Malvaso has a hard time waiting when someone's in trouble."

Casey Malvaso's head snapped up. "Before you go off half-cocked, Allen, he doesn't do stupid things. He's just braver than most."

With the devil in his eyes, Zach chimed in. "Hey, I'm here. You're talking about me as if I'm not."

"So it's an admirable trait, Firefighter Malvaso?" Parker asked.

Before he could answer, Felicia slapped her hand on the table. "This is what I mean. You're gonna skew everything."

Knowing not to suppress this crew, Cal let the scene play out.

Parker tossed back her hair and straightened her slender shoulders. "No, I'm not. For what it's worth, what I saw this morning was incredible."

"But you'll pick up on what O'Connor said."

"I'll pick up on everything, Lieutenant."

For some reason, Cal enjoyed watching the reporter go toe-to-toe with Licia.

"Chow's on," Ramirez called out from the stove. "Cease fire. Truce. No fighting." He said a little louder, "I mean it."

Brows furrowed, Parker looked to Cal.

"Ramirez is our resident peacemaker."

As a group, they rose and crossed to the counter where Tony and Sydney had assembled BLTs with macaroni salad. The scent of the bacon made Cal's mouth water. He waited for everyone to serve themselves and had grabbed a plate when the PA crackled. "Car accident on Mercury Avenue. Rescue 7, go into service."

"Fuck," O'Malley said, throwing back his chair.

Cal headed for the door but said to Parker over his shoulder, "You can stay and eat." God knew why he was looking out for her.

"No," Felicia stated harshly, "she can't. Let her go hungry, too. At least she doesn't have to do anything."

The challenge worked. Allen stood. "I'm coming."

Rolling his eyes to the heavens, he headed out. This was shaping up to be a hell of a day.

• • •

PARKER DRAGGED HERSELF into the firehouse at four o'clock, her shirt dripping with sweat, her face grimy from smoke that had poured out of one of the buildings, and her stomach growling. She was so hungry she could barely stand so she leaned against a wall in the bay and watched the people who had done the work file in, quiet now. They looked almost beaten up. They'd gone to three calls this afternoon, one right after another. A car accident, where they had to rip off the roof of a Mitsubishi to rescue two people, another fire, this time at a house, and they'd assisted on a roof cave-in at a local restaurant, which sent five people to the hospital.

They took off their turnout clothes slowly, not like they'd donned them. His face covered with dirt, sweat soaked through his T-shirt, Malvaso called for their attention. "I know we stink and can taste the dirt. I'm ordering you all to do a quick wash-up and then go into the kitchen to eat before you try to shower. We still have an hour left on our shift and you need to fortify."

No grumbles. No humor. Literally, they dragged themselves into the kitchen. Where every one of them perked up. Because around the table sat five fresh-as-daisies firefighters; they had to be the night shift for Rescue 7, which wasn't due to start till five.

A man stood. Malvaso went right to him. "What's going on, cuz?"

Cuz? Ah, this was the luminous Mitch Malvaso, rumored to be the most beloved firefighter in the district. Tall and dark haired like his cousin, they bore a remarkable resemblance.

Mitch head-locked his relative. "My crew heard the calls on the scanner. You're officially off duty. Every single one of us is here to take over and I'm on for Cal."

Parker took in a breath. Wow! Talk about loyalty. These people seemed to care about each other's welfare. Oh, sure, she'd heard that about the firefighter brotherhood, but she'd also seen TV shows like *Rescue Me* where the guys weren't always nice to each other.

One Malvaso man hugged the other, and each of Gabe's crew did the same for his or her replacement. "Yuck, don't touch me," and "Boy do you stink," came from the recipients, but she noticed they didn't back away from the embraces. Instead, the new group got out food and served the others.

Sure enough, as soon as everybody sat down, the PA blared again. The night squad bounded into action. Felicia took several bites of her sandwich, which had been stored by somebody after they left, then arched a smug brow at Parker. "Ever seen anything like that, Allen?"

She could pretend to misunderstand. But she didn't. "No, actually, I haven't. Selflessness is in short supply these days."

"Not around here," Ramirez added with a smile.

A phone rang and Malvaso took out his cell as he chewed the food in his mouth, then answered. "Hey, sweetheart. No, we didn't have to go again. Yeah, the night guys came in. Uh-huh. Uh-huh. Okay, I'll ask them. Hold on."

The crew members looked up from their sandwiches. "Rachel's off today. We bought half a cow. She's inviting all of you and your significant others to come over for steaks at eight. Sophia's already on board with food for kids. Who's game?"

They all were, with caveats to check with their families. But Parker guessed every single one of them would show up.

As she watched them make calls, speak intimately, smile, she got a hollow feeling in her stomach. It took a while to recognize the emotion—jealousy.

• • •

CAL DROVE OUT to Rachel's feeling good about the day. He'd been worried they'd have one of those tours when everything went wrong, but instead, he couldn't have orchestrated the situation better himself, right up to their replacements coming in early. They did favors for each other a lot, but he'd bet his badge all the members of Group Two had made an extra effort to come in today because they knew Parker Allen was visiting.

He had to smile. She'd looked like a whipped puppy, not that his crew was any better. But they were trained and in shape for this kind of rigorous shift. Still, she'd kept up the brutal pace pretty good.

*She's in shape, too.*

Damn, where had that thought come from? But he knew. He'd watched her face animate with each of the rescues that occurred today. She'd pulled all that hair off her face as she observed and...wondered, he bet. She'd told him as much when he invited her into the office at day's end....

"So, what do you think?" he asked from behind his desk, trying not to notice how her blouse was damp and clung to her.

"I'm impressed. Who wouldn't be?"

"You kidding?" he responded honestly.

"No, I am."

"What impressed you the most?"

"How they did all that work on empty stomachs. I thought *I* might faint and I was a bystander."

"And you weren't carrying sixty pounds of gear and lifting the deadweight of passed-out bodies."

She'd crossed her legs, her hands clasping a knee. He noticed her nails were clipped and unpainted. "I said I was impressed, Chief."

"What will you write for tomorrow's blog?"

"The truth."

"Good stuff, for a change."

She'd inched forward and held his gaze. Her violet eyes had black rims around them. "Absolutely. But know this. When I come here and things go badly, I'll report that as honestly."

"I'll take what I can get, Ms. Allen."

She stood then and said, "Have a nice time tonight."

Cal had noticed how her voice had caught. Recognizing the emotion in it as longing—something he often felt about his son—he had the absurd urge to invite her to the dinner. Which he wisely resisted....

Parking in the visitor lot at Rachel and Gabe's condo on the lake, Cal hefted the case of beer he'd brought along out of his trunk. Carrying it on his shoulder, he made his way around back and found them all there, families, too. Man, he loved this job.

"Ah, here he is." Gabe came to him and relieved him of his burden. "We're waiting with bated breath for a report on Allen's take of the day."

"It was good, very good. We dodged a bullet today."

"Only eleven more to go."

"What, Licia?"

"Only eleven more bullets to go. That's how many visits she has left."

O'Malley handed Cal a beer and lifted his own. "To dodging bullets."

"To dodging bullets," his brother the cop reiterated.

Everyone joined in on the toast.

• • •

AT DAY'S END, Parker practically crawled into her house on the east end of the lake. She'd inherited the place from her mother's parents—who'd helped raise her when her father had gone to jail. The only child of *their* only child, Parker was a rich woman now. In money, anyway.

Damn it, where had that come from? But she knew. She was thinking about the group of firefighters partying across the lake at the condo Rachel Wellington Malvaso owned. She remembered the woman—tall, beautiful, fit. Rachel had written Parker a scathing email after she read the blog's account of her relationship with her captain and what led up to it. But the story lost its punch when they married suddenly.

Stripping out of her soiled clothes in the laundry room on the lower level, she climbed the stairs to the living area, where she headed right to the shower. Her skin prickled at the sting of the air-conditioning but the coolness felt good after a day in the oppressive heat. So did the cleansing shower, and the feel of silk on her skin as she dressed in pajamas. It was only six o'clock.

Why not get ready for bed? She had nowhere to go, she again thought as she pictured the firefighters celebrating together. Parker had never in her life experienced that kind of camaraderie. After her father died and one disastrous relationship that changed her life, she'd chosen to be alone. Even when she was asked to be in Emma Walsh's sorority, she stayed on the periphery. Oh, she dated, casually, but nothing stuck, because she wouldn't let it. She cringed when she thought about how she flirted with men outrageously to cover her innocence, and almost got it on with Brody O'Malley once when she was drunk, but that wasn't the real her. It was just another façade.

Grabbing a glass of Pinot Grigio from the subzero fridge she padded out to the deck—with her tape recorder in her hand. Before she replayed the day's events, she had to think about them. Parker planned out her blogs in her head and then they simply flowed into the computer.

The sun was still bright, but her lot was treed, so she sat in the shade and closed her eyes. Images bombarded her. Of yellow-helmeted, heavily coated men and women running into burning buildings. Of a woman firefighter, she couldn't tell which one, carrying a heavy man and stumbling with his weight. Of the incredible lines of exhaustion on their faces, which then split with smiles when they had what they call a *save*. Several were made today. How normal was that? She'd have to ask the chief.

Her thoughts drifted to him. She'd seen another side of him today. A commander. Excellent at his job. Enthusiastic about it. And—who would have guessed?—fun, as he joked with the others.

*He isn't bad on the eyes, either.* Funny thing about that. Parker hadn't seen him as attractive before today. But in his office at the end of the shift, she found herself noticing the dimple in his cheek when he smiled, the curve of his lips when he talked, the powerful shoulders and biceps peeking out from his smudged officer's shirt.

"Arrgh." Too much good stuff. She needed to dilute it before she wrote the blog or she'd be salivating over them.

So Parker rose, went in through the open French doors to the great room, unlocked the teak armoire and pulled out an album. This was going to hurt, but she'd do it anyway. Then she'd be sober enough to write sanely.

She expected the surge of pain when she opened to the first picture of her father but still it made her stomach clench. His photo was on the front page of the suburban Chicago newspaper, *The Sudbury Sentinel*, being taken away in handcuffs. His tall, always stalwart frame hunched over. Though she didn't notice it then, his hair had gotten grayer in the year he'd been a suspect in an arson case that had ruined all their lives. She stared hard at the picture and made herself remember the day they'd come for him. Her mother was still keeping up pretenses of support for her dad, so she and Parker were at home.

As a fifteen-year-old, Parker was on the brink of womanhood and had all the insecurities that came with being a teenage girl. But it was her father who shepherded her through that time and not her mother. Patrice Allen was a cold woman, even then, and had barely been able to give her the physical facts of life. Her dad had given her the important ones....

They were sitting on the patio, under an umbrella table next to their pool. "I'm sorry if my situation is hurting you," her dad said. "I've done everything I can to prove my innocence. I didn't set those fires."

She'd taken his hand. "I know you didn't, Daddy."

He studied her face, which she knew was taut with worry. "Are you getting grief at school?"

Parker lied. "No, kids are understanding."

Her dad stared at the pool then said, "I haven't seen that boy around lately. Mitchell?"

"We, um, broke up. I'm too young to get serious anyway, Dad."

"I know you are. But listen to this, sweetie. Any man or boy who doesn't stick by you in a crisis isn't worth your time."

That was only one of the many male/female gems of wisdom he'd given her. They were discussing what makes a good man when the doorbell rang. Every time they had a visitor, she and her dad tensed up. Her mother seemed resigned.

But that had been *the* day. She followed her father—against his wishes—to the front door. On the stoop stood a man she hated more than anybody in the world. He was big and ugly with beefy hands and a body like a tree trunk.

"Well, well, well," the arson investigator in Sudbury said silkily. "Nice family time, eh?"

"What do you want, Felk?"

Jonathan Felk gave him an oily smile. "You know that arson investigators are officers of the law, right, Larson?"

Her dad turned to Parker. "Go back inside, Princess. You don't need to see this."

"Maybe she does." Felk stepped aside. "Cuff him," he barked to the officer and followed up with, "You have the right to remain silent…"

"Parker, please, leave." Her dad's craggy face was tortured. "Go get your mother."

Instead, Parker stood back, her hands over her mouth watching the police and fire department manhandle her gentle, loving father. Tears coursed down her cheeks. Felk grabbed her dad's shirt and turned him around. "See what you've done to your little girl, you scum? Look at her. It's not half as bad as what you did to the families of the people you killed when you decided to torch your warehouses."

"Parker, I love you," her father said. "And I didn't do this. Now please go in the house...."

Her mother had finally come into the living room. She'd dragged Parker away but it was too late. She'd never forgotten the images of that night and the fire department's cruelty to her family...

She forced herself to read each and every page of the scrapbook. His indictment, the awful trial her mother had forbade her to attend. How evidence had piled up. And how he'd been wrongly convicted.

Once she'd turned eighteen, she tried to visit him in jail, but he refused to see her. She'd written him letters, telling him how much she missed him, how she believed in him. Her mother had insisted she change her name and had thrown a fit when Parker balked. Eventually, she gave in and took her mom's maiden name, but that almost killed her.

Finally, when she was twenty-five, Nigel Larson was exonerated, but the damage had been done.

She turned to the last page. A small article in the *Sentinel* was the last entry. The headline read, "Wrongly Convicted Man Found Dead in Apartment Ten Days After his Release from Prison."

Parker hadn't even seen him before he took his own life.

Standing, sober enough now, she replaced the awful book and headed to her computer. Finally, she was able to be objective about the fire department.

# CHAPTER 4

CAL STALKED INTO the firehouse the next morning ready to spit nails. Fuck! What did that woman want? He found the Rescue Squad sitting around the outdoor picnic table, each holding a sheet of paper. They were grim faced, despite the warm sunshine and slight breeze, so he knew they'd all read the blog.

"Good morning," he said for lack of something else to say.

"It should have been." He expected the worst from Felicia and could tell by her words and the sour expression on her face that he was going to get it. Her guy, Ryan O'Malley, in his police uniform, reached over and put his hand on her shoulder.

Exhausted already, Cal dropped down into a director's chair that was at the head of the table. He hadn't slept much last night. "I don't know what to say. The blog isn't what I thought it would be."

"Damning with faint praise," Ryan offered. When everyone blanked, he added, "It's from an English poem."

Brody rolled his eyes at his brother. "I suppose you know who wrote it."

"Alexander Pope." He shrugged. "So I like poetry."

Ignoring the byplay, Gabe said, "I'd like to be given credit where credit is due." As captain, he was trying to keep it together, but Cal could tell he was furious. "What more could she expect from us?" He directed his question to Cal.

"My thoughts exactly. Saves, excitement, enthusiasm and the unselfishness of the night shift." He tried to battle back his anger but it was hard. "Jesus."

"She didn't even balk at the housework," Tony put in. He seemed puzzled by another person's selfishness.

Sydney, who'd gotten up to get the coffee carafe from inside, set a mug in front of the chief and filled it. "I don't think it's too bad." She spoke as she refreshed the others' morning brew.

"That's because your head's so in the clouds with Delinsky that you can't see straight." Brody's tone was teasing but there was an edge to it. Must be true love only went so far.

Sydney didn't have a retort.

"I'm not sure how to handle this," Cal told them honestly. "Maybe you were right, Licia, about letting her into the inner sanctum. That she'd twist things. Hell, if she'll do this on a good day..."

Felicia said, "I didn't want to be right." She dragged her laptop in front of her and tapped a few keys. "There are some comments. Holy shit. A lot."

"Read us some." Cal thought maybe there would be community support, at least.

"*The group you spent the day with sounds great. How come your blog isn't?*"

"Well, that helps." This from Gabe.

Felicia read on. "'*I wonder what it will take for you to like these guys. They're our heroes.*'"

"Somebody we know write these?" Tony asked.

Felicia scanned the entries. "No they're signed by legal residents of Hidden Cove but not family."

Leaning forward, Brody peered over her shoulder. "Scroll down. Emma said she was going to write something."

Brows furrowed, Felicia scrolled. Finally she said, "Here it is." A smile. "'*Thank you so much for your effusive praise of our local firefighters. It's appropriate to celebrate that the life of a car accident victim was spared, a child was rescued from a fire and four people were pulled from a cave-in at a local restaurant. Or didn't you know that?*'"

Felicia laughed out loud. "Good for her. She's so sweet I didn't know she had sarcasm in her."

"Easy for you to say." But Brody's grin was a mile wide. "You don't live with her."

Ryan scowled. "They were sorority sisters. I'm surprised Emma would attack her."

"She knows where her loyalties lie." Brody's chest practically puffed out.

Sighing, Tony sat back. "I think the best thing to do is ignore her lukewarm review."

"I don't." This from Brody. "I'd call her on it."

Gabe shook his head. "We'd better decide how we're going to handle this before tomorrow, when she comes again."

Cal folded his arms over his chest. "I think we need to object. But I'll voice our displeasure. The rest of you act like you don't hate her guts." He lifted his chin to conceal his disappointment. "I'll take care of it now."

"Wait a second, chief." Gabe dashed inside and brought out the Joke Jar. "We need a pick-me-up."

A lot of grumbling.

"I don't want to."

"It won't help."

"Not now!"

"Don't be such crybabies," Gabe said. "We'll only do one." He held the jar out to Cal. "Pick it, Cal."

"No thanks, it'll be another chief joke."

Brody winked at Sydney. "We'll wait to get a blonde one."

Rolling his eyes, Cal grabbed a slip of paper and handed it to Gabe. It took three tries to get the female one. He read:

"A fire broke out in a six-storey apartment building last week in a nearby town. A blonde, a redhead and a brunette escaped the flames by climbing up onto the roof. When the fire department arrived, they got out a blanket, held it up and the Chief called to the brunette to jump into the blanket.

"The brunette jumped. As she was falling, the firefighters pulled the blanket away and she landed on the street like a brick. The firefighters then held the blanket back up, and the chief told the redhead to jump. 'No way! I saw what you did to my friend,' exclaimed the redhead.

"'I am sorry,' said the chief. 'My wife was a brunette and she divorced me. I don't like brunettes. We have no problems with redheads. Jump, it's your only chance.' So the redhead jumped. On the way down, the firefighters pulled the blanket away and she hit the pavement like a tomato! The firefighters again held up the blanket and the chief told the blonde to jump. The fire was getting worse and her only chance of survival was to get off the roof.

"'No I am not jumping. I saw what you did to my two friends.'

"'I'm sorry,' said the Chief, 'I explained what happened to the brunette and when the redhead jumped, we were a little distracted. It will not happen again. Just jump!'

"The blonde thought for a moment. 'Okay, I'll jump, but first I want you to lay the blanket on the ground, back away, and then I'll jump into it.'"

Everybody laughed and the sound rang out in the sober morning.

"You got the chief in there, after all." Cal stood and said good-bye. But he was still smiling when he reached his office. His cell phone rang, so he answered, hoping it was Parker Allen. It wasn't.

"Hey buddy, it's Max."

Leafing through the stack of pink phone messages left on his desk, Cal said to his friend, "How are you?"

"I'm having breakfast at The Hidden Cove Diner and thought you'd like to know your nemesis just walked in. Looks as if she's here to stay. She's got her computer. You might want to head over here and, maybe, um, clear the air about the bloody blog she published this morning. Syd said the day went a lot better than that."

"Hmm. Maybe I will. You staying?"

"I can. Come and pretend to have breakfast with me."

"Will do." Cal left his office in a hurry. Never one to look a gift horse in the mouth, he jumped into his fire department Jeep and headed out of the parking lot.

• • •

DRESSED CHEERFULLY IN a summer skirt and matching yellow top, Parker had come to The Hidden Cove Diner for some coffee and to work on her computer because she couldn't stand her own company. For the first time, she felt like she'd been unfair to the firefighters and her lack of integrity bothered her. Last night, she'd dreamed about a visit from the chief. Her hand went to her mouth, remembering...

*There was pounding on her door. She awoke and was afraid. Daddy? No wait, her father was dead. She wasn't fifteen. She was thirty-five and an accomplished woman. Flinging off the covers, she didn't bother with a robe, forgetting about the plunging neckline of her gown. She walked to the front door, checked the peephole and saw the battalion chief standing on the porch. How did he know where she lived? She opened the door. He was dressed in jeans and an HCFD polo shirt that outlined all his muscles. "I need to talk to you." His gaze dropped to her chest. He swallowed hard. Ah, this was good.*

*"You sure you want to talk, Cal?"*

*Suddenly, he grabbed her waist and drew him to her. She was filled with his scent. His arms banded around her. And he took her mouth.*

*She should have been afraid, but she wasn't. She was aroused...*

"Fancy meeting you here."

The voice drew her out of the erotic memory and Parker blinked hard. Hell, what had she done, conjure him? "Good morning, Chief."

"I'd like to talk to you. I was, um, meeting my friend over there"—she followed the direction of his hand—"and saw you when I came in. Let me speak to him first." He walked away, not waiting for an answer. As he talked to Max Delinsky, she noted the breadth of his shoulders in his crisp white shirt, his confident stride, the way his head tilted. And then he was back, seated across from her, taking up her personal space. She wanted to shrink in his presence. Was it because he was so big and male, with his arms crossed over his chest, or because she'd betrayed him? No, no, she hadn't done that. But she hadn't stayed true to herself, either.

The waitress showed up and he ordered coffee. His green gaze was more piercing today, but she held it. Waited for him to speak. He finally said, "I saw the blog. I have to say I was disappointed." His voice caught a bit.

"It's the way I saw the day."

"Don't lie to me, Parker." That was the first time he hadn't called her Ms. Allen. Or worse, probably.

She swallowed hard.

He held her gaze.

"What *did* you expect, Chief?"

"Praise where praise was due. Criticism when it wasn't. Your bias was hard for my crew. Next time, they'll all be looking over their shoulders."

She hadn't thought about that.

"Have you read the comments?"

"Yes."

"Ninety percent of your readers see right through you."

"Through me?"

"That you're not going to give us a fair shot."

"Would you like to cancel my visits to the firehouse?"

"Hell, no. We aren't cowards. Even if you are." He stood then and threw a twenty on the table. "Breakfast is on me."

Unable to watch him walk away this time, Parker sat staring at the money. Her eyes stung. She told herself her reaction came from the fact that he'd called her a coward, something she vowed she'd never be again, not after all she'd been through. But that wasn't it exactly.

There had been hurt in Cal Erikson's beautiful green eyes and *his* reaction bothered her. A lot!

• • •

IT WAS A rotten thing to do to her. Cal knew that in his heart. But when he'd gotten a call from Jeb Caruso, the BC in charge of the Academy, who said that there was a screw-up in scheduling and they needed a crew to refresh Rapid Intervention Training, which his group hadn't done recently, Cal said yes immediately. He believed the training was something Parker Allen should experience. For someone who'd technically won the first round, she'd seemed incredibly vulnerable at the diner yesterday. The plot hadn't hatched in his mind until after he saw her again today, face impassive, wearing black and white, ignoring him.

She sat all morning listening to Ian Woodward give the details of what to do when a firefighter was trapped. Mayday calls were always the worst. Allen had been quiet and edgy the whole two hours of prep time. Now, they were out at the training tower, where a dummy would be rescued by the crew.

Cal insisted she go inside, too, so they dressed her up in firefighter gear first, and O'Malley had even put the air tank and mask on her, so she was totally weighted down. Standing before him looking like a spaceman, she tried to maneuver. "Hell, I can barely move."

"That's why we have daily exercise. I think you called it *personal workouts* on company time, but we need to be in top shape to do our job." Reaching over, he removed the headgear. He snagged her hair, had to untangle it and noticed how thick and luscious it was. "Go in without this."

"No, I want to experience what they do."

"My decision. It's too much for you. You can keep the turnout coat, pants and boots on, but unbutton the coat. It'll be hot in there." Admitting he shouldn't be sending her in, especially alone, chivalry got the better of him. "I could take you inside."

She shook her head, sending skeins of that hair around her shoulders and down her back. "No way. All I have to do is find them, right?"

"It's not that easy. You'll be operating blind. The house is filled with mist, but it's thick and opaque. That's why this training is so demanding. Even seasoned firefighters have trouble rescuing a dummy when it's been pinned down."

"You pinned it down?"

"Of course. They need experience in the worst scenarios. Ready?"

"Yes, I am." She arched a brow. "I'm going to do this, Chief. And do it well."

*Not a chance*, he thought, but said, "I hope so." He handed her a radio. "Call *Mayday* if you get disoriented."

"I won't."

"Take it," he barked, startling her, but she did as he instructed. He watched her disappear into the first floor of the training tower and glanced at his watch. He'd bet on five minutes tops before he got the Mayday.

Across the line, he heard his team inside.

"Jesus, where's the wire on this side?"

"Who's got the cutters?"

"One's free."

"Oops. I feel blood."

"Damn it. There's more wires."

"Hell, I dropped the cutters."

"Feel around for them, Sands."

Listening to the very typical reaction to RIT, Cal knew all was as it should be. This activity was designed to give them a hard time.

He spoke into the radio. "Allen's coming in, guys. She there yet?"

"Who the hell knows?" Felicia growled. "We can't see anything. I don't remember the mist being so thick before." On the same frequency, he asked, "Ms. Allen, you okay?"

No answer. Jesus. He tried again.

"Parker, where are you?"

Nothing.

He glanced at his watch. Seven minutes...not too bad. He kept calling into the radio. After ten, he headed to the door, and as he reached it, he heard a whimper through her mic. Oh, hell. What had he done now?

• • •

HER TEETH CHATTERED, even though the air was suffocating. Her head hurt from where she'd bumped it on something. She found a door, opened it, stepped through and came up against a wall. Oh, God, no. Turning, she reached out. All walls. Where was the opening? *Calm down, Parker. You can do this.*

But there was no opening, no handle. It took her a minute to realize the door had slammed shut. Her heart started to beat so fast, it cramped. She backed up and suddenly she was in another place, and another time....

"Where the fuck are you?" she heard from out in the bedroom. She'd run there, hoping to get away from him. She could hardly move her arm, he'd wrenched it so badly. She tried to stay as quiet as she could as she heard his footsteps. Once light shined in, she saw what was in his hands. A belt...

"No, no, please don't hurt me."

"Open your shirt and I won't."

"W—what?"

"Open the goddamned shirt."

Her hand fumbled on the buttons.

"There, now this will be better."

He raised his arm and she felt the first biting sting of the tip....

• • •

SCREAMS CAME FROM the second room in the house. Mentally picturing the space he'd been in a thousand times, Cal raced into it and the yelling got louder. "No, no, please, no."

Cal threw open the closet door. He couldn't see anything, but he was used to that, and he knew right where she was. "Parker, it's me, Cal."

"No, Mike, no. Please…" She sobbed out the words

Bending down, he felt for the outline of her body. Carefully, he slid his arms under her, scooped her up and held her close. She fought him, hard, but she was weeping uncontrollably. "Shh, it's me. Cal. You're safe."

Oh, Lord, he couldn't be sorrier for sending her in alone. Who knew she'd be claustrophobic?

Hugging her tight to his chest, he made his way quickly and calmly outside. She was still bucking him, but he subdued her and crossed to a tree. In the shade, he laid her out flat.

"Shh, Parker, you're out of there. You're safe."

Her head shook wildly. "Never be safe."

Cal looked her up and down to see if she was hurt. There was an ugly bruise on the temple. The turnout coat was off and she seemed to have ripped open her own blouse. What the hell? A roadmap of scars crisscrossed her torso, old but still very visible, from the plain white bra she wore to the turnout pants.

Holy Mother of God, what had happened to this woman? He had a sinking feeling in his stomach. A tightening of his chest. She'd been yelling as if she was somewhere else, to a guy named Mike. Had Cal been responsible for conjuring up some horrid experience from her past? His heart clenched at the thought.

• • •

REALITY FINALLY DAWNED. Parker came to in a blissfully cool room, the lights dim. Her hand went to her middle and there was no pain. She was lying on a leather couch. As her mind cleared, she heard the low murmurs of male voice across the room. Glancing over, she saw Cal Erikson and a man talking. Slowly she sat up. They noticed. Cal strode to her. Hunching down, he didn't touch her. He was probably afraid to. "I'm so sorry, Parker. I shouldn't have sent you in alone."

She remembered opaque whiteness. Blinding pain.

"I was mad about your blog today. I guess I was trying to teach you a lesson." He shook his head as if he couldn't believe what he'd done.

Mike Cameron had been trying to teach her a lesson when he'd beat the shit out of her, too. It had something to do with smiling at a waiter. What was it with men's egos?

"Please, forgive me."

For a moment, she didn't react. Then she shook herself and looked to the left at the other man in the room.

"I'm Jack Harrison. Cal brought you in here because you were upset and disoriented." Ah, the fire department psychologist. If she recalled correctly, she'd lobbied for his position to be cut.

Parker closed her eyes. Oh, God, she'd remembered every detail of her previous attack. With Cal Erikson as a witness.

"Move back," she said, and as soon as Cal did, she swung her feet to the floor. Her stomach lurched. The chief dropped down on a chair, and the psychologist took another. At least she was eye level with them. Again, her hand went to her stomach, and their gazes followed. She could sense they knew. Ah, yes, Mike had ordered her to open her shirt, and she'd been living in the nightmare.

"You saw."

Cal nodded soberly.

A horrible thought assaulted her. "Did the crew see, too?"

"No, no, they were still in the house. I brought you here because you couldn't settle down. I, um, did up your shirt first. I'm the only one who saw the scars."

"He told me," Jack said soothingly. "Would you like to talk about whatever happened to you?"

A shiver went up her spine. "God, no."

"Have you seen a therapist?" Cal asked. "You took a pretty brutal beating."

"Over a decade ago. I'm fine."

"Parker, you were scared and in pain when I got you out."

"I don't like closed-in spaces."

"I wish you'd told me. I can't say how bad I feel for sending you in."

"I knew what you were doing. I thought I could handle it."

"That's what old trauma does, Ms. Allen," Harrison put in. "It sneaks up on you and strikes."

"Well, it's over now." She stood, though she was a bit unsteady on her feet. "If you don't mind, Chief, I'm going to call it a day."

"Will you be coming back to the firehouse at all?"

Saner now, she managed to cock an eyebrow. "Are you going to tell the group about my dirty little secret?"

"No! Of course not. I'll say you got claustrophobic."

"I can live with that. Okay, I'll be back on your next tour. It's a night shift, right?"

"Um, yeah. But I really think—"

He'd been kind and promised to keep her secret, so she said, "I'm fine Chief, really. I'll go home and swim in the lake."

"You shouldn't be driving, Ms. Allen," Harrison said. "Let Cal bring you home."

"No thanks. I'm used to taking care of myself." With that she walked from the office.

Outside, she leaned against the wall and took in a deep breath, trying hard to squelch the old, familiar feelings of humiliation and shame. She'd never thought she'd feel them again.

# CHAPTER 5

IN DEFERENCE TO the late August heat, Cal dressed in navy shorts and a cotton, white polo shirt. With Dockers on his feet, he headed out to Hale's Haven to get a dose of the joy the HCFD and HCPD gave sixty kids every summer. He couldn't be prouder of them. Even if Rescue 7 had been brutal when they heard Parker Allen had gotten claustrophobic yesterday at the training....

"Wonder how she'll use this against us," Licia had said.

All Cal could remember were trembling lips and wide vacant eyes. "I don't think she will. Claustrophobia happens to laypeople."

"Yeah, well, I wouldn't put it past her," O'Malley quipped.

There had been no blog today and Cal worried about that. About her. All night long, when he couldn't sleep, he put together the pieces. *It was decades ago.* So she was in her twenties when the life-changing event had happened. *No, Mike, don't please.* A guy named Mike had beat her up, viciously.

And Cal would bet his chief's badge the guy had either been a firefighter or a cop. Which, on top of what had happened with her father in the arson case, explained absolutely everything about her vendetta. He couldn't help feeling bad for her and was suddenly glad he and Noah had decided not to dredge up her background.

Once he arrived at the camp, he forgot about the woman and got caught up in the excitement of the kids.

"Hey, buddy, good to see you here." Noah, dressed similarly, but wearing a camp hat, smiled broadly. "We're going out on the water in a few minutes. Want to come for a spin or look around the camp?"

A fast blast of cool air on his face would be bracing and wake him up some. "Water first, then look around."

Ten minutes later, he was seated next to Noah in the big party boat. Kids and counselors crowded into the back, screeching with delight. Cal tried to enjoy the wind in his face and the chitchat coming from Noah. "My in-laws live right there." Noah pointed to the condos on the other side of the lake.

"The Woodwards. Yeah, I know. So do Gabe and Rachel, but down a ways from them."

"Lakefront property is great in the summer. Eve and I are thinking about buying a condo near them. Rick and Faith Ruscio live next door, but believe it or not, the condo on the other side of them is for sale."

"Kismet, then. Go for it." Out of the blue, Cal wished he had a brother or sister to share his life with. He wished he was more important to his son and grandson. And he wanted a woman in his life. He'd been divorced a long time. Hell, must be exhaustion brought on sentimentality!

They sped down the lake to the ritzier section of homes. Huge houses with big windows and expansive decks overlooked the water. "See that wood-and-glass house, rising three levels?"

"It's a beauty."

"The dreaded Parker Allen lives there."

"Really? She has that much money?"

"Uh-huh. Family inheritance."

"How do you know that?"

"I did a little digging of my own."

"Find out anything else new about her?"

"Nothing you don't know. She went to school with Brody's Emma at Northeastern, stayed in Chicago until she was twenty-four, then moved around some and ended up in Hidden Cove. That place used to be her grandparents' home. She's owned it a while."

Hmm. Chicago must be where the incident with Mike had happened.

"Ever visited the Chicago smoke eaters?" he asked Noah.

"Yeah, they're a tough group. A lot like the FDNY." He waited a bit. "Why?"

"No reason."

Which was a lie. But he couldn't tell Noah where his thoughts had gone. He couldn't tell anybody about the obscene scars on Parker Allen's stomach, which went way, way deeper.

Glancing over his shoulder at her millions-of-dollars home, he wondered if she was there today, trying to recover from her ordeal.

An ordeal Cal had engineered. He felt like a first-class shit.

• • •

THE DOORBELL KEPT ringing. Parker huddled in her bed like some freaking coward, afraid of what was behind the door. She'd been in the same spot for thirty-six hours, staring into space, watching some no-mind TV and eating enough so she didn't pass out.

Disgusted with herself, she flung off the covers of her expensive down duvet, which had been protecting her from the icy cold she'd felt since her experience in the training tower. "Damn it, Parker. Quit cowering." As she strode to the steps, then downstairs to the entry, she glanced at her outfit. Light cotton shorts and top. The mail carrier, UPS guy or whoever it was would have to take her as she was—stringy hair, clothes wrinkled—but she didn't care. It was time to face the world.

She pulled open the door and realized she'd made a mistake. It wasn't a delivery. Standing before her was a tall, broad-shouldered man, his green eyes filled with chagrin. "Hi."

"Chief?" She pushed back her hair and toed her bare feet into the tile. "What are you doing here? And how did you know where I lived?"

"I was across the lake at Hale's Haven and Noah pointed out your home." He held up a bag. "I came bearing gifts."

Parker stared at him. She should tell him to go away, but in truth, she didn't want to be alone anymore. And what did that say about her life that she'd keep company with the enemy to ward off her total isolation from others? She dropped her gaze to the bag he carried. "What did you bring?"

"Ice cream. I, um, always eat it when I'm struggling."

Lifting her chin, she asked, "You think I'm struggling?"

"No, I am."

That confession softened her ice-cold heart.

"Please, let me come in and talk. I've been thinking about you since yesterday."

To stall for time, she eyed the ice cream, her weakness. Then she looked over her shoulder at the empty house.

Calling herself all kinds of a fool, she stepped aside, let him in and led him to the lower-floor sitting area.

He glanced around at the decorator's dream—stuffed rattan furniture in front of a triple set of glass doors that looked out on the patio facing the pristine lake. The doors were open, luring in the hot August air and a slight breeze. "This is beautiful, Parker."

"Thanks. My grandparents left the house to me. I redecorated it in my own taste."

He nodded. Did he already know her home had been given to her? She chose not to worry if he did. "Sit." She went to the back, where a small kitchen hid behind the big room, and retrieved spoons. When she returned, she sat adjacent to him on a huge rocker and handed him one. "What kind did you bring?"

He pulled out six different pints of Ben and Jerry's, making her smile. He said, "You pick first."

"The most chocolate thing you have." Maybe the endorphins would lift her mood.

They were silent, staring out at the lake while they ate. She couldn't finish the whole pint, but he downed all of the pistachio. Surreptitiously, she perused him. He didn't have an ounce of fat anywhere that she could see. He was long, lean with world-class muscles. When he finished his treat, she stood and took the extra pints to the fridge. Back in the room, she asked, "Why did you come here, Chief?"

"Sit, please." Leaning forward, he linked his clasped hands in between his knees. "To give you my sincerest apologies. I knew I was sending you in for a rude awakening. I didn't know..."

She was surprised at his candidness. "You got more than you expected, didn't you?"

"I'm afraid so. Parker, truly, I'm sorry."

Ignoring how much she liked hearing him use her first name again, she sighed. "Who else did you tell?"

Eyebrows bleached by the sun rose. "Nobody. I swear. And I won't."

"It's not going to come out the next time you get pissed off at me?"

He shook his head. "We never released your background, and you've been pretty rough on us."

Parker didn't know what to say. Since her father had been taken, she wasn't used to consideration and kindness from men. Her grandparents were as cold as her mother. "I'd appreciate it if you wouldn't. That would be totally humiliating."

His face reddened. "*You've* got nothing to be ashamed of. Whoever did that"—he gestured to her torso—"should be crucified."

"Well," she said without thinking, "he burned to a crisp in a fire, which was probably worse." She gasped. "God, I didn't mean to say that. My defenses are down."

"I figured out he must be a firefighter. Mike, right?" At her surprise, he added, "You used his name. I put the pieces together."

She bit her lip, a nervous gesture. "It was a long time ago, like I told you and Jack Harrison. I've dealt with it."

"But my sending you into that tower, knowing you'd get disoriented, even trapped, brought the nightmare back."

She could only nod.

"Jesus, I'm an ass."

Her head tilted. "Are you always this...responsible? I mean, do you always take things on that you have no control over?"

Easing back in the chair, he crossed his ankle over his leg. He had muscles there, too, corded, with a light sprinkling of hair. "I guess I do." He stared past her shoulder out at the lake. "I have my own demons, Parker."

"Tell me some. Maybe I won't feel so self-conscious then. So exposed."

He waited a long time and she thought he might not answer.

Finally, he said, "The worst thing I did in my life was neglect my son and wife in my quest for the white helmet."

She knew the term from her research. "You want to be Chief of the Fire Department?"

"I did. In any case, my son acted out because I wasn't around and got his girlfriend pregnant at nineteen. The good news is Peter and Sally have been married for years and I have the best grandson in the world. My relationship with Tommy is good, but I can't say as much for my son."

"What happened with your wife?"

"She had affairs." His face turned incredibly sad. "I didn't know about them until the last one, after her best friend died. Then she didn't try to keep them a secret."

Parker didn't say anything.

"The divorce was nasty, even though I gave her everything. She wanted a pound of flesh. She *deserved* a pound a flesh."

"Affairs happen all the time. It's never one person's fault."

"Were you ever married?"

*I have no man, no friends, nothing.* "Ah, no. It's hard for me to trust."

"I can see why. What happened to you must have been horrible."

"I don't want to talk about that, Cal."

"All right. But know that some professional help might make things better."

"I've never had a flashback before. I don't intend to again." She stood. "Thanks for coming over. And for sharing. But I think you should leave now."

He looked disappointed. "The truce is over?"

"Yes." She stared down at the shoulders she'd clutched yesterday, remembering how gentle he'd been. "Again, thanks for the sympathy and care yesterday."

"You're welcome."

She led the way to the foyer. Opened the door. He turned to face her. "Let me say one more thing before we go back to being adversaries. Since I know about all this and not many people do, if you'd like to talk more, I'm here."

Banding her arms around her waist, she said, "Thanks, but that'll never happen."

He reached out and squeezed her shoulder. Didn't let go right away. "Well, just in case." His grip was strong but not threatening. And very male. This close, she could smell his woodsy scent.

Letting go, he turned and trundled down the expansive steps to the driveway.

Parker watched him until he got into his Jeep and drove away. Then she went back into the house, determined not to think about him again. Instead, she climbed the stairs but didn't retreat to her room. Feeling buoyed, she crossed to her computer to write her blog. Clicking into her email first, she found one from her source in the fire department. For some reason, she wasn't thrilled to be hearing more negative things about the people she'd come to know.

• • •

PARKER ALLEN'S BLOG—ANOTHER Day in the Life of Rescue 7

Yesterday, on my second visit with firefighters, the group was taken out of service to train at the Anderson County Fire Academy — something that happens frequently and they obviously need to do. But this begs the question, why are they so against brownouts? A squad is regularly missing for training.

In any case, the classroom session was presented by Battalion Chief Ian Woodward, hurt in 9/11, on what to do when a firefighter or anyone is trapped. His teaching was stellar, his demeanor calm. Given what was done to him. I've rarely admired anyone more.

The guys were typical. They joke, get sarcastic with each other, have fun while training on such a serious topic. I will never understand police and firefighter black humor.

In the afternoon, the firefighters implemented what they learned at the training tower. The building was filled with white mist that was as blinding as dark black smoke, I'm told. And they had a hell of a time rescuing a victim. I was critical, thinking "This is their job, why can't they do it well? The Rescue Squad is the crème de la crème. If they can't execute this maneuver, who can?"

This was my attitude when I was sent in on my own by Chief Cal Erikson. It was a dirty trick on his part, as he knew I would have trouble finding my way. And I did. I got lost, disoriented and panicked. I was terrified. The chief had to come in and get me.

I'm trying to be unbiased here, so I'll just say it. Kudos to Rescue 7 for doing this in their professional lives when no one will come in to save them.

• • •

"CAN I TALK to you a minute, Chief?"

In his office at the beginning of Rescue 7's night tour, Sydney Sands stood before Cal, tall and serious. She'd made his best friend, Max, happier than he'd ever been, so Cal was glad to see her.

"I only have a few before the mayor gets here." It was very odd that the mayor was coming to the firehouse. Bob Johnson had called earlier and said he wanted to talk to Cal, although Cal was usually summoned to his office. "Sit down, Sands."

Sydney sat and fidgeted. She'd become a lot more relaxed around him since her relationship with Max, so he wondered why the nervousness today.

"What's on your mind?"

Her brown eyes were clear and her gaze direct. "I read Parker Allen's blog this morning. I have to register a complaint."

"Against Allen? I thought her blog was fair." And shocking. He'd expected a diatribe against him for sending her into the tower alone and was inordinately pleased by what she wrote instead.

"No, against you." She moved to the edge of her seat. "Cal, I've had a problem with confined spaces since I got trapped in that well. It's better, but it's a hell of a thing."

He knew all this. "As far as Gabe's concerned, this isn't affecting your work." Cal cocked his head. "Or did you have problems in the tower?"

"No, I didn't. But sending Parker Allen in alone wasn't right."

"I know."

"Even if you didn't think she was... Wait, you know?"

"Yes. It was petty. And had disastrous results. If it's any consolation, I apologized to her the next day."

Her face reddened. "Oh, good."

"And I'm glad you feel free to tell me things like this, Syd. I want all my men and women to be open with me."

Nervously, she tucked a strand of dark hair behind her ear. It was a dark brown rather than Parker's near black. "You do?"

"Yes. Someday you'll know me well enough to realize that."

She stood then. "Okay."

Before she left, he said, "I'm running and having dinner with Max later, since I had to come in early for a meeting." Battalion Chiefs took night tours, too.

"I know. Have fun."

He smiled as she left. The woman was going to go far in the department. He half expected her to be sitting in his chair someday.

While he mused about Sands, a brief knock sounded on the ajar door. Cal looked up to see the mayor of Hidden Cove in the entryway. He stood. "Come on in, Bob."

Noticing that Johnson closed the door, Cal frowned. "Can I get you something? I'm sure there's coffee out in the kitchen."

"No, thanks." He sat at the conference table off to the side and Cal joined him. "I want to talk to you about Parker Allen."

Cal nodded.

"I'm glad you went along with Noah about having her visit the firehouse." He fished a paper out of his suit coat pocket. "Today's blog is pretty good. Except for the brownouts part."

"I thought so, too."

"Have any idea why she takes it easy on what happened at the training tower?" Cal watched the mayor. Johnson laughed. "You had to have sent her in alone on purpose. She could have eviscerated you in the blog."

"Well, I did apologize."

"I was hoping that was why. I want you to keep it up."

"Keep what up?"

"Sweet-talking her."

He took offense at that. "I didn't say I sweet-talked her."

"You did something to sway her. Be nice to her, Cal. Change her mind about us."

The latter didn't sound too bad. "I'm trying, Mayor."

"Make an extra effort." He stared at a Manwaring firefighter print on the wall, as if deciding what to say next. "She's a beautiful woman."

What did that have to do with it? "I guess she is."

"Shouldn't be so hard to...get her on our side."

When he realized the tenor of the comment, Cal's temper spiked, but he held his feelings back. Johnson was tough and hard-nosed. But Cal had mostly respected him—before this. "I'll do my best."

Standing, Johnson held his gaze. "Just so we're clear." He turned to go, then pivoted back around. "It's no secret you're on my short list for the deputy chief when Lincoln retires. I like cooperation."

As the mayor left, Cal's mind whirled. What the hell had the guy been suggesting?

He asked Max Delinsky the question as they met to jog before they headed out to supper. They'd stopped running consistently at six o'clock because, Max said, he was often spending his mornings in bed. Cal filled in the blanks. And lately, had been jealous as hell.

Max frowned when Cal told him the story. "Jesus. That doesn't sound good, whatever he meant. Like, what, you're supposed to seduce her?"

A flash of bare legs, slender shoulders and violet eyes to get lost in ambushed Cal. "I don't know, Max. Christ, I hope not."

"That would be totally unethical."

"Of course it would."

They ran a while, then Max asked, "You think she's pretty?"

"What? I'm not blind. Why?"

"I don't know. That night at the Lakeside, there were a lot of sparks between you two."

"Of course there were. We were fighting."

"Maybe. I sensed something else."

Once in a while, Cal kidded himself. Most of the time, he put up a front for others, but he rarely misled Max. They were like brothers. Cal stopped running. "Truth be told, Max, I do find her attractive. I went over there the day after the incident." He described what he'd said and how good it felt not to fight with her.

Halting, too, Max faced him. "Ordinarily, I'd tell you to act on an attraction like that. But if you want to be deputy chief, my guess is any involvement with her could ruin that chance."

"Johnson mentioned the job."

"Ah."

Cal started running again. Faster. He didn't want to talk about this anymore. He didn't want to think about it—or Parker Allen.

And her beautiful violet eyes.

# CHAPTER 6

THE KITCHEN WAS quiet and calm when Parker walked into firehouse on the second night of the Rescue 7, Group 3's, late-shift tour. She carried a small travel bag of things she'd need to stay overnight. Cal had told her to come at five, the official starting time; everyone had arrived and gathered around in the table again. Even when they saw her, they didn't stiffen up or glare at her.

"Hey, there."

"Hi, Ms. Allen."

"Can I get you something?"

The comments flowed from their lips as if they didn't hate her. And for the life of her, she couldn't imagine why that meant something to her.

Sands rose and crossed to the counter. "I'll get you coffee. Nice blog the other day," she called out.

Parker nodded. She didn't know exactly what possessed her to be kind to the department after the ugly trick Cal played on her. She hoped it wasn't because of his visit the next day. Despite her determination not to, she'd been looking forward to seeing him again all week.

"We're gonna put you on KP right away," Tony told her with a genuine smile. "As a sort of sous chef."

"I guess I can handle that. Who's cooking?"

"I am." The deep voice came from behind her and shivers skittered up her spine, literally. Uh-oh. She turned to find Cal, his arms full of bags. Ramirez got up and relieved him of part of the burden. "What are we having, Chief?"

"Shrimp cheese."

"Zach Malvaso doesn't like seafood."

As if summoned, a group of four men and one woman entered the kitchen from the outside door. They were covered in sweat. Razzing each other. "Yeah, Zach. Keep tellin' yourself that. I didn't foul. *You* lost the game."

Zach slapped the woman's butt. "Liar."

Parker's eyes widened.

"They're married," O'Malley announced, catching her reaction.

Gabe Malvaso stood. "Now that you guys are finished with the training field, we're going to do some of our own."

As the whole group of them exited the kitchen, Parker approached Cal, who was unpacking the brown bags. "Where do they train?" she asked.

He glanced at her. "It appears they're headed to the basketball court to decimate each other." His look was intense. "It's aerobic exercise, Parker."

"I understand."

"You wrote a blog once showing you didn't."

"I guess being around them is changing me." She nodded to the stove. "What can I do?"

"Grate the Velveeta cheese." Crossing to the cupboard, he got out the grater and, on his way back, stopped to switch on the radio. Some cool jazz drifted out from the corner.

"You like jazz?" he asked.

"As a matter of fact, I do."

He handed her the cheese but didn't let go of his end. "How you doing today?" His voice was pitched low. Sexy. Like it might get after making love. Of its own volition, her hand went to her middle. She discreetly drew it away.

"I'm better. Temporary insanity that day."

"I'm glad you're okay." He waved his hand around the firehouse. "You sure you're up for this?"

"You mean a sleepover?"

His eyes darkened, then lit with mischief. "Yeah, I guess."

"I am. It'll be fun to witness their night routine."

"I wouldn't exactly call it fun." He turned to the stove.

They worked in companionable silence, broken by comments about the shrimp, the cheese sauce, the rice. She took a few loaves of bread out of the bag, and the scent of dough had her breathing it in. "This smells wonderful. I don't usually eat carbs after two o'clock, but I can't resist this."

"Knock yourself out and break off an end piece now."

Her smile came naturally. "Sounds good. Want some?"

"No thanks. I gotta watch my waistline."

As she bit down on the thick crust, she noticed the waistline he referred to was pretty damn nice. Trim. His white shirt fit him well and tucked easily into his black pants, which covered long and muscled legs.

Dinner was scheduled for six and the Rescue Squad crew filed in, along with the Quint and Midi groups, who'd just gotten back from a run. They let her go first, then Cal, and when they were all seated, the PA went off.

"Rescue 7, fire at 99 Cumberland Drive. Three alarms."

"Shit."

"Damn."

"Might have known."

The five men and women swore but bolted up.

"Ninety-nine Cumberland? Oh, my God." This from Sydney, who hadn't moved.

Everybody froze.

"That's Happy Time Day Care. Daisy goes there sometimes."

Cal crossed to her and touched her arm. "Is she there now?"

"No, but they're open at night. Cal, kids will be in that building."

"Then let's go help."

They raced to the truck, with Parker trailing behind, and climbed onto the rig quicker than the last time; they also drove faster. After a harrowing trip in complete silence broken only by the siren and some radio instructions, they arrived at the site.

Pulling up behind them in his red-and-white Jeep, Cal hurried over to Incident Command. The others got tools out, and she noticed three more trucks had arrived and were doing the same.

Cal conferred with the other white-shirted man and looked at the computer set up on his vehicle. They talked, then the chief jogged over. "The fire was started by an explosion in the back. That exit was immediately blocked. The day care workers handed a few kids out a window, and the rest went for a side entry. But the door stuck. By the time they headed to the front, it was engulfed, too. Four's got water on it now. You're going in."

"How many kids trapped?" Sands asked.

"Six. And two workers."

Suited up, they headed for the front door. From the looks of it, the other company had put out that part of the fire, but she noticed a stream going in the back.

Parker held her breath as she watched the Rescue Squad firefighters enter the burning building like warriors going into battle. She remembered last week when she'd been trapped in opaqueness. They'd be in the same blinding darkness tonight. Would they get the kids out? How on earth would they find them in a big and unfamiliar building?

For long minutes, she stood there, arms wrapped around her waist, biting her lip. *Please, God, let them save the kids,* she prayed silently. *And keep them safe.*

Finally, one firefighter approached the doorway, but Parker was unable to tell who it was because she couldn't see the back of his coat. He carried a baby in his arms. Next, another firefighter with a second baby. They filed out, each with a child or a baby. She counted six.

But only one adult, who was over somebody's shoulder.

Paramedics and an ambulance crew swarmed the group as soon as they reached safety. All six firefighters were relieved of their treasures, and all fell to their knees on the ground. Someone—it turned out to be Felicia White—wasn't wearing her air mask, and when she whipped off her helmet, she bent over and vomited.

Cal approached Parker and tracked her gaze. "She gave a little boy her air. Took in too much smoke herself."

"Will she be all right?"

"In a while. The headache will be the worst. Carbon monoxide brings on a migraine-worthy bout."

As she watched, another firefighter exited. He held a charred body. Oh, no! Parker had to turn away from the site.

After White and O'Malley were checked out by medical staff, they all dragged themselves to the truck. Climbed in. The total silence in the rig on the ride back, the acrid scent of smoke and the *feel* of death was awful. When they reached the firehouse, Cal was already there. Once again, they climbed off the truck—slower this time—and entered the house. No one went to the kitchen for food. Instead they dispersed.

"What will they do?"

"Clean up. Rest. Eventually, they'll have to eat."

Her heart ached for them, for the family of the person killed. How did firefighters routinely experience this kind of terror and loss? "It must be tough when a victim dies."

"More than you know. At least we saved he kids. I lost a little girl once. It haunted me for months."

Suddenly the PA sounded again. Parker couldn't believe it. Rescue 7, Quint and Midi 7 were called to another fire. As she watched them dress in dirty gear and climb onto the trucks, she couldn't imagine how they'd mount yet another daring rescue.

• • •

CAL HEARD PARKER get up about three in the morning. He was still awake himself. They'd had four calls tonight and no one was interested in his shrimp cheese. All part of the job, he knew. But he wondered what she thought of their odd hours and crazy schedule, missing meals and, finally, exhaustion.

Throwing on sweatpants over the boxers he wore with a navy T-shirt, he crept downstairs and found her watching the coffee perk. She turned to him when he said, "Couldn't sleep?"

Her long dark hair was free around the cotton top she wore with fleece shorts. The luscious locks were messy, like a man had run his hands through them. For a brief instant, he pictured that man as himself. "No, you either?"

"Nope. You'll have to catch some during the day."

She poured from the pot—two cups—and handed him one.

"You might be able to take a nap if you don't have that, Parker."

"I won't. Once I'm up, I'm up."

*I'd know how to put you to back to sleep.*

Damn it, where had that come from? He took a sip and trained his thoughts on something less pleasant. "Since you're awake, I want to tell you something."

Her face tightened. "Is it bad?"

"Yes. Someone rigged all the internal doors in the training tower."

"Excuse me?"

"The door that locked you in. The handle was missing; somebody removed it on purpose."

She took a seat at the table. "How do you know this?"

He leaned against the counter. "I got a call from Noah Callahan right before we went up to bed. Eve heard about what I did to you, and after she got royally pissed at me, she wondered about the closet. They drove out to the Academy and found it—and a lot more—had been tampered with."

Staring up at him with tumultuous eyes, she swallowed hard. "Who would do that?"

"The arsonist who's going after us."

"How would he get access?"

"For one thing, the training tower isn't locked up. But Eve has wondered for a long time if the torch might be a firefighter."

"She'd incriminate her own?"

"First off, she came to us from the office of investigation in Albany, so her job there was partly to investigate fellow officers. But if one of our own is targeting us, yes, she'd go after him. We've had some close calls."

"I think I might like Eve Callahan."

"She's a wonder." He scowled.

"What?"

"Well, you might as well hear it all. She hooked up with Noah while she was investigating him."

"I already knew that. Just like your captain and his bride."

Cal scowled. "Yeah, you wrote a blog about them, and O'Malley and Felicia. But nothing about Noah and Eve."

"I didn't want to go on speculation and rumor. I only wrote about what happened on my watch."

The light was dim and the sound of crickets came through the open windows. Cal took a seat adjacent to her and could immediately smell the scent of her. "Can I ask you something?"

"Of course. Seems like there's no secrets between us anymore."

"Are you changing your mind about us?"

"Hmm, I see now how hard you work. You deserve your pay and downtime, after what I witnessed today. But I have some trouble with the closeness of the people here. You're like family."

"And that bothers you?"

"It should affect how you do your job."

"Have you seen it hindering us?"

"Ramirez is very protective of Sands. And he's married."

"To a wonderful woman. And Sydney's happy as a clam in a new relationship."

"To your friend?" At his raised brows, she added, "I heard you on the phone with him."

Cal realized he'd better keep up his guard. "Does that bother you?"

"Some. Can you treat her fairly as the officer in charge?"

"I think so. But their relationship is relatively new. We haven't decided if she should stay at one of my firehouses. There are other battalion chiefs she can work under."

Rising again, Parker walked back to the pot to fill her cup. Her hips swayed in the soft cotton and he got hard. Jesus!

She pivoted and stayed where she was, giving him a bird's-eye view of her long legs. "I don't like these cross connections. It's too much."

"For you."

"What?"

"For you. Though Rescue 7, Group 3 seems more interconnected than most, these kinds of ties bind firefighters in ways lay people can't understand."

"Like Malvaso and his wife. Who also hooked up here."

"Some of that is inevitable. Especially after 9/11."

"What do you mean?"

"We've done some awful work together. It makes us closer."

She waited for a moment before she asked, "Did you go down to Ground Zero?"

He felt for his wallet without thinking. "Yes. It was horrific."

"Want to talk about it?"

"No, not now."

"You don't trust me. But I swear, I wouldn't use it against you in any way. I'm just curious."

"It's not that. It's too hard, is all." Something made him stand, cross to the pot and draw more coffee. She moved down a few inches. He faced her. "Parker, when you work in close quarters, when you experience life-and-death situations together, feelings develop. And grow."

She was so near, he could see her pupils were dilated. Because he knew what that meant, he reached over and took a strand of her hair and slid it between his fingers. "I've been dying to see what this feels like."

Her breath hitched. "W-what are you doing?"

"Not what I'd like to."

Her brow furrowed. "Th-this isn't a good idea, Chief."

"I know." He stepped back. His own breathing had sped up. "Doesn't make it any less than what it is."

"What is it?"

The PA crackled again. "Rescue 7, go into service."

Cal blew out a heavy breath. "Saved by the bell, I guess."

And then he left the kitchen to get into his officer clothes for yet another fire tonight.

His men would be exhausted, but Cal was enervated. Plain old desire did that to you, he guessed.

• • •

AS THE AUGUST sun blistered the landscape the next day, Parker headed to the lake to swim, where she often planned her blogs. This morning's entry had been complimentary. How could it not be? Parker had witnessed a night where it didn't seem humanly possible to do what the Rescue Squad had done. Yet, she'd seen it with her own eyes.

*I don't like to go on gossip. Only what happened on my watch.*

And what had she seen for herself last night? Ah, the million-dollar question. She reached the lake, but instead of going in, she sat on the dock and dipped her feet in. The warm water tickled her skin. She tried to concentrate on the beauty of the day, the purr of boats passing by and the soft swish of their wakes, but she could think about only one thing. What was in Cal Erikson's eyes last night. And if the PA hadn't sounded, what would have happened?

There was no denying she wanted him to kiss her. When was the last time she'd felt so drawn to a man? But it wasn't only chemistry sparking between them. She'd gone and liked the guy. He was gentle, yet firm. Smart. And sensitive. No one knew about her past, and she still couldn't figure out why she told him, but he'd listened and sympathized. And, thank God, didn't try to make things right, like most men would do.

*I don't like the interconnections.*

*Some of that's inevitable.*

Was that happening to her? To them? No, no, there was no *them*.

Sick of this rumination, she stood and dove in. The water was soothing. As her arms cut through the water, she thought about what topic to write about for tomorrow. She was losing her edge and she needed to keep it. She couldn't let Cal Erikson or a group of firefighters she was beginning to like soften her. She had to stay tough.

*Why Parker? Why do you need that?*

*To protect myself.*

*Wouldn't it be nice to have someone in your life?*

*Maybe, but not Cal Erikson.*

After ten laps between buoys, Parker had an idea. It would kill two birds with one stone. She'd call the next blog. "Too much togetherness? You decide."

She needed to distance herself from Cal, from these people, and what better way to do it than to criticize exactly what was happening to her? The blog would take care of his attraction to her. For good.

Parker finished her laps and walked out of the lake. Usually the endorphins kicked in by now but not today. Today, she was feeling unaccountably sad.

Work was a good antidote, she thought as she headed to the house. In reality, that's all she had.

# CHAPTER 7

CAL HELD HIS grandson by the hands and swung the boy in front of him as they wandered around the annual August Firefighter Festival. "Cool, Papa. Do it again."

Ah, he'd gotten himself into something now. But he was glad to have Tommy with him. Everybody brought their kids, and he'd convinced Peter to let Tommy come along. He couldn't talk his son into joining them, though. As Cal held his flesh-and-blood's hands, he vowed to find more ways to make inroads with Peter.

"Papa, look there." Tommy pointed to a dunking booth. "Can we do it?"

"Sure." They meandered over. A group of firefighters were scheduled to sit in the booth. As he and Tommy waited in line for their turns, he tried to concentrate on the event, which would raise money for Hale's Haven. He needed distraction from thinking about Parker Allen. After the call to a false alarm, the rest of the night shift was fairly uneventful and there had been no repeat of their...closeness. Hell, he'd almost kissed her right there in the firehouse! What had he been thinking? The answer was, he *wasn't* thinking. With his head at least. Jesus, he was forty-five and should be past reacting with his dick.

"Oh, just what I was waiting for."

Recognizing the voice, Cal's head snapped up, and he angled his body to see Ed Snyder from Engine 4, two people ahead of him. The guy was not his favorite person.

"There's a lady in the booth," Tommy said.

Cal checked. Rachel Wellington Malvaso, Gabe's wife, had taken the hot seat. And Snyder was a notorious misogynist. Cal surveyed the scene.

The bucket to dump water was triggered by a tennis ball. Nothing bad could happen with that, could it? Still, a skitter ran up his spine as Snyder's turn came up. His meaty fist closed around a ball. Drawing back his arm, he bulleted it—right into Rachel's forehead.

It all happened so quickly, Cal only had time to get Tommy out of the way. Gabe hopped over the fencing of the small enclosure, then vaulted the above-ground pool and waded to his wife.

And two men jumped Snyder. The O'Malley brothers. Glancing around, Cal saw Sydney and Max standing off to the side with their two kids. Syd looked ready to pounce, too. He hurried over with Tommy and said, "Watch my grandson and stay here!"

Max automatically grabbed the boy, and Cal rushed back. Brody had gotten one of Snyder's arms and Ryan the other, but Brody had raised a fist and was about to take his own swing. He lowered his arm when he saw Cal.

"What the fuck is wrong with you guys?" Snyder spat out.

Ryan yanked on Snyder's shoulder. "You hit Rachel in the head on purpose."

"Let me go or I'll kick you in the balls."

Great language for a family event. "I got this," Cal said evenly. "Snyder, you're coming with me."

The guy opened his mouth to speak, then his eyes widened at something behind Cal. He turned to find Noah, his eyes flaming, had come up to them. "I'll take him," Noah said. Under his breath, he muttered to Cal, "I've been waiting for something like this to happen."

Snyder went along with the chief, though he was scowling.

The rest of the day went downhill from there.

Tommy got sick on a hot dog.

Max, Syd and even Amber were sleep deprived from Daisy's teething.

And Gabe was fit to be tied because Rachel had a huge welt on her forehead. Even though the standby paramedics checked her out and put ice on the welt, Cal could see his captain was livid.

But it was when he noticed great legs in a pretty pink skirt that his own heart started thumping. His gaze trailed upwards and to a pretty white blouse.

Parker Allen was smiling up at a tall, good-looking guy. Who, from how he grasped her hand and didn't let go, was obviously her date.

Still—or because of that?—Cal approached them. "Parker, hello."

Her face didn't soften at all as she rested a cool gaze on him and introduced him to Jordan Jacobs, an old family friend. But when she caught sight of Tommy, her body language changed. "Well, hello there." She glanced from Tommy to him. "You resemble your grandpa."

"The spittin' image, my daddy says." Tommy stared at Parker and mumbled something.

"What was that, son?"

"She's pretty."

"I heartily agree," Jacobs commented, sliding his arm around Parker's waist. Cal took satisfaction in the fact that she stiffened—like she *hadn't* that night at the firehouse when he'd held on to a few locks of that lovely hair.

Cal managed to get away from her and soon he and the boy headed home. But he took another emotional jab on the jaw when Peter made a disgusted sound as Cal informed Sally that her son had vomited. Peter's expression said, *You're not any better at being a grandfather than you were a father.*

So when Cal got home and checked his email, and saw one from Parker, he knew she must have sent it before she left. "Thought you'd like to see the new blog."

He smiled. Maybe the day was looking up.

Eagerly he clicked into the link she sent. *"Too Much Togetherness? You Decide!"* jumped out at him. Damn. This couldn't be good.

It wasn't.

• • •

PARKER FELL ASLEEP fine with the help of a pill. She often had to take one to settle down. But she awoke with a start at one in the morning. She'd been dreaming about the festival, only she was with Cal and not Jordan, they'd been holding hands, and he'd kissed her on the Ferris wheel. She was aroused when she awoke.

She lay back onto the pillows, but instead of reliving the dream, which she wanted to, she pictured what his reaction would be when he read the blog. His chiseled features would harden. His shoulders would tense. And he'd be disappointed because he expected better from her. But she had to keep her edge with the blog. And she had to protect her heart. So she imagined every little detail of his anger and disappointment. Not only had she criticized the department, but she'd used some of his own words against him.

Finally sick enough of what she'd done to make her realize nothing could happen between them, she slid out of bed, made coffee and took it out to her deck. The early morning was beautiful, with chirps from cicadas accompanied by the soft whoosh of the waves on the lake. For a long time, she sat watching them crash on the shore. She was enjoying the solitude when she heard the engine of a car. Odd, this end of the lake was not well traveled. Frightened some, she decided to go back inside when a figure appeared at the bottom of the deck in the darkness. Her heart started to stutter. Gripping the arms of the chair, she froze. Parker had made a lot of enemies with her blog. There were any number of people who would want to do her harm and she was totally alone back here. And very vulnerable. Oh, dear God!

"Parker, it's me. Cal."

Expelling a heavy gasp, she fell back onto the cushions. She couldn't take in enough air. He climbed the steps and came into the light shining from the kitchen. "I scared you. I'm sorry. I drove out and saw the light. You said you couldn't go back to sleep once you were up, so I came back to see if you were around."

Still, she said nothing. Just stared at him. In the light from the house and the moon, she noticed he was dressed in shorts with a T-shirt, which was not tucked in. Noting the fact that he was unshaven and messy provoked a different kind of fear in her.

"Parker, are you all right?"

Sanity returned, thank God. She sat up straighter. "Um, yes. You did scare me, though." She cleared her throat because her words were husky. "What are you doing here?"

Without invitation, he dropped down onto an adjacent chair, on the edge, hunching forward. His face was shadowed but she could tell he was looking at her. "You know why I'm here." His voice was raw.

"Because of the blog?"

He waited a beat. "Partly. Who was the guy?"

Caught off guard, she stammered, "I, uh, I told you. An old friend of the family." Who her mother had tried to set her up with for a long time. She'd refused until yesterday, when she needed cover from Cal and called Jordan.

"Are you sleeping with him?"

"That is none of your business."

"Isn't it?" His tone was as rich as the night.

"Why would it be?"

Again he waited.

She blurted out, "Nothing happened the other night between us."

"Something's been happening since I met you at the Lakeside months ago."

"No, Cal, don't say that." Panic welled inside her. "It's not true."

"Believe me. I don't want it to be true."

"Then why did you come here tonight?"

Looking heavenward, he shook his head. "I couldn't stay away."

She stood, more fearful of his words and how he uttered them than she had been of anything in a long time. "I think you should leave."

He rose, too, and came close. Too close. "All right, I'll go if you want me to. After this." Reaching out, he drew her into his arms.

His touch was gentle; one hand slid to her waist as his other cupped her neck. His mouth, when it settled on hers, brushed softly, with no hint of insistence. Even when his tongue probed open her mouth, it was a tender assault, meant to coax and not demand. By the time he drew back, she was trembling, grasping on to the cotton of his shirt. He didn't let her go. Instead, he wrapped her up in his arms. "Don't be afraid. I'd never hurt you."

She buried her face in his chest.

"Please, Parker. I wouldn't."

The gentle lull of his voice settled her, as did the way he massaged her back. She relaxed by degrees. Then other things came to the forefront—how he smelled like man and soap. How big his chest was. How broad his shoulders were. They were so close she could feel his hardness against her. And instead of frightening her, it excited her.

She hadn't felt a man's erection or the gentle wave of desire that swept through her since one cold October morning when the beating that changed her life had happened. Her sensible side, the person who took over that night, told her to pull away and run into the house. But from somewhere, the woman Parker had been at one time surfaced and would no longer be denied. She drew back and he let her.

When she peered up at him, his hand cupped her cheek. "I'll do whatever you want, Parker, but you have to tell me."

She whispered, "Take me inside, Cal. Make love to me. That's what I want."

And she really meant it.

• • •

CAL KNEW HE was a considerate lover, but as Parker led him up a circular oak staircase, he prayed for the gentleness, the tenderness that this woman needed. Her hand in his felt small and delicate, fragile like she was on the inside. When they reached an open door, she drew him into the bedroom. A soft light glowed from the corner, so he took in the spacious suite with a glance, then dismissed the high-ceilinged space decorated in green and white. His gaze focused on her and he smiled.

"Oh, that's nice."

"What?"

"Your smile. It's reassuring. I'm nervous." She was wringing her hands. "It's been...it's been..." Turning her head, she looked away.

Something dawned on him. Oh, dear Lord, could that possibly be true? Stepping close, he placed his hands on her shoulders. He needed to know. "It's been a long time for me, Parker."

Her eyes were dark amethysts tonight and stared up at him.

"You, too?"

She nodded.

"How long?"

She drew in a heavy breath. Let it out. "Since October third, two-thousand-one."

"Oh, honey." He brushed her cheek with his knuckles. "I'm so sorry. And pleased you want to do this with me."

"Can we go slow?"

"Of course. We can do anything you want."

A relieved sigh.

Lifting her chin, he brushed his lips over hers with exquisite care, promising himself he'd do this right, no matter what his body screamed at him.

She fell into the kiss in stages. At first, she kept a space between them. Then she sidled in closer. He let his arms go loosely around her. Still the kiss went on, and she put more oomph into it. He responded but kept control. Need rampaged through him, but it didn't matter. When she looped her arms around his neck and totally gave herself to the embrace, he knew she'd stopped thinking about another time and another place and was only with him.

Drawing back, he smiled again, kissed her forehead and led her to the bed. She stopped next to it, peering up at him again.

"How do you want to do this, love?"

"Can we undress ourselves?"

"Like I said, we can do anything you want." He raised his hands to the nape of his shirt to pull it off.

"Can I watch you first?"

"Oh, darlin'."

Slowly, he slipped the tee over his head. He felt totally self-conscious: he was a forty-five-year-old grandfather, for God's sake, and a well-respected firefighter playing a Chippendale in her bedroom. But he did it anyway. She smiled when he lost his shirt. She stared at his hand when it went to his middle. Undid his belt. Might as well get this over with. He dropped both his navy blue briefs and shorts, kicked off his shoes and stood before her. Totally exposed, with a granite-hard erection, he said, "So, what do you think?"

"I think you're beautiful."

"Thank you."

Standing there, she sighed.

"Need some help?"

"No, not this time." Slowly, she eased off her flowery pajama bottoms. He couldn't look at what they revealed, yet. Then she bit her lip. "Can I leave my top on?"

"Of course. Though I've seen the scars and they don't turn me off."

"They turn *me* off."

"Do whatever you like, but know this Parker Allen, you are one gorgeous hunk of woman."

She grinned this time, as he meant her to. "With a feminist objection to the phrase, thanks for the compliment."

He moved closer to her. Sliding his arms around her, he cupped her bare bottom and inhaled the scent of lotion and shampoo he'd forever associate with this moment.

*Dear God in heaven,* he prayed, *please let me last, let me make this good for her.*

• • •

HIS HANDS FELT good on her. She laid next to him, facing him, touching his chest while he ran his calloused palms over her arms, his knuckles down her cheek, his fingers into her hair. She shivered at his light touch. Tipping her chin, she asked for a kiss and got it. Man, he was a good kisser. He made her belly tighten and her thighs ache with the insistent brush of his lips against hers. Already she felt herself go moist and it was…wonderful. His arm slid around her—she didn't realize how much bigger he was than her until now—and drew her closer. Her legs entangled with his. The feel of them, and his chest sprinkled with hair, were so male her insides went liquid. Even when his hand went under her shirt, to her back, she didn't startle.

"I need to touch you more." His voice was gravelly, hoarse with desire.

"Please, do it."

His hand traveled lower. Brushed her mound in slow lazy circles. Gently he parted her thighs. Wonderful fingers massaged her, opened her and slipped into her.

She came like a burst of summer rain, slowly falling and warming every fiber of her. The pleasure was so intense, she lost consciousness for a moment.

When she came to, she saw him next to her: his elbow crooked, his head resting on his hand, staring down at her. "That was the most beautiful thing I've ever seen in my life."

"It was wonderful. Gentle. Sweet. Just what I needed."

He grinned. Leaned over. "There's more where that came from, love."

• • •

SHE WANTED HIM and he was pulsing with need. "Come inside me, Cal."

Thank God. "Condoms." He reached over to the floor, grabbed his shorts, extricated them. "Fuck, I only have two."

She laughed out loud.

He slid one on, then whispered, "Look at me, Parker."

Her gaze was so wide, so innocent, it gave him strength. He entered her slowly. Man, she was so tight, he was afraid he might come right away. He counted, he thought of world peace, of everything but her, until finally he was fully inside her.

Impishly, she whispered, "You, um, could move."

Taking in a breath, he pushed. Once, twice, and then he felt her spasms. His body reacted with harder pushes, thrusts, and when he heard her call out "Oh, God, yes," he let go. His last conscious thought was he couldn't control his body any longer, and he prayed he didn't hurt her.

She was watching him when he opened his eyes. They were lying on their sides, their bodies still joined. Her violet eyes shining like gems, she looked wanton with her hair in tangles from his hands, a blush on her cheeks and a big fat smile on her face. *Thank you, God.*

"That was wonderful," she said, caressing his jaw. It was scratchy. He hadn't shaved because he never expected something like this to happen. He'd kept the condoms in his wallet for a long time.

He leaned into her touch. "I'm glad. For me, too."

"You spent much of it holding back."

"Some. And certainly not at the end. I didn't hurt you, did I?"

"No, not at all."

He noticed the tank top she'd left on to hide her scars. "Everything okay?"

"I never felt better in my life." But she yawned.

"Sleepy?"

"Yeah, I can't believe it." She nestled into his chest.

Smiling at a memory of that night she spent at the firehouse, of him thinking that he knew how he could get her to sleep, he pulled her to his chest, next to his heart, reached over her to turn off the light and drew up the sheet.

"Before she dozed off, she said, "Cal, will you tell me about what happened to you on 9/11 soon?"

"All right, sweetheart. I will. Soon."

His eyes closed as soon as he felt her even breathing.

# CHAPTER 8

AS SHE DROVE to the firehouse in the bright sunshine, joy bubbled out of Parker; she was happier than she ever thought she'd be again after the devastating events of her past. Making love with Cal had been a real turning point in her life and she was looking forward to the future. He'd left her bed at dawn so he could get to the station on time, and now she'd see him again. She herself was later than usual, but she'd fussed with her appearance, fluffing her hair, putting on a peach sundress and flirty sandals.

As she walked through the once-again ajar door of the building and headed down the corridor, the familiar sights and scents of a firehouse surrounded her: the pervasive odor of smoke, the aroma of coffee and the picture of the homey kitchen as she reached it.

"Snyder was suspended?" Sydney asked.

*Snyder*, she thought.

"Yeah." This from Gabe, his tone glacial. "Apparently Callahan's been keeping a file on him. They've got him on sexual harassment, insubordination and a few other things."

Felicia snorted. "Couldn't happen to a nicer guy."

O'Malley noticed Parker first and frowned. "Hi, Ms. Allen."

Everybody shut up.

She realized she was still an interloper, though she didn't feel like one anymore. Maybe that could change. She'd sent today's blog to Cal last night, but she didn't put it up this morning, so perhaps this was a new beginning. "Before you go any further, I won't write about what I overheard."

Coming in close to the table, she stood before the five men and women she'd begun to care about. "In fact, I'm retiring my blog."

"Why?" Felicia asked suspiciously.

"Let's just say this experiment worked in your favor." She waved to encompass the house. "In any case, my visit today will be my last." She couldn't wait to tell Cal and get this obstacle out of their way.

Sydney smiled generously at her. "Thank you, Parker. We, um, didn't expect you today, though. The chief told us you wouldn't be in until tomorrow."

"Oh." Geez, she was completely distracted to have forgotten when the next visit would be. "Then I won't stay. Is Cal in?"

"I don't know," Gabe told her. "He has a meeting with the mayor. Want me to check his office?"

"No, I will. If he's not there, I'll leave a message and go out the side door." Again she smiled.

After good-byes, and "Hope to see you" from most of them, Parker headed down the hall to find Cal. She wanted to whistle, to tap dance at the thought of being with him again, watching his green eyes sparkle, his face soften and his sculpted mouth turn up at the sight of her.

From the end of the corridor, she saw a man enter the side door and go right into Cal's office — Mayor Bob Johnson. She hadn't voted for the guy, and after she'd started the blog, she'd had some testy calls from him. Deciding to wait outside for Cal, she walked forward and, as she neared the door, still open a crack, she heard, "Congratulations, my man. You've done a good job controlling the prickly Ms. Allen."

Parker froze.

Cal said, "You misunderstand the situation, Mayor."

"What's to misunderstand? She called Noah this morning and told him she wasn't going to be blogging about the fire department anymore. That she learned how wrong she'd been from hanging out with the squad."

"I didn't know that." His voice was gruff, like it had been last night. "Still, I didn't have anything to do with the decision."

*Oh, God, if only that were true.* Parker had to lean against the wall to keep herself upright.

"All *I* know is I asked you to sweet-talk her into getting off our backs and she did. I gotta say that'll go a long way in snagging you the promotion to deputy chief."

He was up for deputy chief? Was all this why...?

Her stomach roiled.

Her head began to swim.

Suddenly, she couldn't breathe.

Forcing herself to move, she inched forward a few steps and then she began running. She made it out the side door and to her car. Where behind it, she lost the contents of her stomach. Afterward came the horrific realization: she'd been had, in more ways than one.

Taking a deep breath, she tried to steady herself like she had that awful day ten years ago. Because right now, Parker felt equally beaten up.

• • •

"LISTEN, MAYOR, YOU have this all wrong. I haven't sweet-talked Parker Allen. But obviously, she's convinced we do a good job and deserve our pay and benefits. Can't we leave it at that?"

The man's face held a knowing, *male* grin. "We can leave it any way you want, Erikson. But you're getting credit."

He didn't want credit. He wanted *her*. Everything was happening so fast, his mind reeled. Last night. The news that she was giving up the blog. She must have called Noah after Cal left her this morning.

Finally Johnson said good-bye and Cal dropped down at his desk. His first impulse was to tell Parker what the mayor thought. But their relationship was so fragile, he was afraid she might bolt. Yet if he didn't and she found out, the result would be disastrous. There was a knock on the door, then Gabe entered.

"Hey, Chief. I saw the big guy leave."

"Yeah."

"Did Parker tell you her news?"

"Parker? No, but the mayor filled me in about the blog."

Gabe was smiling. "She came in the side entrance and down to the kitchen. She was on her way in here to talk to you. She thought she was supposed to ride along with us today."

Oh, God, no. "I didn't see her." But what did she see? Hear? His hands began to shake, his stomach got queasy like he'd gulped in smoke.

"Anyway, she's out of our hair. Although she seems like a good person underneath all the bravado."

"Yeah, she is."

"Cal, are you okay?"

He shook his head as the pieces of the picture fell into place. "No, Gabe, I'm not. Look, I've got to go out. It's an emergency. Can you handle Incident Command if we get a call?"

"Yeah, sure."

"Great." He stood. "See you later."

Cal left the firehouse with undiluted dread accompanying him. Jesus Christ, if Parker had overheard the mayor, how was Cal going to explain himself?

• • •

PARKER WAS NUMB, but not too numb to make a phone call. One she thought she'd never make again. Now, she waited at her house for him and thought of Cal—and his betrayal.

*Congratulations, my man. You've done a good job controlling Allen.*

*I asked you to sweet-talk her into getting off our backs.*

*This'll go a long way in snagging you the promotion to deputy chief.*

How could she possibly have been so stupid? She'd thought that Cal cared about her. He'd made love to her like a tender suitor. Looked like he took the *sweet talk* a little too far. How could he have done that to her?

*Maybe he hadn't. Maybe you misunderstood.*

"Stop it, Parker. You heard the words the mayor spoke yourself. Fool me once, and all that."

So, okay, time to regroup. Time to flee...again. She'd leave town after doing this one last thing. From where she stood on the lower level in front of the open doors, in the place she'd brought Cal the night he'd seen her scars, she stared out at the lake. God, she loved this house, this town in some ways. She'd thought she might live here with Cal. The pain of that loss was so slicing, she was immobilized.

The doorbell rang. She glanced at her watch. Her visitor was early. Well, good, she could get this over with. Very carefully, so she didn't jar herself too much, because she was afraid she'd fall apart, she made her way downstairs and drew the door open.

Her heart slammed in her chest. "Oh."

"You misunderstood if you heard what I think you heard," Cal said without greeting her.

*Get it together, Parker. Have some pride!*

So she folded her arms over her chest, poor armor against what he'd done to her. "Let me guess. You're going to try to *sweet talk* me into disbelieving what I heard with my own ears."

He brushed past her into the house, making his way to the seating area. Well, she wouldn't be so gullible this time, she thought as she followed him. He stood in front of the sliding doors and faced her. Warm air drifted in, but Parker was ice cold.

"A while ago, the mayor came to me and told me to get you on our side. He thought your visits to the firehouse were the arena to do it in."

She stared hard at him, trying to calm her thumping heart.

"And at that time, he told me to sweet-talk you."

"Congratulations, Chief. You succeeded. You sweet-talked me right into bed."

He started to cross to her. She held up her palm. "Don't come near me!"

He halted. "Okay. But you'll hear me out. I was shocked at his suggestion. And disgusted. I had a long talk with Max about it. You can ask him if you want."

"Yeah, I'd believe your best friend. What, Cal? Are you afraid I'll renege on my offer to stop the blog?"

As if he hadn't heard the question, he went on. "The mayor got it all wrong!" He'd raised his voice.

"No, I'm the one that did. I thought we were…" Damn it, tears welled in her eyes.

"Jesus. Don't cry. You thought right, honey. Last night meant everything to me. I want a relationship with you. I want us to have a future."

"Why? So you can keep me under control?"

"No, so we can be together."

She sighed and shook her head. "I don't believe you. And I'd like you to leave my house now. I don't ever want to see you again."

He advanced then and grasped her arms gently, despite her command he not touch her. She literally shrank from his touch. "I've fallen in love with you. Doesn't that count for something?"

"It would if it were true. Since it's not, I'd like you to stop manhandling me" — a lie — "and leave me alone." When he didn't move, she said, "I'll call the police, Cal. And write a blog about how you assaulted me."

His beautiful green eyes rounded. "How can you say that to me?"

Before she could answer, she heard behind them, "The lady asked you to leave, Chief. You'd better do it."

They both looked over to see Ed Snyder in the doorway.

Cal's face reddened. "What the hell?" He looked to Parker. "What are you doing?"

"Getting information for my very last blog. It's gonna be a doozy."

"I can't believe you'd consort with Snyder."

"Believe it, Chief." She wanted to hurt him. "Where do you think I've gotten all my *inside* information?"

He glanced from her to Snyder. His hands fisted. Then, after a moment, he started away. At the entrance to the room, he stopped. "You're going to regret this, Parker."

"Not half as much as you, Chief."

# CHAPTER 9

CAL TRIED TO tell himself she was hurt, that she wasn't far enough along in her recovery from that terrible beating to see what had gone on with the mayor clearly. He tried to convince himself that he could have another chance with her. But as he drove along the lake, he knew in his heart he wouldn't. Whatever fragile trust they'd built up had been shattered by a few misunderstood innuendos. Still he kept driving, trying to figure out a way to make her believe him. Finally, he gave up and as he reached the city limits, he noticed a message light flashing on his phone, which he'd tossed on the seat when he'd gone to talk to Parker. Jesus, how long had he been out of communication? He clicked into voice mail.

"Cal, this is Noah Callahan. Call me, or better yet, get over to my office right away. Eve's here and we want to run something by you."

There were two more messages, each more urgent. Since he was close to headquarters, he drove the few blocks and arrived ten minutes after he listened to Noah's first call. He hoped this was something that would take his mind off his problems.

Hurrying inside, he found his way to the Chief's office, knocked, then heard, "Come in."

When he entered, he found Mitch Malvaso and the other Battalion Chiefs assembled. Eve Callahan had been talking and she stopped abruptly.

"Sorry I'm late. What's going on?"

Noah said simply, "We know who the arsonist is."

• • •

"I'D LIKE YOU to tell me how you feel the department has been unfair to you, Ed." Parker clicked on the tape recorder and batted her eyes at the jerk for good measure. Flirting with him was obscene, but she was a woman on a mission. And this was the man who'd fed her information for months, so she knew how to elicit it.

Snyder's face was drawn, sported a scruffy beard, and his clothes were wrinkled. Even at the distance she'd kept from him, she could smell an acrid scent of alcohol. "I dunno where to start."

"How about when you transferred from House 7."

"They brought that cunt Brennan in. I couldn't stand being around her." He got a faraway look in his eyes. "I showed them, though."

"Excuse me?"

"They got paid back." Another frown. "Then there were those lieutenants who got promoted before I did. Fucking women, even."

"You're a lieutenant, aren't you?"

"Yeah, yeah. Not till after them."

Despite the fact that Parker was starting to get uncomfortable with his swearing and his wooziness, she kept going. "What else?"

"The reprimands started. Goddamned bastards thought they could tell me what to do. Hah! They couldn't control me, though." Again the disoriented, almost maniacal expression on his face. "And today is the *piece de resistánce*. Hey, you got any beer?"

"Sure. I'll go get you one."

Rising, she went out to the fridge, only to find her hands shaking. Shit! Still, she retrieved a bottle and brought it to him.

He lifted the beer to her, toast-like. "Here's to going boom!"

"Going boom?"

"Uh-huh."

Parker's heart started to beat fast. "What are you talking about, Ed?"

"Erikson, Callahan, that prick Malvaso, they'll know…" He glanced at his watch. "Soon enough."

Her reporter instincts, delayed because of her upset over Cal, kicked in. People were in danger!

"Would you like to stay awhile, Ed? Sit outside with me?"

"Too hot."

"We could go in the pool." Though it killed her, she sidled up to him and touched his arm. "I thought I might put on my bikini."

"Oh, man, this is my lucky day."

She nodded out the doorway. There's a changing room with suits of all sizes by the pool. Go ahead, I'll run upstairs to get mine."

"Okay. Bring me another beer when you come back."

"Of course."

He all but swaggered out the door. Parker waited until he went into the small bungalow, then grabbed her purse from the counter, and flew out. She hopped into her car, drove away, and as soon as she could see her house in the rear view, she punched in a number.

*Please answer. Please.*

• • •

CAL WAS JUST heading out of headquarters when his phone vibrated. He grabbed for it. "Erikson."

'Cal, it's Parker."

"Jesus, I'm just on my way out to your house. So are the police."

Together they said, "Snyder's the arsonist."

Stunned silence. Then Cal asked, "Is he still there?"

"Yes, I—"

"Get away from him, honey."

"I did. I tricked him into going out to the pool. I'm on my way to town. There's more. He rambled on about *something going boom*. Then you, Malvaso and Callahan *would know*. Could he have planted a bomb somewhere?"

"He's had bomb squad training. Jesus, did he say where?"

"No. He only mentioned you guys."

"I'm just about to leave the building but I'll go back up. Call House 7 and tell them to evacuate. That's the next likely target if he named Gabe."

"Cal, don't go to Noah's office."

"I'll be fine. Just get to safety and I'll do the rest." After he clicked off, he thought about who was at headquarters. Noah, Eve, the staff. Most of the chiefs. If something happened…

Turning around, he took the steps two at a time and jogged down to Noah's office. The meeting was breaking up when he burst through the door. "Noah, we have to evacuate the building. Parker thinks Snyder might have planted a bomb here."

"A bomb? What the...? All right, everybody out. Now." He picked up his phone. "This is Chief Callahan. All personnel are to evacuate—"

Before he could finish, an explosion rocked headquarters.

• • •

PLUMES OF SMOKE rose from the building on Andrews Street as Parker swerved into the parking lot. Several trucks were on the scene, their sirens blaring. Flames shot out of one whole corner of the structure. As she exited the car, she caught sight of Cal's vehicle a few spaces down. "Oh, no."

Firefighters descended en masse from the trucks. But she didn't care. She headed for the door of headquarters.

"Hey, lady..."

"Don't go in...."

She didn't hear them, didn't stop until she felt strong arms encircle her. "Parker, it's Tony Ramirez. You can't go inside."

"I have to help Cal."

Tony held her close. "We're helping him. You'll only keep us from doing our job."

Somewhere in her panicked mind, Parker got that. She stopped flailing. "Go ahead."

"Get back to where Gabe is. He can let you know what's happening."

As she hurried to Incident Command, she was assaulted by the stink of smoke and chemicals. Gabe was listening into his radio when she reached him. "Okay, okay. Keep me posted."

He put the radio down and faced her.

"Are they all right?" Parker asked.

"We don't know. The bomb you told us about when you called 7 went off in the corner by Noah's office. People evacuated but not everybody got out from that section of the building. After we get water on the fire, several search-and-rescue teams are going in."

She closed her eyes and swayed. He grabbed her arm.

"I'm okay. Take care of Cal and the others."

The wait was interminable. She got updates: fire on the water...ventilation...bomb squad on the scene...evacuees from different parts of the building. Still no sign of Cal. She promised God she'd never say a cross word to him again, she'd forgive anything he did, even if he betrayed her, she promised she'd go to church, she'd...

Gabe touched her arm. "Parker, look."

She pivoted around. From the side of the building came a sight to behold. First, Noah Callahan with a guy slung over his shoulder. Behind him, his wife carried a petite blonde over hers. Several white-shirted men dragged others out, under the arms, by their feet. But Cal wasn't among them.

Parker started to cry.

There was a lull. For several minutes, no one else exited. Parker's heart was in her mouth, and tears were streaming down her cheeks when a figure finally rounded the corner. Even through the blur of tears and smoke, she identified Cal's big shoulders and muscular torso, carrying a woman in his arms.

Parker fell to her knees and sobbed.

• • •

"SON OF A bitch!" He could have sworn Parker would come to the scene. He'd have bet his life on it. But once the smoke cleared, so to speak, she wasn't anywhere in sight.

Not that he'd had much time to look, he thought as he stood under the scalding shower spray in his office bathroom and let the hot water sluice over him, cleanse him of dirt and grime and the despicable fact that a firefighter had been killing his own and civilians, doing untold property damage. He'd never liked Snyder, but this? Who knew?

Instead of taking that on, of feeling guilty for missing the signs, he chose to concentrate on Parker. She'd gotten away from the guy—smart girl—and warned him. She'd do that, though, even if he didn't get another chance with her.

Which he would, or he'd go down trying. Other than the time he went in after Max, Cal hadn't been inside a burning building in years. And once again, like most firefighters, he'd cheated death. The bomb had caused fire and injury, but the entire set of smoke eaters who'd been in that end of headquarters had acted as a unit. Though they were hacking their lungs out, they'd rescued all personnel in the area. It brought a satisfied smile to his face. He was exhausted, and his chest hurt like hell, even after the medics gave him oxygen, but he was going to head out to Parker's house.

He dressed in jeans and an HCFD T-shirt, got his wallet and keys and opened the door.

Only to find five firefighters lined up against the wall. Rescue 7, Group 3. "What are you doing here?" he asked as he checked his watch. "You're off duty."

Gabe pushed away from the wall. "Primarily, we wanted to make sure you're all right."

"Yeah," O'Malley added, "but we wanted to know about Parker, too."

"Parker?"

"Is she okay?"

Sydney blurted out, "Did you do anything to her?"

Tony was unusually grim. "You know, we like her. And we heard what she did with Snyder. And she called to tell us to evacuate." Though a search of the firehouse revealed no bombs.

Felicia, who despised Parker, was scowling. "Even me, Chief. We know something's going on between you and her, and we wanted to tell you we've changed our minds about her."

Cal threw back his head and laughed. Irony, in its purest form, stood before him. "I'll tell you what. I'm going out to her house now. As soon as I find out what's what I'll let you know."

With that he strode to his car.

• • •

PARKER SAT ON her deck, in a lounge chair, watching the lake. The setting out here was lovely, with trees swaying, a few ducks swimming around, the water glistening in the last rays of the sun. She was going to miss it. Inside, she felt better, but...hollow. At least a disaster had been avoided, and she'd been part of that effort. She poured more wine into the glass she held and tasted the dry merlot.

She scanned the area, then glanced at her cell phone. No call. He hadn't come out. Of course, he'd be busy with the chaos the department must be in, but still...

She shivered, picturing his blackened face and his horrendous cough as the officers of the HCFD had trudged out of the building. Of course, not without victims slung over their shoulders or in their arms. They were consummate firefighters, and as she'd cried out her relief, another feeling ambushed her. She'd been ashamed that she'd attacked America's Bravest. For months. Even the last blog, which she intended to write before she left town, wouldn't make up for what she'd done. In truth, Parker was disgusted with herself and her life.

"Well, at least you could have poured me a glass."

Her pulse skittered at the sound of Cal's voice. She looked over at him on the steps. In the last of the light, she could see his face was drawn, his eyes pinched—he probably had a headache—but she was so glad he was here she was temporarily silenced.

"Don't say anything. Let me get a glass and talk."

She opened her mouth.

"No, Parker. It's my turn."

In a minute, he was back, poured himself some red wine and took the chair across from the chaise. "I thought you'd come to headquarters."

"I did."

"You did?" Blond brows shot up. "Then why'd you leave without seeing me?"

"I didn't think you'd want me there."

"You were wrong. I looked for you. To be sure you were safe and for comfort."

She gestured to the pool. "They arrested Snyder before I got back here."

"I heard. But you were in danger." He took a big gulp of wine. "I hate the thought."

"I got out. He never knew I was on to him. I'm sorry, Cal, that the arsonist was one of your guys."

"It'll take the department a long time to recover, I'll tell you that."

A sad half smile broached her lips. "As deputy chief, you'll help out there, I'm sure."

He stared hard at her. "I don't want to be deputy chief anymore."

"Excuse me?"

"Tonight was life changing for me." He gave a little smile. "My son heard about the explosion and called me. He hasn't done that in years. He thought I got blown up when the bomb went off. The close call sobered him, and he said he was sorry for what was between us and he wanted to spend more time with me. To get past this hump."

*So do I.* "Oh, Cal, I'm glad. I know how you suffered over the estrangement."

Again the stare. "I want Peter and his family in my life, and I'm not going to make the same mistake as I did last time by putting my job first." He set the glass down, stood and crossed to the chaise. Pushing her over with his hip, he sat down beside her. Gently, he lifted his hand to her cheek and brushed his knuckles there. Parker melted. She loved that tender, sweet gesture. "And I want you in my life. I want to tell you about 9/11, sit out here with you in the summers and make love to you forever. Know, Parker Emily Allen, I'm not going to stop until I get you."

"I was planning to leave town."

"You're not. You're going to stay here and let me convince you of my real feelings. That I never used you. That I meant everything I said and did."

It was as if a huge emotional yoke was lifted from her shoulders. Her heart lightened and her entire body felt buoyant. "Do you mean that, Cal?"

"Do *I*? You're the one who thinks I did something unconscionable. I didn't, sweetheart, I swear!"

A few minutes ago, she never would have thought she'd say—have the opportunity to say— "I believe you, Cal. Tonight was life altering for me, too." Her eyes welled. "I love you. And I want to make our relationship work."

His grin was thousand-watt. "Thank God. I love you, too." A frown. "But we can start wherever you want, backtrack, get to know each other better while you learn to trust my feelings. Just let me be with you."

She watched him with pure bliss in her soul. Gone were all the shadows. *All* of them. "I know exactly where I want to start." Darkness had fallen and high fences flanked the property. She said, "Push back a bit."

"Excuse me?"

"I said move back down the chaise. I need room."

He slid only a few inches away.

Slowly, Parker set down her glass. Even though her heart was beating wildly, she grasped the hem of her tank top and pulled it over her head. Then she lowered her arms and held his gaze.

"Oh, honey." He moved closer again. His throat worked convulsively, and his eyes were moist. "Thank you so much." Gently, he drew her to him and held her tight.

And for the first time in ten years, Parker felt safe with a man, comfortable with herself and joyful at what the future held.

• • •

# EPILOGUE

## THE HEART OF HIDDEN COVE

Front Page Photo

The Firefighters of Rescue 7, Group 3, from left to right: Captain Gabe Malvaso, Firefighter Brody O'Malley, Lieutenant Felicia White, Lieutenant Tony Ramirez, Firefighter Sydney Sands Delinsky, Battalion Chief Calhoun Erikson.
***Read inside for more on America's Bravest.

Page 2 — Photos of the group

A Brand New Life: Gabe and Rachel Malvaso posing in front of the Fire Academy, where Firefighter Wellington Malvaso now works full-time. With them are Joey and Lilliana and soon-to-be Baby Malvaso. (News flash: it's a girl!)

Brothers, Buddies, Best Men: Brody O'Malley and Emma Walsh O'Malley with Felicia White and Ryan O'Malley, posing in Jamaica, where last month the double wedding took place.

All in the Family: Lieutenant Tony Ramirez and Sophia Ramirez, their children, Miguel, Mari, and tiny little Antonia (Nia), just a few weeks old.

Right at Home: Firefighter Sydney Sands Delinsky, her husband, Max, and the Delinsky girls, Amber and Daisy, in front of a Sold sign at their new home on Hidden Cove Lake.

A Place to Belong: Battalion Chief Cal Erikson and Parker Allen in front of firefighter headquarters, where Parker works in public relations for Hidden Cove Firefighters.

Page 3 Family photos

Mitch, Megan, Trish, Bobby and Sabby Malvaso, held by namesake Sabina "Mama" Malvaso.
    Zach and Casey Malvaso, with their children, Jason, Nicky, Shannon and Lindsay.
    Noah and Eve Callahan with their child Ianna; Eve's brother Captain Ian Woodward and his wife, Lisel Loring Woodward, and their baby, Eva. Looking on are Rick and Faith Ruscio, Godparents to both children, along with the twins, Abraham and David.

Table of Contents

Page 4 My story—How Rescue 7 Saved My Life, by Max Delinsky
Page 7 Life at House 7, by Parker Allen and Max Delinsky
Page 11 Notes from the Brass
Page 19 The History of Women in the HCFD, by Felicia White
Page 22 Rescue Photos—Fires, accidents and other *routine* saves
Page 30 From those rescued or helped by the HCFD

Page 48 Remembering 9/11, by the firefighters of House 7
Page 53 Firefighter jokes (They're bad!)
Page 50 Parker Allen's Blog: *What I Learned about Firefighters: a Tribute to the HCFD*

• • •

**For notification of Kathryn's new work and information about her books, be sure to sign up for her newsletter at** http://on.fb.me/1bLS0bN.

# AUTHOR'S NOTE

PICTURE THIS: A hot, sweaty August afternoon. In the dead center of a large city, firefighters go about their daily chores: They do some in-house training, check out the rigs, make sure their equipment is in working order and mop the bays. A tone sounds over the static-filled PA system and everyone freezes. It's a run, and they're off—shoes flying, turnout gear donned; within minutes the truck is on its way. With me in it!

I began my research on fire fighting years ago when I decided I wanted to write about this truly noble profession. I spent many hours with the Rochester Fire Department, in upstate New York, a five hundred plus organization of men and women dedicated to saving lives. I visited the station houses first, met with firefighters, paramedics, battalion chiefs, and arson investigators; even the top guy, our fire chief, spent an afternoon with me—and he was instrumental in helping me create the chiefs in these novellas. I talked at length with many of them and ate meals with them—firefighters love their food and go to great pains in fixing it. Some invited me to their homes to talk to them and their families. A truck was actually taken out of service for an hour to show me how to use the Hurst tools. From here I went on the ride-alongs, where you ride the trucks to actual calls with the firefighters. Imagine my shock when the first run I went on was a stabbing!

I also visited the Rochester Fire Academy. I met with instructors and recruits and sat in on numerous classes and drills. I can open an oxygen container now and know the basics of cutting through a roof with a K-12 saw. I dressed in their gear, posed for them as a patient in EMS drills, crawled through their maze with them, and participated in night training evolutions.

As I did this primary research, I read about fire fighting: famous books like *Thirty Years on the Line* by Leo Stapleton, *Report from Engine Company 82* by Dennis Smith, *The Fire Inside* by Steve Delsohn, and *Fighting Fire, A Personal Story* by Caroline Paul. I also read books on firehouse jokes, fire fighting lore, fire museums, arson, and fire house cooking. I even subscribed to *Firehouse* magazine, though I confess my husband thought that this was going to an extreme. The most strenuous tome I read was the entire recruit manual on fire suppression (700 pages) and parts of the recruit texts on EMS—Emergency Medical Systems.

When I was looking for a focus for the Hidden Cove series, I remembered reading about a camp for the children of slain firefighters and police officers put on by the renowned Camp Good Days and Special Times on Keuka Lake. I interviewed the chairman (he, too, gave me hours of his valuable time) and asked to volunteer. Though that particular camp wasn't offered that year, I did spend almost a week at a similar one, a camp for kids affected by homicide, at the same residential facility. Much of the setup of my fictional camp in these novellas is based on this selfless, heart-warming endeavor. I go back every summer to help Camp Good Days and Special Times provide a respite for kids dealing with life-altering problems.

My heartfelt thanks to everyone who helped me learn about their areas. Particular gratitude goes to Joe Giorgione, Rochester firefighter and paramedic, who steadfastly spent hours with me explaining techniques, developing plot lines, and figuring out answers to the unending questions I had. He also graciously accompanied me to several book signings. You can see a picture of Joe on my website.

Once again, I think I've given an accurate portrayal of a fire department in upstate New York. Along the way, I took a requisite amount of poetic license — the books are fiction, after all, and they are clearly love stories — but I hope I stayed true to the character of these special men and women. They are among the most courageous, generous, interesting, and exciting people I know. It is my sincerest hope that these books pay tribute to America's Bravest.

**Visit or Contact Kathryn at**
www.kathrynshay.com
www.facebook.com/kathrynshay
www.twitter.com/KShayAuthor
http://pinterest.com/kathrynshay/

**If you liked this book, you might want to post a review of it at** http://amzn.to/vy6mUx.

## Other Kathryn Shay firefighter books

**After The Fire**
After being trapped in a fire, the Malvaso brothers and sister decide to make changes in their lives. Follow Mitch Malvaso as he struggles to get closer to his kids and out of a doomed marriage. Jenn, his sister, wants to have a baby and asks Grady O'Connor, her best friend, to be the father.
http://amzn.to/fwxJBS

**On the Line**
Fire Chief Noah Callahan and Albany Fire Investigator Eve Woodward butt heads while she investigates the cause of accidents at Hidden Cove fire scenes. Who knew they'd fall in love? And watch Zach Malvaso become the kind of man he wants to be with feisty firefighter Casey Brennan.
http://amzn.to/hu66kz

**Nothing More to Lose**
INJURED 9/11 FIREFIGHTER, Ian Woodward (Eve's twin), and a disgraced cop, Rick Ruscio, struggle to salvage their lives with the help of the women who love them.
http://amzn.to/h5QpxS

**America's Bravest — Six Novellas**
The men and women on another Rescue Squad in the Hidden Cove Fire Department have complicated personal relationships due to the nature of their jobs. Each of the six novellas details the love and work of one firefighter, but the stories are tied together with an arson case and a blogger out to discredit them.
http://amzn.to/vy6mUx

**It Had to Be You**
Beckett Sloan is an Iraq and Afghanistan veteran who comes home with PTSD. He joins the fire department and finds the love of his life in army nurse Lela Allen, but his demons keep them apart. http://amzn.to/U4NHIt

**Chasing the Fire—Three Novellas**
In another set of novellas, CHASING THE FIRE, the past catches up with three brave firefighters and they must wrestle with it to find love and contentment. http://www.amazon.com/dp/B00DU1QBTA

To browse Kathryn's impressive list of titles go to http://www.kathrynshay.com/books/.

# EXCERPT FROM *IT HAD TO BE YOU* BOOK 5 OF THE HIDDEN COVE SERIES

# CHAPTER 1

"HELL, IT'S HOTTER in here than it was in Afghanistan!" Beckett Sloan mumbled the words, but his radio mic must have picked them up because he heard his captain, Gabe Malvaso, chuckle through the line.

"At least it's chilly outside for April," Gabe responded. "Thank God for small blessings, Beck."

*Not gonna happen.* To Beck, *blessings* and *God* had become irrelevant words since he'd taken his first tour in Iraq over twenty years ago.

Instead of dwelling on war experiences in Iraq, which still woke him in the middle of the night, he focused on his current job.

"How you doin' back there, probie?" Felicia White tossed out. The tall, slender woman had a core of steel.

Intentionally this time, Beck snorted into the radio. "Just fine, Lieutenant." For most of his adult life, Beck had held officer's rank—from second lieutenant all the way to colonel. No more. Now, thanks to the Hire Our Heroes initiative, he was rookie in the Hidden Cove Fire Department, which suited him fine. The fire service was basically a paramilitary organization, with the same slogan as the armed services: *Duty, Honor, Country*. It was as close to the army as he could get without IEDs going off in his path or the slaughter of innocents happening right in front of him. At least now he was trying to save people instead of kill them.

A timber crashed down in front of Gabe, and all five members of the Rescue Squad jumped back. Sparks flew in every direction and a few embers landed on White, who was in front of Beck. They'd kept him close to officers for the first year. Immediately, he reached out to brush the glowing shards from her helmet. Embers under their Nomex hoods were nasty.

Into his mic, Gabe asked, "Condition of the fire, Chief?"

"Getting worse," their battalion chief shot back, with a note of concern in his voice. "You're close to coming out." The voice belonged to Cal Erikson, who was operating Incident Command.

"We're on the second floor. Let us check the bedrooms."

"Do it fast."

Gabe ticked off orders. "Sands and O'Malley, left. White, go with them. Sloan, you're with me."

"Yes, sir."

Following his officer into a bedroom straight ahead, he dropped to the floor when Malvaso did. It was a furnace in here as heat rose. "Check the left side."

Blindly feeling the wall, Beck connected with a steel post. A bedstead? He reached beyond it and found a soft spongy mass—a bed. Which, when pressed, bounced. "Got one, Cap."

"You carry him out, Beck. My side's clear. I'll be right in front of you to lead the way."

Thankful he didn't have a superior officer who took over when things got tense, Beck identified legs first, a torso, a head. Scooping up the body, he determined the person weighed about two hundred pounds. And had a lot of muscle. Pitching the guy over his shoulder, Beck stood into even hotter air, which could burn the lungs. Using the wall again since he could only see outlines, he slid his hand along the sheetrock until he reached the door.

Stepping into the hallway, he slowly made his way down the stairs, careful to balance his heavy load. His pace was also hindered by the traditional gear of heavy clothing and a breathing apparatus, which weighed about sixty pounds. Halfway there, the horn blew, calling all firefighters to evacuate.

"Pick up the pace, Beck."

"Yes, sir!" Beck tried to quicken his steps, but his balance started to give way; sweat seeped out of him inside his turnout coat; the weight pressed over his shoulder had him stumbling to the exit.

"I'm right ahead of you," Gabe called out. It was pitch-black down here, and Beck couldn't see anything. "Follow my voice."

A bracing rush of cold air, clean air, hit them as they exited the house into the night. Two paramedics from one of the ambulances rushed to Beck, took the body and strapped it onto a gurney; when they left, Beck dropped to his knees. Every one of his muscles pulsed, and his breathing was ragged. Ripping off his head gear, he sucked in deep breaths. Again, he recalled the hot, fetid air he'd been forced to take in after a skirmish in Iraq or Afghanistan.

Brody O'Malley approached him. "Did good, buddy."

"Thanks."

"Gonna hurl?" A woman—Sands or White?—asked. "I have. It's okay."

Once more, he was overwhelmed with these people's *kindnesses*. When a member of the elite Rescue Squad, Tony Ramirez, had been promoted to lieutenant on a different group at the house, they'd pulled Beck up from his six-month rookie position on a pumper. He knew why. Purple Heart. Silver Star. A variety of commendations for his performance on the battlefield. Though those things meant little to him, they gave him an opportunity for a career that suited him. And he'd always admired firefighters for the actions in 9/11, just as they admired soldiers.

"I think I'm good." Sitting back on his haunches, he surveyed the scene. Three alarms, which meant three firehouses were called. Five trucks. Two ambulances. Turning, he saw the structure engulfed in angry yellow-and-red flames. They'd had a close call.

He'd had closer.

"Need a medic?" This time, Gabe came over and asked the question because Beck still hunched on his knees.

White answered. "He says no."

Finally able to stand, Beck felt himself wobble. The lieutenant slid her arm through his. "You should be shaky, Beck. You carried a lot of weight in sweltering conditions."

"I'm okay." He moved away from her.

"Suit yourself."

"We heading to the trucks?" he asked.

"In a minute." Gabe perused him closely, his dark gaze searching, then turned to cross to Erikson.

The others wandered off to get water. Beck started toward the Rescue rig, passing the Midi, a two-person medical truck, which carried supplies. Someone stepped out in front of him. Zach Malvaso. Though he was a nice guy, he was more extroverted, more cocky than his brother, Mitch. "Doin' good, Beck?"

The origin of that question was different from the others' queries. Zach Malvaso was a firefighter with PTSD. "Yep, good."

"You going to the meeting tonight?" All the firefighters in Beck's house knew of his problem, which was necessary because something could happen on the job.

*Afraid so.* "Yep."

"Good." Malvaso grabbed his arm. Zach and all his family were touchers. "The group isn't so bad. I still go occasionally, so I knew about the one that's starting up tonight."

"Sure, yeah. I'm down with it."

After he told the lie, he strode quickly to the truck. Luckily no one was nearby. Circling the end of the rig so he was out of sight, he leaned his forehead against the cold, red-painted metal and closed his eyes.

His attendance at the Trauma Survivor's Group bothered him more than the experience he'd just had inside the burning building. The last thing Beck wanted was to be part of a specialty *support* group, set up by the fire department for its members and including veterans from all walks of life. Society was trying to help the wounded warriors who returned from the Middle East and Asia. One of the conditions of his employment in the HCFD was attendance at the sessions, but it had taken the department about nine months to set up this particular class because of scheduling problems. Then the doc running it had a family emergency, so the new group had kept getting put off.

Beck thought about his PTSD—the emotional shrapnel left in him by war—mostly centered around depression and nightmares, with the occasional flashbacks. The fire department officials believed he could learn to *manage* his symptoms. But he had no inclination to deal with the very thing that had cost him his marriage, his kid and, to a degree, his sanity.

• • •

*LELA ALLEN KNEW she was in a dream, struggled to surface from it, but she couldn't. Instead, pain rocketed through her. The slam of her head against the wood-paneled wall radiated to her nerve endings, and her vision blurred. "Please, Len, don't."*

No response from the man she'd married. Just a grunt as he wedged his arm in her windpipe.

She gagged. Choked. "Len, please. It's me, Lela."

Sometimes yelling her name pulled him out of the fog. Thank God, this was one of those occasions.

He blinked.

His eyes widened.

Then he fell to his knees and buried his head in his hands. Began to weep.

Her struggle to breathe, combined with the wrenching sound of his crying, had Lela bolting up in bed; she was gasping for air for real. Slowly, she became aware of the firm mattress beneath her, the cool April breeze on her arms and the scent of laundry detergent from the bedclothes. Tugging the quilt to her chest, she uttered the familiar mantra: "It's a dream; it's over; he can't hurt you anymore."

The first two points were true. The jury was still out on the latter. Maybe once the divorce came through, she wouldn't be as affected by his problems as much as she was now.

Hating the impotence those dreams engendered, she flung off the covers, grabbed a robe and padded to the bathroom off the hall. Ten minutes later, she crept down the steps, walked through the big living room, noting that it needed dusting and vacuuming. Once in the small but efficient kitchen, she made herself a cup of coffee. Sitting at the breakfast nook, she glanced at her watch. Five p.m. She had two hours to eat and dress for tonight. She calmed herself with slow sips of coffee. And thought about the invitation that had come to her. Her friend and colleague at Memorial Hospital, Sophia Ramirez, had offered it when she told Lela about the spouse-concerns group she attended at the Anderson County Fire Academy....

"Now that Jack Harrison is available"—he was the department shrink—"he's starting another group in a few weeks for sufferers of PTSD and their families."

Lela was confused. "I don't have PTSD. Len does."

"I know, and it's amazing you escaped the malady after what *you* went through in Afghanistan."

Now Lela was a trauma nurse in the ER, but for five years, she'd been a medic, stationed in Afghanistan in a small medical outpost that treated soldiers right off the battlefield. She'd seen some hideous injuries: limbs blown off, faces unrecognizable, evisceration of torsos, as well the vacant look of death in soldiers' eyes. But for some reason, Lela had been spared PTSD. There were three-hundred thousand returning vets with the condition. No one seemed to know why some combat personnel developed it and others didn't. In that area at least, she was lucky.

Sophia had continued, "The group is open to veterans *and* their families."

"That's an odd combination to treat together."

"What, the spouses and the sufferers?"

Lela nodded.

"Jack thinks having people on both sides of the condition together in one group will increase understanding of what each person goes through." She smiled. "And you know how much I adore the man." Sophia had confided in Lela what she'd gone through with her husband last year. She'd gradually become unable to bear the danger Tony was in every day and her fear had almost destroyed their marriage.

"Why is the fire department including veterans?"

"There's a big initiative out there for organizations to help returning soldiers in any way they can. Maybe you should give the group a shot...."

So, after she'd tried to get Len to join instead of her and he'd refused, Lela had enrolled. What could it hurt?

When she'd erased the aftereffects of the dream with high-test coffee, a quick sandwich and a shower, Lela dressed in blue jeans (her Southern mama would have had a fit) and a nice, deep maroon sweater, which brought out the red highlights in her hair. Driving to the Fire Academy made her tense, so she did some shrugs and stretches to loosen her shoulders. All too soon, she arrived at the big glass-and-brick building, servicing several surrounding towns as well as Hidden Cove. Lela had moved to the town, about a hundred miles outside of New York City, after she'd left the service, because Len had grown up here and had wanted to come back home when he'd gotten out. She'd thought being with family and friends might help him. Though Len had moved into his childhood house after their separation almost a year ago, he was still in bad shape.

Lela had visited the Fire Academy once for a refresher training on sunken chest wounds, given by a paramedic. The building held offices, but its main purpose was to train firefighters from several counties. As she approached the entrance a second time, her heart beat a wild tattoo in her chest at what she was in for tonight.

From her right, a man came up flush to the door when she reached it. He was definitely the armed forces. She could spot them anywhere. Impossibly erect posture. Still-short hair. This one had chiseled features, but his eyes were world-weary.

"Ma'am," he said in short clipped tones.

"Sir." She responded unthinkingly to the greeting.

He cocked his head and stared at her a minute. "Army?"

She nodded. "Nurse turned medic. Kandahar. You?"

"OCS, twenty years. Iraq. Afghanistan."

Wow, Lela thought. Len had only been in ten years. *This poor man's wife.*

Together, they took the elevator to the third floor. He gave her a little smile. "Don't much see Southern belles who turn into army medics."

He must have caught what remained of her accent. "My mama would have agreed with you. God bless her heart. But I joined after both my parents died."

He chuckled. The sound was deep, masculine. When they reached the third floor, he held the elevator door so she could exit before him. Chatter drifted out from the first room on the left, so she headed for it, with him behind. As they entered, Lela noted the muted lighting and how the chairs were arranged in two half circles, not one with chairs that would back to the door. The soft blue walls and grass-cloth paper soothed on sight. "I see somebody knows what he's doing."

"Ma'am?"

"Please, call me Lela. Ma'am makes me feel like your mother."

For a brief second, his eyes perused her in anything but a parental fashion. "Lela. Beckett Sloan. I go by Beck."

She held out her hand and they shook. His palm dwarfed hers and his clasp was firm. Since they'd reached the chairs at the same time, he stood while she took one, then dropped down next to her. Sitting, he seemed bigger. Taller. But for some reason, maybe his manners, she didn't feel threatened.

Not so of everyone who had assembled. As she glanced around, she saw in a couple guys' expressions, and one woman's, the confusion and acute anxiety she'd lived with for years. Without her conscious intent, she leaned in toward Beckett Sloan.

Promptly at seven, a good-looking man with a full head of dark hair graying at the temples, entered the room and pulled up a chair facing them, his own back to the door. "Hi, all. I'm Jack Harrison. You can call me Jack, Doc or Dr. Harrison. Behind my back, I hope you're kind."

A bit of laughter.

"I've been the psychiatrist for the fire department for close to two decades. Thanks for coming to this very first meeting of our Trauma Survivor's Group this year. Whether you're a sufferer or related to one, you're all survivors."

Before Dr. Harrison could go further, the door slammed open and Lela gasped. In the entry stood her soon-to-be ex-husband, Len Allen, once again crazy-eyed and, from the looks of him, drunk.

• • •

UNRUFFLED, JACK HARRISON turned and glanced over his shoulder. Then he stood and asked pleasantly, "Can I help you?"

The man said, "Staff Sergeant Len Allen, sir. I came for the group."

Harrison scanned the clipboard he held. "I don't see your name here, Len. Did you enroll?"

"No, but I changed my mind." His gaze scanned the semicircle. "I wanna be here with my wife."

A quick intake of breath from the woman next to Beck.

"I'm sorry, Len." Again Harrison spoke calmly. Almost gently. "We don't allow spouses to take the sessions together." He looked to Lela. "You're signed in, right?"

"Yes, I'm Lela Allen."

Harrison fished something out of his pocket. When he gave the card to the soldier, the guy's hand shook. "Here's my number. Maybe we can schedule some individual counseling."

"Don't wanna. I'm stayin' here."

"No, I'm afraid you're not."

Jack wisely didn't touch Allen, just moved in closer. "Let's go out into the foyer, Len."

The man stood his ground. He sported a medium build, but his physique consisted of a roadmap of corded muscles. Beck remembered working out till he dropped, trying to conquer the demons. "No."

Harrison hesitated and Len started toward the group. Beck took another glance at Lela. Her lips had thinned and her jaw was tight. But she held her head up to face down whatever was coming.

Rising, he stepped between her and her husband. "Atten-*tion*, Staff Sergeant Allen. Colonel Beckett Sloan here."

Reflex kicked in. The guy halted, stood straight and saluted, just as Beck suspected he would.

"We're going into the hall. That's an order, Staff Sergeant."

"Yes, sir."

Turning, he followed Allen out of the room. Harrison said to the others, "Be right back," and went with them.

In the corridor, Beck hadn't forgotten how to lead men. Standing over Allen, he donned a stern expression. "Have you been drinking, Staff Sergeant?"

"Some."

"A lot, from what I can see. Hand over your keys."

"Excuse me?"

"I want your keys. You aren't driving home."

"What do you mean?"

"We'll get you a cab."

The man's chin raised. Expecting belligerence, Beck leaned in some.

"I wanna go in there. I need help."

Beck glanced at Harrison, who had let him handle the situation to this point. The psychiatrist spoke softly. "Yes, you do, Len. Call me and we'll set up an appointment."

"I wanna be with my wife." He sounded like a little boy, and it angered Beck that the disorder could turn good soldiers into whiny children.

"I remember her application now. She said she asked you to come alone, and when you said no, she decided to attend. She also said you're legally separated and soon to be divorced."

"Don't want it." The man began to waver on his feet.

Beck moved in closer. "Come on, Staff Sergeant, I'll get you in a cab. We can talk some more while we wait."

Harrison nodded. "I'll call one of our staffers. He'll drive the Staff Sergeant home."

By the time they reached the elevator, Len Allen was slumping onto Beck's shoulder. He murmured, "It's fucking hard. Sometimes I don't wanna live anymore."

"I felt the same from time to time. You can get better."

"Tried."

"I know what I'm saying for a fact."

"Then why're you here?"

"Requirement of my job." They reached the parking lot, and a fire department Jeep pulled up in front of them. A uniformed firefighter got out. "I'll take him from here."

"Okay." Beck hesitated, then took Harrison's card, which Len still held in his hand, and scribbled on it. "Here's my cell number, too, if you need to talk to someone who's been there."

"Thanks, Colonel. Sorry about the scene in there. See if Lela's okay, will you?"

"Just go sober up. And get help."

Beck watched as the car sped off, then headed inside and took the elevator to the third floor. He walked into the room, and the person speaking halted.

Harrison said, "We're giving our reasons for being here. We've only covered three people, and I'll catch you up later, Colonel."

Beck nodded and took his seat next to Lela. She looked over at him and her eyes were bleak, but she hadn't cried or left. She was tougher than she looked. But, of course, she'd been an army medic. "Thank you," she mouthed and he nodded.

The spouse of a female marine spoke next. He was a big teddy bear of a guy. "Dennis Lewis. My wife's not the same person since she got back. Actually, I'm afraid to leave her alone with the kids. We need help, big-time. And she's not going to be the one to get it."

Two firefighters talked about having been trapped in an elevator that was about to plunge fifty feet. "I didn't think we were gonna make it out," the younger one said. "I can't sleep because of the nightmares."

Next was Lela. Her face was flushed, but she spoke clearly. "First, let me apologize for Len. I'm embarrassed."

Harrison took a bead on her. "Lela, listen to me. Your husband's behavior is no reflection on you. He's sick and needs help."

"Well, y'all know my circumstances. Len's why I'm here. We *are* getting a divorce." She nodded to the husband of the marine. "My son's afraid of him. He won't spend any time alone with his father, and it breaks Len's heart. I encourage him to go to Len's parents' house, so they can supervise, and that's what Josh does now."

"How about you, Lela?" Harrison asked. "What do you do?"

"I'm a trauma nurse at Memorial Hospital. Sophia Ramirez told me about this group. I was an army medic for five years, too, and made NCO status. I met Len over there. I left the service when I got pregnant, but Len stayed in for five more years. He's been home about two years, and things have gone from bad to worse."

"A lot to contend with," Harrison commented. His gaze transferred to Beck. "Colonel?"

Beck's heart started to gallop. His brow got sweaty. Subtle physical reactions happened whenever he talked about his experiences in the war. "Beckett Sloan. People call me Beck. Career soldier. Now a firefighter. Haven't had an episode since I joined the department, but before that, I was..." he glanced to the door "...a lot like the Staff Sergeant."

• • •

"CAN I WALK out with you, Beck?" Lela addressed him as soon as the group ended. His face was lined with more fatigue than when they'd arrived.

He gave a small smile. "Yeah, sure."

They walked side by side to the elevator, stood silently inside until they reached the foyer. Under the florescent lamps, she looked up at him. His eyes were a color green she'd only seen on people wearing contacts.

"They're real," he said sardonically.

"Excuse me?"

"The color of my eyes. No contacts. Everybody asks."

She wanted to say how beautiful they were but figured the remark was inappropriate. "Thanks for what you did."

"You got no business being embarrassed."

"Still, I appreciate you taking charge."

"Can't seem to get over that."

She gave him a smile. "Must be hard being the rookie on a squad, then."

His expression was questioning.

"I see firefighters all the time at the ER. Let's just say *one-upmanship* is a kind way to describe them."

Now a full-bodied laugh escaped him. It was a rusty sound. "I get you there. And I bet they flirt like hell."

She could feel the flush creep up her neck. "Nah, they call me ma'am, too."

"I highly doubt that." His gaze darkened. "I'm sorry for what you've gone through."

They locked gazes for a moment. Something subtle, an all-male scent, drifted over to her.

Then he said, "I gave Len my cell number. Maybe I can help him."

"That was sweet of you."

*Huh!* "I don't know as though anybody has ever called me sweet. Certainly not the soldiers under my command."

Reaching out, she squeezed his arm. "Well, you are, Beck. Thanks again. Good night."

He didn't accompany Lela to her car and she was glad. She'd had a strange reaction to him. She didn't examine it too closely, because for a long time, she'd wanted any reaction to any man to be nonexistent.

• • •

LEN BOLTED UP in bed. What the hell? It was dark in the barracks. Quiet. He grasped on to the mattress. The thing was too thick. When the clock's lighted dial winked out three a.m., he realized he wasn't in Afghanistan. But it took him a minute to get that he was back in the States, in the house where he grew up. Fuck!

Sliding out of bed, he stumbled to the bathroom down the hall, hoping like hell he didn't wake up his mother and father. He'd already put them through hell, and besides, they'd only rag on him about his drinking. He took a piss, brushed teeth that felt like he'd eaten camel dung, and splashed cold water on his face. But when he looked in the mirror, he cringed. Not because his hair was shaggy, a beard roughened his jaw, or his eyes were the color of cherries. He remembered what he'd done tonight.

Poor Lela. He'd hurt her enough. To barge into the Fire Academy and make a scene had embarrassed her. He could still see the shame on her face. The colonel had to drag him out. Jesus.

Once he got back into his room, Len lay down and listened to the sounds of crickets drift in through the open window. When the world stopped spinning, he did what he always did—he made a list in his head of what he needed to do to get better. Go to therapy. Maybe with that Harrison guy who didn't seem like too much of a dick. His mother had also given him AA pamphlets. He'd been to a few meetings before, and a lot of the guys were like him. Vets. Drunks. Bums.

Yeah. He'd do that tomorrow.

But when the dial on the clock clicked to 4 a.m. and then to 5 a.m., the demons came and ate up all his promises.

*You're a worthless piece of shit. You never deserved her. She didn't know you bought black market liquor and how much of it you drank over there or when you got back. Go have some more. You don't deserve any better.*

As always, he listened to the voices in his head. He slid off the bed, and this time went to his top dresser drawer. Out of which, he pulled a pint of vodka.

He gulped a swig back. And another. The taste was tart and cool. By the time the last drop touched his lips, the demons were gone.

**For notification of Kathryn's new work and information about her books, be sure to sign up for her newsletter at** http://on.fb.me/1bLS0bN.

**If you liked AMERICA'S BRAVEST, you might want to post a review of it at** http://amzn.to/vy6mUx.

Made in the USA
Lexington, KY
10 March 2014